D1525562

Savage Journey

BOOKS BY ALLAN W. ECKERT

The Winning of America Series

THE FRONTIERSMEN
WILDERNESS EMPIRE
THE CONQUERORS
THE WILDERNESS WAR

Nature Books

THE GREAT AUK
THE SILENT SKY
WILD SEASON
THE CROSSBREED
BAYOU BACKWATERS
THE KING SNAKE
IN SEARCH OF A WHALE
INCIDENT AT HAWK'S HILL
THE OWLS OF NORTH AMERICA
THE WADING BIRDS OF NORTH AMERICA

Others

SAVAGE JOURNEY
A TIME OF TERROR
THE DREAMING TREE
BLUE JACKET
THE COURT-MARTIAL OF DANIEL BOONE
THE HAB THEORY
TECUMSEH! (DRAMA)
THE LEGEND OF KOO-TAN (SCREENPLAY)
BLUE JACKET (SCREENPLAY)
THE FRONTIERSMEN (SCREENPLAY)

Savage Journey

a novel by

Allan W. Eckert

AN AUTHORS GUILD BACKINPRINT.COM EDITION

Savage Journey

AN AUTHORS GUILD BACKINPRINT.COM EDITION

Published by iUniverse.com, Inc.

For information address:
iUniverse.com, Inc.
5220 S 16th, Ste. 200
Lincoln, NE 68512
www.iuniverse.com

Originally published by Little, Brown

ISBN: 0-595-18171-6

Printed in the United States of America

Dedication

To my stepdaughter . . .

Emily Grace Dent

. . . with love.

Savage Journey

Prologue

THE AMAZON RAIN FOREST, an immense entity with the composure of supreme confidence, stands patiently as it has been standing for countless eons — a living paradox. It is both malevolent and benevolent; silent, yet raucous with chatter and rustle and melodic sound; gloomy, yet alive with vibrant color. The tones of nature become the expression of its moods.

This rain forest, the largest on earth, is a great and powerful volume, filled with a complexity of life and a simplicity of purpose, illustrated with tall dark trees whose straight trunks tower upward two hundred feet to a lofty canopy. Their branches are strung with a confusing network of hanging and climbing vines — the twisted, knotted, cabled, serpentine lianas. Moss-coated boulders jut from the forest floor and occasional flowering trees splash daubs of brilliant yellow, orange and red against a blanket of varied greens.

It is a great unity, within which the pulse and throb of life is constant. It is more than a forest — it is a presence: watchful, patient, knowing . . . and waiting.

The vast green body of this mighty Amazon forest is bisected by a river bearing the same name, a river worthy of this forest. It flows almost on the line of the equator, stretching eastward across the South American continent from its sparkling, crystalline headwaters in the Andes Mountains to its sprawling, sixty-mile-wide mouth at the Atlantic. It is a river draining an incredible two and a half million square miles, carrying a greater volume of water than any other river on earth, pouring into the Atlantic Ocean fourteen times as much water as the Mississippi, staining the sea a muddy yellow for over two hundred miles.

Flowing grandly past the silent trees, the Amazon River is a world in itself — a tenuous passage into the bowels of the rain forest — so deep and broad that oceangoing vessels churn their way upstream past the city of Manaus, a thousand miles from the coast, where the water is still ninety feet deep, and continue their surging, upstream movement in minute, foam-flecked arrogance through the heart of Brazil fully twenty-three hundred miles to Iquitos, Peru. From there, smaller craft can skim upstream yet another sixteen hundred miles. But they are prisoners, these craft on the Amazon, confined by the very forest they penetrate. Although the river has become a familiar passage, mere yards from it there remains a mysterious world, untrodden except by feet that have known no other soil.

An intricacy of tributaries courses sinuously through the lushness of the Amazon basin: eight major rivers, each a thousand miles in length, and many thousands of smaller creeks, brooks and rills — all eventually pouring themselves into the Amazon. One such stream is the Javari, flowing from the Brazilian wilderness to the south and emptying into the Amazon downstream from where Peru, Colombia and Brazil meet. One of the main branches of the Javari is the Itacuaí River, whose upper reaches are only scantily known. A principal feeder stream of the Itacuaí is the Ituí River, practically unknown for its full length of two hundred fifty miles.

The Ituí flows through a wilderness where the leafy canopy is so dense that almost all sunlight is shut out to the ground below, giving the effect of an endless cavern whose roof is two hundred feet above a floor carpeted with mosses and gigantic ferns. Like stalagmites, trees spear straight upward a hundred feet or more before branching; lianas hang like stalactites, and when the breeze, which is not felt on the forest floor, stirs the uppermost canopy, these lianas move eerily, softly moaning and creaking, sighing and groaning, in a multitude of musical sounds; a strange but lovely, sensuous and neverending symphony. This rain forest sings and speaks in a variety of voices. It is redolent with a rich and heady scent of humus lying moist and moldering upon the warm and luscious body of the earth.

Forming the Ituí are a number of trickling little brooks originating on the north slope of an east-west line of low mountains heavily clad with the everpresent forest growth. They are known as *Pequenas Colinas Verdes* – The Little Green Hills.

Here the forest stands waiting as it has always waited. Here, the Ituí is waiting as well; waiting without knowing; waiting for a girl on the threshold of womanhood.

A girl named Sarah Francis.

Chapter One

SARAH FRANCIS WAS AMONG the fortunate few who were not affected by the sickness.

For an expedition begun so auspiciously, this one was abruptly in serious trouble. There had been that unfortunate mishap at the river and then the difficulties between the river and the site of the dig, but since then everything had gone exceptionally well. The extensive ruins had been located just where expected. The beautiful and mysterious appearance of the ancient architecture, covered with lush green jungle growth, was dominated by a small, square-topped pyramid her father called a ziggurat. Sarah, who had recently become reacquainted with the writings of L. Frank Baum, had spoken first.

"Ohhh," she had breathed, "it's like the Emerald City!"

They all had laughed but then the leader of the expedition, Hadley Merchant, had nodded and smiled at the thirteen-year-old, rubbing his wiry gray goatee. "Why not?" he said. "It's as good a name as any. You've named it, Sarah."

Unexpectedly, from the onset of the dig, they had begun finding unusual artifacts. These were mostly stone carvings rendered with an exquisiteness of detail that both perplexed and delighted Dr. Merchant. During those busy days it had become commonplace to hear him murmur, "Remarkable. Most remarkable." Normally taciturn and unexcitable, he had become garrulously enthusiastic when three stone tablets had been discovered by Sarah's father, who was Dr. Merchant's chief assistant at the museum.

Ian MacWilliams Francis, following a hunch, had begun his own particular digging at a point near the ziggurat where an exposed set of stones having the appearance of a walkway suddenly ceased a dozen or more feet from the base of that structure. Digging, he discovered that the walkway actually continued, but angled down as a rampway and had, over the ages, been covered with soil. A tangle of plants and roots made digging difficult. Then, only two feet below the surface and still following the walkway, he had encountered the tablets. With great care, sometimes using a soft camel's hair brush, he gradually freed them, his pulse quickening. The tablets were identical in size — oval shaped, about five inches long and half an inch thick. On each was line after line of symbolic writing, hieroglyphics of a character he had never before seen, although he was quite familiar with Assyrian, Egyptian and Mayan hieroglyphics.

"Excellent, Dr. Francis," the portly Dr. Merchant had said softly, studying them closely. He too, however, was unfamiliar with the peculiar hieroglyphics. They had carried the tablets to where the expedition's coleader, Dr. Anita Cruz, was working with two archaeology graduate students, Pamela Wynn and Tad Roche. Although a noted expert in ancient writings, she was no less baffled and excited by the find, considering the tablets to be of great significance.

As if these stirring discoveries were not enough to spur them on, Pamela Wynn, during the seventeenth day of the dig, voiced a cry which brought the others running. She had discovered an eight-inch-high statue of a winged human in a chariot upon a base six inches square. On this base were more of the same type of hieroglyphics. That was exciting enough, but there was another factor about the little statue that was breathtaking.

It was solid gold.

For the next five weeks after that they had all engaged in the dig with feverish activity, but the days passed with no discoveries more outstanding than finding several more stone carvings of animals or humans. All were of interest and bore a certain resemblance to artifacts of the Inca culture, yet with subtle differences. As the party sat cataloging their finds in camp one night, Dr. Merchant had again picked up the golden statue and inspected it closely. His hands were shaking as he gently set it down and spoke to the group.

"Even if we turn up nothing else, this single find has justified the expedition. It might turn out to be the most significant archaeological discovery of the decade." He waved a hand at the collection of artifacts arranged neatly on the ground, each with its own identification tag, and continued, "I do believe there is the possibility these artifacts may be from a culture superior to that of

the Incas and which predates them." That was tanta-
mount to the discovery of King Tutankhamen's tomb.

It was the next morning that the malady had struck
them. In rapid succession, Dr. Merchant's wife Ruth and
Dr. Cruz were severely stricken, while Dr. Merchant
himself, along with Pamela Wynn, Tad Roche, and
another of the graduate students, Matthew Bruce, were
affected to a lesser degree. The latter four were still able
to function reasonably well, but they felt terrible. Dr.
Cruz and Mrs. Merchant, however, were in serious condition. At intervals they became delirious and when not
in that state they were almost constantly writhing and
moaning with abdominal pain, able to eat little, if anything. Only three were entirely unaffected by the sickness. One of these was the fourth student, Patrick
Houghton, an athletic young man who had taken his
bachelor's on a gymnastics scholarship. The other two
were Dr. Francis and Sarah.

At first the consensus had been that the illness, suspected of being a virus, would pass in a few days and the
afflicted would recuperate. Instead, their conditions remained the same or became worse and they were weaken-
ing from the strain. Ruth Merchant was delirious more
than conscious and it was obvious that she needed a
doctor badly.

Now the decision was made: the four who were partially afflicted would use makeshift litters to carry out the
severely ill women. Conceivably, the energetic Patrick
Houghton, striking out as rapidly as possible, could
make his way through the jungle to Cruzeiro do Sul.
By the time the main party reached the landing place at

the Ipixuna River, eight miles south, Patrick could be back with help in canoes. As for Ian Francis and his daughter, their task was no less important. Pulling his goatee nervously, Dr. Merchant outlined what they were to do.

"We shall take only what is essential in order for us to reach the river, Dr. Francis," he said. His hand left the chinwhiskers and indicated the assembled artifacts. "All these we'll leave under your care, along with the supplies, tools, whatever. We cannot carry them with us and we simply can't afford to leave them unprotected, especially the tablets and gold statue. I hate to leave you like this, but there is no sensible alternative."

"I understand," Dr. Francis replied, nodding. He put an arm around Sarah's shoulder and pulled her to him, holding her firmly. "Don't worry, Sarah and I will be all right. We'll continue the dig as best we can and wait for your return."

"I should think," Dr. Merchant said thoughtfully, "that we will be back, or have someone else here to help, in about ten days — say two weeks at the outside."

The men shook hands and Dr. Francis and Sarah waved to the others, ready with their packs in place. Dr. Merchant shrugged into his backpack while Matthew Bruce waited at one end of the litter containing the semiconscious form of Ruth Merchant. Grunting under the strain, because she was a heavy woman, the two men lifted the litter. Behind them, Pamela Wynn and Tad Roche raised the litter in which Anita Cruz was lying. Patrick Houghton was already gone, having set off at a fast trot following Dr. Merchant's final instructions.

Without further word, Hadley Merchant leading the way, they moved off and then carefully down the rather steep stone-block steps on the north side of the ruins, which were the only access to the Emerald City ruins from the plateau below. At the base of the wall where the steps ended, the trail moved immediately into rank jungle growth, circled the wall to the east and moved across the plateau before beginning the gradual descent toward the Ipixuna River landing eight miles away.

The archaeologist and his daughter watched them until they disappeared into the forest below. As soon as they were out of sight, Ian Francis turned to Sarah and patted her shoulder warmly. "Well, we're on our own now, Sarah." He was wise enough not to ask if she was afraid and thereby plant the seed of fear. "Are you hungry?"

The girl nodded. Her deep, pewter-colored eyes met his unwaveringly. "Sure am. How 'bout you?"

"Ravenous! Come on, let's have a bite to eat before we get back to work."

They walked back to camp and, while Dr. Francis wrote in his journal, Sarah prepared sandwiches, glancing up occasionally to study her father. Though she had hidden it well, she was a little afraid and thankful for his presence. She smiled as she watched him write in the small crisp hand so familiar to her. He was by no means a large man, a couple of inches less than six feet, but he exuded a self-confidence which, in this present situation, was comforting. She had never known him to be other than a rather mild-mannered individual, studious appearing, often almost owllike behind heavy horn-rimmed glasses. Annoyingly myopic, he kept three sets of glasses with him at all times, one for close-up work and reading, another for times when the range of necessary vision was limited to less than about a dozen feet, and a final set for long-range viewing. He despised wearing bifocals or trifocals and the result was a somewhat comic glasses-changing routine. Physically, Ian Francis was a bit bulky, rather Teutonic but not at all fat. Nevertheless, he moved with a marked grace, a fluidity which belied his chunkiness. His ears were well shaped and set close to his head. Although his nose was large, it suited him well, lending character to a face that a smaller nose would have weakened. His mouth was wide and his lower jaw angular, determined, and he showed strong, slightly crooked teeth when he smiled, which was often. His hands, though very strong, could perform tasks requiring great delicacy. He and Sarah were generally alike physically. Where they differed most was in their hair. His retained the soft blondness of youth, bleaching readily under a summer sun, and his eyes were so deep a blue that some people considered them violet; Sarah, however, had dark brown hair to complement her warm gray eyes — these features the only visible inheritance from her mother.

Sarah returned his smile as he glanced up at her from his writing, but she detected a faint pinching at the bridge of his nose and knew he was worried about her, perhaps regretting that he had brought her along over the initial dubious reactions from the others.

"I'm all right, Dad, really. Don't worry. We'll get along just fine."

He chuckled at her perceptiveness and grunted an

affirmative, returning to his writing without speaking. She felt a welling of pride that he accepted and evidently believed what she had said. Early on she had determined that in no way was she going to be a problem to him during this expedition, not after the difficulties he had surmounted getting approval for taking her along.

Dr. Merchant had been strongly opposed to it at first, harumphing and shaking his head, declaring that an archaeological dig in the Brazilian jungle was no place for a child. Dr. Francis was not put off by the predictable reaction. He explained patiently that Sarah was a very self-sufficient girl, not given to selfishness and its accompanying complaints. She was mentally sharp, observant, efficient and could help with any number of details about the expedition that did not require an archaeological background and perhaps even with some that did, once she understood what was required. Further, if she were not permitted to go, then, most regretfully, Dr. Francis would not be able to go either. Sarah was now his responsibility alone. Even had he chosen to do so — which initially he had considered and almost immediately rejected — he could not board her out for the length of time they would be gone. This was not only because he simply could not afford to do so, but because, except for an elderly aunt, he had no family with whom to leave her. He wouldn't even consider trying to make some sort of arrangement by which Sarah's mother would keep her. That would be bad for everyone concerned, Sarah most of all.

Dr. Merchant, having on occasion met his assistant's former wife, Vicki, sympathized with that. He was also dismayed at the thought of not having Dr. Francis along.

Nevertheless, he remained unconvinced that any thirteen-year-old should be taken along on a three-month expedition which, at best, would entail considerable hardship. It was Sarah herself who changed his mind. The expedition was of tremendous importance to Dr. Francis and in near desperation he asked his superior at least to talk with Sarah to get a sense of what she was like. Reluctantly, the older scientist agreed.

The three of them met in Dr. Merchant's cluttered office in the basement of the Field Museum, where the portly curator of archaeology talked with them for close to an hour, primarily questioning Sarah and listening closely to her responses. She fielded the questions well, as Ian Francis had known she would, never looking toward him for help as he sat quietly in a battered wooden desk chair across the room from them. She spoke quietly, with self-assurance, her responses far more mature than Dr. Merchant had anticipated.

"Have you set a goal in life for yourself yet, Sarah, for when you are older?" the curator asked, stroking his goatee.

She smiled. "Without meaning any disrespect, sir, thank you for not putting it into the context of 'What would you like to be when you grow up, little girl?' To answer your question, I'm very interested in what my father does. I've watched him work at home and sometimes here at the museum. I'm fascinated with archaeology and think I might want to study it, but I like anthropology, too, and I'm not sure yet which one I like better. I'm quite certain I'd like to study one or the other, perhaps even both."

Merchant nodded, impressed. "Fine. A worthy ambition." He cocked a shaggy brow at her. "You have a rather extensive vocabulary. Do you read much?"

"Yes sir, quite a lot." She laughed lightly, brightening the fusty room with the sound. "Both good stuff and bad. I've paged through most of Dad's books. There's a lot I don't understand, but I'm gradually learning." She glanced briefly at her father, then back at the curator. "And he's always answering questions for me. But I wouldn't want you to think I'm always buried in his books. I read a good bit of light stuff, too."

"Such as what? What book are you reading right now?"

"Books. I'm reading four at the moment. They don't have much in common. The heaviest one right now is *The Ascent of Man.*"

"Jacob Bronowski's book? That is heavy."

"Yes, but it's very good, too. Sometimes it's difficult for me."

"I shouldn't wonder," Dr. Merchant murmured. "What else?"

"I'm also reading *Dorothy and the Wizard of Oz* for the second time. I'm almost finished with Osa Johnson's *I Married Adventure* — *that* one I really like. The last one is *'Salem's Lot* by Stephen King."

"A wide range. Is your reading always so varied?"

"Usually. Sometimes I'll read more of one kind of book than another for a while."

"Do you read magazines? Romances? Hollywood magazines?"

"Some magazines, but not those. Dad gets *National*

Geographic and I almost always read those pretty well. He takes *Scientific American,* too, but I don't care so much for that. It's too technical. I have a subscription to *Ms.* magazine, but usually I just page through it."

"Let me ask you a different question," Dr. Merchant said, leaning back in his chair and exhaling loudly. "Suppose you were, in fact, on such an expedition as we're planning and you became separated from the group. What would you do?"

"Well, the most important thing is to keep my head and stay calm. Dad says panic will kill people lost in the woods or anywhere else faster than anything. I guess first I'd sit down and think about the situation and try to figure out where the separation happened. I'd probably go back exactly the way I'd come until I found a place where we'd been together and then try to reunite with them. If I weren't able to do that, I'd do what Dad's always advised — be aware of my surroundings, walk carefully so as not to fall and get hurt, stop often and listen carefully, and try to continue walking in what I thought was the right direction until I found them again. Or, if I didn't find anyone, until I came to some kind of waterway — a river or creek or even a little trickle of runoff. Follow it downstream and sooner or later I'd come to where people lived and I could ask for help."

Sarah couldn't tell whether or not Dr. Merchant liked the answer. His face was expressionless and when next he spoke he directed his question to the assistant curator.

"Dr. Francis, what about the school situation?" Before he could answer, Dr. Merchant shot another question at

Sarah. "Where do you go to school and when does summer vacation begin?"

"Maine West High School in Des Plaines," she replied. "I think we get out on June tenth this year."

"Then we have a problem, don't we, Dr. Francis? The expedition is scheduled to begin in a few weeks — the last week of April."

"I don't think, Dr. Merchant, that would be any real problem. Sarah is very high in her class. In view of the educational value of this expedition, I rather think something could be worked out whereby she could leave before the school year ends."

The curator stood up. "All right," he said, "suppose we leave it in their hands. If you can clear it with them, she can go. If you can't, then that's that. Agreed?"

The two men shook hands and Sarah thanked him. Merchant smiled and placed a hand on her shoulder. "I still have certain misgivings," he said, "but as a matter of fact, I rather hope you'll be able to work things out."

Working things out with the school powers had been no problem whatever. The broadening value of such a trip for Sarah, its academic value and the fact that she would be with highly responsible people, including her father, won the full approval of the principal of Maine West, Mason Aldrich. Matters had thereafter moved along rapidly and now here they were in the Brazilian wilderness and thus far, despite the illness that had so unexpectedly disrupted them in the midst of the dig, Sarah wouldn't have missed it for anything.

"Sandwiches are ready, Dad."

Ian Francis nodded, closed his journal, tucked the

ball-point pen into a pocket and changed glasses. He reached over and accepted the thick sandwich Sarah had made of canned ham with mustard on rather heavy slices of bread from the loaves baked a couple of days ago by Pamela Wynn. Her own was somewhat smaller. They both drank tepid iced tea made from a mix in packets stirred into water filtered through the expedition's portable purification machine. They had fresh bananas for dessert. It wasn't elegant, but it was substantial and tasted good. Already Sarah was mentally planning what she would prepare for their dinner, probably the remainder of the ham — canned goods had to be consumed quickly, once opened — fried along with some potatoes and powdered eggs scrambled. Plus some canned pears. They were going to get along just fine.

After her father finished his cigarette, the two walked back to where Dr. Francis had been involved with his own dig until this morning. His work had carried him slopingly downward until now the earth had been removed in a trench about five feet wide and seven feet deep. The excavation was presently within two or three feet of the base of the ziggurat and, though he continued to dig slowly and carefully so as not to damage any other artifacts that might be encountered, the scientist was becoming more keyed up.

Sarah was helping by carrying away and dumping, two at a time, the small baskets of soil he filled. Her hands were dirty and two blisters had appeared, one on each palm, which she didn't mention to her father. Mostly they worked without talking, Dr. Francis often using a makeshift ladder, digging with care and frequently checking to see how close the excavation was to the base of the peculiar structure. By late afternoon he had moved away the earth to within a foot of exposing the entire wall. Above them the stone blocks had been cut and fitted with great precision. No mortar had been used to seat the stones together. It had not been necessary. The cutting had been done so that one abutted the other perfectly, held in place by its great weight and interlocked with neighboring blocks by jutments and indents.

"How did they ever cut such big blocks, Dad?" Sarah asked. She was resting a moment, seated on the sloped earth behind him, studying the construction he was clearing. "How did they ever lift them into place?"

Her father shook his head without looking down at her, continuing his digging. "No one knows for sure, Sarah. One theory is that they drove wooden stakes into cracks in the rocks and then poured water in until the crack was filled. The wood swelled and the resulting expansion created such pressure that the rock split. That," he added, descending the ladder, "may have been true in some cases, but it doesn't satisfy me. It doesn't explain these jutting cuts or the indentations into which they fit. They're not accidental. They've been designed and cut perfectly that way. To accomplish this even with our own technology would take a lot of heavy-duty machinery and there has never been any trace of such machinery having existed."

He had reached the ground and began shoveling the loose dirt into the baskets, continuing to talk. "Besides which, the Incas — if that's what they were, which we're all doubting now — didn't have iron, didn't even know of it until the Conquistadores came under Pizzaro and ravaged the country. So how could they do this? We just don't know. Lifting them into place is every bit as perplexing. These particular blocks must weigh at least three or four tons apiece. Theory is that they built up to the place with fill dirt and rolled or slid the cut blocks up rampways and into place, using the brute strength of slaves or workers or whatever, but there's no real evidence of that, either. I think they may have had some way of easily cutting and moving these stones; some power of which we have no knowledge. Some of the ancient carvings seem to depict individuals using peculiar instruments for such efforts with these blocks, but so far that is only wild speculation. No such instruments have ever been found."

"When you get that last layer cleared away," Sarah said, waving her hand erratically for a moment to shoo away an insect that had begun flying around her head, "what do you expect to find? A door?"

He stuck the point of his shovel into the ground and moved over beside her, sitting down heavily with a faint groan. "Feels good to quit for a while." He dug into his shirt pocket, took out a cigarette and lighted it. Leaning over, he kissed Sarah on the temple and cocked his head at her. "Hard to get used to you, honey, with that short hair. I think I like it, though. I liked it long, too.

"Anyway," he blew out a plume of blue-white smoke, "you asked a question. I don't know, really. I like to hope we're going to find a door or an opening or something.

I can't imagine they'd've built this sloping walk to the wall without reason. I expect we'll find out tomorrow, maybe by noon or thereabouts."

He stood up and held out his hand, pulling her to her feet. "Come on, we'll empty these last few baskets and call it quits for the day. By the time we do that, clean ourselves up a little and finish eating, it'll be dark." He arched his back to ease the ache and groaned again. "I won't have any trouble sleeping tonight."

"Neither will I," Sarah replied, picking up two of the small baskets by their looped handles.

But she did. Long after they had finished eating and crawled into their sleeping bags beside one another in the tent, she lay awake. Outside there were night sounds, sometimes distant, sometimes close, which she could not identify, and she shivered slightly. The faint, almost inaudible peeping sound surely came from bats wheeling about in the darkness, catching moths, night-flying wasps and the multitude of other insects attracted earlier by the tent lantern. But what was that husky, rumbling coughing sound? A jaguar, maybe? That piercing whistle far off sounded like a bird, but was it? If so, what was it doing awake and crying long after dark? Closer to the ruins a deep, mellow and lonely sort of cry could have come from an owl, but an owl would not crack a branch underfoot and that was definitely a branch cracking where the other sound originated. The night was full of sounds and she shivered again, wondering why they hadn't bothered her before, realizing at the same moment this was the first time she hadn't gone to sleep within moments upon turning in, the first time she had stayed awake and really listened. She was sure this wakefulness was because she and her father were alone. The comfort and security of being part of a group was abruptly missing.

The one reassuring sound Sarah heard was her father's faint snoring. Her cheeks swelled with a smile as she turned off the outside noises and concentrated on this nearby comforting sound. She couldn't see him in the darkness, but she felt his presence and it eased her mind considerably. Reaching out until her hand touched the edge of his sleeping bag, she gripped the fabric and lay quietly, glad she was close to him, glad she was able to be close to him, thinking how right it was being with him and how horribly wrong it had been with Mother.

Ian and Vicki Francis had divorced almost four years ago and, at the insistence of Vicki, Sarah had stayed with her mother. That had been a mistake. It had taken two years for Sarah to comprehend what had precipitated the divorce and, once her father was not around to bear the brunt, what an impossible person her mother could be to live with — self-centered, demanding, accusatory, mercenary, faultfinding. Sarah yearned to be with her father and, at the end of the two years, she had hesitantly but reasonably broached the subject.

"Mother," she had said softly, "would you be upset if I were to go live with Dad?"

The reaction from Vicki was so outraged and vituperative that her words had struck Sarah with greater impact than physical blows. She raged against Ian Francis furiously and concluded with a vile hiss: "If you go live with your father, I will hate you for the rest of your life!"

It was a terrible thing to say to a ten-year-old, and Sarah, both cowed and fearful, had not brought up the subject again. But the situation further deteriorated and a year later Sarah had simply walked out and gone to live with her father. The resultant custody battle had been bitter but the court's decision ultimately had gone in favor of Ian MacWilliams Francis after the judge spoke to Sarah privately for over an hour in his chambers.

Sarah finished elementary school in Des Plaines, the Chicago suburb where her father lived, and then, last September, enrolled as a freshman in Maine West High School. There, in addition to excelling in her studies, she had found new companions and was quite popular. She had not yet dated, partly because her father considered her still too young, but mainly because she hadn't been asked by anyone. That wasn't altogether surprising, since she was not really a pretty girl. Her features were just a little heavy and her figure chunky. Her hair was long and rather coarse, but this was a situation that could be remedied by a good professional haircutting with proper thinning and layering. Yet, for anyone who really *looked*, a very distinct beauty was there — an inner beauty which shone through the pewter eyes and was reflected in her smile. There was no vestige of cruelty or smallness about her.

So now, eighteen months after coming to live with her father, she still disliked her mother, but it was a dislike tempered by pity. Vicki Francis was what she was and she would never change; the tragedy was that she made her own life so miserable.

Sarah momentarily started as another weird, unidentifiable sound cut the darkness, but then she smiled and chided herself. They were just sounds of the night. She was safe here with her father.

That's all that really mattered.

Chapter Two

THE SUN HAD CLEARED the treetops only an hour when Sarah and her father were back at work in his dig located in the southeast quadrant of Emerald City. With the knowledge that he was nearing his goal, Ian Francis attacked the work with subdued excitement that transmitted itself to Sarah. The bite of his small, sharp-pointed entrenching shovel, while still carefully placed, was quicker than it had been yesterday.

Because of torrential rains that fell for two hours or so every afternoon, a strong tarpaulin cover had been erected on poles over the dig to afford shelter and prevent newly exposed earth from being transformed into a quagmire. Less than perfect in this respect, it did help and it also shaded them from the blazing sun which, by the time the afternoon clouds rolled in, became all but unbearable. The tarp was rigged in such a manner that during the more pleasant early morning hours it could be rolled back for more light and to let the breezes sweep over them. They had rolled it back this morning.

Father and daughter spoke little as they worked, the archaeologist concentrating on his efforts, Sarah methodically making trip after trip with dirt-filled baskets, carrying them from the bottom of the sloping excavation to the wall thirty yards distant and dumping them over onto the sizeable pile of earth already below. The floor of the jungle came directly to the wall, lush and green, exploring massive stone blocks with viny fingers. Here and there the wall had become a prop for larger trees that had tired as saplings and leaned against it, molding their bodies to the solidity as they grew larger.

Earlier today the surrounding jungle was vibrant with sound. Parrots shrieked in raucous cacophony, diminutive monkeys scrambled about in the treetops with alacrity, scolding anything that moved, and a wide variety of birds painted brilliant but fleeting spots of color on individual leaves and limbs in the verdant depths while trilling and warbling a concert of haunting melodies. But that was an hour ago and already the voices of the larger creatures were stilling as day expanded, allowing the sibilance of insect sounds to replace them.

Inch by inch the portion of the ziggurat that had been covered with soil in the rampway area was being exposed, momentarily damp and dirt stained but quickly drying when exposed to the sunlight. Dr. Francis was methodical in his work, taking time as he proceeded to alternate his digging with use of a broad, soft-bristled paintbrush, whisking away from the stone the residue of dirt as it dried. For the first couple of feet below ground level there was no change in the wall surface. In mute symmetry, massive block rested perfectly against massive block. But then, as he cleared an area at the center of the newly exposed wall only a few inches deeper, the archaeologist suddenly sucked in his breath.

"Sarah!"

There was no reply and he turned around, looking for her. Having just pitched another two baskets full of earth over the wall, she had paused to watch a great black vulture soaring effortlessly on broad wings high above. When he called again, louder this time, she dislodged her gaze and came running toward him. He was already talking excitedly as she entered the rampway, pointing to his discovery.

"Look at it, Sarah. I was right. Look at it."

She looked and her brow furrowed because there was nothing to become excited about that she could detect. The block wall was still a block wall except for a foot-wide arc of earth still clinging to it just above the center of the earth still to be moved. She looked at him with questioning gaze and he threw back his head and laughed aloud at her bewilderment.

"This!" he said, touching the tip of the shovel to the arc of dirt. When she still looked confused, he thrust the shovel inward and it stuck there when he pulled his hands away, the blade half-buried, taking on the appearance of some strangely shaped spear that had been hurled by unseen hands and buried itself in the edifice. Abruptly the blank wonder left her face and she began to realize what was strange about it, what her father had seen at once, and it unraveled itself to her in choppy thoughts. The shovel had stuck. It hadn't connected with impenetrable stone. The earth went into the wall here. The earth was packed into a hole. The hole was an opening. The opening was . . .

"*A doorway!*"

"Yes!" He was jubilant. "Yes, Sarah, a doorway!"

His excitement flooded her and as she stood watching he jerked the shovel out and, with care, began swiftly clearing away the dirt remaining against the solid wall to the sides and below. There was still much to remove and Sarah resumed filling the baskets at the bottom of the rampway and carrying them away. It was noon before the last of the covering soil was removed flush with the wall and all residue on the ground had been shoveled up and carried off. When Sarah returned from her last trip to the dumping area, her father was standing at the surface entrance to the rampway, the shovel and makeshift ladder on the ground at his feet. His shirt was dirty, plastered to his back with perspiration, and he was breathing heavily. She joined him and together they stood looking at what he had exposed.

The earth walls and floor of the sloping excavation were now free of loose dirt and the stone walkway, which had led Ian Francis to this spot initially, continued in regular fashion down the incline for a dozen feet. They were three-foot squares, separated from one another by two or three inches and only half the final one visible, the remainder hidden by earth packed above it; earth that now formed a perfect arch embedded in the great wall before them. The top of the arch was just over five feet from the base and the dirt-packed doorway not quite four feet wide.

"From this point on," Sarah's father said, "we proceed with great care. I'll be removing the remaining dirt with a trowel."

"How far in do you think it goes, Dad? The dirt, I mean."

He shrugged. "I don't know. Probably at least a

couple of feet. Maybe as much as five or six. Maybe more. I just don't know."

"Well, if there's apt to be that much, why don't you continue to use the shovel?"

"There may be artifacts — like the tablets I found earlier — in the doorway. Or, for that matter, there may be only a few inches of dirt packed against another wall on which there could be hieroglyphics. Can't take the risk of damaging anything. We'll just have to progress slowly."

Sarah nodded, understanding, yet unable to see how he could keep from attacking the remaining dirt with his shovel in order to expose as quickly as possible what lay behind it. Her own enthusiasm over what might be ahead made her feel like jumping up and down.

"I can't wait to see what's there," she said. She threw her arms around him and hugged tightly. "Oh, Dad, I'm so excited!"

He kissed the top of her head and then held his hands on each side of her face and kissed the end of her nose. He was grinning broadly when he pulled away and looked at her.

"So am I. However, young lady, it's lunch time. Want a bite to eat before we resume?"

The sun glinted in small highlights from her short hair as she shook her head. "Not really. I'd rather continue working."

His grin became laughter. "Me, too. All right, let's go over to the supply tent and get a couple of steel trowels and we can work together on it. Remember, it'll go more slowly from this point on."

Despite what they'd both said, they did stop long

enough, once they'd reached the tents, to grab a quick bite to eat — a shared can of tuna and two bananas apiece. Within a quarter-hour they were back at the archway digging cautiously with the trowels, Sarah working from the top center and to the left, her father doing the same on the right. As he said, it did indeed go slowly. About every half hour Sarah carried the dirt-filled baskets to the dumping area. Shortly after one return, while she was clearing the left side of the archway where the arch itself ended and began the straight fall to the bottom, her eyes widened as she removed a clod.

"Dad, look!"

He turned and breathed a short exclamation as he saw what she had discovered. A series of carefully carved hieroglyphics were exposed, obviously continuing behind the earth still remaining in place. He gently inserted his trowel and pulled away another clod, exposing more of the strange characters and his eyes were aglow as he nodded, more to himself than to her.

"Just like the others on the tablets," he murmured. "Wait a minute."

He turned and carefully dug into the soil in the area directly opposite on his side of the arch. In a moment he grunted with pleasure. "Here, too," he said, showing her the characters he'd uncovered. "I'd say both uprights are probably covered with them for however far inward the entry blocks go. It's a terrific find, honey. I'm proud of you. Now," he reached into his hip pocket and handed her a straight-handled brush about three times the thickness of a pencil, its bristles flat on the end and medium stiff, "use this for the final clearing away of the dirt. It may be easier if you dig carefully with the trowel first, coming close to the stone but not scraping it, then let the dampness evaporate a while before brushing it. I'll be doing the same on this side."

Sarah was not unaware that he was giving her a great responsibility and she swelled with pride at his confidence and trust in her. She was very careful indeed. The work, which had been going slowly, slowed even more with the extreme care they were taking. Almost before they realized it the sun had become snagged in the leafy canopy to the west and reluctantly they set their tools aside and returned to camp.

While Sarah prepared their dinner, and afterward as they ate, they discussed their momentous find and what might lie ahead. They wondered about how the remainder of the party were faring; if Patrick Houghton had reached Cruzeiro do Sul safely and was returning with help; if the others had reached the Ipixuna all right and were waiting at the landing place for that help. As Sarah's father smoked his after-dinner cigarette, they talked about home, discussing Sarah's future. Her eyes were bright as she responded.

"Before this trip, I was sort of undecided between archaeology and anthropology when I finally go to college. I'm not anymore."

"Archaeology?" He said the word with a mischievous quirk of his lips.

"Uh-huh."

Her father stroked his chin as if he were stroking a goatee and then muttered in perfect mimicry of Dr. Merchant, "I shouldn't wonder," and their laughter silenced the animal sounds in the jungle around them.

Later, again in their sleeping bags, Sarah lay on her

back with her hands clasped behind her head, her eyes wide in the darkness, the steady soft sounds of her father's somnolence reaching her. They had both been very tired from the day's work. After cleaning up, they'd retired to the tent, closing the flap and mosquito netting against insects. Sarah decided she would read during the interval it would take her father to log the day's events in his journal, and started in on a soft-covered volume he had brought along, *The Ancient Civilizations of Peru,* by J. Alden Mason. Though tired, she wasn't really sleepy, but after reading only a few pages she set it aside, preferring merely to lie there and think.

A small moth, which had evidently been inside the tent before the flap was drawn, circled the hissing gas lantern a few times and then came to rest in Sarah's hair. She brushed it off with one hand and it flew directly to the lamp, tried to light upon the enameled lid and immediately fried itself.

Sarah glanced at her father. Intent on his writing, he hadn't noticed. She ran her fingers through her hair and smiled at the shortness of it, remembering how long it had been just a few days before they left on this trip. In all her thirteen years, Sarah had never had a haircut until then. It had been trimmed occasionally, to be sure, but never really cut. When she went to The Hair Affair on Walnut Street that day in late April and announced she wanted her hair cropped all over to within an inch of her scalp, the operator, a slender-hipped wisp of a woman named Wendy, was very upset. Sarah's hair was so long she could sit on it and Wendy had much admired its texture and glossy bitter-chocolate color. The very thought of cutting it, much less cropping it the way Sarah wanted, was abhorrent. She refused until Sarah finally convinced her to call her father at the museum and get his approval and the reasons for doing so. Even then she bemoaned the operation all the way through. Sarah herself was stunned when she viewed the results in the mirror. She suddenly felt almost naked and smiled crookedly at the perverse thought of her mother's seeing her now, since Vicki Francis had always taken such pride in Sarah's hair, as if she had grown it herself. Nevertheless, a short haircut was absolutely essential for the trip. The other females who were going – Anita Cruz, Ruth Merchant and Pamela Wynn – had already had theirs chopped off short. Even Tad Roche and Matthew Bruce, both of whom normally had long hair, turned up with crew cuts. All were aware there were no barbers where they were going and the jungle was no place for even moderate-length hair.

Three days later they were on their way. They boarded the AeroPeru jetliner at O'Hare International Airport, hardly three miles from where Sarah and her father lived on Margret Street in Des Plaines. They were a cheerful, enthusiastic party of nine – originally intended to be seven until the addition of Sarah, a month ago, and the self-invited wife of the expedition's leader, three weeks later.

Ruth Merchant, a heavy-set woman in her middle fifties, had a very outgoing – some called it overbearing – personality. Not only the wife of Dr. Hadley Merchant, she was also a noted Chicago socialite, descended from a grandparent who was of the elite clique known as the Chicago One Hundred, a fact of which strangers were always made aware within the first three minutes of being introduced to her. Enormously wealthy, she was also one of the principal patrons of the Field Museum.

When the three-month expedition to undertake a dig at the ruins was first proposed, there were financial problems. The museum would allocate only about half of what Dr. Merchant considered the bare minimum required. It thereupon had become a joint venture, involving the University of Chicago, which pledged the other half of the requisite amount with an understanding that the head of its esteemed archaeology department, Dr. Anita Cruz, accompany the expedition in the role of coleader and that whatever artifacts were found would, after the required division with the Brazilian government, be divided evenly between the museum and the university. Since both institutions had worked together in previous expeditions, this arrangement was quite acceptable. The budget at that time provided for seven people — Dr. Hadley Merchant and Dr. Ian Francis of the Field Museum, Dr. Anita Cruz, who was also professor of archaeology and ancient studies at the University of Chicago, and four graduate students who had recently been dividing their time between the university and museum, Tad Roche, Pamela Wynn, Matthew Bruce and Patrick Houghton.

It was just before Sarah was included — and one of the reasons which made it possible — that Ruth Merchant magnanimously and without then asking favor in return, had donated the same amount the museum and university together had allocated for the expedition. What had initially promised to be a sparse, no-frills operation, was abruptly altered to include not only whatever was absolutely essential, but nearly all that was desirable. The addition of Sarah, therefore, had been no financial hardship.

The shock came when Dr. Merchant somewhat morosely informed the others only a week before departure that his wife had decided to go along. Although he had at first attempted to dissuade her, citing the hardships involved in any such expedition, even one so well equipped, she was a determined woman and brushed aside the objections. There had really been no way he could prohibit her coming along, not when she was underwriting about half the total cost of the project.

The flight was without incident but very interesting for Sarah, not only because it was her first flight aboard a jet, but because of their discussions en route. For the first time Sarah learned what had originally inspired the expedition. The Field Museum's curator of botany, Dr. Edward J. Fredericks, had returned from a successful collecting trip along the upper reaches of Brazil's Juruá River, concentrating in the area of the village of Cruzeiro do Sul, which straddled the border of Brazil's far west-central provinces of Amazonas and Acre. While there, he had asked how the village came by its name. He was taken to an aged Jesuit priest who lived in sparse quarters attached to a small Catholic church called Santo Antonio. The priest, Father Eugenio Bado, had dug deep inside an old battered trunk and brought out an object wrapped in soft gray flannel.

"Dr. Fredericks said he'll never quite get over his first

view of what came out of that wrapping," Sarah's father told her. "It was a palm-sized object of solid gold, a thick disk, evidently representing the sun with rays emanating from it, set upon a cross — not a cruciform, but rather a cross with arms of equal length. He said it weighed about a pound and upon it, etched with incredible detail and beauty, were numerous animal and floral forms.

"Did it say anything on it?" Sarah asked.

"No, there was no writing of any kind. Father Bado told Dr. Fredericks it had been found twenty years before he came there, about fifty miles north of the village at some ruins atop a long ridge of low mountains. The village had a different name then." He shook his head. "I forget what Dr. Fredericks said Father Bado told him it was, but the old priest whose place Father Bado was taking told him that the villagers thought the artifact belonged to God and they gave it to him for safekeeping in the church. Father Albano, the first priest, eventually passed it along to Father Bado. Anyway, from the day it was brought to the village, the people called it Cruzeiro do Sul — that's Portuguese for Cross of the South — and that's what they renamed the village."

"Well, didn't Dr. Fredericks go and see the ruins for himself?" Sarah was fascinated with the story.

"In a way, yes. At least he tried. Father Bado told him the villagers were very superstitious about the place and would not go there."

"Why not?"

"I guess they did, at first. Gold does tend to attract people and they'll go through a lot of hardship to find it.

Naturally, when it became known that the Gold Cross of the South had been found in the low range of mountains called The Little Green Hills — that's *Pequenas Colinas Verdes* in Portuguese — a lot of people started going there, looking for other gold."

"Did they find any?"

"Not so far as Dr. Fredericks was able to ascertain. Evidently some kind of accident or sickness overtook anyone who went there. So many people became sick — some even died — and so many were hurt or killed in one kind of accident or another, that they believed the place was jinxed. No one will go anywhere near the ruins now."

"Then Dr. Fredericks really didn't get there?"

"Well, as I mentioned, he did, in a way. He tried hiring guides but at first no one would take him. Finally he found someone who could be described, I suppose, as the town drunk, who said, for a price, he would guide him. They traveled by canoe most of the way, first down the Juruá and then up the Ipixuna. There were some difficult rapids and then, when they got within sight of the mountains, they encountered a waterfall — not high, but large enough to prohibit further upstream travel. As they put to shore there, the guide fell while getting out of the canoe and broke his ankle on the rocks. He told Dr. Fredericks then that even if he could have walked, he would have gone no farther, so they got back into the canoe and returned to Cruzeiro do Sul. But the crux of the matter is that before putting to shore, they could see the tops of The Little Green Hills from the river and the guide pointed out the one where the ruins were supposed to be located. All the hills were round-topped except that one, which looked as if it had been cut off with a big knife. Also, Dr. Fredericks said that downstream a little way from the falls, where they came ashore, there was a large gravel bar. There was also a large cube-shaped boulder with a smaller boulder, a round one, balanced on top of it — an excellent marker for the location."

Dr. Francis paused to light a cigarette as the AeroPeru stewardess passed through handing out soft drinks and they each took one, Sarah a Coke and her father a Seven-Up. Under his amused gaze, Sarah drank half of hers without pause. She grinned.

"Good. I was thirsty. Okay, go on — was that as close as Dr. Fredericks came to the ruins?"

"As a matter of fact, no. He was determined to see for himself and procured an even smaller canoe and came back alone. He returned to the landing place below the falls without any difficulty, took a compass bearing on the flat-topped hill and then set out through the jungle. He got there all right and was halfway to the crest when he climbed up onto a large rock to look around. That was when he caught his first glimpse of a ziggurat — one of the square-topped pyramids common to ancient ruins in South America. While standing there, the rock he was on tipped over and he hurt his knee pretty badly. He still limps from it. Anyway, he couldn't continue the climb and he had to cut a crutch in order to limp back to his canoe. Even then he almost didn't reach it because of a whole series of assorted mishaps. But he finally reached Cruzeiro do Sul and came from there to the States. About a week after he returned, he called Dr. Merchant and me to his office and told us the whole story. He showed us pictures he had taken of the gold artifact and the landing place on the Ipixuna. He was convinced it was worth an expedition and we agreed. That was when we started making the plans."

"Do you think we can find it?"

He chuckled. "We wouldn't be going if we didn't think so."

They broke off talking for a while and Sarah stared out her window a short time and then read while her father napped. In less than an hour lunch was served and they chatted while they ate. They were just finishing when Matthew Bruce came down the aisle heading for the lavatory. The graduate student was tall and good looking in a rather sharp-faced way. He was twenty-five and wore his moustache and whiskers trimmed in a manner which reminded Sarah of the Sheriff of Nottingham. This was to be the second dig in which he'd participated and he was hoping for great things. The first, in Costa Rica, had not amounted to much. On reaching their row, he paused and sent the wide, genial smile that was his trademark in Sarah's direction, then spoke to her father.

"I was just talking with the stewardess, Dr. Francis. She said we'll be coming up on the Peruvian coastline pretty soon and will follow it south to Lima. Sarah might enjoy hearing about Chan-Chan when we pass Trujillo."

"Thanks; Matthew, I'm sure she would. How are the others holding up?"

The young man rolled his eyes. "Dr. Merchant is

asleep; I think he's been asleep ever since we cleared O'Hare. He didn't even wake up to eat. Mrs. Merchant — " he leaned closer and his voice lowered, "do you know she's been telling us all to call her Ruthie? *Ruthie! My gawd!* Anyway, she's playing solitaire, at least when she's not nudging Dr. Merchant and trying to get more than a grunt out of him. Tad — he's sitting with me — is asleep. Pamela, Patrick and Dr. Cruz are all sitting together ahead of us. They've been talking shop ever since we took off. I think they're on the Incas now. They've already covered the Aztecs and Mayans. Where's the nearest poker game?" He barked a short laugh, touched Dr. Francis's shoulder and was gone.

Ten minutes later the coast of Peru was passing beneath, and far to the east, partially shrouded in clouds, were the imposing Andes thrusting white-tipped peaks like wolf fangs toward the sky. The western slopes of those mighty mountains, leading to the sea, were bare and scorched, with only scattered small rectangles or uneven lines of green indicating rivers or water sources where vegetation could be supported. Closer to the coast there was more greenery, much of it in geometric patches. Those, Dr. Francis pointed out, were primarily cotton fields. Twice the loudspeaker system came alive as the pilot alerted passengers on the left side of the aircraft first to the city of Talara and then, after another twenty minutes, to the larger city of Chiclayo. The third time he spoke, a quarter-hour later, it was to announce Trujillo.

Staring at the city nearly five miles below, Sarah was unable to make out details, but she could discern its

general shape on the austere hills above the sea. Her
father leaned over to look out beside her.

"That city," he said, "is on the site of a once-great
ancient city called Chan-Chan."

"The one Matthew mentioned?"

"That's the one. The people who lived there were
called Chimú and they predated the Incas, so far as we
can determine. In fact they were still the power in this
area until the Incas came along. The Chimú controlled
an area of about ten thousand square miles; the whole
Peruvian coastline area, from the Ecuadorian border in
the north down to about where Lima lies. One of their
noteworthy accomplishments was the building of adobe
houses having both beautiful designs molded in raised
relief on the façades and brilliantly painted backgrounds.
We still don't know how they did it — what sort of
process they used to make them last so long. The Chimú
were immensely wealthy."

"Gold?" Sarah asked.

He nodded. "Much gold. One of the burial mounds
that was opened — called Huaca de Toledo — contained
over two million dollars' worth of gold. Pizarro's principal object, when he conquered Peru in the sixteenth cen-
tury, was finding gold. He let nothing stand in his way.
He found a highly developed people, the Incas, standing
between him and the gold, so he simply slaughtered them
by the thousands. After stealing their wealth, he tore
down their temples, had their priests murdered and then
set up the cross, justifying all his atrocities as having
been done for God's purpose. From the very beginning
it became common for the Spanish priests to round up

the Indians and work them like beasts in the mines until they dropped dead — and they considered those miserable people well paid by a promise of a white man's heaven that was totally incomprehensible to them."

He sighed and motioned toward the window with his thumb. "Anyway, the Chimú down there were a very sophisticated people, very advanced. They had medical techniques, for example, that still rival some of those of modern medicine."

"Like what?" Sarah asked, looking at him. "Surgery?"

"Yes, surgery, plus other skills. They knew how to do very successful brain surgery using a technique called trepanning and they —"

"If they disappeared so long ago," the girl interjected, "how do we know the surgery was successful?"

He smiled approvingly at her. "Good question. The reason we know is because we've recovered many skulls of trepanning surgery patients. In almost all cases the bone tissue, after surgery, has mended, meaning the patient recuperated and probably lived a reasonably long life after being operated upon."

"What else? In medicine, I mean."

"Well, they also knew how to amputate limbs very skillfully and they were downright masters of dental techniques. They knew how to repair teeth by crowning them, by filling them with silver as we do, and by bridging. In other fields, they knew how to smelt gold, silver and copper. Somehow, though no one yet knows quite how, they mastered the secrets of metal plating. They could do it just as well as we do with our modern electrolytic process. Their art was superb and they did a great deal of mosaic work, using ivory, mother-of-pearl, colored shells and bone."

"Whatever happened to them? Why did they disappear?"

"The Incas rose to power and they were stronger. Their fortress and supposed point of origination was an island in Lake Titicaca, on the present Peruvian-Bolivian border. The Incas spread out and warfare resulted. They conquered all of the Chimú except those in Chan-Chan. That was a tremendous fortress and it held time after time against the Incan onslaughts. The Incas finally realized they'd never be able to take it by direct assault so, withdrawing out of sight of Chan-Chan, they built a dam across the river that supplied the Chimú fortress with water. The situation got pretty bad. What few crops the Chimú had left withered and died. A lot of people were lost from thirst. But Chan-Chan still wouldn't give in."

"Didn't the Incas ever conquer it?"

"They finally took it, yes, when they sent in word to the surviving Chimú that if they didn't surrender they would put out the sun in the same way they had dried up the water. So the Chimú gave in. After that, although the Incas ruled, the Chimú lived in harmony with them for a long while. You'll be able to see a lot of the artifacts from both cultures in Lima at the archaeological museum — it's called the *Museo Larco Herrera*."

Despite her interest, a huge yawn caught Sarah unaware and Ian Francis leaned back in his seat and patted her knee. "Hey," he said gently, "I'm sorry. I've been lecturing as if I were a schoolteacher. C'mon. Here's a pillow. Tilt your seat back and take a little snooze. You'll want to be wide awake when we reach Lima."

She slept for an hour, awakening as the plane was making its final approach to Lima's international airport. Within the hour they had checked through customs and seen to their personal baggage and the expedition gear. After that they checked in at their hotel, the Palacio. It was quite close to the Municipal Palace, in which the illiterate conqueror Pizarro had lived. The city itself, she learned, had been founded by Pizarro three years after his arrival in Peru. During those previous three years he had been exploring, conquering, pillaging and destroying as few conquerors in history before him had ever done.

Making arrangements for their further transportation had consumed three days, with most of the detail work accomplished by Dr. Merchant and Dr. Cruz. The latter, who had been born in Lima and was formerly connected with the *Museo Larco Herrera*, was fluent in both Spanish and Portuguese, which helped in cutting through governmental red tape. A fair amount of time was spent, as well, arranging matters with the Brazilian government through their embassy in Lima.

Sarah was impressed with the old city and the way it had been established. Much as Chicago had been planned, it was laid out in checkerboard fashion with uniform-sized blocks. Specific places were relatively easy to locate by street numbers. The architecture was breathtaking and Sarah, unlike the others who had begun to chafe at the time they were having to spend here instead of at the dig, would have been perfectly content to remain a week or more just seeing the sights and steeping herself in the first foreign culture she had ever experienced.

Many of the old homes could only be described as magnificent. One they visited was called the *Torre-Tagle*. The entry was an elaborately carved doorway of stone, the doors themselves constructed of heavy wood studded with bronze. Immediately inside was a lovely tiled vestibule with a wide variety of ornately potted plants and a great deal of statuary. The vestibule led to a series of patios, and off these were a number of extensive suites comprising sumptuous chambers. Large, beautifully painted oils framed in antique gold hung on brocaded walls. They were primarily portraits of past owners of the *Torre-Tagle* and their families. The parquet floors were exquisite, here and there covered by intricately woven, softly colored rugs from Cuzco. As members of the party strolled through these echoing, highly polished *salas*, it was easy for Sarah to envision the pomp and luxury of the social life that had existed here over the centuries. Much of the stonework was of material brought at great effort and cost from Panama. The inlaid tiles were from Sevilla, and the rich, magnificently finished woods originated in the forests of Central America. Lavish, intricately carved balconies of Moorish design were the final graceful touch for each of the suites.

Briefly, they toured the oldest institution of higher learning in the Western Hemisphere, the College of San Marcos, founded in 1551. This school had passed the half-century mark before the first permanent settlement was made by the English at Jamestown. Its library, over one hundred fifty years old, was of special interest to the group because it contained not only a vast and varied collection of fine books, but also the diaries, journals and manuscripts of early churchmen, especially Jesuit missionaries, who traveled extensively into the interior of the country and recorded their impressions of the people and places encountered.

They strolled through the bustling core of the city, the Plaza. On one side was the Municipal Palace where Pizarro had lived during his reign of terror and where he was eventually murdered; on the other side was the huge cathedral where he is buried; adjacent to that, the palace of the archbishop had deeply carved balconies overhanging its glistening white façade. Religion, Dr. Cruz explained to the party as they walked through the *Plaza de Armas*, always played an integral part in the lives of Peruvians, but especially so in Lima. This plaza was, and still continued to be, the principal scene for all public rejoicing and lamentation.

"There was often good cause for the lamentation," the archaeologist added, "especially during the Inquisition. Terrible time — just terrible. Over in that direction," she pointed, "where the statue of the Liberator stands, is the *Plaza de la Inquisicion*. That building at the end of the Plaza is the House of Congress. During the Inquisition, more than one hundred people were publicly burned to death and over three hundred severely beaten. The Inquisitors, you know, were exempt from all taxation and merchants were required to provide them free of charge anything in their shops."

"Sounds like being an Inquisitor was a cushy job," Tad remarked dryly.

Anita Cruz nodded. "At first there were only twelve such posts here, but the demand for appointments became so heavy that it increased to forty families. It became a reign of terror not unlike Nazism. Heavy pressure was brought by the church upon the faithful. Only the Inquisitors themselves were safe and everyone curried favor from them. Husbands denounced their wives, sisters informed on their brothers, children accused their parents — oh, it was a bad time, all right. Testimony offered against the accused was accepted, but if it was in his favor it was rejected, irrespective of evidence to the contrary."

"When did the Inquisition finally end, Dr. Cruz?" Sarah asked.

She grimaced. "Not soon enough, Sarah. Spain fully terminated it in 1813. Somehow, people always find some sort of justification for their mistreatment of others. Unfortunately, religion in those days was often used as an excuse for inflicting terror and pain. Peru, for example, has always been subject to severe earthquakes and," she stretched out her arm and made a sweeping gesture, "it was right here, following the earthquake of 1655, that Pedro Castillo stood on a pedestal over the heads of the crowd, castigating them for their sinfulness and demanding that they repent if they wished to avert a similar catastrophe.

"Now bear in mind," she told them, "though there had been a lot of damage to Lima in that 'quake, no one had died. However, Castillo whipped them into such frenzy of penitence that a peculiar phenomenon occurred. Everyone rushed to confession and poured out his iniquities into the ears of the priests. Rich men gave the church their entire fortunes and dressed in rags. A general fasting occurred and instead of the Plaza's being filled with cheerful, happy people, hundreds of thousands formed themselves into slowly moving lines circling about right here, many of them walking on their knees, a good percentage of them with blood streaming down their faces from the crowns of thorns they had driven into their own scalps. Most of them wore sackcloth and a large number were in chains and carried heavy wooden crosses. Some walked with their backs bared and bleeding as others lashed them. An unbelievable chorus of groans and sobs and moaning filled the whole Plaza, along with the clanking of chains and hissing whips smacking against flesh. Above it all the church bells were constantly clanging."

As if to clear her mind of the grisly picture, Anita Cruz shook her head and looked around. When she spoke again her voice was so low it was difficult to hear. "Another earthquake didn't come – at least not right away. But though the 'quake they'd just gone through had not killed anyone, hundreds upon hundreds died of the wounds they had inflicted upon themselves or from exhaustion. It doesn't make much sense, does it?"

Sarah's reverie was abruptly cut short as her father closed his journal, looked across the tent toward her and was surprised to find her still awake. He smiled wryly and leaned over to pat her leg through the sleeping bag.

"Hey," he said, "I've been keeping you awake. I didn't

realize it. There was a lot to write about what we uncovered today."

She smiled back. "No problem, Dad. I wasn't sleepy. Just thinking about our trip down here."

He stretched expansively and yawned. "Well, I, for one, am very tired and I'm going to knock off now. Do you want the light on any longer?" At the shake of her head he turned a knob on the lantern and immediately the hissing stopped and the brilliant glare began to fade. He leaned over and kissed her. "Better get some sleep. Another big day tomorrow. Good night."

"Good night, Dad. I'll be going to sleep soon, too."

Her father snuggled down and was asleep before the final glow of the lantern extinguished. Now, listening to his steady breathing, Sarah continued to lie with her hands behind her head and thought about the journey from Lima to Emerald City.

With final arrangements having been made in the Peruvian capital, the party loaded their equipment and themselves into three small planes and set out on a course due northeast from Lima, heading for Cruzeiro do Sul, Brazil. It was necessary to use three planes because only the smallest of aircraft could land at the tiny airstrip at the Brazilian village.

It was just over four hundred air miles to their destination, and in single file the little planes labored to climb over the rugged Andes range. The tops of the eighteen-thousand-foot peaks seemed to be reaching up hungrily for them as they flew past. The whole aspect of the terrain changed dramatically on the east side of the mountains. Where before the landscape had been one of

bare, harsh crags and desert conditions, now the slopes
became covered with dense greenery and the air was
often cloaked with heavy mist. Ahead of them stretched
the seemingly endless mantle of the rain forest — a single, virtually unbroken jungle almost as large as the
continental United States.

As they descended somewhat east of the mountains,
the broad expanse of the sinuously winding Ucayali
River lay ahead. This great stream was the upstream con-
tinuation of the Amazon River, its headwaters not very
far from Lake Titicaca, seven or eight hundred miles
south. The river finally took the name Amazon at the
confluence of the Ucayali and the Marañon rivers, over
five hundred miles to the north. They landed briefly for
rest and refueling at Iparía, on the banks of the Ucayali,
and were amazed at the atmospheric difference. They all
felt weighted down by the moisture-heavy air.

Slightly over an hour after taking off again, they
crossed the border into Brazil, although except for their
pilots' telling them so, they would not have known it.
There was nothing below but unbroken jungle with occasional meandering streams. The ground was still faintly
mountainous, but only in few areas could the rockiness
of those mountains be seen. Most were covered with the
continuous greenery of forest cover, giving them a soft,
rolling appearance. For the most part these mountains
were no more than a thousand feet high and more com-
monly around seven hundred feet. In each of the valleys
were streams, all of them on their meandering move to
become eventually a part of the Amazon and empty,
after many months of steady flowing, into the Atlantic.

Cruzeiro do Sul appeared ahead almost shockingly —

an island of low wooden and adobe buildings encompassed by the dense forest and dominated by the spire of the Church of Santo Antonio. A few small fields had been cleared for the growing of mandioca, tobacco and bananas, and the airfield's runway was nothing more than a long narrow avenue of bare ground not much wider than the planes in which they were flying. Cruzeiro do Sul was situated on the northwest bank of the Moa River, almost within sight of where that stream merged with the larger Juruá, from which point the Juruá flowed northeastward.

This was where certain difficulties began to develop. They had planned on hiring local people to transport them and their equipment by river to the landing place on the Ipixuna and from there overland to the site of the ancient ruins. There had even been hope of hiring a crew of men to remain on the site with them to help with some of the heavier labor of the dig. They had also hoped to get a woman or two to cook for them. Their inquiries met with instant and very firm rebuff and they were immediately treated with a certain indefinable fear or suspicion. Warned not to embark on such a foolish and dangerous venture, they were regaled with stories of the mishaps that had befallen those crazy enough to have gone there in search of gold. The fact that the expedition's goal was not to find gold but to seek knowledge and the artifacts of an ancient civilization did little to ease the emotions they aroused. Under no circumstances would anyone volunteer to help at the site, despite offers of handsome wages. It was only with the greatest of difficulty they were able to hire guides and half a dozen long dugout canoes to transport them and their goods to the point where the overland journey would commence. Even this was accomplished only through offering owners of the boats three times more than Dr. Merchant had anticipated spending for the service.

The archaeological party would be transported to the landing place eight miles from *Pequenas Colinas Verdes*. The boats would be unloaded there and return immediately to Cruzeiro do Sul. When the party was ready to return, a call on their radio transmitter to a ham operator in the village would alert the boat owners to pick them up. There was no other choice.

Hadley Merchant was furious, but the pragmatic Anita Cruz merely shrugged. It was a difficulty, but what expedition did not have to overcome at least one such difficulty? They would simply have to work together, themselves carrying the equipment from the landing to The Little Green Hills. It would not be easy and might require two or three trips, but they could do it.

Much of the heavier equipment brought along was thereupon left behind under the care of Father Bado, stored in an adobe hut in back of the Church of Santo Antonio. They took with them only what was absolutely essential for the dig. That still amounted to a substantial quantity.

"Wouldn't you know," Patrick Houghton commented with heavy irony, "most often there aren't funds enough to really outfit an expedition well. Then, the one time when you have everything you need, you have to leave half of it behind anyway. Jeez!"

Once afloat on the Juruá, however, the sense of disgruntlement vanished. The nine members of the party were in three of the boats, each handled by two paddlers. The other three boats, also paddled by two men each, carried equipment. The river was swift and smooth and immediately after Cruzeiro do Sul was left behind, the jungle closed in right to the water's edge and they slid quietly into a different world.

Hordes of little monkeys scurried about in the tree-tops or sat munching fruit, watching the floating pro-cession pass and occasionally chattering with excitement at such a spectacle. Huge gaudy macaws, screeching in-sults, sailed across the water ahead of them, always in pairs, and occasionally they saw large caimans — the crocodiles of the Amazon — floating with their snouts and backs exposed in the vegetation-cloaked areas close to shore. Hosts of brilliant butterflies flitted in and out of the wall of lower forest growth lining the river's edge. Where occasional sand or gravel bars were encountered along the shorelines, the party startled little herds of capybaras frolicking in the shallows. Looking like mon-strously overgrown guinea pigs, these hundred-pound rodents grunted high-pitched warnings and either crashed off into the forest or plunged into deep water to swim off beneath the surface.

Once, at the mouth of a rivulet entering the Juruá, a snake about twelve feet in length and as thick as a man's upper arm dropped from a branch overhanging the water only a dozen feet in front of Sarah's boat, disappearing with a sizeable splash. The villagers laughed and called it *sucuruju*, saying that it was only a baby. Sarah thought they were teasing and looked at her father, but he shook his head.

"They're not kidding, Sarah. It was an anaconda and a

pretty small one at that. They're constrictors and sometimes grow to enormous size. Biggest snake in the world. As I recall, the largest officially recorded was not much less than forty feet long and as big around as your body. They've been reported up to eighty feet, but that's probably exaggeration. They're not poisonous, though, and reasonably inoffensive if you don't antagonize them."

Tad Roche, in the same boat with them, gave a little snort and looked at Sarah, who shuddered. "I give you my solemn promise, Dad, I won't antagonize any."

Her remark struck Tad as being terribly funny and he brayed with laughter, joined by Sarah and her father. The young man relayed the conversation to those in the boats behind and they laughed too, except for Ruth Merchant who despised snakes, didn't think it was at all funny and looked about nervously for the next hour or so.

Several stretches of rapids were encountered through which the dugouts were skillfully maneuvered. Sarah, who had never been through white water, experienced a sense of exhilaration tinged with fear as great protruding boulders swept past, while the foamy water swirled about them with wicked gurglings. The water of the Juruá was clear but stained brown, and every once in a while Sarah caught glimpses of large fish flashing beneath the surface. Smaller fish sometimes jumped out and fell back with noisy splashes.

Thirty miles downstream from Cruzeiro do Sul, a substantial river emptied into the Juruá from the northwest. This was the Ipixuna — a gin-clear stream that had its headwaters nearly a hundred miles away in the low mountains of the Peru-Brazil border country directly west. They had to ascend the Ipixuna for another eighteen or twenty miles before reaching the landing place where their overland journey would begin. They camped for the night on a broad sandbar jutting out into the river at the confluence of the two streams.

A remarkable change occurred early the next morning as soon as they began heading upriver on the Ipixuna. The paddlers, who until now had been reasonably friendly and gregarious, turned sullen, uncommunicative. With each mile moved upstream, their evident apprehension grew. Dr. Merchant chose to blame it on the increased difficulty in paddling. Some of the passage became very troublesome where the stream narrowed between hills and the pressure of the water was extremely hard to buck. The three younger men of the party — Matthew, Tad and Patrick, each in a different canoe — took up paddles and assisted. While this helped the boatmen considerably, it did not improve their mood. Twice they had to portage around severe rapids, following dim trails of previous portages, everyone helping to drag the heavy dugouts loaded with equipment to where they could again be launched.

The upstream movement was so difficult that by sunset they had gone only two-thirds of the distance to the landing. Once again they made camp on a bar, but this time the twelve men from Cruzeiro do Sul drew themselves apart from the party, building their own campfire — a very large one — and huddling close together around it. When at last they slept, two of their number stood guard. Except for some strange, unidentifiable noises from the jungle, nothing happened during the night.

At dawn's light, amid the customary chattering of

monkeys and birds, they were again on their way. No more than two miles below the landing another rapids was encountered, considerably more severe than the previous two, and again they portaged. As they pushed out into the current again above the rapids, two paddlers in one of the equipment dugouts sent their craft skimming under some low-hanging branches to avoid a large rock protruding from the water. One man accidentally banged his paddle against an overhanging branch upon which was a large wasp nest.

Instantly the angry insects streamed out and descended with stinging fury. The men shrieked and strove to get away, but the wasps followed in a brutal cloud. First one man, then the other, leaped into the water. The unmanned dugout spun with the current and shot back into the midst of the rapids. Twice it struck rocks and remained afloat, but the third time it hit a jagged projection broadside and split in two. Everything in that boat was lost — tools, a couple of guns and ammunition, much of the party's extra clothing, a portion of their food supply, the photographic equipment and, worst of all, the radio transmitter.

Both swimming men also were swept into the rapids but miraculously they survived. One suffered a severely wrenched back and the other a bad gash in his upper arm, which was bleeding abundantly. Both were battered and bruised from contact with the rocks. Well over three hours were lost in helping them back to the other boats above the rapids and in making vain searches for any equipment that might be recovered. Part of the time was taken up by treating the injury of the man who had gotten gashed. Anita Cruz took a suture needle from one of the first-aid kits, sterilized it with the flame of a cigarette lighter and then stitched the wound closed with nylon thread. Sarah watched closely, marveling at the toughness of human flesh and the difficulty Dr. Cruz had in pushing the needle through. The wretched man was no stoic; he moaned and cried with pain at each stab of the needle and Sarah felt very sorry for him. Six snugly tied stitches closed the wound nicely, but the man never even expressed his thanks.

It was only with great difficulty that Dr. Merchant persuaded the guides to take them the remaining short distance to the landing place, which they reached just over an hour later. Only fifty yards ahead and in clear view was the waterfall. It was thirty feet high and sixty feet wide. A great volume of water poured over the entire edge and the roaring was so loud they had to raise their voices. Before they came ashore on the bar near the landmark boulders there was a glimpse of the hills, including the flat-topped one. A compass reading verified the report that it was due north of the landing.

With unseemly haste the men from Cruzeiro do Sul unloaded the boats, dumping equipment in a hodge-podge pile on the gravel bar. They didn't even want to talk with Dr. Merchant and Dr. Cruz, but the two scientists flanked their leader and Dr. Cruz conversed with him heatedly in a torrent of Portuguese accompanied by much gesticulation. With the radio lost, arrangements had to be made for these boats to come back for them at a specified time. At first the man shook his head violently and replied angrily to everything said, but at last he became less argumentative, hunched his shoulders a few times and finally nodded reluctantly. Having been promised double what they'd already been paid, a quarter of it now and three-quarters later, he agreed to have the boats back at this same bar in exactly ten weeks. Within moments of his collecting the advance payment, the five dugout canoes were paddling swiftly downstream.

Sarah could remember no time in her life when she had worked so hard as during that first week. No one had anticipated this sort of difficulty. Time became a blur of loading, carrying, and hacking a trail through the jungle. They found the ruins where expected, atop the flat-topped mountain at an elevation of six hundred sixty feet, eight miles from the river, and Sarah had dubbed the place Emerald City, but that whole first week comprised little more than getting all the supplies from the river to the dig site and setting up their camp.

Sounds from the jungle filtered to Sarah's consciousness again and she turned on her side in the sleeping bag and closed her eyes. What her father said a little while ago was true — tomorrow was going to be a big day and she'd better get some sleep. Unlike last night, the sounds tonight filled her with a sense of comfort and her last waking thought was, "I could come to like those noises."

In the morning, Sarah Francis and her father were back working in the dig while the monkeys were still chattering breakfast greetings to one another. The father and daughter concentrated on the stone portal and by noon they had it all but cleared of earth. The hieroglyphics on both uprights of the doorway were extensive and Dr. Francis was very excited about them.

"Before we quit today, Sarah," he said, "I want to

copy these down exactly. It's quite possible they could provide a key for translation of what's on the tablets and the base of that statue."

"Do you want me to get your notebook and pen?"

"No, I'll copy them later. I really don't want to stop right now. Tell you what — are you game to go rustle up a bite for us while I continue working?"

"Sure."

"Good girl. Let me know when it's time."

He was already back at work with his trowel as she left the excavation. Opening another tin of ham, Sarah made sandwiches again, using the last of the bread and deciding that she'd have to bake some tomorrow. She'd also suggest that Dad try to shoot some more of those big grouselike birds Tad had been shooting to provide the party with fresh meat. There were still tins of canned goods, but they were becoming tiresome and some fresh meat and fruit would be good. She prepared two cups of the iced tea mix and strolled back to the dig. When she looked inside, Ian Francis was on his hands and knees, furiously pawing dirt behind him.

"Dad! What's the matter?"

He grinned up at her through dirt-speckled glasses, panting heavily. "Matter? Nothing's the matter, honey. Everything's great. Just great! Look here."

He stepped aside and she saw that the earth that had covered the whole inner portion of the archway between the hieroglyphic uprights had apparently fallen in a pile at his feet. Beneath the arch and downward for half the distance to the base was a flat gray face of stone just like that of the wall. But where it ended, about thirty inches above the floor, there was still loose dirt, much drier than before, and this was what her father was clawing away. He dropped back to his knees and continued scooping it out, sometimes to the side, sometimes through his legs like a dog digging and scattering the soil behind. Sarah watched a few minutes and then she spoke hesitantly.

"I've got our lunch ready, Dad. Don't you want to stop for a while?"

He answered without turning. "Sure. Sure. Give me another five minutes here. I think I'm about to break through to whatever's behind. Just five minutes more, okay?" She didn't respond and he looked around. She was there behind him on her hands and knees, helping to toss the dirt farther back, making room for what he was still scooping out.

"Oh, you are a real doll," he laughed. "I love you."

"I love you, too, Dad. Take your time. Lunch will keep. This is more important."

Two minutes later, as his arm was outstretched to its farthest reach under the stone block, he gave a sharp cry. His hand had just broken into an empty space beyond. He dug even faster then, pulling the dirt away swiftly, letting it crumble to some degree from the sides down into the gap he was making and thrusting it behind him.

"Now I know what a mole feels like," he said with a short laugh. In another few minutes he had enlarged the interior opening enough to admit his head and shoulders. He wriggled back out to clear away the mound of dusty soil about his knees, trembling with excitement, and his breath coming in harsh gasps. From a pocket he withdrew his cylindrical butane cigarette lighter and used his thumbnail to push the flame adjustment lever over to the highest pitch. When he flicked the wheel a steady, bright yellow pencil of flame three inches long sprouted from the end of it. He nodded and turned it off.

Sarah touched his arm. "Dad, do you want me to go in? I'm a lot smaller. I could get through easier."

"No. Not till I make sure it's safe. I'll take a quick look with this," he held up the lighter, "and if it seems all right, we'll clear out the rest of the entry here and get flashlights. Then both of us can go in."

He assumed a prone position on the ground and squirmed forward with the unlighted cigarette lighter at arm's length ahead of him. He crawled farther inside until only his lower back, hips and legs were still outside. Sarah heard the flick of the wheel and then the glow of the yellow light past his silhouetted forequarters became visible to her through tiny niches in the soil at his sides.

"What do you see, Dad? What's inside?" She could scarcely contain the excitement bubbling in her and she came up close behind him on hands and knees, leaning her head down in a futile effort to see past him.

His voice was muffled but hollow sounding and no less excited than her own. "Oh, my God, Sarah, wait'll you see what's here. You won't believe it. It's *incredible!* There's —"

A deep, torturous screeching sound of heavy stone against stone obliterated his words and then, like some monstrous guillotine, the enormous block in the archway directly above Dr. Ian MacWilliams Francis dropped.

Chapter Three

F OR THE FIRST FEW SECONDS after the stone dropped, Sarah could not comprehend the enormity of what had occurred. Then she screamed. The piercing cry ripped from her throat and rolled out of the excavation, so filled with horror and despair that it silenced all other sounds nearby. It was as if all the jungle creatures had frozen in place, stricken by the intensity of it. The forest listened with stilled leaves and even the breeze held its breath. An unnatural quiet prevailed long after the desperate, anguished cry dwindled and disappeared. Even then the memory of it hung.

In the excavation, still on her knees beside him, Sarah gripped her father's leg and shook it, blinded by tears, her thoughts inchoate with a mélange of agony, despair and fear. She buried her face on the backs of his legs and her shoulders heaved with the eruption of wrenching sobs.

Then the legs moved – a shuddering, spastic movement causing the toes of his shoes to gouge the earth. She jerked erect and stared at them. *He was still alive!*

Sarah lunged into action, tearing at the ground with her hands, spewing the earth behind her in a veritable spray. Her fingernails broke and tore and her fingers

bled, but she didn't notice. After a while she snatched
up the little shovel and attacked the earth, repeating the
same phrase time and again as she did so, without even
realizing the words were leaving her.

"Hold on, Dad, hold on."

At first the digging was automatic, undirected, merely
an effort to move the earth, to free him from his entrap-
ment. Then there was a return of reasoning, an analysis
of what had happened, where he was and what she was
doing. If she persisted in digging at the earth to the side
of him, that would only undermine the mass of stone
block above and allow it to settle more heavily upon him.
Immediately she began to dig beneath *him* instead, trying
to remove enough of the dirt to enable her to free him
from below.

Almost at once she struck the stone block of the walkway he had followed. A new wave of fear gripped her as
she backed off a little, searching for the end of the block.
Perhaps by digging down its edge, she might find it thin
enough to be removed. She found the edge and dug
around it, exposing the corner of it near the hieroglyphic
upright, then dug straight down. The block seemed endless, going down and down until finally she was more
than a foot beneath the upper corner and had not yet
reached the bottom. The sick realization struck her that
even if she encountered the bottom now, there would be
no way she could even budge such a block.

She paused, thinking, thrusting aside the grief and fear,
concentrating only on what she could do. Abruptly she
lunged for the shoulder pouch which lay on the ground
on the other side of him and tore it open. A rock ham-

mer, several chisels, a tape measure, brushes, a two-inch magnifier, a package of cigarettes, a notebook, a pen. That was all.

She put two of the longest chisels on end, their bases on the block beneath him. They were too short to reach the block above. She snatched the steel tape and measured the gap. Just under eight inches. Leaping up with the tape still clenched in her hand, she scrambled out of the excavation and ran to camp, her eyes searching for anything — *anything!* — she could use as a prop. Her gaze fell on a number of flat rocks that had been used to help hold down the tent flaps. She gathered some and measured them. Too short. But they were flat! One atop another would do it. She stacked them and measured carefully, discarding one for another until she had six flat rocks, each about the diameter of a saucer. When stacked in two piles, they were just about the correct height.

She thrust the steel tape into the pocket of her khaki trousers, scooped up the rocks in her arms and carried them back to the excavation. She touched her father's leg but there was no answering movement. Removal of more earth from the surface of the base rock was necessary and she used both shovel and trowel to scrape dirt away on both sides of the stone doorway close to the hieroglyphics. She tried various combinations of the rocks atop one another until there were three which fit perfectly, so close she had to wedge them in with taps of the rock hammer. The other side was more difficult. Before she could get them to fit, she had to use the hammer to chip off a nodule on the surface of one. Again she tapped them in place, jamming them so tightly they could no longer be budged. Then, sometimes kneeling, sometimes lying on her stomach, she began digging again.

Not until her knees began sliding about beneath her did she realize it was raining and the earth was turning to mud. For herself she didn't care, but for his protection and in an effort to keep the dirt dry and diggable, she climbed out of the excavation and unfurled the tarpaulin as best she could. As usual, the rain had started as a light fall but now was becoming torrential. The tarpaulin cover wasn't perfect, but at least the rain did not fall directly upon him. She skidded on the slickened surface as she reentered the sloping rampway and fell, sliding and rolling to the bottom. Caked with mud, she scrambled back to where she had been before and resumed digging. The earth there was still dry and crumbled away easily. She was on his left side and his arm there was pinned beneath his body. Bit by bit she pulled the earth away, her efforts directed mostly to that side, her arm aching from stretching so far, her hand cramped and fingers clawlike from digging. She didn't even notice when the rain stopped. She dug with a singlemindedness that precluded everything else.

At last her probing fingers reached the point of his left shoulder. She scraped and dug the earth away from his neck, felt the hair of his nape, touched the lobe of his ear and pulled the soil away from it. *His ear!*

"Dad! Dad! Can you hear me? If you can, move your feet, anything. Just move. Please, Dad, move!"

Sarah straightened out of the hole and shook his buttocks, his legs, begging him to move, but there was no response. She stretched out on her stomach again and reached far in. As she resumed pulling away more of the earth, she noticed it was no longer easy to throw out behind her. It had begun clinging stickily to her fingers and she thought at first that somehow the rain had seeped in and was turning it to mud. She brought a handful of it close to her eyes and saw that it was a bright reddish mud and she knew that the moisture was not rainwater. She wept again, as she had at intervals, and the fresh tears carved clean little channels through the dirt and mud on her face, then fell in discolored drops from her chin and from the tip of her nose.

She reached in again and her groping fingers found his head. It was not tilted, but face down, mashed into the layer of earth still covering the block beneath him. Her fingers traced the back of his head, past his ear, moved up over the unnatural bulge of his cheek and into his hair again. Then they touched something very jagged and sharp and she realized it was his skull, broken, crushed. The horror descended upon her again and she jerked her hand away. A terrible sound filled the excavation and in some remote corner of her mind she realized she was screaming again and couldn't stop.

How long Sarah sat there beside him, her hand on his back, she had no way of knowing. Awareness returned slowly and with it the realization that it was dark. How long ago nightfall had come, she didn't know. Shock cloaked her and everything had nightmarish quality. She moved her hand and felt a scattering of dirt on him and she knelt beside him, methodically brushing it off the small of his back and from his trousers. One pantleg had pulled halfway up his lower leg and she carefully pulled it down, her hands brushing against the skin of his calf and noting remotely that the warmth and living elasticity of skin was gone and that it was now like cool plastic, pliant to a degree but lifeless.

She leaned back against the excavation wall and looked up. Beyond the edge of the covering tarp there were stars of intense brilliance against the dark of night. She watched them for a long while without really seeing them, suspended in a vacuum precluding thought or sensory perception. Once she drew up her knees, folded her arms across them and leaned her forehead against them. If she dozed, she didn't know it, but neither did she know if she were awake. She simply was not aware.

The first sense to return was hearing. She was nudged into awareness by the chattering of monkeys amid a background chorus of birdcalls. It was daylight again. She was infinitely weary, her muscles aching as she came stiffly to her feet. She looked down at the body of her father, but the horror was gone; all that remained was an encompassing grief. She turned and made her way slowly up the slope and walked mechanically back to camp.

The two sandwiches looked terrible, having remained exposed on the tiny camp table for so long under the rays of the sun and the following downpour. She realized she was hungry and it embarrassed her. How could she be hungry when her father lay dead in a hole fifty yards away? She picked up one of the sandwiches and began to eat it, dimly aware it might be spoiled, that it might make her sick or even poison her, but she didn't care. It had no taste to her, good or bad, and she automatically ate it. The two cups of tea were still there, one of them with a dead bee floating on the surface. She reached for the other one and accidentally knocked it over. The liquid splashed over the tabletop and began dribbling off one edge. She watched it with vapid curiosity a moment and then picked up the other cup, fished the insect out with a muddy finger, flicked it away, and drank half the contents. Then she picked up the second sandwich, ate that and finished off the tea.

"What do I do now?"

The thought had become a vocal expression and the sound of her own voice startled her, drew her back into a greater awareness of reality and her present situation. There was a peculiar comfort in just the sound of her own voice and she wished someone were here, anyone, just so it was somebody to talk with, someone whose voice she could hear. There was no one, so she talked to herself, sometimes aloud, sometimes mentally, sometimes not knowing the difference between the two.

"First I've got to see to Dad. I can't leave him like that. I'll have to bury him or at least cover him somehow, right where he is. The others will be back before too long. Ten or twelve days. I should just wait for them here. But what if they didn't make it safely to Cruzeiro do Sul themselves? What if no one comes back? What's going to happen to me?"

She shook her head. No, she wouldn't wait. Didn't *want* to wait; not with Dad there in the hole. They hadn't been gone all that long. They were probably at the river landing, still waiting for Patrick to come back with boats to help them. Who could know how long they'd have to wait there? Maybe days. Maybe a week or more. They'd been gone only two full days. This was the beginning of the third. Chances were if she walked the eight miles to the landing place, she could still find them there. At least it would be something to do. She couldn't just stay here and wait, day after day, hoping for their return. But the fear was a cold hand twisting her insides and she began trembling so badly that she sat down, feeling sick with it. The spasm passed and she clenched her fists.

"No," she told herself. "You will *not* act this way. I won't permit it. Think! What would Dad want me to do? The first thing he'd say would be to stay calm. Reason things out. Act sensibly. Decide what needs to be done and *do* it. Don't let fear master you. It can kill you quicker than anything else. Just *think* — and then act."

Sarah Francis thought. Fear was an entity within her, struggling to get out, to be given expression, but she held it in check. After a few minutes more she got to her feet and returned to the excavation with a larger shovel from the supply tent, steeled herself at the entry and then went down. She leaned the shovel against the earth wall and replaced the contents of her father's strong nylon pouch she had dumped yesterday. One by one she emptied his trousers pockets: wallet, handkerchief, pocketknife, nail clipper, a nickel and dime, several Peruvian coins, a set of keys. These, too, she threw into the pouch, then tossed the pouch and little entrenching shovel outside and began digging in the left wall with the larger shovel.

She worked in an almost trancelike state, forcing her

mind away from what she was doing, not watching as
shovelful after shovelful covered his shoes, his lower
legs, his upper legs. An hour passed, during which she
thought of her mother, her friends, her school; she
thought of the members of the expedition; she thought
of the Chimú and their defeat by the Incas; she thought
of Lima and of Iparía and Cruzeiro do Sul; she thought
of the artifacts that had been found. . . .

Abruptly she stopped, frowning. The artifacts. They
were supposed to have been taken care of, protected by
Sarah and her father. They rested now in the supply
tent and she knew she musn't leave them there. She left
the excavation and returned to camp, emptied a satchel
partially filled with miscellaneous gear and filled it with
carved stone heads and figurines. She took them to the
trench with her and laid them on the ground carefully at
the right side of her father, then went away and came
back again with the rest, including the stone tablets
her father had found and the gold statue Pamela had
unearthed. These she left in the satchel, carefully placing it at his left side. Then she dug again. Now she
was aware of what she was doing, carefully scattering the
shovelfuls of soil over the artifacts and satchel until they
were covered. In the process she covered the remaining exposed part of her father's body.

By this time the hole she had made in the left wall of
the excavation was rather deep. Her hands were blis-
tered and her back and shoulders ached. She came out of
the hole, walked over to the ruins wall and breathed
deeply, looking but not seeing. For ten minutes she stood
there quietly and then the impact of it all struck her

anew and she sat on the edge of the wall, burying her face in her hands. Her shoulders heaved and she rocked back and forth, a low moaning issuing from her. It was a reaction, but it was also a catharsis, cleansing her of the grief and fear and self-pity that had been mounting throughout the morning. When the reaction abated, all that remained was a clean and healthy sorrow — not grief, which debilitates — and a keen awareness of her situation coupled with a determination to act sensibly, maturely.

Though she had heard nothing, when she returned to the excavation, Sarah found that the whole left embankment, undermined by her digging, had caved in, dumping tons of earth over the form she had been covering. The entire stone arch had been covered as well. It was far more than she would have been able to do in a full day's digging. She didn't dwell on the fleeting thought of what would have occurred had she still been there when it fell. It had happened as it did and she was thankful for it. The shovel was buried but it made no difference now.

Sarah stooped and picked up the pouch and entrenching shovel, then paused a moment, considering, her gaze on the raw earth. Neither her father nor mother had been churchgoers but both had, in their own ways, expressed belief in a greater Power, whom they called God. For her own part, Sarah had never really doubted that there was a Supreme Something, but she had been extremely dubious about the existence of any God — or Goddess, for that matter — perched up there somewhere keeping track of every move she made and listening in on everything she said. If, in fact, there was a God, then He-She-

It had much better things to do than hover overhead listening to whatever consignment murmurings Sarah Francis might now utter or supplications she might beg of Him-Her-It. In the end, she simply stood there and said what was most natural, most heartfelt.

"Good-bye, Dad. I love you."

When she returned to camp she stripped and washed herself thoroughly from the camp's water supply and dressed in fresh clothing, tossing to one side the mud-caked garments, knee-high socks and tennis shoes she had been wearing. Since she would be doing considerable walking, she decided against wearing the tennis shoes and instead laced on the sturdy ankle-high hiking boots that she hadn't worn since arriving here.

Next she concentrated on what she would take. There were backpacks in the supply tent but she didn't want to be that encumbered and decided she would simply use her father's tough nylon shoulder pouch for whatever necessaries she took. She estimated she would require enough food and other items for one or two days, but decided she'd better take enough for twice that time, just in case anything unexpected happened. She emptied the contents of the pouch onto the ground and then began picking through the camp's supplies. The items she selected very rapidly became a formidable pile and she had to readjust her thinking. She divided the collection in two parts — one of absolute essentials, another of desirables. There were still too many items in the essential pile alone when she finished, so she eliminated more and finally completed her selection. Canned goods were heavy so she packed only a bare minimum — remembering to take a can opener — and instead took more of the dried fruits: apricots, peaches and prunes. Though bulky, she also took a couple of packages of crackers. By this time the pouch was half filled. One change of clothing — another set of pima cotton khakis, plus socks and underwear — were tightly rolled and stuffed into the pouch. She finished by packing insect repellent, a two-cell camp flashlight, a bar of soap in a plastic container, a toothbrush, a round tin of waterproofed farmer's matches, a small first-aid kit, and her nylon, hooded poncho, tightly rolled up. She had difficulty snapping the pouch shut.

Still on the ground were a few things from her father's pockets and pouch. His pocketknife, nail clipper and magnifying glass she put into her side pockets. The wallet she carefully buttoned into one of her shirt pockets. She put two fresh handkerchiefs into her hip pockets and then hung a sheathed machete on one side of her belt and a canvas-covered canteen of fresh water on the other.

There were a shotgun and shells but she decided against taking them, mainly because she didn't like guns and knew little about how to use them. Besides, they were very heavy and she already had all the weight she wanted to carry. Only one other thing remained: her bright red, lightweight sleeping bag. She rolled it up and adjusted the straps so she could slip them over her shoulders and allow the sleeping bag to ride on her back, but she didn't put it on immediately. Instead, she cleaned up the camp, stowing everything of any value in the supply tent, securing the flap. On the verge of stowing the rock hammer, she decided to take that too, hanging it in its belt sheath next to the machete.

Sarah stood for a long moment looking over the site of the dig. Again she considered remaining to await the return of the others, knowing she would be safer doing so, but when her slowly moving gaze abruptly anchored to the site where her father was now buried, she knew she couldn't stay. The image of the ruins began swimming as her eyes filled again. How could it be that just yesterday he had been alive and well and excitedly digging there, and now he was gone? She sniffled and shook her head, pushing the thoughts away and, with them, the hysteria that immediately began to blossom. No, whatever the hardships might be in moving out and finding the others, they would be preferable to remaining here and waiting. At least she would be doing something.

By now it was well past noon and the customary clouds were rolling in, darkening the sky. She wished they hadn't shown up today, as occasionally they didn't, and the sky had remained bright. Perhaps it wouldn't rain; now and then the clouds would form such a dark ceiling low above the trees but no rain would fall. Far more often, though, the rain began gently, quickly increasing its intensity to a heavy downpour. Usually it lasted for a couple of hours before tapering off, sometimes longer. Afterward the sky always remained overcast until nightfall. Then it would clear and the stars, as if newly washed, would sparkle with unbelievable brightness.

Sarah opened her pouch and readjusted the packing

somewhat so that the rolled poncho was handy on top, then snapped the flap closed again. She picked up the rolled sleeping bag, shrugged into the straps, perching it comfortably high on her back, and then adjusted the pouch over her left shoulder. A smaller strap trailing from the rear of the pouch she pulled snugly around her waist and clipped it to a metal eye loop on the front of the bag. This would keep the pouch from bouncing annoyingly and slipping off her shoulder as she walked.

She thought about leaving a note in the supply tent for the others in case she missed them but decided that was pointless. Turning away from the camp, she walked to the north edge of the Emerald City ruins and descended the stone steps to the jungle-grown plateau below. Without hesitation she entered the forest along the trail they had made when they had so laboriously carried their equipment up here from the river; the same trail upon which Dr. Merchant and the others had departed three days ago.

"I wish I had gone with them," she said aloud, a rather frightening loneliness now filling her.

Within a dozen yards or so the vegetation was so thick she was having difficulty. Numerous long woody vines called lianas had fallen and were draped across the path, and she climbed over or ducked under them frequently. Even in the path itself, which they had cleared with such difficulty when they first arrived, there was much new growth. Though the Merchant party had passed along here quite recently, it was difficult to follow the trail. Sarah took out her machete and began whacking the larger growths out of her way.

The leafy canopy shut out much of the daylight and caught the rain when it began its first gentle fall. Because of the noise she was making in her passage, Sarah was unaware it was raining until a large drop struck high on her forehead and ran into her eye. She stopped and looked up at the interlocking canopy of leaves and branches high overhead. The sky itself was hidden. In the heavy silence she heard other large drops spattering as they struck the leaves around her. Immediately she removed her dark green poncho from the pouch and tried to put it on, but found it would not comfortably go over the rolled sleeping bag. She took the sleeping bag off and ducked into the poncho again, pleased when it covered the shoulder pouch without binding. She picked up the sleeping bag and tucked it under her left arm on the outside so that it rested on the bulge of the pouch. Still using the machete with her right hand, she continued along the trail. By this time it had grown much darker and the rain was falling more heavily. Thunder rumbled and occasionally lightning cracked harshly, but shed little light where she was walking. The downpour became so heavy the canopy was no longer a protection and the whole forest was engulfed by the sound of the rainfall. She paused again and pulled up the hood of her poncho, tying it snugly around her neck. There was a small bill on the hood over her forehead and she was thankful for it. Without that, her face and eyes would have been soaked immediately. The rain poured off the hood in such volume she could see scarcely a dozen feet ahead, and she wished she had not left her pith helmet back at camp.

Swinging the machete at vegetation blocking her way was becoming a problem because she became heavily sprayed with water each time she struck a leafy plant or vine. She used the tool less frequently and, where possible, stepped around obstructions. She trudged on determinedly, as if in a dream, the rain drumming on her poncho monotonously. The sleeping bag held under her arm had become saturated. Its surface material was purportedly water repellent, but it certainly wasn't waterproof and, soaked as it was, it had become a heavier weight to carry. Chances were she really wouldn't need it more than a few times anyway, so at last she decided it was too much of a burden. Wishing she had left it in the tent, she set it on end against the bole of a large tree and left it. Even soaked the way it was, and despite the dimness of the forest floor here, its scarlet color was so bright she was certain there would be no difficulty in locating it when they came back.

Relieved at the elimination of that burden, she moved along more easily, glad to have her left arm free to help thrust aside the growth through which she was passing. She knew that once she was down the south slope of the mountain the passage would be easier because there the forest floor was much more open. There was something about that thought which stuck in her mind, plaguing her until she suddenly jolted to a stop. The slope! She should have been descending it long ago, but she was still on relatively level ground, meaning she must still be on the plateau of the small mountain. But that was impossible. It was only a ten-minute walk on the trail around the wall of the ruins to where it began to descend the south slope and she knew she had been walking at least half an hour, perhaps even longer. It had surely been ten minutes ago that she had left the sleeping bag behind.

Sarah began to pay closer attention to the ground around her. What she was following, which appeared to be the trail, was clearly not the trail at all. She turned around slowly and discovered that in all directions it looked the same, that no matter where one turned, one could imagine a trail leading that way. She studied more closely the area near her and could detect no marks of passage save her own, no older slash marks machetes would have made.

With crashing suddenness she realized that somehow she had strayed from the trail. She was lost. A paralyzing fear began rising, engulfing her, and she stood frozen there, a diminutive speck in the vastness of the forest. The rain pelting her had now become an ominous thing, a malevolent force responsible for her straying. Sarah leaned against a tree and then slowly slid down to a hunched position at its base and her tears merged with the rain on her face.

"Dad. Help me. Please, help me!"

The torrent of rain drowned out her words and panic became a tangible thing, flooding her mind with abject fear such as she had never known. Her whole body trembled and her intestines churned and writhed as if gripped by a powerful hand twisting them unmercifully. Bladder control was lost and her pants were suddenly warm-wet. For a moment she thought she would vomit and a strand of mucus hung from the end of her nose and bounced weirdly with the violence of her trembling.

"Think, Sarah, *think!*" The words came into her mind as if spoken aloud and she let them fill her. "Remember, the thing that will kill you sooner than anything else is panic."

Were they her own thoughts? Were they somehow a communication with her father? It was almost as if he were standing here beside her, comforting her, and she let the words continue filling her mind, dredged up from somewhere within, where they had been indelibly imprinted.

"You have to keep your head. Think. You *must* think! Panic destroys reason. Don't run, don't walk, don't even move for a while. Just think about where you are and where you came from and where you are heading. Remember your good answer when Dr. Merchant asked what you would do if you became lost. You told him you'd stay calm, keep your head, think. Do it now. Stay calm. *Think!*"

Sarah Francis thought. She thought about where she was at this moment and she thought about the direction from which she had come. She knew she could retrace her steps to the sleeping bag. Perhaps that was where she had unknowingly left the trail. All she had to do was go back to the sleeping bag. Then she'd be all right. The incipient hysteria relaxed its hold, the rising panic faded, the trembling eased and then left.

The rain was still falling very heavily when she came back to her feet. She stood still, looking around, afraid to move from where she was until she knew positively from which direction she had come. She wished she had used the machete more. She saw a foot-mark in the thin layer of moldering debris. Hers. She saw, beyond that, a small plant crushed down. Her doing. She moved to them and looked more closely. Ten feet ahead a woody vine marked by the bite of her machete and another just beyond that. She moved to them, reassured. She continued to move in that direction, certain she would soon see the brilliant red of the sleeping bag. She was so positive it was just ahead of her, she concentrated her attention on that to the exclusion of her own trail marks, losing them again without realizing it for several minutes.

The rain was pelting down so hard that sometimes even just breathing was difficult. She wished now she had remained crouched at the tree until it stopped, but then reasoned it would have been foolish to have done so, because the downpour would have helped erase her own trail. Aware that she was no longer following her own marks, she started walking in a wide deliberate circle, paying close attention to the ground, watching for when she would cross her own trail again. She found nothing and, once more, the tendrils of hysteria clutched at her heart.

Sarah stood still, using great mental effort to force down the panic. After a few minutes she calmed and her mind threw off the fear again. She took stock of the situation, deciding what to do. She turned in a slow circle, wishing she had taken her father's compass because then she could simply head due south until she hit the Ipixuna River. Without it she could only guess which way might be south. She continued turning slowly until she had a sense that *that* was the right direction. She than walked slowly and very straight in the direction she believed was south.

Fearful that she would start walking in wide circles, she began to align her gaze on a tree as far ahead as she could see and walk directly to it. Repeating the process with another distant tree and then another, she kept on a straight course. After fifteen minutes the ground suddenly began sloping sharply downward and a sense of exultation rose in her. She was certain she was heading in the correct direction, and this sense was intensified when she encountered a little erosion gully in the forest floor, so small she could step across it easily. It was simple to deduce that by following the tiny stream it would eventually empty itself into the Ipixuna.

By slow degrees the rivulet became larger as she descended beside it. Other rivulets joined and the runoff became a clear bubbling brook dashing itself over rocks and roots, winding sinuously around huge trees. By the time she had followed it for half an hour, she could no longer step across the ravine it had formed. By the end of another hour the stream was three feet wide and its ravine was six or seven feet across. She began growing excited, thinking the Ipixuna must be just ahead. Occasionally she paused, listening for the roar of the waterfall just above the landing place, but all she heard was the persistent drumming of the rain.

At last the downpour tapered off, almost three hours after it had begun. There was no way for her to tell when it ceased altogether, for a steady fall of drops continued long afterward from the dense blanket of leaves overhead. The ground was more level now but it was also much darker, the approaching twilight deepening the gloom of the forest. Tree frogs had begun singing and their chorus seemed to come from everywhere at once. Occasionally birds flitted past, dark shadows silently heading for their night's roost.

Sarah continued to walk, but it became so dark that she had difficulty seeing. She fell several times and, fearful that she would stray from the stream, she stopped at a huge tree with enormous buttressed roots and curled up in the recess where two of them joined at the tree.

The air was cooler and she kept her poncho on. She was very hungry, having eaten nothing since the stale sandwiches. She turned on the flashlight and rummaged in the pouch. Finding a can of tuna, she opened it and used the blade of her father's pocketknife to spear the chunks of fish. Nothing had ever tasted so good. When the big pieces were gone, she brought out the crackers and spread the residue of the tuna on them. Finished with that, she neatly buried the empty can in the humus beside where she sat and put the remaining crackers away. With a handful of dried apricots, Sarah finished her meal and took a long drink from the canteen.

Full dark had come and she was momentarily startled as a huge hawk moth swooped past, its great wings the size of both her palms. It flew past the glow of the flashlight again and was gone. Movement on the ground attracted her attention and she swung the beam down, impaling a cockroach the size of a mouse. It spread leathery wings and flew off into the darkness. She looked at the beam of light and was appalled at seeing how much dimmer it was than when she had first turned it on. Berating herself, she clicked it off, allowing the almost palpable darkness to close in. Immediately the sounds from the forest seemed amplified and, with her arms drawn in from the sleeves of the poncho and wrapped around her legs, she shivered.

The frog and toad symphony was louder than it had been before and set to an accompaniment of a weird variety of insect noises. Stridulations from crickets and katydids became a string section as they drew saw-toothed leg shanks across wing edges and created a perpetual buzzing on several tonal levels. Here and there the deeper, throatier calls of owls and goatsuckers added a bass section to the étude. Once, far up near the canopy, a branch snapped loudly and fell, crashing against other branches and lianas as it dropped, finally striking the earth with a heavy, muted thud.

Had there been someone knowledgeable on hand to identify the sounds they would have been fascinating to hear, but to Sarah they were little less than frightening and, as she cowered between the roots, a soft frightened moaning occasionally escaped her. Her head jerked erect when, very close at hand, there was a heavy cry, almost like the bray of a mule, and she had no way of knowing that it was just a little tree toad which she might easily have held in the palm of her hand. A little later a different amphibian, a tree frog, expanded the air sac under its chin and, though no larger than the tree toad, erupted in a brief and astonishingly loud roar. The hairs on the back of Sarah's neck tingled the flesh as they came erect, and her anxiety was in no way eased by the call of a larger brown frog in a small pool of the stream she had been following. It sounded almost as if someone had struck a wooden barrel with a mallet six or seven times in succession.

A larger animal of some kind squealed loudly and then there was the thrashing sound of something chasing something else, ending in a piercing shriek as the pursuer caught the pursued and killed it. From high overhead, in the now invisible canopy, the din was constant. Again it was the tree frogs and tree toads creating the greater part of it, issuing a cacophony unlike anything Sarah had ever heard, each variety with its own particular call. Some of them sounded like short grunts, others were melodious trills or penetrating whistlings, and still others rattled or croaked or made tinny hammering sounds.

A dozen times or more Sarah dozed, only to come awake as some louder, closer sound punctuated the pervading din. She wished desperately that she had not abandoned the sleeping bag, longing for its warmth and comfort, wanting nothing more than to crawl into it completely and be encased in its haven until daylight returned. She wished the night would end, wished the dawn would come, wished someone would find her, wished she would find someone, wished most of all that her father were here. And suddenly he was . . . in a way. A conversation with him surged up out of her memory; a day about a year ago when she had expressed a wish for something and he had turned to her with a wry smile and spoken not unsympathetically.

"Wishing's no good, Sarah," he said. "It seldom accomplishes anything, and more often than not it's self-defeating. What's far more important is the determination to get something done. In other words, intestinal fortitude – plain old guts!

"Most people don't have any," the archaeologist had declared, "and that's what's wrong with the world today. Having guts is not the same as never being afraid. Sarah, any person who tells you he's never been afraid is a fool or a liar – probably both. It's what a person does *when* he's afraid that's important. The one with guts does what has to be done or endures what has to be endured.

"Sarah," he had touched her cheek softly, then cupped her chin in his strong hand with great gentleness. "Somehow I know you've got what it takes to make the mark. More, in fact. I happen to know that whatever comes up in your life, good or bad, you'll always meet it head-on. Sometimes you'll be afraid. We all are. But whatever happens, Sarah, I know you'll face the situation, no matter how difficult it is. In doing so, pretty soon you'll discover that most of the things scaring you are worse in your mind than in reality. And pretty soon you'll realize the futility of sitting around wishing for what's not possible. If you remember that, honey, you'll make out just fine."

Sarah remembered it now. The sounds coming out of the darkness were no longer quite so frightening. Mostly they were the sounds of small creatures that were essentially harmless – crickets and frogs, katydids and toads and night birds – and when you *listened* to them, they were really rather pleasant.

She moved out of her crouched position and lay on her side, her back to the forest, knees drawn up, her head pillowed on the pouch. The chill of the rain was dissipating and the forest was warm and comfortable. She might have felt better in the sleeping bag, but she was warm enough with the covering of her poncho. The scent of the decaying wood and vegetation had the same rich humus smell she remembered from inside Chicago's Garfield Park Conservatory, and that too was friendly and comforting.

Just before she fell asleep a final time, the memory of her father rose and engulfed her and, though she tried not to think about him and what had happened, she couldn't help it and there was a terrible welling of pain in her breast. She didn't want to cry, tried to keep the tears in check, but they came anyway and she sobbed herself to sleep.

Chapter Four

A BELL WOKE SARAH. The sound penetrated her sleep, crisp and sweet, a clarion note resounding in the early morning light. She sat erect at once, listening intently. There were many other sounds, close and far, with which she had become familiar each morning at the Emerald City dig: monkey chatterings and parrot shriekings; multitudes of parakeets moving through the canopy and voicing subdued chitterings interspersed with occasional harsh little screams; the throatier and more grating cries of the macaws.

The single bell note came again, explosively loud, a musical metallic peal overriding the more distant sounds in its stark clarity and sweetness. Getting to her feet, Sarah moved to the outer point of the buttressed root flanges of the giant tree between which she had slept and tried to pinpoint where the peal had originated. A flash of pure white caught her eye and she focused on it. A bird about the size of a blue jay perched on a long hanging loop of liana some thirty feet above the ground and not more than fifty feet distant from her.

It was snowy white with the exception of a very peculiar black fleshy spike projecting straight up from the base of its upper beak. Even as Sarah stared at the bird, it fluffed its feathers and the black spike swelled. The mouth gaped wide and that incredibly sweet bell-like note pealed forth. Sarah was amazed that such a sound could issue from a bird and she immediately thought of it as a bellbird, not realizing that this was actually its name.

While pleased at the sighting, she was also disappointed. What she had expected to see was some person walking along and at intervals tapping a well-made brass bell with a little metal hammer. The thought of that reminded her of the isolation and the need to get to the Ipixuna River as soon as possible. The air was close and warm and she removed her poncho and rolled it up. The little stream running past the big tree where she had slept was considerably smaller now than yesterday, but still running very clear.

Hungry again, Sarah considered eating more of the dried fruit, but then changed her mind. Her trousers were still damp in the crotch and down the insides of the legs from when she had urinated during her brief panic yesterday and she was distinctly uncomfortable. She picked up pouch and poncho and climbed down the bank of the ravine to where the water flowed around a large flat rock projecting above the surface. It created a small eddying pool on the downstream side. Here, removing the canteen, machete and rock hammer from her belt, she placed them, along with the poncho and the pouch, on the rock and then sat on it herself, removing her shoes and socks. The socks, too, were damp.

She reached down and felt the water. It was mildly warm and pleasant and, on an impulse, she cupped her hand and filled it, bringing the water to her mouth. It tasted sweet and good, even though warm, but she was accustomed to that same warmth in the camp water and it did not disturb her. She stretched out on her stomach on the rock and leaned her head down, her mouth to the water, and drank deeply. When she was finished she removed the canteen from its canvas cover, dumped out the slightly metallic-tasting water it contained, and submerged it until the air bubbles ceased coming out of the top. She recapped it, replaced it in the cover and stripped herself.

The water in the pool was shallow, not quite reaching her knees. It felt very good and she sat down, letting the gentle current lave her. She looked about and saw, sitting on the opposite bank and perhaps six feet up-stream, a medium-sized greenish-brown frog. It was regarding her with steady bulging gaze, apparently not at all afraid.

"Good morning, Frog," she said. "Are you the one who made some of the awful noises last night?"

The frog didn't move and Sarah tilted her head, smiling as she looked at it. "I don't suppose," she went on, "that you're one of those frogs who would turn into a prince if you were kissed, are you? Well, we'll never know, will we?" She laughed lightly, cupped some water in both hands and tossed it toward the amphibian. At that, the frog croaked a guttural sound, leaped into the water, kicked a few times when it got to the bottom and hid itself under a little rock ledge.

Sarah reached over and removed the soap from the pouch and used it to scrub her panties thoroughly. The foam she created, especially as she rinsed and wrung them out, was carried downstream in a small white cloud and she thought, in a detached way, "I'm polluting the water." After spreading the clean panties flat on the rock, she picked up the trousers, emptied the pockets, washed the garment and then did her socks. The shirt she left alone.

Wading a few steps downstream, out of the eddy and into the moving current, she stopped where the water was only ankle deep and there she squatted in midstream, moved her bowels and urinated. She splashed water on her bottom when she was finished and returned to the pool.

Now she concentrated on cleaning herself. She briefly ducked her head under the water, came up sputtering and spouting, then lathered her hair and scrubbed it with stiff fingers, thankful for its shortness. She rinsed thoroughly twice, stood up and soaped her body.

At thirteen, Sarah's breasts were firm and well rounded, though not yet fully developed, so that the aureoles seemed overly large — a fact which had distressed her lately. Her body was chunky, still with a semblance of little-girl plumpness, but only recently her waist had become narrower, more trim, her hips fuller, more womanly. Her pubic hair, which had first sprouted when she was ten, was already full and heavy, a curly black triangle of which Sarah was inordinately proud. She was much less pleased with her thighs, which she felt were too heavy, but they and the lower legs were also gradually becoming slimmer. She was sure she would never have the long, lean, graceful figure that

American men seemed most attracted to, but her concern in that respect had been alleviated by her father. He had sensed it and sat down with her one day, explaining that while the svelte figure was popular in the United States, almost everywhere else in the world the female figure most admired was the type Sarah was almost sure to have — a full, healthy, strong body, well fleshed but not fat.

Sarah returned to the reality of her situation at this thought of her father and, more soberly, she finished her bathing quickly and stepped up onto the rock. She hung the damp clothing on a root projecting from the ravine embankment and, with no towel on which to dry herself, sat down and ate her breakfast of crackers and a handful of dried prunes and peaches. She could have eaten much more but rationed herself carefully, conserving the food she could carry with the hope of finding edible things as she traveled.

Half an hour later she was still damp and the clothing was virtually as soggy as when she had hung it. The humidity was so high that things just did not dry well, not even skin. She noted that on her hiking boots a faint sheen of mold was forming in every seamed groove. This had not been a problem at Emerald City because there they had enjoyed direct sunlight, but here in the rain forest it was an entirely different matter. It had been daylight for some time, yet the dim, filtered quality of the light remained the same. Almost no sunshine reached the forest floor and, for the first time, Sarah became acutely aware of the remarkable thickness of overhead foliage and that the forest floor was nowhere near so dense with low-growing vegetation as she had expected.

She had walked all day yesterday through the rain forest, yet she had not really seen it. The more she had descended into the level area, away from the mountain, the thicker the woods had become and the less jungly undergrowth there was. Now, as she looked around, she was really seeing her surroundings for the first time. The trunks of the trees were unbelievably tall, rising straight and pillarlike, without any branches at all for well over one hundred feet.

Most of the mature trunks were relatively slender, from one to four feet in diameter, and the fact that they rose so high before branching created the unreal effect of a colony of ship masts. Here and there, rarely close together, were trees that were truly gigantic. They monopolized the area in which they stood and nothing else grew close to them. They had cylindrical trunks, usually about twelve feet in diameter but sometimes twice that thick, soaring upward in grand fashion to a huge crown, often two hundred feet above. The crown itself was so thickly leaved it took on the appearance of a gigantic green cauliflower. These larger trees, such as the one Sarah had slept beneath, all had the great buttressed roots which formed spacious chambers large enough for five or six people, the flanges rising straight up from the ground sometimes to a height of ten feet. Rarely more than a few inches thick, these roots — usually three or four to a tree, but sometimes up to ten — created a cartwheel effect at the base of the tree since they extended outward in all directions for six to ten feet. Sometimes the buttresses were straight but occasionally they were incredibly gnarled and angular; without their support the gigantic trees could not possibly remain standing.

In many cases, the bark of the trees was difficult to discern because the trunks were well covered with bromeliads and epiphytes as well as being draped with curtains of lush climbing plants such as pothos with deep green, heart-shaped foliage and the giant-leaved philodendrons. Only rarely could Sarah see areas where she could trace the line of one of the tree trunks to its uppermost area. In most cases the layer of foliage began thirty or forty feet above the ground and the trunks just disappeared into it.

The majority of the lower foliage sprang from the incredible tangle of lianas which interlaced and looped, stringing themselves from tree to tree. Creating a world of themselves, they twisted in great cabled strands, knotting themselves together, sometimes spreading apart in zigzagging fashion, every once in a while becoming indented as if they were stairsteps leading into the roof of foliage. Not uncommonly, there were lianas hanging straight down, having broken at one end above and still anchored by the other.

For Sarah, the effect was like being in a vast, endless cathedral, where light and sound were muted, where the grand tree trunks formed supporting columns, where only a very small percentage of full daylight filtered down to the forest floor, where only a few varieties of plans could grow — primarily ferns, some of them ten feet tall. There were also many mosses, along with unusual plants Sarah could not identify. All these ground-growing plants obviously required little sunlight. But compared to the density of the overhead foliage, the forest floor was relatively open and there were few areas where the ground was thickly overgrown. The sunlight that did manage to penetrate the upper leafy barrier appeared only as small flecks, slowly moving about, changing in size and shape, appearing and disappearing as the position of the sun changed. Much of the light that reached the cathedral interior was sunlight already reflected once or twice from light-colored tree trunks or from glossy leaves, many of which looked as if they were lacquered or stamped out of shiny sheet metal.

The ground was well littered with debris from the canopy. There were leaves dislodged by wind or rain or living creatures; a multitude of gigantic bean pods from the lianas; fruits of strange appearance and texture which ripened and fell naturally or were plucked and dropped by monkeys, birds or other animals; limbs that had crashed down from on high and also quickly underwent deterioration; nuts in hard kernels, which defied decomposition best, but ultimately gave way to it. The whole effect was one of a complex cycle of life and death. There was no time here when simultaneously, different plants were not sprouting, blossoming, producing fruit, dropping leaves, and dying. Everything that fell was decomposing rapidly, providing sustenance to the soil, and that sustenance in turn was being absorbed by the great trees and lianas in order to produce more fruit, nuts, leaves and limbs, which would, in their turn, eventually fall. Now and then there was a great log lying on the ground where one of the towering trees had lived out its life span and had fallen. Even this soon returned to the soil as the wood became coated with ferns and mosses, while beetles and other insects combined with moisture to turn the hardness to spongy material that gradually flaked away to nothingness.

Sarah felt very small and insignificant in the grandeur of this mighty forest, knowing that what she was seeing at ground level was only a small fraction of the life, vegetable or animal, living here; that most of it lived in the vast and much more expansive world of the many-layered canopy and that this was a hidden world she probably would never know well.

Behind her there was a heavy splash and she whirled around, startled. In the pool where she had bathed was a peculiar-looking fruit surrounded by rapidly disappearing concentric ripples. Glancing up, she saw nothing stirring in the canopy and could not tell whether it had fallen by itself or been dropped by a monkey. She stepped into the water to get it and brought it back to the rock for closer inspection. About the size of a large apple, the fruit had an oddly scaled skin bearing a resemblance to the skin of a tortoise. The rind was thin enough that she could feel the softness of pulp beneath, but so tough she could not tear it with her fingers.

Using the pocketknife, she cut it open and found a cluster of dark, mahogany-colored seeds, each about the diameter of a dime and perhaps a quarter of an inch thick. They were surrounded by a lemon yellow pulp very much like custard in appearance and with a pleasant, pungent aroma. Hesitantly she scooped some out on the blade of the knife and took a very tiny taste. Her eyes widened. Delicious! Unlike anything she had ever tasted before, it was, she thought, most like a combination of lemon and pineapple, faintly tart yet very rich. She ate the whole fruit, spitting out the seeds as she mouthed the pulp from them. Finally, she scooped the remaining pulp from inside the rind with the knife blade, enjoying every morsel. She scanned the surrounding area for any others that might have fallen. There were a few but all were badly rotted and she was disappointed.

An hour had passed since her bath and, except for her legs, which had just gotten wet again, and her hair, she was fairly dry. The nylon panties were damp but the other clothing was almost as wet as before, even though the pima cotton trousers ordinarily dried quickly. Unwilling to delay any longer, she put on the shirt she had been wearing and took the fresh trousers, panties and socks from the pouch. Within a few minutes she was fully dressed, with the canteen, rock hammer and machete again suspended from her belt. The pouch, now containing the rolled-up poncho, was strapped over her shoulder. She picked up a short length of branch and whacked it against a tree to dislodge any bugs. She shoved it through the waist and one leg opening of the still damp panties, arranging them to hang in the center of the stick, leaving room for the trousers to drape over the end. Sarah hung her socks between the two other garments. With the branch held on her shoulder as if she were carrying a rifle and the clothes flopping soggily like battle-weary flags, she struck out again downstream, following the rivulet. Far above a unicorn bird sang three heavy sounds like the braying of a jackass. She glanced up at it briefly and then walked on in the dimness.

The gloom of the forest did not bother Sarah. In fact, she rather liked it. She walked carefully, to avoid stumbling over logs or branches, paying attention to what was around her and still feeling a turn of her stomach when there were unexpected sounds or something moved suddenly nearby. Not infrequently she encountered giant toads which flattened their bodies and regarded her balefully. Some were enormous; long as her forearm and easily weighing five pounds apiece. They were ugly amphibians, covered with horny protuberances. She didn't think they posed any danger but, nevertheless, she always circled them widely. Sometimes as she passed one it would utter a dull clucking sound.

A part of Sarah's consciousness remained infinitely sad in respect to her father, but by willpower alone she set that aside and concentrated on the task of getting reunited with the other members of the party. When that was finally accomplished, when she no longer had to have her wits about her every moment, when she had opportunity to think and to reminisce and relive, then it would all crowd in upon her and she could let the full impact of it flood her, engulf her.

More than once she had been told of the extreme dangers rampant in the Amazonian rain forest. Hundreds, thousands of people had been swallowed up in its depths, never seen again. Others, lost for only two or three days, had been found in terrible condition, torn and bleeding, suffering from thirst and exposure — many of those had died also. She was not foolish enough to believe that because thus far she was in good condition, without accidents, she could move about for very long without serious difficulty. Despite that knowledge, she was not terribly concerned. After all, it was only a matter of a short time until she rejoined Dr. Merchant and the others.

Sarah did not become concerned until the afternoon. She had been following the rivulet for three or four hours, the going becoming progressively more difficult, causing her to observe much less of what was around her and concentrate instead on thrusting her way through areas where mere walking demanded full attention. Part of the reason for the difficulty was that the stream, having been joined by several of similar size and itself merging into a somewhat larger creek, had shores that were becoming very overgrown. Ever more frequently she was forced to circle widely around huge clumps of bamboo near the water's edge; stands so thick, the stems grew within mere inches of one another with no way to slip through. Multitudes of whiplike saplings and fiercely thorned tangles of bushes screened the waterway from view and, even had she been able to get to shore, she could not have walked along it. The vegetation not only grew to the water's edge, it even extended well out over the surface.

The reason for the change was that the waterway itself had changed. Earlier, when it had just been a tiny rill or brook, it had wound along past the trees in the dimness of the forest, rarely seeing a spot of sunshine. Without the sun's light most plants could not grow. Practically everything that grew there strove to reach direct sunlight, and this was the reason for the elongated tree trunks and the extensively draped lianas, where one vine often stretched for a hundred yards or more. All were competing for the available sunlight, thrusting leafy hands higher and higher to get above their neighbors to bask in the life-giving sunshine.

As the stream grew larger, so did the ravine it gouged. It detoured less often around trees and, when swollen by the daily rains, roared and pulled and bit at their roots, undermining them until they collapsed. When this happened, a gap was created in the forest and the rays of the sun could reach the ground. Immediately a host of seeds that had lain dormant germinated and grew with astounding swiftness, competing with similar plant sprouts of many kinds for the available light. The larger the stream became, the less anything could withstand its onslaught. More trees in its path were toppled, letting in additional sunlight and contributing to the growth of even more dense jungle vegetation near the stream.

No longer able to walk the stream bank, Sarah was forced to follow as closely as possible the thick vegetation flanking it. Thorns tore at her clothing as she passed; several times she was tripped by roots or vines and fell headlong. When she finally stopped to have something to eat, wondering why she had not yet come to the Ipixuna River, she briefly burst into tears when she discovered the branch she still carried had nothing on it but the panties — badly shredded. There was no way she could force herself to backtrack and look for the lost socks and trousers. She would simply have to make do with what she had.

She felt weak with hunger and ate not only an entire tin of deviled ham on crackers and the remainder of the dried apricots, but two cans of pork and beans, washing everything down with half the water in the canteen. She justified this extravagance by reasoning that she'd soon be with the others and they would have food to share. Unaccustomed to such difficult, extensive walking, her legs were aching and her feet were sore. The travel was no longer in any way pleasant. She had no thought for appreciating what she might see around her, only an overriding desire to get to safety. Where was the Ipixuna?

Less than fifteen minutes after she began walking again, her movements jerky because of stiff, sore muscles, the forest became even gloomier and, with the increased heaviness in the air, she knew the afternoon rain clouds had covered the sky. A peculiar, pregnant stillness settled throughout the forest, then the rains came pelting down, almost before she had a chance to get into the poncho. Heavy as the rain had been yesterday, this one was heavier, although it didn't last quite so long. Sarah plodded along, blinded by it, still trying to keep the riverine growth in sight. When the rain tapered off and then ceased, two hours later, she had covered less than three miles from where she had been when it started. She removed her poncho and put it into the pouch, planning to walk on, but she was so weary she could hardly move.

As she had done the previous evening, Sarah crept into one of the buttressed root chambers of a big tree. She fell to the ground and pawed through the pouch for something to eat but even before she took anything out, there was a sudden sharp pain on her left hand, followed by an intense burning sensation. She jerked her hand up and looked at it. An enormous black ant clung there, its powerful jaws biting and its body hunched as it drove the stinger at the rear of its abdomen into her flesh.

Sarah screamed and swatted it off, then leaped to her feet as she saw several more crawling on her trousers. She brushed them away and looked at her feet. The ground was alive with them and they were crawling on her shoes, trying to bite and sting them. Another bit and stung her on the heel of the same hand and she screamed again and smashed it, snatched up the pouch and ran. Thirty yards away and still running, she put a foot down in a hole and tumbled over and over, the contents of the pouch spewing in all directions.

The pain in Sarah's whole left arm was intense, her hand burning and a steady throbbing coursing up to her armpit. It was far worse than the sting of a wasp. She was sobbing as she checked her clothing to make sure no more ants were on her. There was one — fully an inch and a quarter in length, its jaws tightly gripping the fabric of a belt loop and its tail searching for a place to drive the venomous stinger home. Afraid to touch it, she took the knife from her pocket and cut the insect in half. The abdomen fell to the ground, still twisting and trying to sting. The front half released its hold on the belt loop and grabbed the blade of the knife. There was a faint grating sound and Sarah could feel the vibrations in the handle as the fierce jaws clenched and ground on the steel. She rubbed the oversized ant off against a tree and, moaning with pain, picked up the scattered items, replacing them in the pouch.

Visibility was becoming very poor with the approach of evening and Sarah walked only long enough to find another huge tree with buttressed roots. This time she entered one of the chambers carefully, illuminating the ground before her with the flashlight, making sure nothing of any consequence was there.

Her hand and arm up to the elbow were badly swollen and the pain was not diminishing. She sat down in the angle where a flanged root joined the tree, and held her arm in her lap, for a long while rocking back and forth with the agony of it. After an hour had passed the pain seemed to be easing. She took two aspirins from the first-aid kit and gulped them down with water. Sarah had long since stopped crying but her moaning persisted and did not end for another hour. By then the pain had nearly ceased and the swelling was going down. It was dark and she was tired and hungry and miserable. Despite the aspirins, for one of the few times in her life she had a mild headache; she suspected it had been caused by the venom from the ants' stingers.

Using the flashlight sparingly, she took another can of beans and one of corned beef from the pouch and the last package of crackers. As soon as they were opened and close at hand she turned off the light and sat there, eating in the dark. Even after finishing the tins of food, half the crackers and the remainder of the water, she was still hungry, but ate nothing else. Her food supply was disappearing rapidly and this frightened her. What was she going to do when it was gone? And where was the Ipixuna River? And where were the other members of the party?

She slapped her cheek where something was irritating her, then the other side of her face. Her neck and ears were also becoming irritated. She continued to rub them, but then her hands began to itch and smart. She groped in the darkness, found the flashlight, switched it on, but at first could see nothing. The irritation continued and she resisted the inclination to rub and scratch the backs of her hands. Instead, she shone the light on them, looking closely. Then she saw the flies. A half dozen or more diminutive flies were crawling about, sporadically pausing to bite. They were almost invisible, not only because they were hardly so large as the head of a pin, but also because they were flesh colored.

Sarah recognized them. She had encountered similar flies twice before, once during a vacation to Florida where they discouraged campers and fishermen upon whom they descended in clouds. The second time was the night the expedition had camped on the bar at the point where the Ipixuna had emptied into the Juruá. In Florida they were called sand flies. "Here in the Amazon country," Anita Cruz had told her, "they're called *piums*, and they differ somewhat from the Florida sand fly — they're meaner. The Florida ones just cause an annoyance and no lasting damage. That's not the case with these rascals. After about fifteen minutes you'll get a little inflamed spot at each place you've been bitten, in the center of which will be an even tinier red, blood spot.

After a day or so the red center will become black from coagulated blood and the inflamed area will subside."

She had been correct. Fortunately, there had been none of the *piums* at the Emerald City dig, but all the members of the party had had the distinctive little black spots on their skin for a week or more. These had finally flaked off during the normal course of washing.

The present annoyance was growing worse as hordes of the minute, biting gnats attacked her, and so Sarah dug into the pouch again and found the insect repellent. It was a thick cream in a small squeeze bottle. She put a healthy dollop into one palm, rubbed her hands together and then transferred the repellent to her face, ears and neck. It helped considerably and she rubbed a little more over the backs of her hands, then pulled her head and arms inside the poncho, tucked in her legs, and fumbled about until the garment was snugged in pretty well around her. She was not terribly comfortable, but neither was she pestered by the *piums* any longer.

Sarah slept poorly this night, often thrashing about and on two occasions waking herself with her own screams. The nightmares were frightening, yet she couldn't remember what they were about after waking. She awoke a final time before the break of day and sat hunched under her poncho, very alone, very frightened and with a burning thirst. She was sorry she had drunk all her water last evening. In this interval just before dawn, the night sounds of the jungle gradually died away, leaving behind a pressing silence. For the first time she realized there was a sense of comfort to be gained in the normal sounds of the night.

With no forewarning, she found herself crying again and was angered at her own weakness. Why couldn't she be strong, like her father? Despite the tears, the thought of him brought a wistful smile to her lips. Sarah remembered with remarkable clarity almost every conversation they had ever had, a tribute to the unforgettable nature of her father's character. One such conversation now came to her with great impact. Sarah had asked him how a person could become strong. He had considered carefully before answering.

"Sarah," he'd said at last, "first you have to know what strength is and what it isn't. We're not talking about physical strength and we're not talking about guts, either, although those having guts usually have strength and vice versa. No, strength has a lot to do with tenacity. Stick-to-itiveness, that's what a lot of it is. You have to have the will to hang in there, come what may." He had hugged her, kissed the end of her nose and then continued. "That's not easy much of the time. It also has a lot to do with selfishness. Generally speaking, people who're selfish aren't very strong because they're thinking too much about themselves, their own comfort. As soon as something gets rough and they get scared or uncomfortable or are in some kind of pain, they back off and take the easy way, whatever it is. Strength? I'll tell you what it is, honey." He looked into her eyes steadily. "It's mostly just not giving up no matter how bad things get. It's not just telling yourself that you'll *try* to see it through, but that you damned well *will* see it through because there's nothing that can stop you."

The memory of it brought a warm glow to Sarah now,

but she wasn't sure she had that kind of strength. The going was getting very rough and she wanted nothing more than to be safe and comfortable.

"Maybe," she whispered in the darkness, "those people who got lost in the Amazon died so fast because, like Dad said, they didn't have the will to go on. Maybe they believed they weren't going to make it, so they just didn't." She was silent for a long while, thinking, and then she spoke again, louder this time. "Well, I *will* see it through because I *am* going to make it!"

A few faint chitterings of birds were piercing the gloom, tenuous and cautious, as if testing to see if it were safe to burst into full voice. But in that last short span of forest silence remaining before the day creatures began stirring in earnest, a faint sound came to Sarah's ears that made her first cock an ear to hear better and then stand up, listening. It was a deep, muted rumble, constant and just at the lower limit of audibility. She stood perfectly still, not even breathing for half a minute in order to hear better. A slow smile touched her lips and her eyes brightened.

"The falls!" she said. "It's the falls above the landing. I've made it. Everything's going to be just fine."

The lift in her spirits was phenomenal and Sarah could hardly contain herself to wait for daylight. The *piums* were gone, the rain forest smelled marvelous, birds and monkeys were awakening and bringing the canopy to life with their callings and everything was wonderful. The poor night of sleep was forgotten and, suddenly very hungry, she snapped on the flashlight and dug, once again, into her pouch for food. There were two cans left, one of tuna and one of ham. She opened both. The half-pack of crackers she placed on the ground beside her and, pleasantly unconcerned with the food supply, sat cross-legged in the dimming glow of the flashlight, eating until she was quite full. A small chunk of ham was left when she finished, which she tossed on the ground for whatever animal discovered it. She dug a small hole with the rock hammer and buried the cans and cracker wrapper. She was still very thirsty but confident she'd soon have all the water she needed when she reached the Ipixuna.

Sarah's muscles were stiff but quickly loosened up as she began walking. As before, she followed the thick line of undergrowth fringing the small stream she had been following — the going no less difficult than it had been the day before. In addition to tangled, thorny thickets and extensive clumps of impenetrable bamboo, there were many very tall, spindly palms in this area, their supple trunks curving weirdly as they tilted their shuttlecock heads toward the stream opening for their share of the precious morning sunlight. She heard, more than saw, flock after flock of garrulous parrots and macaws flying raucously over the stream.

At one place she found two more of the strange custardy fruits with the tortoise-skin rind, newly fallen and lying amid the rotting remains of others. She picked them up and put them into her pouch for Dr. Merchant and the others to sample when she joined them. Quite a few unusual beetles were crawling about on the spoiling fruits and eating them. Primarily they were dark brown or black thumbnail-sized insects, but here and there were some which were startlingly different: brilliantly iridescent green, fully an inch long and somewhat oval shaped. Others of the same shape were iridescent blue or reddish-bronze. They looked like animated precious gems as they moved about the spoiling fruit. The strangest, however, was a splendid beetle fully two inches long, its back colored orange and black and pale beige in an attractive harlequin pattern. Its two front legs were each almost four inches long and the remaining four, colored in the same manner, were about half that length. All the legs were similarly colored, black with a bright orange band. Projecting from its thorax on each side were two sharp spines and an amazingly long antenna grew from above each of the two large compound eyes. As this insect consumed the disintegrating fruit pulp it made strange grinding sounds.

Sarah found the beetles fascinating and would have liked pausing to watch them for a while, but the desire to reunite with the others of her party was too strong and she moved on. Here and there the ground was littered with very sharp, strong spines of a particular palm tree, the trunk of which was surrounded by a bristling armor of the same sort of spines in peculiar whorls. The tree itself was about fifty feet tall and had a shaggy crown of feathery leaves, which very little light penetrated. The spines that had fallen to the ground were each several inches long, jet black and exceedingly hard. Often as she walked through them, they stuck to Sarah's shoes and in one case, when she scuffed her foot, a spine plunged right through the tough shoe leather and into her big toe. Fortunately, it did not penetrate very deeply into her flesh.

She limped to a nearby mossy log and sat on it, then grimaced as she pulled the thorn out of her boot, not without considerable difficulty. After discarding the palm spine, Sarah took stock of herself and shook her head ruefully. She was a mess. The sturdy hiking shoes were already coming apart at the seams and her trouser legs were badly tattered. Her shirt was torn in several places as well. The skin of her face and neck was blotched with the reddish spots of inflammation from *pium* bites, also scored here and there with scratches. Her arms and legs were much worse, deeply crisscrossed with gouges she had suffered, mostly from encounters with cactus while hacking her way through thorny thickets. Her left hand had only a little swelling left from the bites and stings of the giant ants, but it was still very sore. Once again she was thankful she had such short hair, shuddering at the thought of the problem it would have been — and what it would have looked like by now — had it still been long. While sitting there she ate a few of the remaining dried peaches and prunes. Then, too anxious to rest any more, she came to her feet and began walking once again.

Ahead, the sound of the waterfall had become a deep continuous roaring and she quickened her pace. Within another hundred yards the small stream she had been following for so long emptied into a much larger one and Sarah's spirits soared. The Ipixuna River! She caught a glimpse of it through the rank undergrowth of the shore where one of the giant buttressed trees had recently crashed across the river, forming a natural bridge. Surrounding foliage had been crushed flat and new growth had not yet had time to fill the inviting gap this created.

Then minutes later Sarah saw the falls. It was rockier here, with much less undergrowth and she was able to pick her way carefully to a broad rock ledge at the very lip of the falls. She was dazed by the first bright sunlight to fall upon her since leaving the Emerald City ruins. It was in such strong contrast to the perpetual dimness she had been experiencing in the forest that at first she had to squint and shade her eyes. The power of the waterfall made the ledge she was standing on vibrate and the tremors course up her legs. Her heart was hammering with excitement, but also with a certain fear. The niggling worry she had been harboring ever since she began this savage journey suddenly rose up in strength, filling her mind with dread: a fear that Dr. Merchant's party would already be gone. She steeled herself for that eventuality, clenching her fists at her sides and telling herself that if such were the case, she'd try not to be too disappointed and would simply follow the easy trail from the gravel bar landing back to the dig and wait there for their return.

Sarah turned and looked downstream. The jungle growth came right to the water's edge on both sides, a thick green wall sixty or seventy feet high, the individual leaves glistening from sunlight reflected on the droplets pebbling their surfaces, droplets formed by the billowing mist rising from the foot of the falls.

No one was there. No Dr. Merchant and no reclining forms of the ailing Ruth and Anita. Tad wasn't there, nor Pamela, nor Matthew. Patrick was not there nor were the canoes from Cruzeiro do Sul. There wasn't even a gravel bar!

Could it have washed away? Sarah turned her head slowly and one by one she noted differences. This waterfall was lofty, easily over a hundred feet, but the falls on the Ipixuna had not been over forty feet high. The Ipixuna falls had been at least seventy feet wide and this one was no more than thirty. Here there were more jagged cliffs and more rock ledges. The river downstream from the falls here was relatively narrow and filled with rapids, but the Ipixuna had been quite broad. As she stood looking downstream, she realized that the sun, which was now well up over the trees, was to her right, meaning this river was running north. The Ipixuna ran directly east to the Juruá.

The realization struck Sarah with devastating impact that this was not the Ipixuna at all. She buried her face in her hands and fell to her knees, the sound of her wrenching, anguished cries lost in the roar of the waterfall. In a moment more she flattened herself against the ledge, lying there on her stomach, her eyes tightly closed and her whole body heaving with the shuddering sobs she could not contain.

Heedless of the girl lying there in abject despair, the Ituí River continued to plunge noisily over the brink and then onward below toward the Amazon, flowing through the wildness of a wholly unexplored jungle.

Chapter Five

How long she lay there on the rock ledge at the falls of the Ituí, Sarah had no idea. The emotional shock of realizing that, after all her wandering and difficulties in the jungle, she had been going in the wrong direction had sapped her. That, coupled with her poor night's rest, caused her to cry herself to sleep.

What awakened her now was being struck by drops of falling water. In her befuddled half-sleep state, she thought she was back in Des Plaines at Rand Park swimming pool, dozing on the warm concrete, and that one of her friends had climbed dripping from the pool and was playfully sprinkling water on her.

"Don't," she murmured and the word was lost in a heavy rumble of thunder. Then the continuing booming of the waterfall brought her back to reality and she sat up. Above her the sky — how she had missed seeing the sky these past few days! — was the color of old zinc and the spattering of raindrops was becoming heavier. She looked around and saw that upstream from where she was lying the ledge ascended in layers almost like steps. About twenty feet higher than the rock surface she was on there was another ledge, much smaller, with an overhang above that. Trees were growing atop the overhang and quite a number of roots and leafy vines curtained the opening.

She ran that way at once, holding the pouch tightly against her side. Climbing to the next ledge was not difficult, but the rain was turning into a downpour by the time she reached it and her back was soaked. She scrambled onto the upper ledge and, panting, crawled back to where she could press against the rear wall. It was a cozy niche, perhaps ten feet long and six feet deep. The rear wall of rock rose straight up for about four feet and then curved outward and farther upward to form the projecting overhang.

Outside, the rain had become torrential and Sarah could scarcely see the trees on the opposite side of the river, but not a drop was falling inside her haven. Sitting with her back against the wall, she hugged her knees, delighted at finding such a nice dry place. The thought struck her that a short while ago she was in the depths of despair at her predicament and now she was feeling a sense of elation at the simple good fortune of finding this shelter. Without even knowing it, she was learning a very elemental lesson: in a situation where survival is the issue, nature does not permit the luxury of emotionalism. The *now* of surviving becomes paramount, taking precedence over reflection on past failures or successes, or future problems.

For a long while she watched the rain, marveling at its heaviness and at the fact that it fell almost straight down instead of slanting. Torrents of water poured off the roots and vines hanging like a sparse drapery from the upper ledge. She remembered she was thirsty and so she removed the canteen from her belt and, stretching far out, held its open mouth beneath a little stream pouring from a root. Within moments it was filled and she pulled it back inside and drank greedily. She refilled it, screwed on the cap and replaced the vessel in its belt pouch.

She sighed deeply. It was so good to watch the rain and hear it, yet not be in it. In these few minutes she had formed a close attachment to this niche and fleetingly wished she could just stay here, warm and dry, until some rescuer found her. She pondered the pleasant thought until a slight movement at the left outer corner of the rocky cavity caught her eye.

A strange little creature, thoroughly drenched, was laboriously crawling into the dryness. No more than two and a half inches long and dirty gray in color, it held its long narrow tail straight behind. Eight sticklike jointed legs raised and lowered deliberately in dainty succession and a pair of much larger arms equipped with pincers were extended partially in front, each crooked outward at the elbow. Its body was squat and segmented, with similar segments continuing down the length of the tail. The final one, black and rather bulbous, diminished quickly in a tapered curve to a needle-sharp point.

Though she had never seen such a creature alive before, Sarah had often seen mounted specimens of them in the Field Museum and pictures in books. It was a scorpion. She knew it was a venomous animal but somehow the knowledge didn't bother her. As a precaution, she slowly unsheathed the machete and sat with it across her lap.

The scorpion detected the movement and instantly its

tail curved up over its back in a parody of a question mark, the sharp end poised to be jabbed with pointed accuracy at anything that threatened. The claws drew in close to the head, as if protecting it, and the scorpion waited. Sarah did not move and, after a few minutes, the scorpion, evidently deciding there was no immediate danger, began moving across the rim of the opening without lowering its tail.

Midway on the ledge it paused for a long moment, then extended its foreclaws forward as it had them at first, lowered its tail and continued the rest of the way to the opposite outer corner of the cavity. There it found an elongated crack in the rock and, though to Sarah it looked too narrow to squeeze into, the scorpion did just that.

Sarah released a breath she hadn't even realized she was holding and smiled faintly. Almost as if he had spoken them aloud to her again, she recalled the words her father had spoken one day in the reptile house as they were strolling through the Lincoln Park Zoo.

"There's really very little to fear from most wild creatures if you just sit still and observe them, Sarah. People have the idea that such animals as snakes and wolves and the big cats, or even smaller things like spiders and wasps and bees and so forth, are just moving about actively looking for people to bite, claw or sting. T'ain't necessarily so, honey. Most times when people have been hurt by them, it's because they've disturbed the animals, either accidentally or deliberately. Then they get hurt because the animals believe they or their nests or young are in danger. That doesn't mean you shouldn't respect many of them and keep your distance, if possible, but you really don't normally have to be afraid of them if you keep your head and stay quiet."

This present situation involving the scorpion underlined what he had said. Obviously the scorpion could have caused a problem and might have stung her with serious consequences if she'd reacted with fear and tried to thrust it out or mash it. But *it* hadn't because *she* hadn't, and she was pretty sure that even had it crawled across her, she would have remained still and it probably would not have bothered her at all.

As the rain continued she thought more about her father and, though sadness was still strong in her, she didn't dwell on it. She thought, instead, of what he might have done in a situation like this; that thought evolving into, better still, what he might have advised her to do. She was at first tempted to make an effort to return to the Emerald City ruins, but she immediately rejected that plan for two reasons: first, she doubted she would be able to find it again; second, even if she found it, there was the possibility that Dr. Merchant's party would have returned by then and, finding no one there, departed again, this time taking all the supplies with them.

No, she was sure that at this point her father would have advised her to continue following the river downstream until she came to habitation. Further, as always, he would have cautioned her to keep her head, to think about what she was doing and proceed slowly and carefully. Fear was the enemy, along with ignorance and haste, not the jungle itself. It didn't really make any difference whether she traveled a mile or ten miles in a day. The important thing was that she didn't panic, didn't

overdo herself and become so obsessed with getting to
safety that she hurt herself or let herself become weak
because she neglected to take care of herself. Ignorance
she couldn't help — she knew nothing of jungle survival
— but she would just have to hope she would not make
too many mistakes.

In the jungle there were all kinds of things to eat if
you really looked for them, just like the custardy fruit
she had already found, so there was little likelihood she
would starve. The river had plenty of water to drink and
even if she could not easily get to the river, it rained
practically every day, just as it was raining now, and it
would not be difficult to keep her canteen filled.

Insects might be a problem. She shuddered a little,
remembering the giant ants and the horde of minute
piums she had already so unfortunately encountered.
The ants had attacked, it was obvious now, because she
had inadvertently disturbed them by stumbling into an
area where they were. The lesson to be gained there was
to be sure what she was walking into before she did so.
Where *piums* were concerned, it was obvious they were
concentrated in rather limited areas. If possible, she must
keep out of such areas or, if that were not feasible, then
she had to take refuge from them in whatever way she
could. She shuddered again at the prospect of running
out of insect repellent.

No matter what else engaged her, part of what she
must do each day was look for food, rest often and keep
alert for any possibility of danger. If she were successful
in doing these things, she felt chances were good she
would eventually reach habitation and safety.

"I won't give up," she said aloud, her jaw at a determined angle. "No matter what happens now, I won't give up."

Having reasoned this way and come to her conclusion, Sarah Francis found she felt much better. As the rain continued, she planned what she would do next. The principal thing, of course, was to follow the river, keeping as close to it as she could but not so close, as she had been doing recently, that it created special hardships for her. Wherever necessary, she would make her way to the river to bathe or get drinking water. As soon as the rain ceased, she would leave this shelter and look for food, then return and spend the night here. Tomorrow she would continue her journey at dawn.

With a definite plan in mind, Sarah relaxed. She was hungry again and thought wistfully of the chunk of ham she had thrown away. All she had left to eat were the two custardy fruits in her pouch. She took them out and placed them on the ledge before her. Using the pocket-knife, she cut them in half and casually ate the contents of both, again delighted with the taste but still hungry when she was finished. The residue of rind and seeds she tossed out into the stream below. Then she moved closer to the rim of the ledge and sat there cross-legged, merely watching the rain and the river.

Not infrequently branches floated past and vanished over the edge of the falls. At one point an entire tree drifted into sight, caught and momentarily held several times, but eventually plunged over the falls. Half an hour later another tree, even larger, came drifting past and also was washed over. This gave her an idea. Supposing tomorrow she went down to the bottom of the falls and waited for another tree like that to be carried over the cataract? She was a good swimmer. Might she not swim out, climb onto it and just ride downstream until she reached habitation? The thought was tempting, but then she shook her head, rejecting it. No, not only would the current be very difficult and possibly dangerous for her, but she would be hampered by her clothing and the pouch and everything would get wet. She was well aware of how long it took things to dry here. Her shoes were already in bad condition and that would help ruin them even faster. Besides, there was no telling what was in the water here. Weren't there supposed to be piranhas in these rivers? And what about perils unknown to her? No, she wouldn't do that.

The rainfall lasted at a downpour for two hours, then tapered off and stopped, leaving behind a dull gray overcast. Sarah left her ledge and returned to the forest the way she had come. Using her machete, she hacked blazes into both sides of certain trees as she reentered the gloom. She did not intend to go far, confident that the sound of the waterfall would guide her back and her tree marks would direct her to where the ledge was located.

One of the trees she marked had ragged reddish-colored bark with deep, rough scorings. Nearly six feet thick, it rose straight up like the others and was lost in the canopy, but by moving around it she could see the tree was close to two hundred feet tall. She was surprised to note that a sap the color of milk had begun flowing freely down the trunk from the place where she had struck it with the machete. She wondered if it might be a rubber tree, since she recalled that rubber tree sap was supposed to be milky white, but she was sure that such sap was much thicker.

She found her first food after about fifteen minutes of roving. Near the base of one of the loftiest trees she had yet encountered were several large, heavy pods. They bore a remarkable resemblance to rusty cannonballs. Six or seven inches in diameter, they had faintly pebbled surfaces and were very hard. At first she thought they were balls of solid wood. Then she saw the remains of some older ones that had been attacked by mold and mildew and were disintegrating. She poked at them with her machete and found inside a large number of quite symmetrically shaped seeds which at first glance looked like sections of an orange. These, too, were dark and moldy and they fell out easily at her poking.

Sarah gave a short exclamation. Brazil nuts! She was overjoyed. Those from the decayed shells appeared in bad condition and, fearful they were spoiled and could make her sick, she did not take any. Instead, she shoved two of the fresher pods into her pouch. They were very heavy and so she tossed one of them out, believing that one alone would have enough nuts to feed her well. She began walking away, changed her mind, went back and put the second one in her pouch after all. It was a load to carry but she might not again find this tree or another like it, so it would be worth the extra effort to keep them.

The sound of the falls was still clearly audible and so she moved farther into the woods. Most of the trees had peculiar plants growing out of their trunks, usually from natural indentations. They were mainly ferns and huge sharp-leaved plants that looked much like the leaves atop a pineapple, though more compact. These were bromeliads and, though Sarah could not identify them, she pulled a low one off a tree with her machete, thinking perhaps there might be some sort of fruit inside. She found instead that the construction of the leaves was in the nature of a rosette, overlapping at the base and forming a reservoir that collected rainwater. The whole front of her right leg was soaked as the plant tumbled down, releasing about a quart of water as it inverted. She carefully cataloged the oddity in her mind, seeing this as a possible source of water if her canteen became dry. She thought wryly of how thirsty she had been yesterday and this morning and how she had unknowingly been passing these receptacles of water frequently.

There was also an abundance of cacti growing both on the forest floor and on the trunks of trees. Several trees she passed had twenty or more different species of the epiphytic cacti on a single trunk. She had no idea what the varieties were, but most of them had sharp spines and, wherever possible, she avoided contact with them, having been stuck and scratched by them often enough over the past few days.

There was surprisingly little wildlife encountered. Here and there small lizards scurried out of sight at her approach and occasionally she saw insects, mainly beetles and butterflies. The sounds of birds from the canopy were almost continuous, but rarely did the avians come down to ground level and any she saw were momentary shadows flitting along through the leafy cover, zigzagging expertly among the tree trunks and vines.

With the sound of the falls becoming faint behind her, Sarah turned and began making a wide circle toward it rather than backtracking, hopeful of finding something else to eat, such as more of the custardy fruits. She had gone only another hundred steps when she jolted to a stop, hardly believing her eyes. Ahead on the ground was a large plant with narrow, widely spreading, spearlike leaves. In the center of the plant, on a thick stem, was perched a pineapple about half the size of those she was accustomed to seeing in the market. It was green near the top, but the sides and bottom were yellowish brown. Without hesitation Sarah lopped it off the stem with her machete, but at the price of a rather nasty little gash on her wrist from one of the saw-toothed edges of the leaves. She chopped off the small cluster of sharp leaves on top of the fruit and the aroma of fresh pineapple caused her to begin salivating. She placed it in her pouch, very pleased with her find, and moved on.

At one place she saw an inch-thick ropelike material plastered to a tree and at first took it to be a vine. Her eyes followed its progress up the tree and she saw that it ended about twenty feet up the trunk in a large football-shaped construction that was dark brown. Tentatively she poked the machete at the ropey material and it broke and flaked off, revealing that it was hollow and constructed of mud. Immediately, several fairly large brown ants emerged from the broken section and began moving about confusedly. Deducing that the construction on the tree above was the nest and wanting nothing more to do with ants, she moved quickly away from the tree.

Sarah had gone farther than anticipated from the falls

and by the time she returned to its vicinity and found her blazes on the trees without having found anything else edible, dusk was approaching. She passed the tree cut earlier that bled milky sap and noticed that it had sealed itself reasonably well. The sap had become very thick, coagulating into a mass that was now becoming ivory colored.

"Maybe it's rubber after all," she said, pausing to look curiously at several dark beetles that had been attracted to it and were entrapped by the coagulation.

Although it was not difficult for Sarah to find her way back to the ledge, darkness had come quickly, as always in the jungle, and little daylight remained as she climbed up to the niche. As a precaution against scorpions or anything else, she shone her flashlight briefly on the floor and back wall of the cavity. It was as she had left it. Her feet hurt and she considered taking her shoes off, but decided to do so later. Right now she was too hungry. She took off her pouch and sat down beside it, salivating again as she brought out the little pineapple. She pared off the outer covering of the top half where it was green, cut out a chunk of the almost white pulp and speared it on her knife blade. She popped it into her mouth and bit once, then spat it out, the sourness making her grimace. Disappointed, she cut away the entire top half and found that the lower portion had more of a yellow coloration. Again she cut out a piece and tentatively nibbled at it. The taste was tart but not unpleasant and she ate the rest of the piece. The closer she came to the bottom, the better the taste became and the final portion was deliciously sweet.

Sarah's hands had become very sticky, so she removed a handkerchief from her hip pocket and, wetting it well with water from the canteen, scrubbed the stickiness away from mouth and hands alike. She was still very hungry and wished there had been more. Again she tried to eat the top portion but the sourness was just too much and she finally tossed all the pineapple residue outside. The fruit had made her thirsty and she drank half the water remaining in the canteen.

Darkness had come, but a full moon newly risen above the trees on the opposite side of the river helped her to see. She concentrated next on one of the heavy woody fruits from the Brazil nut tree. Placing it before her she tapped it with the blade of the machete, hardly making a dent. She struck it again, harder, and the blade bit in a little, though not much. For her third attempt she raised the machete high overhead and brought it down with all her strength on the ball. The blade struck it slightly off center and the nut case caromed to the rear wall, bounced back and rolled toward the edge of the niche. She lunged for it and missed. It dropped off the edge and she heard it bump several times on the way down, terminating in a splash barely audible above the sound of the falls.

Angry at herself, she took out the other one and sat on the rock floor, holding it firmly between the soles of her shoes. Again she lifted the machete and brought it down. Again her aim was slightly off and the blade chopped into the husk with enough force to dislodge a chunk, but it also continued with the force of the blow and buried itself in the side of her right shoe at the ball of her foot. It hurt and for a terrible moment she thought she had cut herself badly. She turned on the flashlight and it shook in her grasp as she inspected the damage. She freed the blade from her shoe and found it had sheared through the heavy rubber rim of the sole and into, but not through, the leather. She thought of how her first inclination when she got back had been to remove her shoes and was weak with relief that she had not. The mental picture of what it would be like to have a badly injured foot under her present circumstances was frightening.

Using the machete with greater care, she chopped away a few of the leafy vines overhanging the entry to her rocky haven, allowing more moonlight to enter, and once again concentrated on opening the nut case. Her blows with the machete were less strong but better directed. Chunk by small chunk, she chipped it away. The husk was much thicker than she had thought it would be and it took her the better part of an hour to get it open to the point where she could gouge out the actual nuts. There were two dozen of them and she placed them in a pile and shoved all the husk debris out of the niche.

Sarah attempted to bite one open but it was too hard. She then whacked it with the machete and cut it in half. One of the halves shot away outside; the other bounced over to the back wall. She picked it up, but the half kernel still in the shell was solidly wedged. By using the smaller blade of the pocketknife she was able to chip away little pieces of the nutmeat, but it was a laborious and unsatisfactory process. Abruptly she thought of something and set the machete down, shaking her head.

"Good grief," she muttered, "if you keep being this stupid there's no way you're going to survive."

She now did what she should have done in the first place. Under the dim light of the flashlight, she took the rock hammer from her belt and used the hammer face of it to tap open the shells of the Brazil nuts one by one and then used the pocketknife to remove the kernels, sometimes whole and sometimes in large pieces. She ate all the nuts and, though they were very good and helped to ease her hunger, she didn't like the idea of having to go through this kind of effort for a handful or two of food. Tomorrow she would renew her efforts to find something to eat on a regular basis — something easier to come by. She drank a few more swallows from the canteen, saving some for during the night, then scrubbed her face and hands again with the damp handkerchief.

Irrespective of how attached she had become to the protective little niche in the cliff, it was certainly not comfortable for sleeping. She took off her shoes and covered herself with the poncho, but trying to get any real rest while lying on the hard rock surface was difficult. Tired though she was, Sarah spent a very restless night, constantly changing position and never becoming really comfortable. During the night she awoke with stomach cramps and a strong desire to defecate. The moon having gone out of sight overhead, it was now much darker in the cavity and she was reluctant to attempt climbing down to some other area. For a while she tried to hold it in, but the discomfort became intolerable. Lighting her way with the flashlight, she finally moved over to the far outer edge of the niche and relieved herself onto a pile of leaves she stripped from the vines still overhanging the opening. She used similar leaves as toilet tissue and then pushed everything off the edge with one of her shoes.

As she was pulling up her trousers, she inadvertently kicked the flashlight and watched with dismay as it rolled off the ledge, clattered against the rocks as it fell and then plopped into the river below. The faint glow quickly disappeared underwater. She was greatly dejected at the loss, but felt her way back to where she had been before and eventually fell asleep while thinking, with her usual pragmatism, that since the batteries had been getting weak, the light would not have lasted much longer anyway.

With the coming of morning it was not the monkeys and birds that awakened Sarah, their distant sounds being overridden by the pervading thunder of the falls, but rather the heat of direct sunshine. Directly exposed to the rising sun, the rocky shelter had become something of a natural oven. Stiff and sore and not feeling at all well, she hardly took note of the fact that this was the first early morning sun she had seen since leaving the Emerald City ruins. While reaching for her shoes to put them on again, she knocked one over and recoiled sharply with a little gasp as a scorpion skittered out, tail aloft and ready to strike. It looked like the same one she had seen yesterday, but there was no way to tell for sure. She pursed her lips in a silent whistle as she envisioned what would have happened had she unconcernedly put her foot into the shoe.

With the blade of the machete, she shoved the little

creature far to the side and watched with satisfaction as it crawled into the same crack the other one — or perhaps this one — had disappeared into before. She banged each of the shoes with the tool and when nothing more came out of them, picked them up one at a time and hit them against the rock, then shook them well before putting them on.

With the nearly empty pouch over her shoulder again, she left her haven a few minutes later, pausing on the lower ledge only long enough to lean over and refill the canteen from the clear river water rushing by. A short distance away a gorgeous golden-yellow parrot swooped down and landed, strutted imperiously to the water's edge and drank. When finished, it fluffed its feathers, screeched loudly and then became a reflected ball of sunlight rising out of sight over the trees. Yesterday's rain had created a little pool of water where the rocks gave way to forest floor. As she approached it there was an explosion of brilliant color as scores of butterflies leaped into flight, whirled about in a little storm and began settling again. Sarah sucked in her breath. They were just gorgeous. Huge morpho butterflies, the upper surface of their seven-inch wings an incredibly iridescent blue, flashed with lightning brilliance in the sunlight. When they landed and held their wings together over their backs, the brightness was gone; the undersides of the wings were a soft rusty brown with subtle patterns, undoubtedly providing superb camouflage for them in jungle cover. Others of the butterflies were bright yellow, black and green, red and black, stark orange, all red, silvery-green, deep lavender, and pure white. It was a glorious display and its beauty made Sarah feel much better.

Back inside the depths of the forest, she moved along steadily, hacking cactus, thorny bushes and other low growth out of her way where it was necessary to do so, careful to keep the much denser growth of the riverine foliage in view to her right so that she did not wander away from the stream. She knew if there were habitation on the other side of the river she would miss it, but there was no help for that, since walking along the banks was not possible. She reasoned that if there were such habitation, then the people living there would surely also be on this side of the river at times and there would be paths. If she encountered such a path, she would simply follow it to the water.

A small branch thumped to the ground just ahead of her and she stopped immediately and looked up. In the lower portion of the canopy the leaves were moving. A few of them fell and several piercing shrieks dwindled away and were supplanted by a low excited chattering. A small wrinkled black face appeared from behind a screen of leaves. The brow projected heavily and the large eyes were bright and black. Small, human-type ears were set at the sides of its head, and in one arm, cradled against the chest, it held several identical fruits. It stepped into full view on a thick horizontal liana and sat down. The long tail, which Sarah had not at first seen, wrapped around the vine tightly.

It was a monkey and Sarah immediately recognized it as one of a variety of monkeys they had seen either at the ruins or while en route there. This particular species had been seen while they were afloat on the Juruá and their guides had pointed at it and cried *"Barrigudo!"* One of the men had immediately fitted an arrow to his bow to shoot it, but the monkey had vanished in the foliage. Later, when they had camped on the sand bar, Anita Cruz had told Sarah that *barrigudo* was Portuguese for bag-belly, the name by which they knew the woolly monkey, because of its distinctive potbelly. She said they had attempted to shoot it because they considered *barrigudos* excellent eating.

Looking closely at the one perched above her, Sarah saw that its hair was short and very dense, imparting something of a teddy-bear appearance. It was brownish-black on the body, frosted with a scattering of white hairs. On the head, the hair was very nearly as black as the hairless face, and the whole head seemed abnormally large for its body. The head and body were about two feet long and the tail more than doubled the total length.

Leaves rustled and the *barrigudo* looked around at the sound but was not alarmed. Another of the monkeys came into sight, then more until twelve were gathered together in a companionable group. They moved with slow deliberation and, unlike the treetop monkeys Sarah had often seen leaping about with great agility and playfulness in the trees near the ruins, these seemed to have very serious demeanor. Each was carrying the same kind of fruit.

They continued murmuring softly among themselves until Sarah moved and was spotted by them. Instantly there was a shriek of alarm from the one Sarah had seen first. It leaped up, dropping its fruit, and climbed quickly out of view in the canopy. The others followed at once and some of them dropped part or all of the fruit they were carrying.

Sarah walked forward a few steps, picked up one of the fruits and studied it. Six inches long and about half that at its thickest part, the oval-shaped fruit was a dull earthy color with a thin woody rind. It had split from the fall and inside were a few small seeds similar to orange pips surrounded by a juicy pulp, in color and texture like that of a peach. It had very little aroma. Deciding that it must be edible if the monkeys were gathering it, Sarah scooped out some of the pulp on her finger and tasted it. The flavor was very pleasant, remindful of the mangoes she had eaten during that vacation in Florida. At once she stooped and began picking up others that had been dropped, putting them into the pouch. Above, the monkeys were in view again and were screaming. They began throwing small sticks and leaves and more of the fruits at her, all the while bouncing angrily on their perches.

"Go ahead, throw them at me!" she shouted. "That's just fine. It's wonderful!"

The sound of her voice stilled them and they scurried out of sight, this time moving far upward in the canopy. When Sarah finished picking up the fruit her pouch was bulging. She walked to a moss-covered rock and sat down. Without pause, she ate seven of the fruits. There were at least a dozen left, but she planned to eat them later.

After resting a little while longer, Sarah began walking again. The food had helped but she still felt the same sense of unwellness that had bothered her earlier. Every now and then a little wave of nausea would rise in her, but she did not vomit.

In the afternoon, when the forest darkened more, she fumbled in the pouch, took out her poncho and donned it long before the first raindrops began to rattle in the leaves. She thought she would continue walking despite the rain but before long it was falling in such a deluge that her only thought was to find shelter. A heavy log leaning against a living tree had become a sloped mossy platform from which were growing some large broad-leaved ferns. She crawled beneath this log and was suitably sheltered from the direct fall of the rain. She leaned her arms on her knees and laid her head on her arms, remaining in this position for the duration of the rainfall, her mind a vacuum.

When the downpour ended, Sarah came to her feet again and left the shelter of the sloping log without a backward glance. She plodded on with the ribbon of dense growth indicating the river to her right. A few birds were moving about in and just below the canopy but she paid little attention to them. At one point, as she passed the buttresses of one of the forest giants, she startled a small mammal.

Although she had never seen an agouti before and had no idea what it was, Sarah knew intuitively she had nothing to fear, perhaps because it was no more dangerous appearing than a rabbit. Except for its small ears, there was even a superficial resemblance to a hare. It had coarse but glossy orangish-brown hair and the tail was vestigial.

The agouti was sitting upright on its haunches when Sarah appeared, nibbling a bit of vegetation held squirrellike in its forepaws. For just an instant the rodent and the girl stared at one another. After only a heartbeat, the agouti dropped to all fours, beat a brief little tattoo on the ground with its hind feet and then raced off toward the river in a speedy, rather bounding gait. Its rump was a brighter orange than elsewhere and a wisp of a smile touched Sarah's lips as she moved on.

An hour or so later, as visibility began dimming even more in the forest, she found another snug little shelter in the angle of two buttressed roots. She followed her now-standard procedure of checking the ground carefully to make sure it was free of the large stinging ants or anything else that might cause her problems. She sat there for a long while without moving, making no attempt to eat or drink. At last she reached into her pouch and took out one of the dingy-colored fruits and ate it slowly, then ate a second one.

She was terribly lonesome. After a few minutes she leaned her head against one of the huge roots and sobbed convulsively for a long while. She cupped her face in her hands and a low, melancholy sound left her.

"Ohhh," she moaned, "I want to go home."

Sarah Francis was very close to giving up at that point. She hardly remembered lying down and though she slept heavily, it was not a good sleep, punctuated at intervals by faint groanings and once by a sharp outcry.

In the morning she ate nothing but drank a large amount from her canteen, relieved herself and moved on. A small bird, a chatterer, flitted past and alighted on a fern frond which bobbed with its slight weight. The bird was a rich glossy purple with snow white wings, but Sarah paid no attention to it. She was dizzy, light headed, only dimly aware of her surroundings as she walked. Now and then she blundered into thickets that tore her clothing even more and scored her flesh in numerous places. From the knees down her trousers were flapping rag strips and only a little better than that from hips to knees. Her shirt was still relatively intact on the body portion, but the sleeves were badly torn. At one point she passed through an area where several large reddish flies with bright green eyes circled her head closely, annoyingly, occasionally alighting on her head, neck or arms and biting savagely enough to make her cry out. Clothing fabric did not stop them and twice they bit right through her shirt. She managed to slap and kill one that was biting her arm, but the needle-sharp half-inch proboscis was buried in her arm and the dead fly just clung there until she pulled it away with thumb and forefinger and dropped it. The others finally gave up and vanished.

By late forenoon the fever that had been building in Sarah was peaking. She finished what remained of her water and was still thirsty. For a while she thought she should hack her way through the undergrowth to the river and fill the canteen but felt too weak to do so and plodded on until she found a low-growing bromeliad on a tree trunk. She weakened its base with the machete and tilted it until the water it was storing began to run out. It was filled with bits of vegetable debris, small insects floating dead on the surface and a collection of minute living tree frog tadpoles, but she didn't care. She filled her canteen anyway, allowing it to run over so at least the floating material washed out. After the canteen was full she capped it and returned it to her belt, then tilted the plant again and held her mouth under the water trickling out. Momentarily she could feel the movement of tadpoles inside her mouth but she steeled herself and swallowed anyway, drinking deeply.

An armadillo, nearsighted and slow in reaction, watched her approach and did not move until she practically walked into it. Then it merely waddled off in armor-plated unconcern, a miniature tank trundling off into the brush, the jointed, sharply tapering tail dragging straight behind. After it was gone Sarah recalled hearing that people ate armadillos and extolled their virtues as food. Too late, she realized she could have easily killed it with her machete.

Shortly after that she found one of the larger trees that had recently toppled, dragging down a number of lianas and breaking several smaller trees in its fall. The roots were an asterisk spreading out from the base, and in the earth where they had formerly been anchored, there was a large crater. A gaping ten-foot hollow in the trunk remained as mute testimony to why it had weakened and fallen. Sarah stopped and looked inside the horizontal hollow. A split twenty feet long and a foot wide had occurred in the lateral length of the trunk from the force of the fall and enough light entered through the split to let her see that no large creatures were inside. She climbed into the wide hollow at the base and found it was roomy enough for her to stand. She could also crouch and then crawl on hands and knees a good bit farther inside. The interior wood was spongy but dry and when she lay on her side, she could see outside perfectly through the foot-wide split.

It was not raining and Sarah felt a twinge of guilt at

stopping so early in the day, but she just couldn't go on. Her legs felt weak and her cheeks were unnaturally flushed. There was a sense of buzzing in her head and a degree of disorientation. Realizing she was sick, she fumbled in her pouch, took out the little first-aid kit and opened it: small adhesive bandages and gauze squares in individual wrappings, a tin of aspirin, a roll of inch-wide gauze, a small roll of adhesive tape, a tube of burn ointment, a bottle of Mercurochrome, a rubber suction kit for snakebite, a small package of cotton, a curved suture needle in cellophane, and braided nylon thread, a bottle of Chloraquin tablets for prevention of malaria.

She took four aspirin tablets from the tin this time and washed them down with water from the canteen. She propped her head on the pouch and lay there, not uncomfortably, on the bed of soft wood, staring unseeingly out the crack. Her last waking thought was, "I'm going to die in here and no one will ever know what happened to me." It didn't seem to matter much. She slept.

Later she awoke briefly and realized that the heavens had opened again and heavy rain was falling, but for the second time she had found a dry haven and felt very removed from the outside world. She got up again during the night, burning with thirst, drank only a few swallows of the remaining water and immediately fell fitfully asleep again.

Somewhere near dawn, Sarah's fever broke. She awakened feeling better, the flushed, light-headed feeling and nausea gone, but with a great weakness still prevailing. Once more she dozed off and this time it was a deep and restful sleep which continued until the afternoon. A shattering crack of lightning startled her awake and she saw it was raining again. Her bladder was painfully full and she crawled back toward the gaping cavity where she had entered the trunk. When she stood up there, the top of her head barely touched the wood above. Here she squatted and urinated, the fluid quickly absorbed by spongy wood fibers.

Rainwater was streaming off the tree in several rivulets at the opening and she held the canteen under one, rinsed it thoroughly and then refilled it. She drank half of that, topped it off again and then moved back to where her pouch lay, aware that she was suddenly terribly hungry. The fruit was not what she craved and trying to pretend that it was a McDonald's burger, french fries and a milkshake didn't work. Nevertheless, she ate all but two of the fruits and did feel better.

Her father's wallet was still buttoned in her breast pocket and now she took it out and looked through it. The plastic divider inside contained some credit cards, driver's license with her father's picture on it, museum identification card and three photographs. One of these was her own school picture from last fall; Sarah with long, gently waved bittersweet-chocolate hair, lively gray eyes and standard photographic smile. Another was a snapshot of Sarah with two of her closest friends, standing at the entry of Maine West High School, all of them smiling, happy. With a strong stab of homesickness, Sarah wondered if she would ever again see any of her friends.

The final picture was one taken on the steps at the front entrance to the Field Museum — Sarah and her father grinning at one another, happy to be together. It had been taken only a week or so after Sarah had left her mother's house. A lump rose in her throat and the photo swam in her vision. She flipped it out of sight and looked inside the billfold pocket. There were two fifties, three twenties, a five and six one-dollar bills.

Sarah closed the wallet and returned it to her jacket, buttoning it in securely. She lay back, listening to the drumming of the rain and thinking of Ian Francis and of home and school and Des Plaines. It was as if these were fragments of dreams that had never existed in reality. The only reality was the here and now of the rain forest. She fell asleep again and what had seemed to be dream fragments became dreams indeed.

Daylight was filtering in through the split in the log when she woke again. Her hunger was strong and the first thing she did was to eat the remaining two fruits in the pouch. It was while she was finishing the second that a movement caught her eye. Her breath caught and the hair at her nape prickled as she saw what it was.

An enormous jaguar had come into view and stopped, looking back the way it had come. Sleek and heavily muscled, everything about it bespoke a tremendous, unleashed power. Its head was massive, seeming to be overlarge for its body, and the thick black-tipped tail was disproportionately short. Head and body combined with the three-foot tail made the magnificent animal fully nine feet long and its weight was about three hundred pounds. In color it was light yellowish tawny underneath and a rich cinnamon buff on sides and back. There were black, rather tigerlike stripes on the breast and numerous irregular black markings on the legs and body. Those on the sides formed large rosette patterns with a black spot in the center of each.

The splendid cat showed no awareness of Sarah's presence and continued to look behind. A deep rumbling rolled from the throat, ending in a short husky cough. Another movement caught Sarah's attention and two roly-poly cubs gamboled into view, tussling with one another as they approached the female. One bowled over the other and then continued a short run and launched itself at its mother, clung to her back and nipped at the base of her spine in mock attack. The female rolled over with it, evidently enjoying the little game and wheezed heavily as the second cub joined in and pounced on her exposed stomach. They continued to roll and play a few moments more and then the female regained her feet and loped off in the direction from which Sarah had come, her every motion graceful and easy. The kittens followed at a run, the one behind biting at the other's tail and haunches. The sounds they made gradually died away, but for fifteen minutes afterward Sarah remained inside the tree trunk, shivering slightly with an admixture of fear and excitement.

She would have remained in the trunk longer, but a deadly looking centipede appeared. Fully eight inches in length, it crawled past her like an animated chain of yellow-green beads, heading deeper into the log. It encouraged her to leave the log without further delay, but when she did so it was with great caution, the machete gripped firmly in her right hand and her gaze sweeping back and forth in the direction where the jaguar and her cubs had gone. There was no sign of them, but still she moved away as silently as possible, not feeling reasonably secure again until she had traveled half a mile without incident.

She was still very weak and tired easily. She paused frequently to rest and her hunger pangs were constant. During one of her brief stops there was a flash of wings ahead and a large heavy-beaked bird, three feet long, sailed to the ground on powerful wings. It shrieked in a hoarse, gravelly scream and Sarah recognized the sound. It was the cry of a macaw, largest of the parrot family, but this was like no macaw Sarah had ever seen before.

In a moment the bird was joined by a second, slightly larger. Both were the most lovely shade of lavender-blue ranging to deep purple and both had the massive hooked black beaks typical of the gaudy gold-and-blue macaw. An ivory-colored rim of flesh encircled each eye and the base of the lower beak. Their tailfeathers were two feet long and they raised their feet high and spread the strong toes wide with each step they took. These were hyacinth macaws and they were a noisy pair.

They squawked and screamed with each step taken and vied with one another for something they were finding on the ground. Sarah, peering from behind a tree only a dozen yards from them, opened her eyes wider when she saw they were picking up Brazil nuts. The heavy pods that had fallen and finally burst from decay had scattered the strong, three-sided nuts all over the ground here. Many were coated with mold or fungi, but this was of no concern to the macaws. One after another they picked up the nuts and, with powerful pressure of their beaks, easily snapped them in two. With greater facility than Sarah had ever had in opening peanuts, a bird would grip a half nut in one foot while its hooked beak, curved to just the right angle, slid in between shell and kernel and popped the nutmeat into its mouth. The birds hopped about, continuing to shriek as they devoured the nuts.

When Sarah stepped into view, both birds exploded into flight and arrowed through the maze of lianas and tree trunks, disappearing into the heavier foliage and screaming terribly with each flap of their wings. In moments the cries grew faint and were lost. Sarah walked over to where they had been feeding. A scattering of twenty or thirty Brazil nuts still lay here and, only too aware of the difficulty of opening them, she nevertheless tossed them into her pouch. Also on the ground were two halves abandoned by one of the macaws when startled. She dug out the meat with her pocketknife, trying to use the blade as the birds had used their beaks. She was rewarded with two nearly undamaged half kernels and ate them immediately.

Half an hour later she passed an area of jumbled rock outcroppings coated with moss. The usual very large trees were fewer in this area and there was an abundant growth of smaller trees, especially palms. She saw several of the latter with heavy clusters of fruits hanging from just beneath the fronds, but knew of no way to get to them. The palms were tall and, in looking up at the fruit clusters, she very nearly missed something extremely important closer at hand. There was a little grove of perhaps thirty or forty palms with heavy, broad leaves of deep green which sprang from the trunk at a height of five or six feet and went almost straight up. Each leaf was from eight to twelve feet long and well over two feet wide. Hanging down from bloom pods on several were huge pendant-shaped reddish-purple blossoms. Growing in rings around the blossom stem were successive rows of deep green podlike formations at which Sarah looked curiously. They seemed vaguely familiar to her.

Stepping closer to the grove, she abruptly came to a halt as one of the most welcome sights ever to greet her eyes appeared before her. One of the trees had the same sort of unusually thick blossom stem, but the little green podlike forms had fully developed and they were no longer either green or podlike. They were eight or nine inches each, very plump and brilliant yellow.

Bananas!

Gorgeous large ripe bananas by the score were on that single stem and now she saw that there were others all around in various stages of development. Some were large and green, others beginning to yellow; a few, like this cluster, were at their peak, and still others were turning a dark brown.

The huge bunch which was just in front of her was one of the lowest, but still well over her head. With machete outstretched, she could just touch the lowermost bananas. She looked around for something to stand upon, but there was nothing, so she went to the trunk of the tree. She discovered then that, while called a banana palm, it was neither a palm nor a tree; also, it had a stem, not a trunk. The stem was thick, to be sure, about the size of her leg, but it was of crisp vegetable matter, not hard bark and woody material. It was as if the broad leaf material had been rolled up into a tight cylinder.

Excitedly, Sarah swung the machete at the stem and was delighted when the blade sank in a third of the stem's diameter. She worked the machete back and forth to pull it out and then struck the stem again at another angle and a large chunk flew out. Several more well-placed blows were all that was necessary before the whole thing crashed to the ground. She ran to the banana cluster, severed it from the plant at the top and tried to carry it away. She was flabbergasted at its weight. She could barely lift it clear of the ground and carrying it any distance was ridiculous.

Unable to wait any longer, she ripped one of the bananas free, peeled back the skin and took a huge bite. It was so good, so *meaty*, that she almost cried with joy. She chewed and gulped, devouring the banana with un-caring greediness. As soon as it was finished she ate an-other, almost as rapidly. The third and fourth she ate at a reasonable pace and she was barely able to finish the fifth.

Sarah sat on the ground, holding her stomach with one hand, resting the other against the banana clump. She couldn't remember when anything had tasted so good. While sitting there she cut from the main clump a large bunch of the bananas and stuffed them into her pouch. There was room for more and so she cut off another bunch of similar size and stuffed them inside also. Then, one at a time she shoved individual bananas into every unfilled cranny of the bag until it was so stuffed she could not close it. Even at that, she had removed only about a third of the bananas from the stalk. She hefted the pouch and grunted at the weight of it. Carrying such a load would not be easy, but she didn't care. She even broke off more individual bananas and stuffed them into her pockets and inside her tattered blouse.

It was only with great reluctance, after eating one more banana from the clump, that she left the area and continued her journey, laboring under the weight. She rested even more often but she ate well and was amazed at how quickly she felt stronger with food of a more solid nature in her stomach.

The bananas lasted her into the fifth day after finding them. During that interval there had been one day when it did not rain at all and she covered many miles. On the other days, she had given up slogging through the rain and instead, as soon as clouds moved in, searched for a suitable shelter under which to sit it out. Usually this was beneath a leaning log or in sheltered crannies among rock outcroppings. Sometimes the rain ended early enough for her to continue another hour or so before finding a place to spend the night. Sometimes she just remained where she was all night.

There were several other encounters with animals, though nothing quite so breathtaking or potentially dangerous as the appearance of the jaguar with her cubs. Once she saw a group of seven or eight capybaras, the largest rodents in the world. The biggest ones in the group must have weighed one hundred fifty pounds and, considering their size and dumpy shape, they were quite agile. As soon as they saw Sarah they scattered in all directions while voicing a succession of cries and grunts.

Another time she saw a paca, which in body shape looked much like its smaller cousin, the agouti. But unlike the orangish-brown of the latter, the paca's hair color was a deep brown liberally sprinkled with white dots and a white line down each side.

The most fascinating thing she saw occurred yesterday morning, the fourth day since she found the bananas. Had it not been for a small bird, Sarah might have walked into some serious trouble. She was moving briskly through an area of tall trees with narrow trunks, most of them less than a foot in diameter even though upwards of one hundred feet high. Her route of travel would have taken her between a dense clump of ferns and a small jutting of rocks from the earth at the base of one of those slender trees. The distance between the two was about six feet. Just as she was approaching it, a small, quite brilliantly colored little bird about the size of a sparrow flew past her shoulder, going in the same direction she was headed, its wings making a strange wooden clatter as it flew.

In the space between the tree and the dense ferns, it stopped abruptly in midflight and hung in the air at shoulder height, flapping its wings furiously and uttering sharp chipping cries. It took a moment for Sarah to realize that it had flown into a huge, poorly made spiderweb and, despite all its strugglings, was securely ensnared. On the verge of stepping forward to free the bird, Sarah gave a sharp little cry and remained rooted.

A spider of enormous size sped from a cranny in the

rocks and raced to the bird. The body of the spider, covered with coarse gray and reddish hairs, was two inches long, but the spread of its legs was fully seven inches. Two huge shiny black fangs projected downward from its head and these it buried in the bird immediately and held them there, injecting its venom, while at the same time anchoring the bird more securely with tough webbing unraveling from the spinneret at the rear of its abdomen.

The bird cried out sharply one time more, trembled for several seconds and then went limp. After another moment the spider released its bite and stepped back an inch or so, surveying its catch. Whether or not it would have eaten the bird at this point, Sarah did not discover. Almost as the bird had done, something else flew past her shoulder and directly at the spider.

It was a female wasp of very large proportions, though not so big as the spider. Blue-black with greenish undertones, the wasp made a pass at the spider but missed as the spider made a great leap, covering half the distance back to its rocky lair. The wasp was too fast for it. Veering sharply around, she launched a new attack, coming after her huge adversary from the direction of the lair. However, the spider itself was not slow to react. It leaped off the web to the ground and immediately rolled over onto its back, fangs ready, spinneret prepared to entangle and all eight hairy legs poised to grip when the wasp came within range.

Fast as she had been before, the speed and maneuverability of the wasp now became phenomenal. So fast that often Sarah lost track of her, the wasp flitted in and out at the spider, spearing at it with the deadly half-inch stinger at each rush. At first the spider parried every blow and once it even managed to grapple briefly with the wasp, but the poisonous fangs did not reach their mark and the wasp broke free.

The spider slowed and either was tiring or had been stung, Sarah could not tell which. The pauses by the wasp at the spider became longer and the insect was definitely stabbing the spider repeatedly. Her own venom was powerful and in less than thirty seconds the spider could no longer defend itself. At the end of a minute it was perfectly still and the wasp landed close beside it, cleaned her own antennae and legs and then walked around her large victim several times. Enthralled by the whole tableau, Sarah couldn't imagine what the wasp would do now.

As if to answer her question, the wasp gripped the spider by the head in her two front legs and then her wings began moving. The buzzing grew louder and louder as she increased the strength and speed of the wingstrokes, and then suddenly she lifted free of the ground, carrying the much larger spider below her. Unbelievingly, Sarah watched as she droned away with her great burden and disappeared into the gloom of the forest.

As clouds began filling the sky again on this afternoon of the fifth day since leaving the banana grove, Sarah still had eight bananas in her pouch. She had, by this time, grown a bit tired of them, but they were much more satisfying and filling than the other fruits she had been eating. Early this morning she had found more of the tortoise-skin custardy fruits and ate four of them. Two others were also in her pouch. She still had a dozen Brazil nuts; so, while she might not have a repast, at least she had something to eat. More than anything else, though, she craved cooked meat or fish and potatoes.

Sarah's gaze swept back and forth as she walked. She was looking with a more practiced eye than previously for a shelter to keep her dry and comfortable for the duration of the rain. She no longer had any desire to put on the poncho and continue walking through the rains as she did in the beginning. It simply wasn't necessary and it only compounded her problems.

As she searched, Sarah wondered idly what she was going to do about her clothing. The trousers had become so badly shredded in the legs they were more an annoyance than a protection. The shirt was rapidly getting into the same condition. Her knee socks could no longer be called socks by any stretch of the imagination. Yesterday, following her witnessing of the dramatic encounter between the spider and wasp, she had sat out the afternoon rain very comfortably between two trees that had fallen parallel to one another over a huge old moldering log. Using her machete, she had cut fronds from some low palms and also from some giant ferns and, interlaying them over the gap between the two trees, formed a dry and pleasant little shelter beneath. A few trickles of water ran through, but they were of no consequence. She utilized the time, after eating four bananas and having some water, to cut the tatters of her trouser legs off about six inches above the knees. The shirt sleeves were next to go, all the way to the shoulders, since they were very nearly as ragged as the trouser legs. She lopped off her socks just above the shoe tops, retaining the feet portions to help prevent blisters.

There was little Sarah could do about the condition of her shoes, and this was a problem she thought about with concern now while searching for the day's shelter. The stitching had pulled away in a number of places and they were falling apart. She was apprehensive about how she would get along once they were no longer wearable. She shrugged and sighed; that was a situation to which she would have to adjust when it became reality.

A rather large outcropping of rock loomed through the trees ahead to her left and she headed in that direction, slowing as she approached to look it over well. Numerous small trees, ferns and mosses had taken root on the sides and top of the outcropping, encrusting it until the rock surface itself was mostly hidden. One face of it, however, was relatively sheer, broken only by an indentation at its base and, a yard or so from that, a vertical split about four feet in width which rose from ground level to a height of six or seven feet, then moved off horizontally, rapidly narrowing until it disappeared.

Sarah checked the niche, disappointed to find it much too exposed and therefore of little benefit. The wide crack was better. It went in about ten feet and ended at a blank wall. A moderate coating of humus on the floor would make it comfortable enough for sitting or lying upon and, except near the entrance, little if any rain would penetrate.

She inspected it carefully, probing here and there with the machete for ants, scorpions or anything else that might create problems. There was nothing to be concerned about so she settled down to wait, sitting cross-legged about five feet inside, facing the entrance. She took a swallow of water from the canteen and momentarily deliberated over whether she would eat one of the custardy fruits or a banana. She chose two bananas, placed one in her lap and was contentedly munching the other when the rain began.

This time it didn't start slowly, as usual; one moment it wasn't raining at all and the next it was a downpour. Thunder rumbled heavily, causing the ground to vibrate. Two rapid-succession cracks of lightning nearby made Sarah wince, closing her eyes tightly for a moment. When she opened them again, she very nearly choked on her bite of banana.

Silhouetted in the entryway was a nearly naked dark-skinned man.

Chapter Six

SARAH FRANCIS, petrified with the fear that filled her, turned ashen, her mouth slightly agape. But she made no sound.

The man standing in the entry, effectively blocking any possibility of her escape, might have been something from one of her nightmares. A thin black thorn, sharpened on both ends, perforated his nostrils and a well-curved conical tooth of some kind dangled from his right earlobe. Blue-black tattooed lines, one from each mouthcorner, ran to the temples. Three short straight lines of the same color were tattooed on each cheek. Other tattoos were on his upper arms and thighs as well as his chest and belly. These were mainly series of vertical or horizontal parallel lines, but one on his chest was in the shape of a large X, the diagonal lines double and intertwining much as lianas intertwined in the trees. His chin was dyed bright red and diagonal lines of the same color were on each side of his neck.

At first he looked huge to Sarah, because he was standing and she sitting, but then she realized he was not really very tall at all, probably no more than four inches over her own height of five feet three inches. He was very broad across the chest and his arms and legs were thick and muscular, with rather small hands and feet.

His only item of clothing was a breechcloth which was not cloth at all but a wide strip of the soft inner bark of a tree. This was suspended from a narrow waistband of the same material. He carried several different items, including a very long pole in one hand, a bow across one shoulder and several long arrows in a crude quiver. A knife was in his waistband, the handle made of wood tightly wrapped with thin vine, along with two pouches, one large and one small, made of plaited fibers of some kind.

Sarah noticed all these things instantly but, as she looked more closely, two other things became evident. He was quite a young man, probably no more than fifteen or sixteen, and he was as much startled by Sarah — and perhaps as much afraid — as Sarah was of him.

Masking her fear and attempting to smile, prepared to snatch up the machete which lay beside her and defend herself with it if necessary, she slowly picked up the banana in her lap and extended it toward him with her left hand.

"Banana?" she asked.

She could see his tense muscles relax a little, but he remained expressionless. She continued holding the banana outstretched and then he came toward her and accepted the fruit. Immediately he stepped back to the entryway, placed the long pole on the ground and, without taking his gaze from her, peeled the banana and ate it in three huge bites. His teeth, Sarah noticed, were short and even, stained blue. He flipped the skin of the fruit outside behind him without removing his gaze from her, his jaws working regularly as he chewed.

Sarah swallowed the residue of banana still in her own mouth and then finished the remaining bite of the fruit she was holding. The fear still rode her, though not so strongly as initially. She studied him more closely now.

His skin was a deep coppery-brown and his hair very black and straight, hanging to his shoulders and chopped evenly across the brow, framing his face in a sort of primitive pageboy manner. It was similarly chopped at the sides to expose his ears and she noted that the left one was in two sections. It seemed evident that long ago he had suffered an injury that had nearly severed part of that ear. His face was round and the cheeks flat, without prominent cheekbones. There was no obliqueness to the eyes, which were steady and very dark. The black thorn through his nostrils seemed to be a permanent ornament. On the upper left quadrant of his chest, almost where it joined his shoulder, was a deep gash about four inches long, very wide and quite recent. It was not bleeding but she could see exposed muscle tissue and it looked very painful.

She pointed to it. "You've been hurt."

His gaze flicked briefly to the wound and then he looked back at her, still without expression. Behind him the rain was falling very heavily, but neither of them paid any attention to it. Sarah's smile was a little less strained as she spoke again.

"You don't understand English, do you?" When he didn't reply, she tried out her high school Spanish. "*Hablas Español?*" Still no response and she cocked her head. "Portuguese?"

Sarah sighed. "I guess we'll just have to start from

scratch," she said. She tapped her chest. "My name is Sarah. Sarah." The humor of the Tarzan-Jane routine struck her and she smiled broadly and tapped her chest again. "Me Sarah. Sar-ah." She pointed at him. "What . . . your . . name?" Again she tapped her own chest and said "Sarah" and then pointed at him. "Name?"

He did not smile in return, yet there was a sense of his expression relaxing, as if he were smiling mentally. His head made the faintest of nods and he touched a finger to his own chest.

"Juma," he said. "Juma *heh*." He pointed at her. "Sa-rah?" He placed strong emphasis on the first syllable, and used a broader *a* sound.

Sarah nodded, pleased, patted the ground and made motions. "Sit down," she said. "Sit."

Cautiously, maintaining his distance from her, Juma slowly sat down in cross-legged fashion. When Sarah reached into her pouch, his expression became tense and his hand went to the haft of his knife, then fell away as Sarah brought out the remaining six bananas attached in one bunch. She broke it in half and extended a trio of them toward him. After a slight pause he reached out his knife hand and took them from her.

With an air of casualness she did not really feel, Sarah peeled one of hers and began to eat it. Juma watched her and did the same, eating this one less greedily than he had the first. He smiled faintly and began to peel a second. When the flesh of the fruit was exposed he pointed at it.

"*Pacova*," he said.

"*Pacova?* That's what you call a banana? Okay,

pacova it is." Sarah laughed lightly, peeled another and ate it. They spoke no more until the bananas were gone. Then Sarah reached into the pouch again and brought out the two scaled fruits and handed one to Juma. He smiled and nodded.

"*Jabuti-puhe*," he said.

"*Jabuti-puhe*," she repeated.

Sarah watched to see how he would eat it. He took the knife from his belt and prepared to cut the fruit, then paused and held up the implement for Sarah to see.

"*Parati*."

She nodded and touched the machete on the ground beside her and repeated the word. Immediately he shook his head. He pointed at the machete and said, "*Terzada*." Again he displayed the knife and repeated, "*Parati*."

Sarah said, "*Terzada*," tapping the machete with her finger, then reached into her pocket. He seemed amazed at such a thing as a pocket and watched curiously as she brought out her father's knife, opened a blade and showed it to him, saying, "*Parati*."

He was very impressed with it and held out his hand. She gave it to him and he looked closely at the stainless steel blade. He pushed on it and the blade snapped closed, nicking his finger and he dropped it in surprise, immediately suspicious. She moved a little closer to him, putting up her hand in a reassuring gesture, picked it up and showed him the proper way to open and close it. Then she opened both blades at once, their tips pointing in opposite directions. He took it from her and looked at it closely again, then cautiously closed each blade in turn. He grunted appreciatively as he handed it back to her and turned his attention to the *jabuti-puhe*.

Using his own knife, which had a dull blade of beaten iron, he cut the fruit in half, flicked out the seeds in one of the halves with the tip of the blade and then used the tip again to free the pulp, running it around inside the rind. When it was loose he speared it with the knife blade and put it into his mouth, then turned his attention to the other half.

Sarah used the larger blade of her pocketknife to emulate his actions on her own *jabuti-puhe* and found it much simpler to eat that way than by cutting off the rind by bits and pieces and gouging out small chunks of the pulp as she had done previously. She could not put it into her mouth all at once as he had done, but ate it like a pared apple. As she ate it, she studied the young man across from her. She was no longer afraid of him and gratified to have someone near. Communication was a problem, but she was sure she could quickly pick up enough of his language to be able to converse to some extent. She wondered if he would be able to help her reach a town somewhere and became excited at the thought of it.

When they were finished with the fruit, Juma tossed his rinds and peels outside and Sarah did the same. Then he reached into the larger pouch at his waist and withdrew two rather large, irregularly shaped pieces of meat. They were blackened on the outside, as if they had been tossed onto living fire. He handed one piece to Sarah and immediately bit into his own piece and tore out a chunk. The meat was pinkish and the good aroma struck Sarah. How she had missed having meat!

Without hesitation she bit into the piece he had given her and the taste was even better than the smell. She chewed it up and swallowed, then rolled her eyes appreciately. "Oh, Juma, that's so good!"

He didn't understand the words but her meaning was clear and when she smacked her lips and patted her stomach, he laughed aloud for the first time. It was deep, hearty.

"What is it?" she asked, talking around another bite.

He was looking at her uncomprehendingly and she tapped the meat with a forefinger and then hunched her shoulders and looked at him questioningly.

He nodded then. "*Gauriba*," he said. "*Gauriba*."

She shook her head, unfamiliar with the word. He grinned and made motions over his head with his hands. Then he shoved his head forward, opened his mouth wide and gave vent to a penetrating screaming sound. She knew he was trying to help her picture whatever the animal was the meat had come from, but she still had no idea what he meant.

"Maybe I'll find out sooner or later when I can understand you better," she said. She began eating again and, uncomprehending of what she had said, he resumed his own eating. The meat was tender and delicious, with a single large bone through the center. Sarah was sorry when it was finished. She brought out the canteen, unscrewed the lid and offered it to him. He frowned, not knowing what she meant, so she put it to her own mouth and took a few swallows, then offered it to him again.

He took it and tasted gingerly. "*Paranah*," he said, then drank more deeply.

"Okay, that's another word," Sarah said. "*Paranah* means water."

Juma looked at the canteen curiously when he finished and tapped a finger against it. Obviously, he had never before seen a metal container. He tried putting the lid back on but failed and she took it from him and showed him how to screw it on and off. She finished drinking what remained in it and went to the entryway, held it under a small stream of water pouring off a thumb-width root hanging there from atop the rocks. When it was full, she capped it and put it away.

Sarah pointed at the nine-foot-long pole he had placed on the ground, which still extended a considerable distance outside. He picked up the end and showed it to her. She saw at once it was not just a straight stick. Two long, half-round pieces of wood had been bound together with a tightly wound spiral of very tough viny material not unlike brown hardware store twine. Before they had been bound, a groove had been scooped out of the center of each piece of wood down its entire length. So precisely cut were the grooves that when the two pieces were fitted together for binding, the opposing grooves met and formed a perfectly round hole running through the center of the pole's entire length, making a tube of it. The whole outside of the tube had been smeared with a waxy substance impenetrable to the rainwater. The tube tapered and was almost twice as thick at one end as at the other. At the thicker end there was a cup-shaped piece of wood with a hole in the bottom that aligned with the hole in the tube.

Juma tapped the tube with his finger and said, "*Pu-cuna,*" then held the pole horizontally, placed the cup end to his mouth, and his cheeks puffed out with the force of the breath he blew through it.

"Oh, it's a blowgun!" Sarah exclaimed. "I've heard about them. *Pucuna.* I never realized they were so long."

Swelling with pride over her enthusiasm, Juma showed her the darts he used in the *pucuna.* He was very careful in handling them. They were in a special little quiver of their own within the larger arrow quiver. Each was almost a foot in length and very slender, about half again the diameter of the lead in a pencil. One end was snugly wrapped in a limber leaf. The back end of the dart was fletched with a little oval mass of fluff that looked like cotton, but much finer and lighter. The leaf-wrapped tip tapered down to a needle sharpness and was coated for about an inch with a dark gummy substance. Sarah assumed this was some sort of poison and must be very potent, considering the caution with which Juma handled it and the fact that the tip was wrapped.

When he finished, Sarah showed him the rock hammer from her belt. Interested, he inspected it closely and repeated after her, "Ham-mer," then handed it back. Immediately he showed her his bow and arrows, which he called respectively *iranpahn* and *mereres.* From the smaller pouch he extracted a little clay pot which he called *yaahn.* It was tightly leaf-wrapped and contained about an inch of the same dark gummy substance coating the dart point. Sarah could see where the points of darts had been stuck into it. Juma was very sober when he told her the material was *wourali.**

Throughout this time, Sarah had been glancing at the

* Wourali is a South American Indian term for the deadly poison more familiar as curare.

gaping wound on Juma's chest. She touched his arm and, when he looked at her, she indicated the gash.

"How did this happen, Juma?"

He looked at it and then at her and broke into a rapid string of words she could not understand. Realizing this, he broke off and made a helpless gesture. He touched the lip of the wound and winced faintly, then said a few more words. The injury looked as if it had occurred no more than a few days ago and that his movements were continually causing it to split and widen.

"Juma, sit down again." He didn't understand and she had to enact it for him, sitting down herself and patting the ground. He sat as he had before and she put her hand on his right shoulder, indicating he should stay. Then she rose, took the cleaner of the two handkerchiefs from her hip pocket and soaked it under the stream of water running from the root at the entry. She returned and knelt beside him and very gently began to daub at the wound. The edges were caked with scabrous material and it took a long while to soften. Every so often she would return to the entryway, soak the pinkened cloth, wring it out, shake off any bits of the scabby matter and then return with the handkerchief newly saturated again.

When at last she had the wound clean, she went to her pouch and dug out the first-aid kit. She used up several of the sterile gauze pads drying his wound, although now it had begun oozing again. She rolled another gauze pad into a tight cylinder and soaked one end of it well with Mercurochrome and daubed the wound thoroughly with it. He made no move, though she was sure that the medication and her cleaning of the wound must have caused him pain.

He pointed at the little bottle and said, "*Ucuru.*" Smiling, he pointed at his red-painted chin.

"I guess it is paint, in a way," she said, still daubing it on and knowing he wasn't understanding what she said but finding pleasure in talking to him anyway. "It's called Mercurochrome and it'll help kill germs and prevent infection. What you really need is to have that stitched up before it gets worse."

She paused, considering. There was a suture needle and nylon thread in the kit. She remembered quite well how Dr. Cruz had stitched up the injured boatman back on the Ipixuna and she thought perhaps she might be able to do it. Whether or not Juma would want her to try was another matter.

"Juma, look here." She held her thumb and index finger parallel to one another just over the wound, then squeezed them together as if they were the lips of the wound. With her free hand she made motions of sewing them together. He understood at once, looked at the wound again and nodded.

Sarah extracted the cellophane-wrapped needle from the kit, along with the thread. She showed them both to Juma and then withdrew from her pouch the cylinder of waterproof farmer's matches. She took one out and showed it to him but he evinced no understanding of its purpose. When she struck the match against the rock wall, his eyes grew wide and for just a moment showed fear again. Still he made no effort to move away.

As best she could, Sarah sterilized the full length of the needle in the match flame. Then she threaded the nylon through its eye. When she indicated he should lie on his back near the entryway where the light was better, he hesitated at first but finally did so. Kneeling at his left side, Sarah began the job.

The needle was very sharp but it was still a job forcing it through Juma's skin — first down through the tissues a quarter-inch from the wound, curving to come out at the bottom of the laceration, then up the other side from the bottom of the wound and out the skin surface, again a quarter-inch from the edge. A small amount of blood flowed but there was no utterance from Juma. She made a loop in the thread, drew the first stitch tight and tied it off. After cutting the thread close to the wound, she started the second stitch. Because of the depth of the gash and its gaping nature, she put the stitches close together. It took an hour for her to finish; a total of thirteen stitches. She finished off by again daubing the wound with Mercurochrome, covering it with two gauze pads and fastening them in place with adhesive tape. She had done a commendable job and it was obvious that Juma was both pleased and awed.

The rainfall lasted until dusk and during this time Sarah continued to learn new words from Juma. He easily fell into the spirit of teaching her and as Sarah pointed to various things, he spoke the names and she repeated them.* She was remarkably retentive and rarely had to ask for the word a second time.

* The language spoken here is Tupi-Guarani, which is essentially the intertribal language of South American tribes, much as Swahili is the intertribal language of African tribes.

They concentrated first on the human anatomy, beginning with the extremities, and Sarah soon learned that all the body parts were words beginning with the letter *H*. The little finger was called *hepunhy*, the other fingers were called *hepun* and the thumb was *hepunhuh*. Fingernails were *hepuapeh*. The hand was *hepo*. The arm was *hediwah* and its elbow was *hediwah-renangeh*. Where the lower extremities were concerned, the toe was *hepuhan*, the foot was *hepeh* and the sole of the foot was *hepetahn*. The calf was *heretamaken*, the knee *herenapahen*, and the thigh was *heu*.

One by one she learned them, committing them to memory and then, when they had gone through them all, testing herself. She gripped her own hair and said, "*Han*," and Juma nodded in affirmation. She cupped her whole head in both hands and said, "*Hanke*," and was correct again. Forehead, *heruan;* ear, *henamhy;* eyebrow, *herupehan;* eyelashes, *herepepy;* eye, *herehan;* nose, *hetsin;* cheek, *heratupe;* mouth, *heyruru;* tongue, *hapekun;* tooth, *heren;* chin, *heradiweh;* throat, *heahn;* shoulder, *heyatiapeh;* chest, *heyarukehn;* breast, *hekehn;* belly, *herauheh;* back, *hekupeh;* buttocks, *herewy;* penis, *herankuh;* vulva, *hnekutyeh*. Even the largest organ of the body, the skin, was a word beginning with *H*— *hepireh*.

As dusk deepened and the rainfall ceased, sounds of the night began. Crickets and katydids, tree frogs and tree toads, and night birds of various kinds blended their voices and sounds in a great chorus, accompanied by a mélange of unidentifiable noises. To Juma they were obviously so commonplace that he paid little attention to them. For Sarah they were still a fascinating and somewhat frightening composition and she thought she would never really take them for granted, wishing she had the ability to converse with him in order to learn more about him and his people and the rain forest.

Juma was an enigma. What was he, a youth only now entering manhood, doing alone in the jungle? How had he been injured? Would he stay with her and help her, or would he merely pick up his weapons and disappear in this wilderness where he could travel with facility and direction and she could not? If she could speak with him, could she perhaps impress upon him the desperateness of her dilemma and the urgency she felt to return to civilization? She knew none of the answers, but resolved to spend every waking moment learning his language and, at the same time, not knowing when he might leave her, learning what to do or not do in order to survive.

She experienced a thrill of fear shortly after the rain ceased, when he stood up and, without a word or gesture, walked out of their shared haven. For a terrible moment she thought he was gone. Then she realized he had left his equipment here and her fear subsided. A moment later she could hear him urinating outside. When he returned, she went out for the same purpose, staying somewhat longer than he had, simply standing still after relieving herself and absorbing the essence of early night, beginning to be able to differentiate between sounds, cocking her head to listen more closely to those unfamiliar, raising her head to sniff the scents that drifted to her nostrils and were so much fuller on the night air than during the day.

When Sarah reentered the shelter, Juma was stretched out, his head toward the entry, his breath coming evenly. She thought she had moved soundlessly, yet when she neared him his breathing changed and she knew he was awake. He made no move and she slipped past him close to one wall. In the deeper recesses, she too lay down, taking off her shoes and stretching out with her feet toward his. She was sure she would lie there a long while, unable to sleep, thinking about this encounter and what would happen next. She did not feel particularly drowsy, yet hardly had she settled herself than she was asleep.

In the dim light of early morning, Sarah awoke and found that Juma was already up, standing at the entryway, his head cocked for sound and turning his gaze toward whatever interesting noise reached him. He already had bow and quiver over his shoulder but had not yet picked up his blowgun. He looked her way as she made a slight sound and greeted her with a faint smile and almost imperceptible dip of his head.

"*Sa-rah. Apotare hahoh heiruhm?*"

He was asking if she wanted to go with him. Although she could not understand, there was something about the query that imparted the sense of what he had asked.

"Let me get my shoes on, Juma," she said. In turn, she held each shoe upside down and knocked it against the wall to dislodge anything that might have taken refuge inside during the night. Juma watched approvingly. She put them on quickly, pulled her pouch strap over her head and shoulder and slid the machete back into its belt sheath. Juma had picked up his blowgun and was inserting a dart into the tube through the cup-shaped mouthpiece. As she stepped toward him, he moved out into the open and Sarah followed.

She had a moment of consternation when he headed away from the Ituí, but then realized at this point it didn't matter; staying with Juma was far more important now than remaining near the river. She walked where he walked, keeping about ten feet behind, studying the way he moved, trying to emulate his sureness and stealth, looking where he looked.

Most often, Juma's gaze was directed overhead. Now and then he paused, watching and listening. Twice he began to raise the blowgun, only to lower it again at once and continue walking. The third time was different. Although Sarah had neither seen nor heard anything, Juma stopped and stared into the canopy. Far above through the interlacing leafiness, little patches of blue sky were occasionally visible. For the most part, however, the ceiling was a multilayered pattern of different tints and tones and shades of green, interspersed with the deeper grays, browns and blacks of tree trunks and branches and lianas.

Without looking at her, Juma signaled with a backward-turned palm for her to stand still. Step by slow, cautious step, his movements all but imperceptible, he eased forward, toes feeling for anything that might make a sound before allowing his weight to settle. Three steps, four, five and then he stopped again. With infinite slowness he raised the *pucuna* until it was straight up, held by both hands close together a foot above the mouthpiece.

Without moving his head he brought the mouthpiece into position.

Her own head back and looking upward, Sarah tried to detect what he had seen. A tiny flash of color caught her eye and she saw it. The bird was a toucan, perched on a slim branch at a height of around one hundred twenty feet. It appeared to be black. The flash of color she detected was from the oversized orange beak. At first the bird was sitting motionless except for brief turnings of its head, and Sarah wondered how Juma could ever have spotted it in the first place. As she watched, however, the toucan began silently hopping about, peeping into cavities of the trunk or in crevices of the branches. Every now and then it would pause to crane its neck, looking for danger. Seeing none, it resumed its probing, accompanying the action with a sound like the croaking of a frog.

Holding very still, Sarah rolled her eyes to look at Juma and was just in time to see his cheeks abruptly inflate with the same sort of distended tightness that appears on the cheeks of a tuba player striving to hit a high note. There was a distinctly audible pop as the dart shot from the muzzle and sped upward so swiftly that it was very difficult to follow its flight. Only the oblong tuft of white fuzz serving as fletching marked its flight, a blurred speck that arrowed through the complex maze of leaves and branches and vines, touching nothing until it found its mark.

Sarah saw it strike the bird in midbreast and lodge there. The toucan spread its wings and made a little jump, but did not fly. Its wings closed again and it ruffled its feathers. The bird stood high and in succession raised and lowered its feet several times, stopped, shuddered violently and then pitched forward off the branch. It struck several limbs and vines as it fell, crashing noisily through the foliage, then thumped to the ground only a few paces from where Juma was standing.

Speechless at this phenomenal marksmanship, Sarah joined him at the fallen bird. Juma was removing the dart, which had penetrated over an inch into the bird's breast. At once he checked the point, saw that it was undamaged and took the little poison pot from his smaller pouch. He unwrapped it and stuck the dart tip into the thick, salvelike *wourali*, twirled it to coat the point evenly and then replaced the missile in the *pucuna*. He rewrapped the pot, replaced it in his pouch and picked up the dead bird.

"*Toco,*" he said, extending it toward her. He was grinning broadly.

"*Toco,*" she repeated, taking it from him by one leg. It was a heavier bird than she had anticipated, and much larger than she had thought when seen from a distance as it was perched high above. It was easily two feet long from the end of the tail to the tip of the beak. Its tail was short and rather square; its plumage solid black except for a bright red patch on the underside just in front of the tail and a larger patch of white on the lower half of its face, extending down its short neck to the upper breast. Its dark eye was surrounded by a narrow circle of gray-blue flesh and a wider circle of orange flesh. The bird's most startling characteristic by far was the size of its beak. About as long as the bird's entire body, it was brilliant orange and had a large elongated black mark covering the end of the upper mandible at the sides and tip. The base of the beak was rimmed with the same black all the way around. That beak had every appearance of being a formidable weapon, yet when Sarah felt it she was amazed at its lightness, as if it had been carved from balsa wood and then painted.

Juma took the bird back from her, expertly opened it with his knife just below the breastbone and scooped out the viscera. He separated liver and heart and cut the gall off the liver. Indicating that organ he said *"Hipyahn,"* and placed it back inside the body cavity. He held up the small heart for her to see, calling it *"Heyimbeh,"* and put it with the liver.

Sarah followed as before when he strode off carrying the bird. As they walked he picked up newly fallen branches and Sarah began to help. When they had a large number of them in their arms, Juma led Sarah to one of the giant buttressed trees where he dropped the *toco* and branches on the ground between two of the roots. He stood his *pucuna* up carefully against the roots and removed his bow and quiver. Sarah dropped her branches also, putting her pouch on the ground near his weapons. He then motioned her to come with him and moved a short distance away to where a peculiarly slim-trunked palm tree grew. It was about fifty feet high, crowned by a clump of pretty fernlike leaves. Beneath the crown hung a cluster of small fruits or seeds. Tall as it was, the stem of this palm at the base was only three inches thick. Juma placed his hand on the trunk and patted it.

"*Bacaba*," he said and then, lest she think he meant only the trunk, he indicated the entire length of the tree and repeated, "*Bacaba.*"

She said the name, too, but when he began hacking at the tree with his short-bladed *parati*, obviously to cut it down, she stopped him and took her machete from its sheath.

"*Terzada*," she said, handing it to him. "Better. Use it."

He chuckled and took it from her, then whacked the tree with strong blows. In less than a minute it leaned, cracked and fell with a whoosh to the ground. They walked to the crown and Juma plucked a few fruits from the cluster and handed them to Sarah. They were the size, shape and color of ripe olives. He took one himself and showed her how to bite into it, not solidly through the middle, but more in the manner of nipping it at an angle. The reason became clear. There was only an eighth-inch of pulp surrounding a large hard seed, again like an olive. He gnawed off the pulp and tossed the seed away.

Sarah did the same and smiled. The pulp was dark brown, of olive consistency, but somewhat juicier, tasting like a combination of cocoa and peanuts. By motions of his hands in crude sign language, Juma showed her how the pulp could be scraped into a container, then mashed and the juice poured off and drunk. She nodded her understanding and wished they had a vessel for that purpose. They tossed a few handfuls of the fruit into Sarah's pockets, but getting the *bacaba* palm fruit was not the reason he had cut down the tree.

Juma used the machete to cut off three of the fernlike fronds and took them back to where the wood had been dumped. Returning the *terzada* to Sarah, he looked around, searching the forest floor. He did not see what he wanted and began circling, with Sarah following closely. At last he grunted in a satisfied manner as he saw a small brown ant mound. It was about a foot high and the same in diameter, although some Sarah had seen in her wanderings were as much as twelve feet across and three or four feet high.

The young Indian kicked it over and immediately a frenzy of small brown ants scurried about, many circling aimlessly, others snatching exposed eggs or larvae to carry them to safety. In the center of the portion Juma had kicked over was a fist-sized clump of grayish material, much like felt in texture and softness. He freed it with his knife, brushed the ants away and showed it to Sarah, calling it *"isca."* They took it back to the tree.

Kneeling there, with Sarah watching every move he made, Juma used his knife to scrape a fair-sized pile of shavings from the underside of the midrib of two *bacaba* palm fronds. Taking the *toco* a few steps away, he swiftly plucked it, the feathers drifting down in a miniature black blizzard. He did not cut off the head and feet. A few steps away he cut down a willowy, green-barked sapling and trimmed it to a four-foot length with one end sharpened. After removing the heart and liver from the body cavity, he thrust the stick lengthwise through the toucan, entering through the vent and emerging from the mouth. Shoving the bird well down on the stick, he then impaled the heart and liver. Leaning the spitted bird against one of the large-flanged roots, he knelt again by the shavings. From inside his smaller pouch he withdrew a little box made of bamboo strips. Inside was a two-inch bar of iron a quarter-inch thick and a flat-surfaced chunk of flint.

Juma tore the feltlike *isca* material in half and put one portion of it into the box and the other he tossed on the ground. Taking out the fire-building equipment, he leaned close to the ground and struck the flint cupped in his left hand with the iron bar in his right. Bright sparks rocketed into the tinder and at once a faint wisp of smoke curled upward. As he blew on it gently, it burst into flame, consuming itself with great rapidity, but before it could go out he tossed on the fine *bacaba* shavings. They ignited rapidly, burning with hot, almost smokeless flame. He finished by breaking twigs and branches and tossing them on the fire. The whole process took only a few minutes and Sarah was very impressed.

The spitted toucan looked much like a chicken and Sarah watched with interest as Juma held it in the living fire, constantly turning it. After several minutes he withdrew it, used his knife to force the blackened and smoking liver and heart off the end of the spit onto the third palm frond, then put the bird over the fire again. He motioned Sarah to eat and she cut each piece in half with her pocketknife. Inside they were pink and steamy. Since Juma was occupied with turning the spitted bird, she fed him half-pieces of the heart and liver and he murmured appreciatively as he chewed. When she ate her own halves, she found them delicious, although the heart was a little chewy.

After about twenty minutes the bird was black. Its skin had crisped and curled and then charred. The outer meat also had blackened, but when he removed the spit and cut the bird in half, the inner meat was well cooked. To Sarah its aroma was heavenly and she could not remember chicken ever having tasted so good. The lack of salt did not bother her at all.

As they ate, Sarah again prompted Juma to talk, to tell her his words for things. She was beginning to learn subtle differences. A single tree, for example, was called *euireh* if it were sapling-sized and *hooweh* if mature, but the forest itself was called *ca-ahn* and wood used as timber was *acapu*. A woman was called *kunyahn*, but a girl was *kunyimuku*. A man was *kumbe eh*; a boy, *kurumi*.

While the lessons went on they continued eating, but when they had finished and Sarah reached for the canteen, Juma touched her arm and stopped her, beckoning her to follow. Perplexed, she went with him and they finally stopped at a huge tree with rough reddish bark. She recognized it as the same sort of tree she had blazed near the falls, the tree that had exuded milk-white sap she thought might be rubber.

"*Massaranduba*," Juma said, slapping the bark. He pointed to her belt and added, "*Terzada*."

She nodded and when she handed him the implement, he struck the *massaranduba* tree two hard chops. A chunk of bark flew out and immediately the white sap began pouring down the trunk. With the machete he lopped a heavy flat leaf from a plant nearby. Rolling the leaf into a cone, he folded up the point and held the open end under the flow until the receptacle was half full. He handed it to Sarah, making sure she gripped the bottom tightly so that it wouldn't leak, and indicated she should drink.

With no hesitation, she did so, though tasting it gingerly at first. She couldn't believe it. Had she not witnessed that it came from a tree, she would have sworn it was cow's milk. The liquid was rich and filling, of excellent taste. She drank all he had given her — certainly more than a pint — and wanted more, but Juma frowned and shook his head, saying, "*Anih!*" which she supposed meant no.

He took the cone from her, refilled it with about the same amount he had given her and drank it himself, then tossed the leaf aside. Picking up the wedge-shaped chunk of bark he had chopped out of the tree, he forced it back into the cut. It stuck there, cutting off almost all the flow. Where some still dribbled out along the edges, it began rapidly coagulating. Very quickly it sealed itself and all flow ceased.

As they walked back to the tree where the fire was dying, Sarah wondered why Juma had not allowed her to drink more of the milk and wished she could question him. It wasn't necessary. By the time they reached the fire, she knew. She was feeling giddy and light headed, wanting to run and dance and sing. Everything looked better somehow — the leaves were greener, the tree trunks more richly dark, the veins and serrations on individual leaves more sharply delineated, crisper and more beautifully intricate. With something of a shock she realized what had happened: she was high — not really drunk, but certainly not far from it.

"Wow, Juma," she giggled, "that was some tree!"

Not comprehending the words except for his own name, he nevertheless smiled along with her. They recovered their gear by the fire and Sarah saw that the pile of bones at the base of one root was already crawling with ants. Most were small and either brown or red, but at least two of the large black stinging ants were there and Sarah shuddered. She pointed at one with the tip of her machete.

"*Tukandero*," Juma said, and Sarah knew it was a word she would not forget.

They resumed walking as they had done earlier this morning, Sarah following Juma and still asking him to name things as they passed. Gradually she was learning more than merely the words for objects. Often he would respond in phrases or sentences and she began making sense of less definite terms — adjectives, verbs and personal pronouns. She did not know quite how she was figuring them out, only that somehow she would suddenly understand what he meant when he used such words and she would file them away in her mental lexicon for later use. She was sure that when she spoke to him her construction of sentences was very poor and difficult to understand, but he seemed able to grasp her meaning most of the time and that was the important thing. She knew she would improve with time and practice.

This was another day when it didn't rain. Juma and Sarah covered a great deal of ground, finding more fruits along the way, which Sarah put into her pouch. Late in the afternoon, Juma stopped unexpectedly and motioned Sarah to silence. His gaze was directed at a clump of low-growing bushes with dense foliage some thirty yards ahead. For fully five minutes he stared without moving. Sarah had no idea what he was seeing but she remained as still as he.

From his right ear he removed the curved boar tooth, which Sarah had thought was just ornamental, and put the base of it to his mouth. A tiny hole had been bored inside the curve halfway to the tip and he placed a finger over it. Blowing into the end, he raised and lowered his fingertip rapidly and produced a strange intermittent squeaking sound. Sarah thought she saw some kind of movement ahead on the ground but could not be sure. Juma, however, was satisfied.

He replaced the tusk in his ear and very slowly brought up the long tubular *pucuna* until it was horizontal, bracing himself and the weapon by leaning against a tree. He aimed it carefully, then puffed his cheeks and the dart leaped from the muzzle with that characteristic popping sound. Sarah watched it speed away in a flat trajectory but then lost sight of it against the bushes. Still, Juma held his place for another minute.

Sarah fell in close behind him when he began walking. At the edge of the dense bushes he paused and pointed. Not until that moment did Sarah see what had attracted his attention and even then she had difficulty making it out, so perfect was the protective coloration. It was a bird about the size of a pheasant, with slightly ruddier plumage. The dart had entered its right side and the bird was quite dead. The tail was rather short and the body shape similar to that of a guinea fowl.

"*Tinamou*," Juma commented, then grasped the bird by the head and lifted it. Where the fowl had been sitting was a nest, a simple affair made of grasses bent down and molded by the shape of the bird, partly lined with down from the parent's breast. Within it were ten of the loveliest eggs Sarah had ever seen. Only slightly smaller than the average chicken egg, these were an intense wine red and so glossy they seemed to be made of porcelain.

Juma removed the dart from the bird, recoated the point with *wourali* and put it back into the blowgun. He gutted the bird as he had done with the toucan, but this time plucked it immediately and gave it to Sarah to put into her pouch. It was plump and appetizing and she looked forward to trying it. While she was putting it away, Juma carefully placed the eggs in his own pouch and then they moved on.

Half an hour later, again having gathered newly fallen branches along the way, they came to a small creek not unlike the one Sarah had followed initially. The ravine was not so deep, however, and on the opposite side, slightly upstream, the creek wound around the base of a large overhanging embankment. Beneath it there was an area of barren dry ground sheltered from rainfall. This was where they stopped for the night, wading across knee-deep water to get there.

They built their fire and cooked the *tinamou* in the same way the *toco* had been prepared. As good as the *toco* had been, this bird was far superior. The meat of the breast, white like that of a chicken's breast, was very tender, definitely sweeter and with much better flavor. Juma scooped up thick clayey mud from along the edge of the stream and one by one coated the eggs until each was a ball about two inches in diameter. These balls he placed in the coals of their fire to cook while they ate fruit.

Just as the sun was setting they heard a strange screaming sound from a multitude of voices. It was originating a long distance away and, startled, Sarah glanced at Juma. He was smiling and nodding.

"*Gauriba*," he said, patting his stomach. "*Gauriba*."

And Sarah knew that whatever the morrow would bring, she would probably find out at last what a *gauriba* was. Later, she dropped off to sleep with blossom-fragrant moisture hanging heavily in the pleasantly cool jungle night. She slept deeply and well.

Chapter Seven

IN THE MORNING a heavy mist curled about the trees —
a convention of wraiths, appearing and disappearing
smoothly, flowing and pausing, rising and lowering — a
host of phantom dancers moving to the rhythm of the
awakening forest, at once eerie and beautiful. Normal
sound was muffled, the crying of birds taking on a for-
lorn quality and the muted chattering of monkeys imbued with a melancholy undertone. There was an other-
worldly unreality to it and, at the same time, a pervading
peace.

Sarah and Juma moved soundlessly among the giant
trees as if treading through another dimension. A fine
sheen of the mist glistened in minute droplets on his
shoulders and the increasingly tattered clothing Sarah
wore clung damply to her skin, yet it was not unpleasant
to either of them.

Small trees were covered with huge spiderwebs which
had been transformed into bejeweled bridal gowns in
celebration of the marriage of air and moisture.

They moved with steady purpose toward the unearthly
chorus of shriekings and screaming in the distance north
of them. It was that sound, clear and sharper then, that
had awakened them at dawn, setting them on the move.

Following closer behind Juma, Sarah was puzzled and just a bit frightened by the cries. It was as if a great crowd of people, somewhere ahead, were undergoing unspeakable torture. The air had been clear at daybreak but, within minutes of their departure, the mist had begun draping itself from tree to tree like a great filmy drop curtain poised to open for a drama being performed on a vast primordial stage.

The cries were closer this morning than they had been last evening and Juma appeared pleased. When the mist expanded about them Sarah thought he would become gloomy; instead his reaction was the opposite and he moved with such purposeful strides, she sometimes had difficulty keeping pace.

There was a gradual change in the forest, and Sarah attributed this to the fact that since her journey began there had been a vague general downward sloping in the direction she was traveling. Here the sense of the jungle was increased; a greater variety and number of lower trees and gigantic ground plants grew beneath the towering taller trees forming the canopy. The leafy ceiling itself was slightly more open, still interlaced with foliage and intertwined with drapings of lianas, yet not so dense overhead as it had been and, consequently, there was more greenery on the forest floor.

Banana palms — *pacovas* — were abundant, growing in masses amid the taller trees, spreading broad, erect leaves in bright emerald fountains, dimpling their lushness here and there with enormous, fuchsia-colored teardrop blossoms and punctuating the verdancy with bright yellow fruit. Throngs of giant ferns rose from the soil to heights of ten or twelve feet before bending their arms gracefully to cascade in a lacy green spray to the ground. Many other forms of low palms and thick-leaved plants abounded and the air was heavy and humid, redolent of jungle growth. To Sarah, it was like walking through an endless botanical garden and, when Juma occasionally paused to listen, it seemed she could *hear* the plants growing.

Though never abundant, gorgeous orchids were visible, growing from the boles of living trees and from densely moss-encrusted surfaces of moldering logs. Some had blossoms large as two outspread hands, others were so tiny that, except for their vivid colors, they would have gone unnoticed. Some were single blossoms and others grew in dense clusters on stems like fairy wands. Purples and lavenders, whites and pinks, pale blues and red and salmon and flamingo; petals that were checkered or spotted or barred in bold patterns; blossoms shaped like butterflies and delicate seashells and strange insects; orchids that were smooth petaled or noduled or amazingly frilly. Sarah never tired of seeing them and wished they were more abundant.

The mistiness anchored birds to the lower layer of branches and leaves, and large flocks of parakeets noisily complained to one another. There were toucans of a variety she had not seen before, with lustrous greenish-black body plumage, red and yellow tail coverts, white throats and red gorgets and great beaks of lemon yellow and ebony; flashy red, blue and green trogons sat unmoving, loud triple whistlings erupting plaintively from them sporadically, their trailing two-foot-long frilled tailfeathers trembling with the effort of calling.

Unseen bellbirds filled the heavy air with sweetly ring-ing calls, as if signaling the beginning of Act One. The curtain deposited itself in twinkling beadlets, highlighting the brightening day in a billion tiny flashing diamonds, illuminating a phantasmagoric world.

It was the rain forest jungle as it should be experienced, rich and warm, lush and verdant, overflowing with color and scent and sound. For the first time Sarah felt as if she belonged here, wanted to stay, wished to share and become a part of the great encompassing wonder of it all, not knowing where she was or where she was going and, most important, not caring. The *now* of existence was all but overwhelming and she felt she must weep with the sheer exquisiteness of *being.*

The sounds of the eerie shriekings and screamings, toward which Sarah and Juma headed, slackened with the dissipation of the mist, but by then they were close by and Juma's movements had become more stealthy. He handed his blowgun to Sarah, took the bow from his shoulder and flexed it several times. Withdrawing one of the four-foot-long arrows from his quiver, he inspected the tip. The shaft was a single section of smooth, very straight reed; its fletching, three thin leaves, stiff but leathery rather than brittle, each of them nearly a foot long, terminated only a half-inch from the nock. The nock itself was a slot cut into the end of the reed. The arrowhead was a neatly carved piece of the tough, horny fiber from the base of a coconut palm frond. Cut when the frond was still green, it had been shaped into an elongated V with a series of barbs notched into both blades. Allowed to dry, it had become tan in color and very hard, but had been further hardened by holding it over a fire.

Juma squatted beneath the bole of a large tree with an immense gall-like swelling twelve feet above the ground. Taking the pot of *wourali* from his pouch, he scooped out some of the poison with a twig and smeared it onto the arrowhead. Carefully rewrapping the pot, he put it back into his pouch, clenched bow and arrow in one hand and beckoned Sarah to follow him. She imitated his moves, stepping where he stepped, pausing and crouching where he paused and crouched, a careful shadow.

A heavy rustling came from the canopy ahead and Juma froze, watching intently. He motioned Sarah to stay and eased forward with movements so slow and smooth he seemed to flow rather than creep. Twenty yards from her and only barely in view through the undergrowth, he slowly stood upright, fitted the notched *merere* to the taut, twisted fiber string on his *iranpahn* and pulled the bow to full draw. As the muscles of his shoulders and back ridged and knotted, Sarah became fearful he would tear out his stitches. Though the pressure was tremendous, he held the bow at full draw for fully a minute. At his release the *merere* whirred upward with an ominous buzz. It disappeared from Sarah's view almost immediately.

She thought she heard a faint thump and at once the frenzied shriekings and screamings and unearthly howlings she had heard from a distance burst in unbelievable cacophony from directly above. It sounded as if the canopy were filled with roaring lions — each roar beginning as a pumping growl erupting into a series of booming sounds, the cries from different animals overlapping, the resultant din so loud and frightening, Sarah was sure a colony of monstrous creatures would descend and tear her and Juma to pieces. Instead, nearly as quickly as the sounds began, they ended, replaced by a great rustling through the foliage.

Branches cracked and broke, falling noisily to the ground amid showers of leaves and scattered falling fruits. There were brief, inconclusive glimpses of speeding dark bodies and, at last, an uneasy silence.

Juma was still looking up fixedly when Sarah moved to his side. He gripped her wrist and, pointing upward, tried to show her something. She could not make out whatever he was indicating.

"*Gauriba*," he said, obviously pleased. "*Gauriba*."

Still Sarah could see nothing. Even when the animal swayed and toppled she did not see it until it was falling freely, a reddish-brown blur dropping through the branches. For just an instant it lodged itself on a branch and Juma groaned; then its fall resumed and it thudded to the forest floor thirty feet away.

It was a huge howler monkey with a long, three-foot, tufted tail. Head and body together were also three feet long and it was sturdily built, with relatively short legs. Its body was thickly haired — the hairs on head and neck so long, they all but formed a mane. The head was quite large, the face naked and a deep grayish-brown. The mouth was turned down in a perpetually forbidding expression. The bottom of the prehensile tail for the last third of its length was bare of hair and served as a fifth palm for gripping branches. There were five digits on each hand and foot.

The arrow had struck the animal in the left side near the hip and had gone through, emerging from its back to the left of the spine. The shaft had snapped during the fall and the fletched portion was missing.

For a moment as they inspected it, Sarah felt a little queasy. *This* was what she had eaten? A *monkey?* As if to verify her conclusion, Juma crouched beside it and patted its haunch with one hand.

"*Gauriba*," he said, grinning widely.

The queasiness did not last; Sarah was gifted with a strong sense of the practical. She had eaten the meat and it was very good; she knew she would eat it again — the fact that it had come from a monkey made little real difference. In certain respects, eating the meat from a hog was more distasteful, if one thought about it. And what about frog legs and eels and snails? People ate such things all the time, considering them delicacies. It was all a matter of viewpoint; in these few minutes Sarah adjusted without qualm to the idea of eating monkey, knowing she would not be bothered again.

Juma pulled the exposed arrowhead and broken shaft of the *merere* the rest of the way through, severed the reed shaft with his knife, carefully wrapped the barbed arrowhead in a leaf, and stuffed it inside his quiver. He discarded the broken piece of shaft. Rising, he grasped the animal's foot, lifted it off the ground, hefted it and grinned more, offering it to Sarah to do likewise. She took it from him and was surprised at the weight, estimating it must be about thirty pounds.

Juma took the monkey back and quickly, expertly cleaned it, skinning off the hide and cutting the meat into chunky portions much as a butcher might have done. Wrapping the fresh meat in sections of *pacova* leaf, he gave them to Sarah to put into her pouch. Then he indicated the special oversized resonating chamber in the monkey's throat, a sort of bony drum-shaped box, and she knew he was showing her how this type of monkey was able to make such horrendous vocalizations.

A variety of insects were being drawn to the scent of blood and viscera. By the time Juma was finished, the offal was covered with wasps, beetles, ants, flies, bees and even a surprising number of butterflies.

Juma and Sarah did not travel much farther. As they walked, Juma's gaze went back and forth and at one point, for no reason Sarah could determine, he turned abruptly eastward. Within the hour Sarah could hear, far ahead, a deep rumbling sound familiar to her – the sound of a waterfall. They were returning to the Ituí.

The thunder of the cataract was much greater than that of the falls where Sarah had first encountered the Ituí and as they approached, beads of moisture became visible on all the leaves and the bark of trees was damp. The ground became liberally studded with great jutting rocks and before long, all but a scattered few trees were left behind and they emerged into sunlight in a rugged area of cliffs and jagged ledges. The river was below them several hundred feet. For a considerable distance they followed a narrow ledge, the swirling, powerful, and now much larger Ituí sweeping far below, dashing itself against fearsome black rocks projecting from the water.

Just a short distance downstream the river split around a craggy wooded island, merging again at the island's lower end before plunging out of sight over the falls. A great plume of white mist, sparkling in the sunlight, boiled up from beyond the falls. Sarah thought briefly of her abandoned plan at the other falls to climb aboard a floating tree and drift downstream, shivering at the thought of what would have happened when she reached this place.

The ledge they were following was only four feet wide, gradually angling downward. Now and again Juma had to assist her in climbing down especially treacherous places. At one place they had to step across a three-foot gap. By the time they reached a point overlooking the lip of the falls they were about a hundred feet above it and the vista was spectacular.

The Ituí was two hundred feet in breadth here and the volume of water pouring over the edge was tremendous. It fell in a sheer drop for three hundred feet, crashing furiously against a jumble of house-sized boulders at the bottom and sending up vast clouds of white spray and mist. Below, the water rushed off in a sharply narrowed chasm, the two-hundred-foot breadth of the Ituí squeezed into a rampaging channel less than fifty feet across. The power of this water was awesome to behold. It had been churned to milky white and did not regain clarity for a quarter mile or more. A mile downstream the river curved out of sight to the northeast. As a final touch, a stationary rainbow was painted in the mist between the base and the lip of the falls. The entire scene was the most stirring sight Sarah had ever witnessed and she was giddy at the grandeur of it.

The ledge they were on had broadened somewhat. It curved westward now, still descending, then swung northeastward again and reentered the forest a hundred yards away. Behind them, at the point where they were standing, was a concavity in the face of the cliff, an indentation forming a level little plateau roughly semicircular and thirty feet wide at its greatest extent. They stopped to rest and Juma reached into his larger pouch. He brought out the ten baked mud balls; when he tapped one of them with the spine of his knife blade the outer material cracked and broke away easily, exposing the *tinamou* egg inside. It had split in the baking but the shell retained its red-porcelain characteristic.

Juma handed the egg to Sarah and she peeled it as she might have peeled an ordinary hard-boiled egg. She was not quite prepared for the baked half-developed embryo she found inside. Juma was openly puzzled at her expression of distaste. While she continued to hold it, he tapped one of the balls open for himself and peeled the egg as Sarah had done. It was identical to hers inside. With undisguised enjoyment he popped it into his mouth, chewed it up and swallowed. Sarah had watched, fascinated, then turned her gaze back to the one she was holding.

"Well," she muttered, "when in Rome . . ."

She put it into her mouth and chewed vigorously, holding her breath and trying not to taste it. She wasn't successful, but neither was she revolted. It was a bit bland and she had the fleeting thought that it could well stand a pinch of salt, but other than that it was quite pleasant. She swallowed her mouthful and extended her hand toward Juma for more.

"Good," she told him. "Very good." She rubbed her stomach and Juma laughed and nodded, handing her one of the balls to open for herself. She broke it against the ledge on which they were sitting. The eggs were a good snack and when they had each eaten five, Sarah was disappointed they were all gone.

Moving on, they reentered the forest. The ground sloped sharply here and walking was difficult. Occasionally they slid on the damp soil and had to grasp at trees to maintain balance. Once Sarah fell, landing on her rump and splitting the remains of one trouser leg to the waistline, but she wasn't hurt.

After half an hour they reached more level ground and walked in a wide semicircle that took them back to the Ituí a half mile below the falls. There were still great rocks here and many ledges and projections. A number of the projections provided space beneath them that Sarah more than once would have welcomed as shelter for the night, but Juma seemed to be looking for something in particular. He found it a few hundred yards farther downstream: a flat shelf of rock projecting twenty feet over the ledge upon which they were walking. It formed a ceiling seven feet high covering an area about twenty by fifty feet. The spacious natural room was only ten feet from the edge of the cliff overlooking the Ituí rapids. It was far enough away from the falls that it was not damp, yet there was a superb view of the waterfall upstream, the rapids seventy feet directly below, and a beautiful expanse of the river downstream.

Almost in the middle of this natural room were the remains of a fire; bits of charred wood and ashes. When Sarah looked from them to the youth he nodded and tapped his own chest and said, "*Tata ihe Juma.*"

He pointed toward the river at a forty-five-degree angle downstream, adding, "*Inyahteihn heh koh emeh iwuyhuahn.*"

She shook her head, not understanding, and he repeated the sentence while making waving motions with his hand and arm held horizontally and moving forward. She thought perhaps he was describing a snake, but then decided he was telling her something about the river, but she was not sure. They would need much more talking together before she would be able to understand other than individual words.

Juma made a motion with his hand, dismissing the subject. He removed his larger pouch, bow and quiver, setting them on the ledge inward from the fire, indicating she should do the same with her gear. When she gratefully put down her pouch, heavy with monkey meat, he turned and walked off. Sarah followed. They went into the forest and gathered wood, returning a quarter hour later with large armloads. Juma had also gotten some more *isca* — the anthill tinder — and a large *bacaba* palm frond. They dumped them on the ledge and returned to the forest, coming back again with more armloads of branches. Juma seemed to think that was sufficient. He motioned Sarah to stay and walked out of sight around some rocks. Sarah was sure he was merely going out of sight to relieve himself.

Moving swiftly, she covered a tuft of the *isca* with shavings she scraped from the *bacaba* midrib, broke a few twigs on top of that and then took a match from her pouch and lighted the tinder. She was not concerned about using her matches. Once they were gone she could still start a blaze by using her father's magnifying glass which was in her pouch.

By the time Juma returned, she had a nice fire going and he grunted appreciatively. It was not yet midday, but the remainder of the daylight hours were spent in roasting the monkey meat over the fire, eating their fill of what they had cooked, and further cooking what was left to better preserve it for later consumption.

The skies darkened shortly after they had begun cooking and a steady downpour was soon falling. It did not end in two or three hours, as it usually did, but continued well into the night. That did not bother them at all. They were safe and dry and comfortable. Their stomachs were well filled and Sarah had decided monkey meat was exceptionally good. The remainder of the time until they went to sleep, Sarah applied herself to learning more of Juma's language.

With her facility for learning, both from experience and through being taught, Sarah grasped the language very quickly. Within another week she could converse with Juma in a broken manner so that at least ideas could pass between them. It was only the beginning. By the end of a month she was reasonably fluent, although there were still many words Juma would use she could not understand, concepts she could not grasp, things he would describe which she had never seen or heard about and to which she could not, therefore, relate. Day by day her knowledge expanded and, most of the time not even realizing he was doing so, Juma taught her well.

After about ten days his chest wound was so well healed that Sarah cut the stitches with her pocketknife and pulled them out. Juma was greatly impressed with the way the wound had grown together. There would be only a thin scar.

They remained at the broad overhung ledge above the Ituí for just over a month. After the first day, Juma and Sarah had made sleeping pallets on the hard rock ledge more comfortable by putting down deep layers of *pacova* leaves atop soft plant materials. Every two or three days thereafter, as the broad leaves dried and began to crumble, new leaves were added.

The muted thunder of the falls to the south and the rapids below them was pleasant and Sarah came to love this place. During bright sunshine the cloud of white vapor hung sparkling in the air like a friendly genie and when the sky was overcast, the cataract lost the deep lustrous green of the water which plunged over the brink in sunlight, and showed deeper opalescent hues of amethyst and topaz. Always, under any conditions, it was a breathtaking spectacle and, in honor of her companion, Sarah had named the magnificent cataract Juma Falls.

During their stay they made daily forays into the surrounding forest for food and firewood, experiencing many small adventures together and a few harrowing ones, Sarah delighting in her own adaptability to this existence, Juma pleased at having her for a companion. But where Sarah's mind was like a sponge, absorbing and retaining the multitude of things which occurred, Juma's was narrow, confined, concerned primarily with day-to-day existence, not only with little thought of things past but, equally, with little concern for the future. He showed minimal interest in or aptitude for learning English. He was a simple young man, content with the basic skills he had been taught as a child — primarily hunting and surviving the wilderness — but with little scope for speculation and an appalling lack of curiosity. When Sarah, after having learned his language enough to converse, attempted to tell him about her world, there was almost total lack of interest on his part. Yet his knowledge of the Amazon rain forest was phenomenal and he could read nature with greater facility than Sarah could read a book. For Juma, every tree and every plant told a story; each broken branch, each trace of a mark on a tree, each mark on the soil, revealed important things to him, telling him accurately who or what had passed, where they had come from and where they were going. Every inch of ground, whether covered by leaves or overgrown with brush or even barren, spoke volumes to him.

Sarah could not hope to learn all the lore that was second nature to Juma, yet she absorbed a great deal. When she considered her first days alone in the jungle she was amazed she had been able to survive at all; the rain forest was a beneficent provider, growing an abundance of food there for the taking, a variety of materials that could be converted to use as clothing and implements and weapons; but the rain forest could also unleash a great variety of malignancies, some overt and frightening, others subtle and insidiously deadly.

On one of their meanderings through the forest, Sarah was in the lead, walking along unconcernedly when Juma suddenly leaped forward and caught her arm, stopping her, his expression reflecting fear.

"*Baah derekoh?*" she asked: What is the matter with you?

"*Assacu,*" he replied, pointing to a strange looking tree ahead of them. "*Anoh ehe curupira, hooweh assacu*" — That is the assacu tree, which contains an evil spirit.

Uglier than any other Sarah had seen, the tree was squat and gnarled, its bark a dingy greenish color, bristling with an array of very sharp, venomous-appearing spines. Its leaves were small, curled as if withered, though they were not. They were dark olive-colored, and appended from the tip of each was a droplet of sap. From time to time the droplets fell with small audible plops and, almost immediately, others formed to take their places.

The *assacu*, Juma explained, was a terrible tree. To remain in the vicinity of one, where its rank smell could reach the nostrils, would result in serious sickness for which there was no cure. Walking beneath it and having the sap drop upon the skin or touch the bare feet would result in painful stinging, rapidly developing into ulcerous sores that would not heal. Stopping for even a short while beneath the tree meant certain death within a few days. To be pricked by one of its thorns meant instant death, as did the tasting of its sap or fruit. Sarah had shuddered, thinking of how simple it would have been for her, before meeting Juma, to have blundered into such a tree without realizing its deadliness. She had wondered how anyone who knew nothing of this jungle forest could survive for very long.

One of Sarah's great fears had been that she would have serious encounters with venomous snakes. After all, wasn't the jungle full of them? Yet, she saw few snakes of any kind, venomous or not. The *sucuruju* — anaconda — she had seen, of course, and a few briefly glimpsed snakes of other kinds in the trees, but few beyond that. One of the strangest was a vine snake which Juma pointed out — a brilliant green snake with huge eyes and unusually long tapered head and snout. No larger than the diameter of a pencil, it was five feet long and fed most often on anoles — the smooth little lizards Sarah had seen sold in pet shops as chameleons.

Once, as they walked through the forest in the relative stillness always occurring at midday, a terrible, agonized scream came from the canopy far above. Juma said it was the death cry of some animal caught by *giboia* — the heavy-bodied boa constrictor — but they saw neither the predator nor its prey. Far more life existed in this forest than she, or even Juma, saw.

Another time, during a two-day foray, Juma used his bow to down a short-antlered deer having a peculiar goatlike appearance. Fairly small and dull gray, it weighed about sixty pounds — the largest animal they had downed thus far. Juma said they were seldom seen and this was only the second one he had ever killed.

As he bent to the task of dressing it, he had no more than slit the belly skin when he jerked to attention, listening intently. After a moment a small gray bird flitted by, twittering excitedly. A second came past; it was warbler sized, black with long, fluffy back feathers and a patch of white underneath. Juma's expression turned to one of dismay. When a third bird like the second flew past only a moment later, equally twittering like the others, he leaped to his feet shouting, "*Tauoca! Tauoca!*" Snatching Sarah's wrist, he virtually dragged her to a dead tree nearby that had toppled and was now leaning at a sharp angle, held up by neighboring trees.

"Climb!" he demanded. "Climb fast!"

Frightened by his actions and tone, she scurried up the sloping trunk, once nearly falling, Juma at her heels. When they were twenty feet off the ground he stopped her and they perched there, looking down.

"*Ko tam baheh, Juma?*" she whispered: What is it?

"*Tauoca,*" he replied grimly. "Coming fast."

"But what is *tauoca?*"

"Watch and see."

More of the tiny birds — they were thrushes — flitted into view, some flying through, others pausing to land briefly and then fly on. And then Sarah heard the sound. It was almost indescribable. A sinister whisper gradually growing in volume, like that of a sheet of coarse sandpaper pushed slowly across a tabletop. Even more of the thrushes came in sight, along with a variety of other birds — tanagers, woodpeckers, barbets, flycatchers. They jumped and flitted, pecked at the ground and flitted again, moving forward at a steady pace, chirping and twittering incessantly, traveling as a troop.

As the birds passed beneath them, Sarah could see they were snatching up insects of many kinds that were appearing in great numbers on the ground — running, jumping, hopping, scurrying across the surface, erupting from tiny holes in wood or the ground, or rushing out from beneath dead leaves and moldering forest debris. And then she saw the *tauoca.*

They appeared in a moving reddish flood, flowing over the surface of the ground and everything upon it. The *tauoca* were army ants, countless hundreds of thousands of them and, so far as Sarah could see, moving in three distinct columns. Perhaps there were more that were hidden by the undergrowth. Each column was twelve feet wide, with smaller, less distinct flanking lines of scouts on each side and a leading phalanx as well. They moved swiftly, swarming over every plant, every rock, every object in their path, investigating every hole or cranny or crevice, climbing every vine and tree to a height of ten feet or more, devouring all things edible.

The ant-thrushes and other birds flitting ahead were snatching up insects in the path of the columns — insects which had heard or sensed the approach of the processions and were attempting to escape. They had little chance. What the birds did not get, the ants themselves enveloped. They were not terribly large ants, no larger than some species Sarah had watched as a little child, except that certain individuals in the mass were larger than others and traveled on the outer fringes of the columns and at the van, as if guarding the majority of smaller ones. These larger ones were about half an inch long, about twice the size of the others, and with much more formidable mandibles. They bit and stung, Juma told her, like the *tukanderos*.

Any insect or other creature not making its move swiftly enough to escape the fearsome columns was instantly attacked and engulfed, stung repeatedly, and chewed to bits in moments. This included wasps and bees, centipedes, scorpions and spiders, whose own weapons were ineffectual at combating this peril. The flanking columns were running from side to side with as much speed as their forward movement. Wherever they encountered anything worthwhile the information was immediately transmitted to the column; sections of that column bulged out in pseudopodian manner, encompassing whatever it happened to be.

They were cinnamon-colored ants traveling in a formation so dense that it created the strong illusion of a flowing stream; a single entity rather than one made up of countless insects. When they discovered the carcass of the newly killed deer, it disappeared beneath the blanket of ants, becoming a seething mass of deep dull red. When they left it, long before the column had finished passing the spot, no vestige of the animal remained except bare white bones and antlers and bits of hoof. Even most of the cartilaginous material joining the bones had been devoured and the bones fell in upon themselves in a jumble unrecognizable as a skeleton.

They mounted the leaning tree upon which Sarah and Juma were perched and scurried upward to within about eight feet of the pair before turning back. Once again Sarah envisioned what would have happened had she been in the path of such a migration before meeting Juma and she trembled at the thought. It took close to an hour for the columns to pass and disappear from sight. When Sarah and Juma returned to the ground at last and recovered his bow and knife and her machete, the two left the area quickly, speaking little, sobered by the awesome sight they had witnessed.

The trips they took into the rain forest usually lasted

half a day or more and nightfall would find them back in the safety of the ledge overhang above the Ituí. Now and again they would become caught by rain while in the open. When that occurred, Juma would swiftly make a shelter of great *pacova* leaves overlapped against a log or rock, beneath which they would crouch until the rain passed. Now and then they took two- or three-day excursions, camping as before in rocky clefts or under buttressed roots upon which they had again placed the giant leaves.

The drama of forest life was unceasing, usually seen in brief vignettes leaving memorable impressions. They saw a huge harpy eagle, heaviest and most powerful of all the eagles, flash through the tangled growth of the canopy with incomparable skill, snatch a full-grown spider monkey from its perch and carry off the screaming primate in its fierce talons; they paused to watch a battle between two huge black beetles with horns like rhinoceroses, a contest of pushing and shoving until one lifted the other off balance and toppled it off the log upon which the duel was being fought; they saw a silky anteater, a beautiful golden-furred animal the size of a squirrel, with its prehensile tail wrapped around a liana, using strong hooked claws to tear apart a termite nest and devour the insects inside; they unexpectedly encountered a giant armadillo, five feet long, weighing about one hundred pounds — the animal fled from them with surprising speed, knocking down plants and saplings, caroming off larger trees as it raced away, unheeding of Juma's hastily shot arrow which bounced harmlessly off its armored back.

Juma always provided them well with meat, downing a wide variety of birds with his blowgun and mammals with his bow. Sarah became familiar with the taste of meat from capybaras and pacas and agoutis, along with smaller animals related to the pacas, which Juma called *cutia, moco* and *punchana*. One day he killed a white-lipped peccary, a fierce and formidable wild pig usually traveling in large bands, but which had appeared to be alone. When the arrow struck and plunged into its heart, it screeched loudly and died quickly, but the sound it had made brought sixty of its companions in a rush and Juma and Sarah only barely made it to safety at the top of a projecting rock. They were held at bay there for hours with the peccaries milling about below, snorting and grunting and gnashing their short tusks.

Sarah's clothing gave out very quickly. Weakened by mildew and mold, her hiking boots fell apart and she became accustomed to being barefoot, as Juma always was. At first it was difficult and her tender-skinned feet became scratched and punctured and cut, but gradually they hardened and, except on rare occasions, she did not miss having shoes. Her trousers, cut into shorts, disintegrated. Her shirt was not much better. Juma used her machete to chop off huge sections of bark from the tree he called *amusi*, showing her how to peel out the inner bark that was soft and strong as woven cloth and looked much like linen. From this she fashioned a sort of skirt and pullover blouse, sewing the necessary seams using palm thorns as needles and a strong thread Juma got from the midrib fibers of a palm he called *ubassu*.

The items she had carried in her pockets, including

her father's wallet, she transferred to her pouch. These days, she wore the pouch constantly during waking hours, fearful that if she took it off she might lose it.

It became commonplace for Sarah and Juma to talk long into the night, sitting or lying on the ledge beneath the silvery sheen of the moon and the glory of a multitude of brilliant stars. Their fires were used for cooking, not for heat. They were rarely uncomfortable due to temperature change — there was little variation between day and night. Any lowering of temperature after dark, whether or not it had rained, was never experienced as more than a delightful coolness after the warmth of the day. The heat, Sarah noticed, was nowhere near so oppressive as the heat in Chicago during the summer months and at night it was always comfortable. With such constancy, therefore, it was pleasurable to sit and talk.

Juma told her that the daily rains were ending and the dry season beginning. Rains would come sometimes, but they would be fewer and of less intensity. That was when the rivers would lower and it would be *"pitiu eh kua praia"* — turtle time on the sandbars. This seemed to be of great significance to Juma and, when Sarah asked why, he told her she would see before long.

Little by little she drew Juma out. So far as she could tell, his people had no conception of religion or a supreme being. There were only four supernatural beings he referred to: *Usinamuy* was a good spirit, upon whom he placed credit for good things which occurred. That spirit's counterpart was *Taifu*, blamed for bad fortune. Another was *Cucupira*, a "wild man" who was responsible for all unaccountable noises heard in

the forest. The final one was *Curupira*, who was simply
an "evil spirit." Such concepts were neither easy for
Juma to put across to her, nor for Sarah to grasp.

Although they talked of many things, there were still
many words and phrases Juma used with which she was
unfamiliar. Sometimes he would begin speaking very
rapidly and she would have to stretch out a hand, touch
his arm and say, "*Ende nyeng apu ahihare, Juma. Ani
akuan*" — You speak too fast, Juma. I do not understand.

At first they had spoken mostly about natural things:
trees and plants and fruits, birds and mammals, fish and
insects. His knowledge of the machinations of nature
was extensive and Sarah enjoyed listening to him speak
of them. One day out in the forest they had stopped
and watched a large brown-and-green-striped caterpillar attach itself upside down to the bottom of a *pacova*
leaf. Not many months before, Sarah had seen a movie in
her freshman biology class showing the caterpillar of a
monarch butterfly doing the same thing and she knew
that this caterpillar under the *pacova* leaf was pupating.
She was about to explain this to Juma when he pointed
to it and said, "*Para-para curi*" — butterfly by-and-by —
and Sarah was surprised that he understood the process
of metamorphosis.

Another time he pointed out the large cocoon of a
moth, hanging from the canopy above by a long silken
strand. He told her the caterpillar had spun the cocoon
in suspended fashion so the birds could not find a purchase in order to open it.

With communication between them constantly im-
proving, enabling them, at least to a limited degree, to

discuss concepts and intangibles as well as realities, Sarah finally learned about Juma's background and why he had been by himself in the jungle.

Juma became expansive when he spoke of his people and about the village where he had lived until recently. He talked about his childhood with animation, and his love for his family was evident. He pointed to his split ear and laughed about it, telling her it had been torn in half when he was a little boy; he had been drinking from the river when a small caiman — the Amazonian crocodile he called *jacare* — had snapped at him, catching his ear. There were many *jacares* in the river near his village. That village, downstream from here on the Ituí, was called Kaumo and his people were Aramoki, an offshoot of the widespread Huitoto tribe. When he spoke of a neighboring tribe called Nhambiquara, he trembled with fear. They were mortal enemies of the Huitoto, savage and powerful, a tribe against whom they had warred since time began, though Juma did not know why. It was an established pattern of life and Juma showed surprise when Sarah asked him why they fought. The reason was simple: they fought because they had always fought.

The young man's face darkened as he told of the most recent trouble, taking on a fierceness Sarah had not seen before. His nostrils flared and the decorations on his face — the black thorn through his nose, the red-dyed chin, and the tattooed lines from mouthcorners to temples, to which Sarah had become so accustomed that she hardly noticed them any more, made him appear almost malevolent.

The fortunes of the Huitoto, especially the Aramoki,

had paled in recent years and their numbers had sharply declined. Only a short time before Juma and Sarah met, the Nhambiquara, armed with spears and knives, had launched a surprise attack against Kaumo. The village had been unprepared and essentially wiped out.

"They took the heads of many of my people, Sa-rah," Juma told her, "including my father and my mother and my brother. Those of us who were able to flee scattered and were chased. I took up my weapons and ran to the river and paddled upstream in my *montaria*" — canoe — "but two of the Nhambiquara warriors came after me in the *inyahn*, which is a larger *montaria*. They were two and I was one, but my boat was small and light and theirs was heavy and so I was able to keep ahead of them. I traveled very far. Two days. Each day I thought I was safe but each day they would appear again behind and chase me. I became very tired on the third day. I came to shore but they followed me and found where I had hidden my *montaria* and they chased me more."

He paused and pointed toward the sound of the waterfall, a muted rumbling in the darkness. "The Huitoto and the Nhambiquari do not go past that great *pancanda* which you call Juma Falls. It is unknown country and those who have tried to go beyond have never returned. But they were chasing me and so I went beyond and still they chased me and I was sure I would be one of those who never came back. Instead, it was they who never went back."

"What happened to them, Juma?"

"I killed them."

"You . . . killed them?" Sarah's eyes went wide.

He nodded. "One of them caught up with me and I fought with him on a cliff far upstream from there," again he pointed toward the waterfall. "He cut me here," he tapped the new scar tissue on his chest, "with his *parati*, but I was able to push him over the edge and he fell into the river. I saw his body swept away toward the *pancanda*."

"Where was the other one who was chasing you?"

"He had fallen behind because his companion could run faster, but now he was coming toward me along the same ledge. He threw a spear at me but I jumped away from it, and when he came closer I blew a *pucuna* dart at him. I had aimed for his chest but I was excited and it struck him here." Juma slapped his thigh.

"Did he die right away?" Sarah's voice was only a whisper.

Juma shook his head. "*Anih*. The dart had poison for smaller animals and it would take him longer, but he knew he was dead. He sat down with his back against the rock and I joined him and we talked until he died."

Sarah was flabbergasted. "You joined him and talked? About what?"

"Many things. War. Hunting. About how he had led a good life and was sorry that it was now over. He asked me if I would throw his body into the river after he was dead so that it could swim downstream and over the *pancanda* and into the river below, where it could then swim down with the current and he could once more pass his home far down the river, far down below where the Aramoki — my people — live."

The nonchalance with which this young man treated

the matter of having killed two men momentarily non-plussed Sarah. It was all so taken for granted. She had a hard time accepting it. The thought struck her that, frightened as she had been when she first saw Juma in the entryway of her shelter, how would she have felt had she known that only a short time before he had killed two grown men?

"Did you do it?" she asked at last. "Did you throw him into the river after he died?"

"Yes. And I watched him swept away with the current toward the *pancanda*, too. I knew he was happy now, and I was happy for him and his friend."

He tossed a little twig on the coals of the dying cook-fire and watched it begin to smoke, then burst into a brief bright flame. "After that, I went into the forest to look for *aningui* leaves to stop the loss of my *hewy*." *Hewy*, Sarah knew, from the animals Juma had killed and cleaned, was blood. "My wound was deep and so much *hewy* was being lost that I was becoming weak. I found the *aningui* leaves and killed a *guariba* at the same place and rested there with the crushed *aningui* leaves in my wound until the *hewy* no longer flowed. I rested and ate *guariba* until my weakness was gone and then I began moving back through the forest so that my feet would some time take me back to this *pancanda*. On the way," his eyes crinkled with silent laughter, "the *amuy* came — what you call rain — and I found a hole in the rocks for shelter and in this hole was a *kunyimuku* whose name was Sa-rah."

They laughed together and Sarah was profoundly thankful he had found her, feeling certain that if he had not, she would probably have been dead by now. It might have been under the claws of a jaguar or the millions of bites of army ants or by innocently blundering beneath the fatal embrace of the *assacu* tree. However it might have happened, she was sure that it *would* have happened. There were many aspects of the jungle rain forest Sarah had come to like very much, but the knowledge was always there that at any moment it could unleash deadly forces. Being alert at all times was a way of life here and she yearned for the simple security of her former life. This train of thought brought her father vividly to mind and her eyes filled with tears. That was when she broached the subject always foremost in her mind — the possibility of Juma's helping her to get back to civilization. There were still difficulties with the language and it was not easy to put across to Juma the concepts she wished to convey. It did not come off well. At first Juma listened closely, but soon he became impatient.

"I do not know of these things," he told her shortly. "The men of our village have spoken of strange people far beyond where the Nhambiquara live. Before long we will go back to my village and then you can ask them. We will not speak of it again until then."

He rolled over on his side, his back toward her, and spoke no more. Sarah felt again a stab of the loneliness and fear she had been experiencing before she met Juma, and the weight of her present situation crowded her mind. The heavy breathing close by told her Juma had already fallen asleep and Sarah lay back with her arms behind her head, looking up at the stars and telling herself that she would not think about Ian MacWilliams Francis. But she did. Despite all her determination not to do so, she cried herself to sleep.

In the morning, Sarah experienced her first menstrual period.

She and Juma strolled to the little brook nearby which emerged from the forest and flowed across the ledge to fling itself over the rim in a miniature waterfall to the river below. It had become their habit to come here to bathe and drink and fill the canteen before beginning their day's wanderings. Sarah always brushed her teeth and had been pleased when Juma showed her how to dry and crush into powder the stalk of a plant he called *carujuru* to sprinkle on her toothbrush. It had a slightly sour taste but did an excellent job of cleansing her teeth. Once in a while Juma used some on a little stick with one frayed end, which he used much in the manner of a toothbrush.

Sarah's panties were becoming ragged but were still wearable and she washed them in the brook every morning. Her soap had long since been used up but she had found that by scrubbing her skin or clothing daily she kept clean enough. Her panties, rinsed and wrung out several times, stayed fresh. A brief hanging ·in the sunlight always dried the filmy nylon quickly.

From the very beginning, there was a singular obliviousness to the civilized concept of modesty between Sarah and Juma. While the natural functions of urination and defecation were normally accomplished with some degree of privacy, it was quite natural and unaffected for them to bathe close together in the brook.

His nakedness and hers at such times were of no consequence to either of them, except for an initial shyness on
Sarah's part. But he had been so natural about it that
her slight discomfiture disappeared quickly. He did not
stare at her, nor she at him. Bathing was just another
function accepted as normally as gathering wood or
fruit. Not infrequently they played and laughed and
slapped water at one another.

All of that ended abruptly now. Earlier, just after
they had awakened, when each in turn had gone behind
the nearby rock for relief of night-filled bladders,
Sarah had noticed nothing different about herself. But
now, following their brief walk to the brook, she removed her barkcloth blouse and skirt and was slipping
out of her panties when she noticed some rust-colored
stains in the crotch, along with a few bright red spots
of blood.

Even though it had never happened before, Sarah
knew immediately what it was. She was neither frightened nor dismayed. The girls at school had talked about
menstrual periods, and sex education classes had given
her a clear and healthy knowledge of human biology.
A few of her classmates had referred to it as "the curse,"
comparing notes and giggling – activities for which
Sarah had little patience. Others, Sarah among them,
had not yet begun to menstruate, wondering when
they would, experiencing a faint sense of something
akin to guilt that they had not started; as if they were
not so mature, so *adult*, as those already experiencing
this natural function.

The problem for Sarah here and now was what to do

to prevent the obvious messiness which would occur, if not this time, then during subsequent periods as the flow became heavier. At school the girls had discussed the relative merits of sanitary napkins and insertable devices, their use, their absorbency, their effectiveness. But what did one do in the jungle where no such conveniences were available? Surely they did something, used something. Hoping Juma might know, she asked him.

He frowned. "You are no longer *kunyimuku*," he told her. "Now you are *kunyim buku* — a young woman — and soon you will be *kunyahn*. After today we can no longer bathe together. If you were in my village, the other *kunyahns* would take care of you. There are things they do at a *kunyimuku's* first dropping of blood which I know, but other things I do not know. All are important for the *kunyimukus*, but you are different from them and whether or not those things should be done for you, I do not know. You must be the one to decide if they need to be done. If you believe they should, then I will try to do them for you."

"Well first, Juma, what do the women — the *kunyahns* — do about the flow of *hewy?*"

"You remember the giant tree I showed you in the forest, the *samauma?*"

"The silk-cotton tree? The one from which you get the soft white fiber you call *kahpahk*, that you put on the ends of your *pucuna* darts?"

He nodded. "That is the one. It is the mother of all trees."

Sarah remembered it well. Although there were taller trees in the rain forest, there were none greater in diameter. It was another of the trees with a shallow root system and great buttresses at the base extending outward from the tree for thirty feet. One of the silk-cotton trees Sarah had seen was easily twenty feet in diameter and soared over a hundred feet. It had rose-colored flowers and leaves very similar to those of a horse chestnut. Most important, the tree produced a thousand or more pods, each shaped like a plump banana about eight inches long. The pods were green and each was filled with a water-resistant fluff even softer than the fluff found in a milkweed pod. Often the ground under such trees was littered with these pods after a storm.

"The *kahpahk* fiber has many uses, Sa-rah," Juma had told her, "among them what we have talked about. I will get you some when we go into the forest. The *kunyahns* use a handful of it at a time, holding it against them by palm fibers tied above their hips and down between their legs. Each day it is changed for fresh *kahpahk* and the old one is burned in a special fire kept for this purpose."

"*Maitahme?*" Sarah asked: Why?

Juma shrugged. "Because that is what is done."

"You said the *kunyahns* do certain things when a girl has her first . . ." she paused, ". . . what do you call it when the bleeding comes?"

"*Hewyekuht.*"

"Okay, *hewyekuht.* We call it a menstrual period. What do they do when it first comes?"

"It is important," he said. "Boys get things done to them, too, when they become men, which are similar."

A far-away expression enfolded him. "It is sometimes painful. What they do for boys helps them to become good hunters and fishers and strong fighters, but what they do for girls helps them become good mothers and tenders of their men and makes them successful in preparing food and medicine."

He paused, watching as she rinsed the panties and wrung them out, then began spreading the garment across a low bush to dry. When she glanced at him questioningly, he continued.

"You remember the *tukanderos?*"

Sarah nodded as she stepped into the clear warm water and sat on the flat rocky bottom, letting the current wash over her legs and lower body. She remembered the vicious black ants only too well.

"When *hewyekuht* first appears, the girl must stand and let *tukanderos* held between little sticks be placed against the palms of her hands, her lower arms, the soles of her feet and each buttock. They bite and sting her and the pain is very bad, but while she may have tears if she wishes, she must not make loud cries."

Sarah was appalled. "Why would they do such a cruel thing? Oh, Juma, they hurt so badly."

"Yes. Boys get them even worse and the pain is sometimes so much that it is hard not to scream."

"But *why*, Juma? Why do they do it?"

It was obvious that the thought of questioning the rite had never occurred to him and he shrugged again. "It is what must be done. After that she has marks like these made on her." He indicated the blue tattooings across his cheeks from the mouthcorners. "That is so she will be beautiful and so we can tell friends from enemies. Our enemies do not mark in this way. In other ways, but not in this way. It is the mark of the Aramoki and it is good."

He removed his breechcloth and stepped into the water a few feet from her and sat down also, splashing water up onto his chest briefly. "But in one way the markings for girls are different. The dye is made from the ashes of burnt honeybees mixed into a paste and stuck into the skin with sharp thorn points from the *carana*, which is a palm tree that grows only along the riverbank. They do this so that later, when she makes *kashiri*, it will be . . ."

"What's *kashiri?*" Sarah interjected.

"It is what we drink most. It is brewed by the women in clay vessels called *tucunas*. It is made with fruit and leaves and chewed mandioca cakes and other things put together and left covered with *pacova* leaves for two days. It bubbles and gets thick on top, but when the thickness is taken away, it is clear and yellow and if you drink too much it makes you feel like the milk of the *massaranduba* tree makes you feel, but it will not kill you if you drink too much, as *massaranduba* will. But the marks of the women are made with honeybee ashes because this will make all the kashiri she brews as sweet as honey. Next, all the hair at the back of her head is cut off and she is taken to her hammock and she must lie in it there until the *hewyekuht* is finished. Then her *murihahn* . . ."

"What's *murihahn?*"

"The mother of her mother. Then her *murihahn*, if she has one, or another old woman, makes her some woven foot coverings from water reeds and paints the girl's

whole body with red juice from the *ucuru* like this."
He pointed at his own red-colored chin. "On the girl's
face she paints special patterns.

"When the *murihahn* is finished with that, the *kunyimuku's heramuhm* — the father of her mother — comes
with a whipping lash made of the fibers of a palm
called *mauritia*. She must stand up and he lashes her,
beginning at the shoulders, and gradually works his way
down until her feet are reached."

Sarah was shaking her head, not sure she understood.
"Do you mean he just hits her lightly with it?"

"No, he must strike her very hard and, again, she
may have tears but she must not make loud cries. Most
of the time the marks he makes become swellings and
are sore. Sometimes, if her skin is very soft, the swellings
will break into open wounds as he whips her. When he
is finished she must return to her hammock and remain there. Many of us live in the same *maloka* and we
take care that no stranger upon entering can see her, for
if that happens, she will lose all sense of shame and
womanly modesty and she will never find a husband
who is happy with her. All the time she is secluded
there, she is forbidden to do certain things and cannot eat
certain food."

"What isn't she allowed to do?" Sarah asked. She was
both fascinated and repelled by what Juma was saying.

"She must not run her hand through her hair, but
instead she may use a kind of stick made from the stem
of the *inaja* palm. She may not cry out at any time, nor
engage in loud talk or a quarrel."

"Juma, I just don't understand. Why can't she do such
things? There must be reasons."

Juma dropped a leaf into the water beside him and watched the current whirl it to the rim where it disappeared over the ledge. "It is our way. Our people have always done this and it is good. Our girls become good women because of it. Just as our boys become good men because of what is done to them."

"Well, what can't they eat?"

"They cannot eat anything except certain small fish. Even then they must be careful not to eat any fish that are very active in the water, for this will increase the flow of *hewy*. They may drink *mingau*, which is a warm brew, but at no time may they drink *kashiri*."

"These restrictions are only during the time that she has her first *hewyekuht*?"

"No, they must be continued until she has finished her sixth *hewyekuht*, but after the first she may leave her hammock. Then there are other things she cannot do. She must not carry a burden basket or touch a knife or a *machadinha* — an ax. She still must not cry out or argue, and she must not blow directly on a fire, but must use only a fire fan."

"But what if she refuses to follow these rules?" Sarah questioned. "What happens if she eats something she is not supposed to eat, or if she blows on a fire or argues with someone or touches a knife?"

"She would not do so."

"But what if she did?" Sarah persisted.

He shook his head. "She would not. But if she did she would become very sick with pains inside and she would faint. Perhaps she would die. After each of the first five *hewyekuhts* she is given a new name and after the sixth one she is given a special mixture which she must rub into her hair so that it will grow long again. Finally, she is given the objects she will use from now on — an ax, different knives, stirring sticks, baskets and other things, all of which are first given magical spells so that no harm will come to her in any way from using them."

Sarah shook her head violently and spoke with some degree of heat, "Well I think those customs are just awful. Nobody should be treated like that! And you wondered if I would want you to do those things to me? No. Not ever! My customs are different, Juma, and it would be wrong to do such things. Wrong and cruel. All you need to do is help me find some of the *kehpahk*. After that I can take care of my *hewyekuht* in my own way."

Juma stiffened and seemed offended. He stood up abruptly and went to the shore where he put on his barkcloth. He appeared to be concentrating on something and when he turned his eyes to Sarah again there was an expression in them she could not fathom.

"That is your choice and I would not ask you to change your customs. Come," he said, "we are leaving here."

"To go into the forest again?"

"No, we are going down to the river. My *montaria* is there and the *inyahn* of the enemies I killed."

He started walking back toward their overhung ledge and she came to her feet and stepped out of the water, calling after him. "Where are we going, Juma?"

The young man paused and looked back, his face older than it should have been. "We are going to Kaumo to see if any of my people are still alive."

Chapter Eight

THEY FOUND JUMA's hidden *montaria* without difficulty and, close to that small dugout canoe, the larger *inyahn* which had belonged to the two Nhambiquara warriors who had pursued him. In it were several calabashes — large dried gourds with open tops — in which they had carried food, but these had been cleaned out by ants. Several weapons were in the boat — a knife not unlike Juma's *parati*, and two *terzadas*, both of them larger than Sarah's machete; a pair of bows were there, one longer and one of the same size as Juma's *iranpahn*, two quivers with five or six *mereres* that had longer shafts than the arrows Juma used but with similar, wicked-looking barbed heads. There were also two short, broad-faced paddles.

Both the *inyahn* and the *montaria* had been chiseled from single logs, but the Nhambiquara's craft was twenty feet long and quite heavy, whereas Juma's was not more than twelve feet and constructed from the trunk of the *itauba* tree, a much lighter wood. The *inyahn* was roomier and looked safer. Sarah was surprised when Juma asked her to help him thrust the *inyahn* into the current to set it adrift.

"Aren't you going to take the things out of it, Juma?"

"They are not mine," he said.

"But you killed the men who owned it," she protested. "You need a *terzada* and there are two good ones here. And other things. The *mereres*. The *iranpahns*."

"They are not mine," he repeated firmly. "I will let the currents of the *paranah* carry their *inyahn* back to their own country so that their people will know what has happened to them and that the Aramoki are not to be attacked without great danger to the attackers."

Not entirely sure she approved, Sarah helped him slide the heavy craft back into the water. Juma shoved it far out into the river, and at once the swift current of the Ituí gripped it, whirling it downstream. They watched until it floated around the river bend below, then loaded their own things into Juma's *montaria*. There was only one paddle, much like the ones that had been in the *inyahn* and Sarah held it up.

"We should have taken one of these from the *inyahn*," she said. "I could have helped you."

"The *iaby cuytahns* were not mine to take," he reminded her.

Among the items they loaded were several *pacova*-leaf parcels of monkey meat from a species Juma called *whiapu-sai*. They had encountered a small group of five in the forest just after leaving the ledge on their circuitous route to the river's edge. Much smaller than the *gauriba*, it was a long-haired, gray-brown monkey with whitish hands and an ugly, beady-eyed face. They had located them by the peculiar yelping sounds they were making. Juma had brought one down with a dart and they had cleaned it, built a fire and cooked it on the spot.

Uncooked meat, Juma explained, would spoil in a very short time.

They also loaded a good supply of other food collected along the way. Several were fruits and vegetables Sarah had not tasted before and she tried them all as they were found. One was a little black fruit which looked and tasted much like a damson plum. Juma called it *umiri*. Another was the *aapiranga*, a bright red berry with a sweet but rather oily pulp enclosing several little seeds. They had also gotten several fruits Juma said were *cuma*, that looked like small round pears with a hard rind and somewhat gummy milk but with pulp which tasted much like an apricot. Twice Juma had used the machete to cut down small palm trees he said were *assaby*, from which he extracted the young inner shoots. Sarah nibbled at one, delighted with its crisp taste – like a combination of raw cabbage and celery.

In addition to *pacovas*, they collected two other fruits with which Sarah was familiar. One was the avocado, for which Juma had a name similar to the English – *abacate* – and the other was a papaya, which he said was *paunapa*. One other item of food was collected which, at first, Sarah decided she just wouldn't eat unless she were starving – perhaps not even then.

Juma had stopped at a moldering log and used Sarah's rock hammer to hack it open. The wood was very soft, much like wadded moist tissue, the pulp riddled with holes as large in diameter as her middle finger. These holes were made by beetle larvae – huge, brownish to ivory-colored grubs the diameter of her thumb and four or five inches long. There were many of them in the log. He gathered nearly forty and would undoubtedly have gotten more except that a blow he made with the pointed end of the rock hammer knocked off a whole section of the log and Juma jumped back with an exclamation.

"*Jararaca!*" He nearly collided with Sarah when he recoiled so unexpectedly.

She looked where he pointed and saw, curled up in a hollow, a rather thick-bodied snake with a long, triangular-shaped head. It was dull in color and pattern, a pit viper three or four feet long, primarily dark olive-green and mottled brown.

Juma stayed a safe distance away and repeated the snake's name: "*Jararaca!*" — Lord of the Forest. He told her it was very dangerous and a bite from its long fangs brought agonizing death within a day. All the more dangerous, he added, because its coloration blended so well with the forest floor that one might step on it before realizing it was there.

Sarah thought he would want to use her *terzada* to lop off its head. She offered it to him but he refused it. "It is not good to kill without cause," he told her. He moved off, Sarah followed, and they walked several hundred yards before stopping. Juma reached into his pouch and removed a grub.

Immediately popping it into his mouth, he chewed it with evident relish. The sight of that nearly made Sarah ill and she refused the one he extended to her. His brow furrowed, but then he quickly built a small fire, impaled a half dozen of the black-headed grubs on a sharp thin stick and roasted them. Still Sarah did not want to try them but so earnest was Juma in his entreaties, she finally gave in and gingerly accepted one. Cooked, it resembled a French-fried potato. Sarah broke off the tail end, held her breath and placed the grub in her mouth. It was crisp on the outside, juicy within and, to her surprise, had a taste very similar to coconut meat. She grinned and nodded, finished off the one she was holding and then quite willingly shared the others. But she still did not want to eat them raw. Juma cooked about thirty more and, wrapped in *pacova*-leaf, they also took their place in the pouch.

They had reached the river three quarters of a mile below the falls and about a quarter of a mile in a direct line from their ledge. However, what with stopping to hunt, cook, and gather fruits, as well as to collect a large supply of *samauma* pods filled with *kahpahk* for Sarah's menstrual use, it was noon before they came to where the canoes had been pulled up on shore.

The water here was beautiful — a clear greenish-blue which darkened with depth. The rocks and fish far beneath the surface were quite visible. A few little rafts of floating foam from the falls and rapids still swept past, but they were dissipating quickly. The current was very fast and smooth with a cheery sound as it swished past the shore, gurgling over rocks and tugging at tendrils of plants and vines drooping into the water.

As soon as everything was loaded, Sarah took a position in the prow of the *montaria*, with Juma in the stern, wielding the short flat paddle. The freeboard was no more than two inches and Sarah was at first nervous at having the water so close to pouring over the gunwale. Yet the craft was surprisingly stable — much more so than the aluminum canoes she and her father had enjoyed on the lagoon at Lincoln Park in Chicago. Her nervousness disappeared within the first few minutes.

The exhilaration of floating along downstream with the current, Juma not paddling but merely using the paddle to guide them, was like nothing Sarah had yet experienced. It did not take long to discover that the world of the river was vastly different from the world of the rain forest interior. The sky was a brilliant clear blue, reflecting in lovely highlights from the water's surface. By the time they slid around the first bend, most of the rockiness of the shoreline had disappeared and there was no longer a visible shoreline at all. The vegetation was a solid green wall, rising from the water to a height of seventy or eighty feet then sloping upward away from the river to the higher trees towering to two hundred feet. The density of the vegetation at the water's edge was such that there was no view at all of the more open forest beyond. It was hard to believe that only a short distance inward the forest floor was so open that one could see clearly for sixty yards or more. Here along the river the eye could not penetrate more than a few feet.

Now and again dark caverns appeared in the greenery and swept past; areas where the river's greedy fingers had dug into the soil at the bases of larger trees and they had toppled into the water and been swept away. The vegetation competed fiercely for the sunlight and no such opening in the green wall remained unfilled for long. It was the only place where a great variety of low

plants could flourish, free from the stunting shade of the
forest giants and the canopy they created. There were
long stretches of tangled bushrope, the *sipos* festooned
with enormous green pods, some a yard in length. Delicate mimosas with pinnate leaves in crocheted clusters
reached for the sunlight and when, on occasion, Juma's
paddle brushed against them, they instantly shrank
from the touch, closing their leaves tightly, withdrawing
into themselves in drooping mute accusation at the dis-
turbance.

By far the most abundant growth along the water's
edge was the great variety of palms, most of them types
Sarah had never seen before and she asked Juma about
them as the canoe passed them. The one he called *hori-
tana* was slender stemmed and bedecked up its entire
length with short, thick thorns. Often, in cases where
the base of the tree had been undermined by the current
and then had splashed into the water, it continued to
hang on, part of the trunk well beneath the surface
and the feathery crown quickly compensating by turning upward out of the water, appearing to grow from the
river bottom. The pressure of the water made the trunk
vibrate incessantly, sending tremors up to the crown,
the shivering fronds rustling, constantly whispering little
secrets. One of the more spectacular palms was the *ju-
pata*, with individual fronds spraying outward fifty feet,
overhanging the river in broad, graceful archments.
Ubussu palms with huge, tufted heads, comprised of
wide, undivided leaves, were a vivid light green, con-
trasting sharply with the generally more somber hues
surrounding them. Uncommonly tall palms which Juma

called *miriti* and *ubim* and *marajae* had gracefully curved trunks and broad, fan-shaped leaves. The *assai* was shorter, but among the prettiest, growing in little clumps, forming frilly tufts set in the circular mass of the tree's foliage. Others were palms with which Sarah was already familiar, such as the tall, stately *bacaba*, with its smooth straight stem and rich, elegant, deep green fronds.

The current moved them along with the speed of a steady, fast walk through long tranquil stretches; a broad blue-green avenue at the base of a green-walled gorge. Oddly, there were few flowers. Only here and there were trees in bloom, usually with small blossoms amid the uppermost branches, drinking in the sunlight and sprinkling the upper level with isolated groupings of vermilion or yellow pinpoints. Less often there were blossoms in orange or lavender or white. Low in the screen of undergrowth rimming the river were clumps of rose-colored begonias; also bromeliads with stiff stems projecting from their centers, topped by scarlet bloom clusters. Despite such floral displays, the prevailing hue was green in an incredible mélange.

As they skimmed along smoothly, silently — Sarah caught up in the wonder of all she was seeing and Juma essentially impassive, though his restless eyes missed nothing — the character of the Ituí gradually changed. Smaller rivers, creeks and brooks merged into the stream, their presence sometimes given away by no more than a faint indentation in the screen of growth. Such waterways, large enough for a canoe to travel in, Juma told her, were called *igaripes*. At one point he paddled directly into one of the *igaripé* indentations and almost immediately the sun went out. It was as if they had entered a deep green tunnel. After a hundred yards they found themselves in the more open gloom of the forest, the *igaripé* they were following barely large enough for the *montaria*, and winding sinuously among gigantic trees. Near the base of an enormous *massaran-duba* they stopped and got out, relieved themselves separately, then ate portions of monkey meat, roasted grubs and fruit. They finished by drinking about a pint each of the *massaranduba* milk.

Returning to the river, they were momentarily blinded by the brilliance of the sunlight and Sarah turned her eyes to the cool depths below. That was when she noticed the change in the river. It was no longer quite so green. While still very clear, the water was becoming more amber colored, stained by the tributaries, which themselves had been colored by decomposing vegetation and roots. Also, the size of the Ituí was increasing and there was an all but imperceptible slowing of the current. There were occasional sandbars, especially just below the mouths of the tributaries.

Juma and Sarah talked considerably during the first hour or so of travel, and, as usual, he often attempted to answer her questions. Later, they became quiet, and this, along with the silence of their mode of travel, permitted them to see an abundance of wildlife, some familiar but much of it animals Sarah had never seen.

At intervals the trees bordering the river became alive with diminutive grayish-brown capuchin monkeys — the pretty, delicate, furry little monkeys of organ grinder fame. Juma called them *caiarara*. They were usually in troops of about fifty, whining and chirruping gently among themselves until they became aware of the two humans beneath them in the boat. At such times they went almost crazy, leaping frantically from branch to branch, making weird purring sounds intermixed with a confused combination of chatters, shrieks and squeakings. They shook the branches in their rage, causing leaves to shower down upon the travelers. While moving they carried their tails curved downward, coiled inward at the tip, or sometimes used them, not too effectually, to grasp branches. They were consummate scratchers, digging and pawing through their own or a neighbor's hair almost instantly upon stopping and continuing the grooming practically without pause until they moved again.

"Do you eat *caiarara*, Juma?" Sarah asked after they had passed such a troop.

"I have eaten them," he replied, "but not very often. They are small and the meat is not so good as *gauriba* or *barrigudo* or *whiapu-sai*."

At one point they rounded a bend at the mouth of a small river and on the head of a glaring white sandbar, fully a quarter mile long, they disturbed a band of about twenty collared peccaries.

"*Cuyam!*" Juma shouted and snatched up his bow, but he was too late. The bristly-haired wild pigs had seen the canoe immediately and, with a chorus of sharp squealings, the hair on their backs and necks standing stiffly erect, they raced from the sandbar and crashed through the riverine growth, vanishing in an instant. In moments even the sound of their passage had ended.

"It would have been good to get one," Juma remarked as they floated past the place where the peccaries had been rooting in the sand. "*Cuyam* are very good to eat and with much meat."

Birds flitted about among the river-fronting trees in considerable numbers, far more than they had seen in the forest. Others were observed briefly as they crossed from the trees on one side to the other. Great gold-and-blue macaws and scarlet macaws, always in pairs or quartets, their long tails streaming behind them, sailed across, scolding as they flew. Green parrots and many-hued parakeets passed in larger flocks or chattered in the trees close by. Hummingbirds flitted and hovered frequently, pausing at trumpet blossoms to sip nectar through the long tapered straws of their beaks.

"Juma!" Sarah exclaimed, pointing, "What in the world is that?"

He paused with his dripping paddle out of the water and looked at several families of hoatzins at their di-lapidated nests overhanging the river. The adult birds were about ten inches long, dark brown on the back and wings, speckled with white at the neck and shoulders, the three longest pinions of each wing and the belly feathers a rich cinnamon, the breast and strange crest a tawny beige. The crest was a disorganized cluster of long thin feathers across the top of the head from the base of the beak to the nape. The beak was grayish and thick and the scarlet eye was set in a broad area of naked bright blue flesh.

The young birds were odd in the extreme. Dark brown, they appeared to be furred more than feathered. At the outer leading edge of each wing they had two curved claws. Using these and their beaks and over-large feet, they climbed about awkwardly in the bushes and, as the half-dozen parent birds were doing, hissed angrily at the intruders.

"They are *ikafu*," Juma said. "Not good to eat. They stink."

Sarah continued to watch them as the boat passed. The adult birds took alarm when the canoe reached its closest point and burst into noisy, extremely clumsy flight. It seemed as if the wings could barely sustain the heavy bodies, and their flights were short — the longest only about twenty yards — at the termination of which the birds stupidly crashed to a stop, evidently having no conception of how to land. At the same time the young birds clawed and scrambled frantically to climb up out of reach and in the process two of them fell into the water. At once the narrow, long brown wings became paddles and the fledglings quickly skittered across the surface out of sight in the dense shore cover.

There was no rain during this first day on the river and late in the afternoon Sarah saw the largest animal she had yet seen in the jungle. The tapir was standing in ankle-deep water beside a sandbar, munching on water hyacinth in a small backwater. It jerked its head erect and for an instant looked their way.

"*Tapira!*" Juma whispered, reaching for his bow.

To Sarah it looked to be some strange combination of pig, rhinoceros and elephant. Well over six hundred pounds, it was brownish and very heavy bodied, built like a hog. Its head was sloping and the nose and upper lip were elongated into an elephantlike trunk about ten inches long, at the end of which were the nostrils. Its eyes were small and piglike, the naked, five-inch tail hanging straight down. The ears, like those of a rhinoceros, stood erect and were oval shaped. The animal was three feet high at the shoulder and eight feet from snout to tail.

As Juma brought up his bow the tapir burst into action. It leaped from the shallow water and onto the bar, crossed it in a bound and plunged with a tremendous splash into the main part of the river. For just a moment it swam on the surface, surging powerfully toward midcurrent with its head high and the elongated snout squirming. Then, just as Juma pulled his bow to full draw, the tapir submerged and was gone.

For half a minute they drifted without seeing it until, far behind, they heard it erupt from the water on the other side of the river under the screen of vegetation and thunder up on shore. For a brief time it sounded as if a tank were tearing through the underbrush and then there was silence.

"He found one of his trails through the heavy cover," Juma explained. "That is the way of *tapira*. Very big. Very strong. No meat in all the forest is better. That was a big one. His meat would have fed my whole village very well."

An hour later, with the sun behind the western trees, Juma pointed the canoe toward a broad sandbar and beached it, telling Sarah they would spend the night there. They ate well of the food they had brought and, while eating, Sarah suddenly gave a low exclamation and pointed across the river. There, wedged in the growth of vegetation that reached the water, was the *inyahn* they had set adrift hours earlier.

Juma frowned and when he looked at Sarah there was a deep-rooted fear lurking in his eyes. "You saw it and I did not. I was not allowed to see it." He shook his head. "They are with us yet. One of them sits in the *inyahn*, waiting. He knew where we were going to stop and he waited for us. He will stay with us, whether we see him or not. His companion has gone on with the current and has told the Nhambiquara we are coming."

Sarah made an attempt at levity, snorting lightly. "Oh, Juma, you're just trying to frighten me with ghost stories! You know, as I do, the *inyahn* just happened to get stuck there. No one is in it. And no one, especially a man you killed, has swum to the Nhambiquara to tell them we are coming."

Juma looked at her balefully and then sighed. "They know we are coming," he said flatly. "You are learning very well about the trees and the animals in the *ca-ahn*, but you do not yet understand about the people. The Nhambiquara have great powers. They see through the eyes of the animals and they listen through the leaves. The river whispers things to them and they know. They know we are coming."

He lapsed into silence and ate no more of his food and the fear in him transferred itself to Sarah. Intellectually, she could not accept what he was saying and put it down as mere superstition. Subliminally, however, an indefinable apprehension had taken root and the unease it created in her could not be shaken.

She was not sure how long they sat there on the soft

warm sand, each drifting with his own thoughts, or
exactly when the sound began. It was not a sound
which suddenly struck the ear and made one look
around to identify it. Rather, it was a growing awareness
of a sound that had begun below the level of conscious
hearing and, in swelling, impinged itself gradually until
the awareness of it was there and one could not say
when it had begun.

The sound was a deep throbbing which at first might
have been mistaken for the pulse of blood coursing
through the system instead of having external origin. It
came on two tonal levels and stirred a sense of primi-
tivism in Sarah that she could not explain. She looked at
Juma who sat close by, his knees drawn up, his hands
clasped across his ankles, staring in the deepening twilight at the *inyahn* wedged in the vegetation across from
them. She thought he was unaware of the sound until
he spoke softly.

"They know we are coming, Sa-rah. They are saying
so on the *manguare*."

"What is the *manguare*, Juma?"

"It is the sound you hear."

She nodded. "I understand that, but what does it
come from?"

"From two hollowed logs hung just above the ground
and struck with special sticks. In this way we send messages long distances."

"A drum, then," she said, a wash of relief flooding her
at the unknown's having been identified. It was clear
now that the muted throb could be nothing else. "It is
what we call a drum. Is it in your village? Kaumo?"

"Yes. And the message is from the Aramoki."

Her relief increased. "But those are your people, Juma, not enemies. What are they saying?"

"The message is in two parts." He was still looking across the river but the far shore was now no more than a deep shadow and it was no longer possible to clearly see the *inyahn*. "The first part says, 'Juma is returning with a *kunyimuku*.' "

Sarah wondered how they could possibly know that. "What is the second part?"

He turned his head and looked at her, his expression masked by the growing darkness. "It says, 'The Nhambiquara know they are coming.' "

The fear came back with a rush and Sarah felt herself blanch. "Oh my God," she breathed. "What can we do, Juma?"

"We will do as the *manguare* says. We will return to Kaumo. Tomorrow. My people will be waiting and they will have a feast prepared for us. There will be rejoicing and they will want to hear of how I killed the two who pursued me. And they will want to hear of you."

"But what about the Nhambiquara?"

"They will come. In time."

"What will they do?"

"Kill us if they can. Take our heads. Or else we will kill them, if we can. That I do not know. We are weak now. Not many of us remain to fight them."

"How many people in your village, Juma?"

"Before the Nhambiquara attack, fifty-two, counting children and babies. How many now, I do not know. The Nhambiquara are many more and they will come again to Kaumo."

"Then why go back? Why don't we just turn around and return to where we were, Juma? It's safe there and no one will bother us."

"My people need me. So I must return."

His implacability angered her. "Then why don't we go there and tell them all to come back upstream to the falls with us, where the Nhambiquara will not bother them?"

"Because our home is not there, it is at Kaumo. They would not leave it and I would not leave it."

They fell into silence then, the sounds of the night swelling and overriding the faint continuing throb of the *manguare*. Frogs lifted their voices in an imbalanced medley and the sibilance of the night insects provided a background theme. A sound she had not noticed before came out of the darkness along the river margin from several places — deep barking noises — and she asked Juma what they were.

"You will see soon enough," he replied shortly.

Juma rolled over onto his side and Sarah lay down too, but still wide awake and deeply frightened. She was sure she would not sleep, but before long she did. The last sound she heard was a strange, unearthly wail; a sobbing, almost human cry of immeasurable sorrow and desolation from close by. It was an Amazonian owl and Sarah recognized it as a sound she and Juma had heard before and which he had identified as "the mother of the moon." The melancholy cry articulated what she could not and, after it faded away, she slept.

In the morning the *inyahn* was gone. To Sarah it was evident that the tuggings of the current had eventually dislodged it and the craft had drifted away. Juma grunted when she told him this, but it was clear he did not share her view. However, he said no more about it and acted very cheerful.

The morning was beautiful. They had been awakened at dawn by the ungodly roaring of a troop of *guaribas* at some distance but, since the supply of food was still ample, Juma was not inclined to hunt them. A small indentation in the sandbar below them formed a shallow backwater with a nice sandy bottom and Sarah said she wanted to bathe. Juma nodded and told her he would bathe also when she was finished. Turning his back toward her, he sat down with a parcel of the monkey meat and began to unwrap it. With a little pang of sorrow that he would no longer bathe with her, Sarah took a couple of the *samauma* pods to the backwater and undressed.

The *kahpahk* she had placed inside her panties yesterday was slightly stained with rust and red but there were no spottings on the panties themselves. Nevertheless, she rinsed the garment, wrung it out and spread it on the sand to dry. The water in the little pool was only a couple of feet in depth and clear, but so tinted with brown that her feet looked amber. She sat down and washed herself thoroughly, then noticed a number of tiny fish circling about her, attracted by her splashings. An inch or less in length, they were thin as toothpicks and swam with queer little spurting motions. She thought they were minnows of some kind.

"Juma," she called, "you should see the school of little fish in the water here. They're cute. They're swimming all around me."

Juma leaped to his feet, consternation in his expression and thudded over toward her, calling as he ran for her to get out of the water instantly. She had long ago learned to obey implicitly Juma's imperatives. She thrashed to her feet and left the water. By then he was beside her and he stopped, looking into the water, and saw them.

"*Candiru!*" he said savagely. He scooped up handfuls of sand and flung them at the water. The tiny fish spurted about in little jumps but were not greatly alarmed. He waded into the water, kicking furiously at them and Sarah, wholly bewildered, watched curiously as she stepped into the still-damp panties and pulled them up.

Juma came out of the water, muttering, stalked past without looking at her and returned to where he had been sitting. Sarah opened the *samauma* pods and scooped out the five little bundles of *kahpahk* from each. Freed from restraint, the bundles expanded into a fluffy mass which she thrust into her panties and adjusted for comfort. The softness was pleasant and the garment held the fibers snugly against her. Putting on the barkcloth blouse and skirt, she returned to where Juma was again eating and dropped to the sand beside him.

"What," she asked, reaching for a parcel of the meat, "is the danger from *candiru?* They're so small. Are they poisonous?"

He shook his head and while she ate he explained the hazard to her. The *candiru* were parasitic catfish. Primarily, they were parasitic upon larger fish, squirming inside their gill plates and attaching themselves to the gills, remaining there for long periods and existing by devouring sucked blood from the filaments of larger fishes' gills. The *candiru* had two sharp spines located behind and below the eyes. These were held flat against the head when the *candiru* were swimming but the fish could, at will, raise them into erect, backward-pointing barbs. When people were in the water the *candiru* swam to them and, if possible, entered the urethral opening, swimming directly into the penis of a man or the vulva of a woman. Immediately the spines would come erect and it would squirm far inside the body. The resultant irritation and pain was excruciating, with no way to dislodge the parasite because of its spines. The little catfish existed on blood sucked through the walls of the urethra and soon the area became inflamed and infected. The only way the *candiru* could be removed was by cutting into the flesh to get at it, a procedure that could cause death to the human host.

It all sounded perfectly awful to Sarah and she began wondering how many other hidden hazards there were around her, disguised in seeming innocence. Over the past few weeks she had been growing rather smug with what she had learned about the jungle and now this simple little incident had demolished that conceit. She felt incredibly ignorant and was more than a bit subdued as she finished eating her meat and fruit.

The morning air was heavy with moisture and at intervals, as they resumed their downstream drifting, they floated through patches of dense mist, the walls of the forest on either side looming dimly, with an intensified sense of mystery. Juma kept the *montaria* in the center of the river, steering with the paddle and using it occasionally to avoid a break or swirl in the flat river surface that indicated a hidden log or boulder just beneath.

Ever more frequently the river, especially along the wall of vegetation resting on the water, was becoming cluttered with drifting logs. Most were underwater but with the highest part of the deeply grooved bark projecting just above the surface. Sarah had noticed some yesterday but did not think much of it. Now it penetrated that if there were logs, someone had to be cutting them. For an excited moment she envisioned a sawmill somewhere nearby and, if that were true, then there would be civilized people and perhaps a means for her to get out of the jungle. On the heels of that thought she realized how ridiculous it was, but the presence of the logs still perplexed her.

"Where have all these logs come from that are floating on the river, Juma?" she asked and then pointed. "Look how thick they are along the shore."

For the first time this day the familiar pleasant grin cracked the young man's lips. "They are not logs, Sarah," he said. "You asked me last night what was making the sounds. I told you you would see today. The sounds came from them." He pointed. "They are *jacares*."

She looked again, this time more closely. This time she *saw*. "Oh," she exclaimed, "they're alligators!"

It was close enough. They were caimans, some of them ten or twelve feet long, mostly six or seven feet, their ridged backs raised an inch or so above the water. They were essentially motionless, simply lying in the water waiting patiently for something edible to appear.

"Very bad," Juma went on. "They wait for animals to come to the edge to drink or for people to bathe. Then they swim below water to attack and drag them away. Very bad. Worse in dry season. That was when the small one grabbed me." He touched his split ear at the memory, then went on. "During the wet season many, especially the bigger ones, go far from the river into marshes and swamps, but when the dry season comes and the water begins to drop, they come back to the river. Then even small boats like this are not safe and river travel has to be in *inyahns*, which they do not attack."

Within the hour the sun, which had been a dull red orb through the fog, turned to gold and then blazing white as it burned away the mist. The sky was deep blue and birds were again on the wing, hurling screeched insults at the monkeys who chattered at them. The river, which had been sixty or seventy feet in width, broadened to eighty and the current slowed slightly.

At midday Juma swung into an *igaripe*, and they followed it upstream for half a mile until further progress was blocked by a large tree that had long ago fallen and was now rotted and moss covered, but still an effective barrier. It was pleasant to be in the cooler forest interior again. They left the canoe and Juma led Sarah down the length of the log to its root system. There he stopped and pointed at a dense patch of fungi. They were armillarias and the largest mushrooms Sarah had ever seen, easily a foot high and eight inches across the crown, with stems more than an inch thick.

"I sometimes came here as a boy to gather these *iuwyapara* for food. They are very good when picked small and young."

Those he considered small and young were half the size of the largest and there were a great many of them. He plucked one and handed it to Sarah and told her to eat. She did and liked the taste. They sat on the ground near the congregation of mushrooms and ate what remained of their meat and most of the fruit. Then they filled their pouches with the young armillarias to take with them.

When they returned to the boat and started back downstream, Juma suddenly snatched up his *pucuna* and blew a dart nearly straight up before Sarah even realized he was shooting. The dart penetrated the upper leg of a huge bird which Sarah at first thought was a turkey. Essentially black, it had a large patch of pure white on its belly and long white-tipped tailfeathers. There was a curly crest of black feathers atop its head and the bright yellow bill had a black tip and a bean-shaped knob, also bright yellow, at the base of the upper beak.

The curassow squawked and flapped its wings, then ruffled its feathers. After a moment its head drooped and its eyes closed. It shook again and then fell, dropping directly into the boat and very nearly hitting Sarah. Juma removed the dart, quickly put new poison on it and reinserted it in the *pucuna*. While he was doing this, Sarah lifted the big bird by its feet to inspect it and was surprised at how heavy it was.

"What is it, Juma?"

"*Piuri*," he said. "It has such good meat. Very white. We will take it with us to Kaumo. They may be hungry if there are no men left to hunt."

He took the bird from her and cut off its head, letting it bleed out through the neck while he slit the belly and removed the viscera. As he had done with the *toco* on their first day together, he saved the liver and heart, thrusting them back into the body cavity.

They had been drifting all this while on the sluggish *igaripe*, Sarah using the paddle in front to shove them away from shore whenever they drifted close to it. Juma finished with the *piuri*, put it down, leaned forward and extended his hand.

"I will take the *iaby cutahn*," he said, and Sarah handed him the paddle.

"Don't you ever miss when you shoot, Juma?" she asked.

"Sometimes." He smiled. "Not often, but there are many who shoot better. Many. I am still learning."

"Do the Nhambiquara shoot well?" As soon as the question left her lips, she regretted it and groaned inwardly, but it was too late. The smile on Juma's face vanished and he grunted an affirmative and said nothing more.

When they were back in the main stream of the Ituí, Sarah attempted to draw him into conversation, pointing to various things and asking questions, but Juma was not inclined to speak. He no longer was content only to guide the *montaria* as it drifted, but dipped and swept the paddle steadily and the boat slid rapidly through the water with a faint gurgling sound.

Not ten minutes later they rounded a bend and Sarah was stunned at seeing a suspension bridge ahead of them. It was a clumsy affair, strung from shore to shore, constructed of three heavy *sipos*. Two of these were essentially parallel to one another on a horizontal plane, con-

nected at about one-foot intervals with cross-branches
lashed to them with *chambira*, a tough cordlike palm
fiber. The third one hung five feet above these two and
was obviously a sort of handrail, stabilized in the walkway portion with tough, thumb-thick vertical strands
of *maguey* fiber at intervals of five feet. At its closest
point to the water surface, the bridge was three feet
high. The shores at the terminal points of the bridge
were relatively cleared and the bridge was anchored ten
feet high on two large opposing trees, with handholds
and footholds cut in the trunk to gain access to the
bridge.

Juma thrust the *montaria* toward the right-bank landing and as soon as it scraped to a stop, Sarah hopped out
and pulled it farther up. Juma stepped out and helped
her pull it up even more. They took everything except
the paddle, and Sarah followed behind Juma as he strode
off on a narrow footpath winding into the interior. After
several hundred yards they came to a clearing.

"This," said Juma, "is my village — Kaumo."

Sarah had not known what to expect, but it was hardly
what she saw here. There were four large, low, rectangular huts constructed of palm leaves overlapped on frame-
works made of branches. The roofs, seven feet high,
angled slightly on both sides from a center ridgepole.
Each hut had only one entry, so small and low that it
would be necessary to enter it on hands and knees, one
person at a time. There were no windows.

The residue of past cookfires was in a center location,
with a scattering of clay pots and wooden implements. In
an area by itself was the drum device Juma called a

manguare. Two large hollowed logs of different diameters were suspended a foot off the ground and three feet apart. The larger one was six feet long, the smaller about four. They were barkless, their surfaces well worn from the pounding they had taken, and the interiors blackened where they had been hollowed out by fire. Each log was suspended by *sipo* ropes attached to two heavy posts sunk in the ground, one at either end. The two *manguare* sticks leaned against one of the logs — each two inches in diameter and over three feet long, each with the handle end worn shiny smooth and the other end capped by a heavy oblong shape of congealed blackened rubber wrapped onto the stick tightly with *tecuna* palm strands.

There were other things to see in the clearing, but at the moment Sarah did not have eyes for them. What struck her with greatest impact was the fifty or more ornamental objects strung on *chambira* fibers, not only from the roofs of the huts but from the uprights of the *manguare* and equally from a scattering of poles stuck in the ground. Some of these objects were painted red with *ucuru* dye, others were blackened by soot, a few were smeared with a yellow ocher. The majority, however, were bleached white.

They were human skulls.

Chapter Nine

JUMA AND SARAH dropped their pouches and the large
bird, and she remained with them while he inspected
each of the huts in turn. Her gaze was still on the human
skulls and she noticed now that the lower jaw of each
was missing, along with all the upper teeth. She was
frightened by the sight and relieved when Juma, finding
the huts empty of people, returned to where she still
stood at the edge of the clearing. He wore a concerned
expression.

"It is worse than I thought it would be," he said.
"They are hiding, even though they know it is Juma who
has returned. They must be very few since the attack.
Perhaps no men at all."

Sarah found it difficult to understand. "If they knew it
was you returning," she asked, "and these are your people, why would they hide from you?"

"They are not hiding from me, Sa-rah. They are hiding from you. You are very different and they are afraid
of you, just as I was afraid of you at first."

"But why should they be afraid of me?" Such a possibility had not occurred to her.

"You are different," Juma explained patiently. "Your
skin is different. You wear clothing to cover you, which

they do not, and that is different. You carry a *terzada* and other things they do not carry. Your face and body are not painted with *huitoc* or *ucuru* like theirs. What is different, they fear, because what is different is usually dangerous."

"How can they know I am different? They haven't even seen me yet."

"They have seen you, Sa-rah. They are watching you now. And they are afraid."

Juma turned from her and cupped his mouth with both hands. A high-pitched ululation issued from his throat, repeated twice more with a harsh single barking sound at the end of each call. Then he stood waiting.

There were only eleven of them and they came in slowly, fearfully. Two were men, one very old and frail, the other, a man of about thirty, short, thick bodied and deep chested, who was badly injured and hobbling painfully with the aid of a staff, helped by two women. There was a boy of about seven and a girl around five. There was one suckling babe and the remaining six, including those helping the injured man, were women.

The men wore barkcloths similar to Juma's but the others were nude. Those two men had black thorns through their nostrils just as Juma had and both wore necklaces of human teeth. Sarah suspected they were some of the teeth from the skulls. Both men had their chains stained red with *ucuru* and they also had tattoos, but different from one another's and different from Juma's. The man who was injured had a large dull blue circle tattooed on each cheek and three blue lines across his forehead, while the old man had thin blue lines radiating outward from the midpoint of his nose and a series of concentric circles from that point. The effect was like a spider web. They also had geometric designs tattooed on the chests, backs, upper arms and thighs. The little girl and boy were neither tattooed nor painted.

The women were not tatooed at all, but they were all painted alike with a deep red-brown stain from the *hui-toc* fruit. There were curved brow lines and their eyelids were painted. Swirly designs of individual lines originating at the shoulders passed over their breasts and stomachs, converging low on their abdomens, passing directly to the pubic areas and continuing around to the buttocks, expanding somewhat there, ending in a hollow circle at the small of the back.

All the women had long and scraggly hair on their heads, hanging in black, unkempt strands. They had neither eyebrows nor eyelashes and no hair anywhere else on their bodies. The hair of the men, like Juma's, was shoulder length and equally unkempt.

The old man came forward as the others stopped in a cluster. He approached to within a pace of Juma and held out his arm toward the young man, palm down. Juma placed his hand atop the skeletal hand and then turned his own hand over, placing it beneath so the old man's palm rested on his.

"We thought you were dead, Juma. *Usinamuy* has smiled on you and helped bring you back to us."

Juma nodded. "The good spirit was good to me, Jarana, but it was *Taifu* who rode with the two who chased me and he took them away. I have been beyond the *pancanda*."

Jarana's eyes widened. "No one, not even of the Nhambiquara, has ever come back from beyond the great dropping water." His eyes shifted to Sarah. "This strange *kunyimuku* is what you brought from there?"

"Yes. No longer *kunyimuku*. She has just become *kunyim buku*. Her name is Sa-rah. I found her in a hole in the rocks when I was weak and hurt. She first gave me *pacova* and then she closed up my wound," he touched the thin new scar on his chest, "and she healed it without *tatahy* and *mariteh*."

Tatahy was fire, Sarah knew, and *mariteh* was pus; the two words together meaning infection.

Jarana pursed his wrinkled lips and made an approving sound. "Then she is good and she is welcome here. Will she heal Temarau?"

"I do not know," Juma said. "I will ask her soon. Are these all who are left?" he said, dipping his head toward the others.

"We are all."

"They killed forty of us?"

"Yes."

"Then what can we do now?"

"We have two choices." His speech was weary and his mannerisms listless. "We can stay here at Kaumo and perhaps they will leave us alone."

"They will not do that. They know I am back. They would come again even if I had not come back."

"That is probably true," Jarana sighed. "Or we can move to Sehlok and live with the Huitoto there; they are still strong."

"No," Juma said, "that would be worse. Then we would no longer be Aramoki."

"We *are* no longer Aramoki!" For a moment the old man's eyes blazed. "Once we were strong and as much as we were afraid of the Nhambiquara, *they* were afraid of the Aramoki." He swept out a bony arm to point at the many skulls. "They knew we could kill them. We fought our wars in the forest when we met by accident and we did not dare to attack their villages or they ours. Then we grew weaker and they grew stronger and they no longer feared to attack Kaumo. Three times they attacked us here and three times we killed some of them, but they killed many of us and we became what we are now. The Aramoki no longer exist. We are *anih baah* — nothing."

Now it was Juma whose eyes blazed and he shook his head violently. "No, Jarana. You are old and cannot fight." He pointed at the injured man. "Temarau is hurt and cannot fight. Our women would not know how to fight them. But I am now a *kumbe eh* — a man, a warrior. I have killed two of them. I am *still* Aramoki. *We* are Aramoki! We are weak, as you say, yes, but we can grow strong again."

Juma indicated the group standing transfixed. "We are not finished. Little Kaiwa will become a man. Ceroyh has a boy baby who will become a man. Temarau cannot fight, but he can make more babies. *I* can make babies. We will grow strong again. For now, we will have to move away from them when they come toward us and keep out of their reach, but one day we will not move from them. We will fight again. We are Aramoki!"

The old man did not reply and after a moment Juma pointed at the goods on the ground. "We have brought some food. It is not much. One *piuri* to roast. Many *iuwyapara* from near the great fallen tree."

"It will help," Jarana said. "We have not had much

food. These are bad times for us." He shifted his gaze. "Will you now ask Sa-rah to heal Temarau?"

Sarah was frightened. She shook her head and told Juma she was not a doctor and did not know how to heal people, but he tapped his chest-scar with his finger and said her words did not agree with her actions, that she should come and look at Temarau's wound.

Unwillingly she did, very nearly becoming sick. The man was in bad shape. Unable to stand any longer, he had sat down, the injured leg stretched out before him, his hands on the ground behind propping himself. Jarana spoke briefly to the women and they went to where Juma and Sarah had dropped their things, and began to prepare the big bird and mushrooms for eating. As Sarah bent to inspect the leg, Jarana rejoined them.

The leg was gangrenous, almost black, the affliction stemming from a horrible gash that had cut the calf muscle nearly in half. The stench was revolting. What she first mistook for muscle tissue turned out to be tiny maggots seething in the flesh. Both lower and upper leg were so swollen that the tightly stretched skin looked as if it would soon split. Temarau's eyes were glassy and he was feverish, but not delirious. There was absolutely nothing Sarah could do and she knew it. She also knew she was expected to do something, perform some sort of miracle to make the man well. She was frightened about what would happen when they learned she could not. Tears were dribbling from her chin when she looked up at Juma and Jarana. She could not speak and merely shook her head. It was Temarau who spoke. He addressed Juma first.

"I am happy you are back, Juma. When I knew you were coming I sent the message on the *manguare*. You heard it?" When the young man nodded, Temarau smiled faintly and said, "Good." He shifted his gaze and continued. "You know I will soon be dead, Jarana. *Kamaytohn* or *kauma kamaytohn*" — Tomorrow or after tomorrow.

Jarana knew what was coming and opened his mouth to speak but Temarau stopped him with a shake of his head. "Do not prevent me," he said. "Only I can say it and if I say it, it must be done. I say it now: *Hembara ahreteh. Zerah hemba-eah-hy. Ayoheh eh-embrahn iwuy priauah.*"

Sarah understood the first two sentences: "I am very tired. I am sick." The meaning of the third was unclear to her, except that he was asking for something. "*Ayoheh*," in the sense he had used it was, "I want . . ."

The old man groaned faintly and touched the top of Temarau's head, then turned to Juma. "Will you do this? I would, but I am too weak."

"I will do it," Juma said grimly. "Sa-rah, remain here with Jarana and the others. You are a guest and they will take care of you. I will be back soon. Let me use your ham-mer."

She removed the rock hammer from her waistband and handed it to him. Before she could say anything, he strode away with only the tool and his blowgun, quickly disappearing in the undergrowth beyond the clearing.

Temarau lay down on his back with his eyes closed, a moan escaping him at the movement. Jarana touched Sarah's arm and told her to come with him and they joined the women who had started a fire and were now impaling the plucked curassow on a sharpened stick six feet long. More than ever the large bird looked like a turkey. Some of the women had placed broad *pacova* leaves on the ground; on these were the mushrooms, now cut into smaller chunks and in a large heap. There were a few fruits as well — *pacova, abacates* and *paunapa*.

Jarana instructed Sarah to sit down by him and when she did so he spoke to the women. "Sa-rah is our friend. She helped Juma. She could not help Temarau. He wishes *eh-embrahn iwuy priauah*. Juma is preparing."

Immediately the women, while continuing to do their work began to wail and moan. The little girl and boy, however, stared at Sarah curiously, no longer with any trace of fear. Unable to understand what was bothering the women, Sarah smiled at the two children. They smiled back and approached her. The women, still upset and a few of them crying, watched closely but without alarm.

"What is your name?" Sarah asked the girl, putting her pouch back over her shoulder.

The five-year-old looked toward her mother, a heavy, sag-breasted woman who nodded. Turning back to Sarah, she said, "Cicaih."

"And yours?" she asked the boy.

"Kaiwa," he replied. "Why is your skin white and your hair brown?"

"For the same reason yours are the colors they are. This is how the people are colored where I live."

"Where did you come from?"

"Far away. From a land called the United States."

"Is that beyond the *pancanda?*" he asked.

Sarah laughed lightly. "Oh, yes, Kaiwa. Many times beyond."

They had come closer to her and Kaiwa reached out and touched her arm tentatively, then more boldly when she did not pull away. He rubbed her skin, intrigued by the color of it and surprised when it pinkened slightly where he rubbed. On a sudden impulse Sarah reached into her pouch and felt around until she located her father's magnifying glass. She brought it out and showed it to him, then held it up an inch or so in front of her own eye to show him and Cicaih how it magnified. Instantly upon seeing the greatly enlarged eye, both children burst into tears and fled to their respective mothers.

Sarah was chagrined. "I didn't mean to frighten them," she said, looking from Jarana to the women who were now regarding her with hostility. She held up the glass and turned it over so they could see both sides and tapped it with a finger. "You see, it's just glass, that's all."

Having no conception of what "glass" meant, their fears were not assuaged. In an effort to reassure them, Sarah attempted to show them what the glass could do. She held it steadily a few inches over a thick dry leaf on the ground near her, focusing the sun's rays to an intense spot of white light the size of a pea. A faint curl of white smoke began rising from the leaf as the concentrated rays burned a hole. She looked up with a smile, certain they would be impressed.

They were even more frightened now and Jarana, too, had begun edging away from her, his expression fearful. Sarah's smile faded and she realized she had made another mistake. Replacing the glass in her pouch, she apologized again.

"You have magic," Jarana said. It was an accusation and his tone was unfriendly.

"No," Sarah objected, "it is not magic. It was just a glass. I'm sorry if it frightened you."

Jarana frowned. "I am not frightened," he said, but the fear still rang heavy in his voice. He pointed a bony finger toward a bare patch of ground about twenty feet away. "Take your magic and go to that ground and sit there. When Juma returns, we will discuss with him what is to be done with you."

She did as she was told, a new fear growing in her. She wished Juma would return and felt very small and vulnerable sitting on the ground apart from the others. Sensing that it would be a mistake to show them how she felt, she made a strong effort to keep her expression calm, quietly watching as the women continued their cooking.

The curassow spitted on the stick was being turned over and over in the fire by two women, one on either side. The aroma of the cooking bird wafted to Sarah and she found she was hungry. They cooked the bird for a long while, until it was blackened on the outside and juices bubbled and dripped from splits in the crisped skin. At last they removed it from the fire and cut it apart. A whole section of the breast meat was given to Jarana on a *pacova* leaf, along with a heap of cut mushrooms. He fell to eating his meal without a glance at Sarah. At the fire the women clustered around the remainder of the bird, putting some pieces of it aside on a *pacova* leaf, then falling hungrily upon the rest themselves. The realization struck Sarah that the moderate portion set aside was for Juma and that no provision had been made for her, nor for Temarau.

It was hot sitting in the sun and she grew increasingly uncomfortable, aggravated by the fact that she had to urinate, but was afraid to move from where Jarana had told her to sit. For over an hour she sat there while the Aramoki devoured all but a very little of the food she and Juma had brought. She leaned her head on her knees and closed her eyes, becoming dissociated from what was around her, not really thinking but more in a strange state of limbo.

Juma did not return alone. Sarah first became aware of his approach when the fearful excited chattering of the women's voices penetrated her consciousness. The afternoon glare hurt her eyes when she opened them, but then she saw what was causing the commotion.

Ahead of Juma, walking unsteadily and guided by Juma's nudging, was a short, dark man of about twenty. In physical stature he resembled Juma, but his face was not so round and bore neither tattooing nor red-stained chin. His skin was more of a bronze coloration than coppery-brown and his only garb was a piece of supple palm-fiber cord tied around his waist. His nasal septum and upper lip were both pierced, with a light-colored straw or thin stick projecting from each hole. His hair was cropped shorter than Juma's, about two inches above the shoulder, but longer at the nape than elsewhere. A large jagged scar ran diagonally upward from his navel to high on his right side. His eyes were open wide but they were glazed and he appeared somnambulistic. It took a moment for Sarah to see the reason: a blowgun dart was sticking in his right shoulder.

Intuitively, Sarah knew he was a Nhambiquara. She watched closely as Juma and the man stopped in the center of the clearing and Juma spoke in undertones to Jarana, who had moved to meet them. While they talked, the stranger stood weaving slightly and then he sat down. Juma and Jarana squatted beside him and asked him questions, but the man did not respond. After a few minutes Jarana said something to Juma, who nodded and, while Jarana continued to question the captive, went to where the women were gathered. He picked up the *pacova* leaf containing the mushrooms and the roasted bird and carried it to where Sarah was sitting. His arms and legs were dirt-stained but he did not seem to notice. Sarah smiled, relieved that he was back. Squatting beside her, Juma began to eat without smiling in return or saying anything. Sarah thought he would offer her some of the food but when he didn't, she frowned and spoke.

"I'm hungry too, Juma."

He looked at her, surprised. "You have not eaten, Sarah?"

She shook her head. "Jarana told me to sit here and they didn't offer me anything."

Juma handed her his food saying, "Eat," and then called to Jarana, asking why none of the food had been shared with Sarah. Jarana looked up from his questioning and told Juma about the incident involving the magnifying glass, making it sound worse than it had been, as if she had tried to hurt them. The women murmured in accusatory agreement. Juma turned back to Sarah.

"Why did you try to harm my people?" he asked.

"But, Juma," she protested, "I didn't. I just showed the children a magnifying glass and they became frightened."

"Where is this thing?"

Sarah dug in the pouch and produced it, showing it to him. He did not take it from her, only watched silently as she showed him how it made things appear larger. She detected a fear in him, too, though not so pronounced as in the others.

"They said," he told her, "that you brought smoke from a leaf with it, without fire."

She tried to explain in simple terms. "If you hold it just right toward the sun, Juma, it sort of squeezes the sunlight all together in a tight beam which gets very hot. Shall I show you how it works?"

"No!" He was abrupt. "Put it away. Why did you not tell me in all this time we have been together that you could make the sun do as you wished?"

She realized he could not understand, no matter how she tried to explain, so she merely shrugged. "I just did not think to show it to you, Juma."

"Do not use that magic any more," he said. "It is not good to frighten people. Eat your food."

She tore off a piece of the meat and found it to be juicier and more flavorful than turkey. She offered him some. "Aren't you hungry?"

"Yes, but I will eat later, after we see to Temarau and this Nhambiquara." He tilted his head toward the darted man, whose head was beginning to loll.

Sarah's voice was small. "Where did he come from and what are you going to do with him?"

"He was watching what I was doing in the forest a little way from here. He did not know I saw him. I put a dart in him. As for what we are going to do with him, there is nothing to do. He is dead. He knew he was dead when the dart touched him."

Even as Juma spoke the Nhambiquara Indian slumped over on his side, his whole body quivering. When the involuntary motions stopped less than a minute later, Jarana walked back to the women and talked to them, gesticulating toward the dead enemy. Four of them went to the man, picked him up and carried him back near the fire. The other two women went with Jarana to where Temarau was lying supine.

"Come, Juma," Jarana called.

Juma stood, pulling Sarah to her feet by an arm. "You come with us Sa-rah."

She followed mutely, an unknown fear gnawing at her insides. Juma seemed so strange, so unlike himself since they had arrived here. She sympathized with what he felt upon learning that about eighty percent of his people in Kaumo had been killed by the Nhambiquara, including his own family, yet the change in him went beyond mere grief. He was more aloof, unreachable, and it frightened her.

They tried to carry Temarau, but the injured man waved them off and sat up with great effort. He held out his arm to Juma and the young man took it, helping him to his feet. With one of his arms over Juma's shoulder and the other over the shoulder of one of the women, they moved away slowly in the direction Juma had taken earlier. Jarana was behind them, with Sarah beside him and another of the women following.

A path led through dense undergrowth into the dimness of the more open forest floor and they followed
that, a silent procession in sepulchral solitude. No more
than eighty yards from the village they came to a newly
excavated hole. On the pile of dirt to one side lay Sarah's
rock hammer and she knew now where Juma had gone
and what he had done. The hole was more in the nature
of a trench, over three feet deep, two feet wide and four
feet long.

They stopped at the excavation and helped Temarau
to a sitting position with his legs inside the trench. In
turn, Juma and Jarana knelt beside him and briefly
hugged his shoulders. The two women, weeping silently,
did the same and pressed damp cheeks against his. No
one said anything. Temarau eased himself into the trench
in a sitting position, his back against one of the narrow
walls, legs outstretched, and said, "I am ready."

When Juma stooped and picked up the rock hammer
from the pile of earth, a terrible certainty dawned on
Sarah — that he was going to use it to kill Temarau. Instead, he walked over to Sarah and wordlessly handed
her the tool, then returned to the others. Confused, Sarah watched, still with a sense of disquiet. The two
women and Juma knelt in the dirt and, with Jarana
standing at the foot of the trench watching, they scooped
up double handfuls of soil and began tossing them down
onto Temarau's legs. The pain of the dirt striking the
distended, gangrenous leg must have been intense, yet
nothing in Temarau's expression indicated he was even
aware of it — he merely stared straight ahead. The
thought struck Sarah that this was some sort of strange

ritual treatment to cure the injury, but she couldn't fathom how. Not until the legs were well covered and they continued to throw in dirt, not until the trench was half filled and the level of the earth was to midchest on Temarau, did she comprehend what was really occurring here.

"Juma!" She ran to him. "Juma! Stop! You can't do this. He's alive. You can't just bury him alive!"

They had stopped at her rush of words and were staring at her. Jarana was scowling and Juma stood up, sighing. He stepped closer to her and placed a dirt-coated hand on her upper arm.

"Sa-rah. You must not interfere."

"But you can't bury him alive. You *can't!*"

"It is Temarau's own wish Sa-rah. It is our way. Whenever our people grow very old and cannot care for themselves any longer or become sick or hurt beyond recovery and become a burden to those around them, they have the right to request *eh-embrahn iwuy priauah* — burial alive. It is an honorable death by choice and those of whom it is requested cannot refuse."

"But . . . oh, Juma, *he is alive!*"

"Yes, Temarau is alive. That is part of it. Would you be kinder to let him stay alive with his leg rotting and the poison of it filling his body? Would you want to hear his screams when the pain became even worse than it is now, and know that it would do nothing but become more painful to him? What kind of people are yours that they would not do this?" he asked, indicating the grave. "What kind of people would be so cruel as to stand by and watch a friend or a relative dying in great pain by little bits and not want to help end his pain? Move away now, so we may continue our work."

Juma motioned to the women and then, with them, returned to tossing dirt into the grave. Sarah watched, not wanting to, yet transfixed by what was occurring. She cupped her mouth and nose with both hands and watched until the level of the dirt crept up to Temarau's chin. He was having trouble breathing now because of the weight of the earth against his chest and his respiration was shallow and rapid. Still he looked straight ahead without expression. His mouth was a thin, tight line and, when the dirt began covering it, Jarana raised a hand to stop it.

"Good-bye, Temarau," he said softly. "Sleep forever well."

He dropped his hand and, at that, the activity of Juma and the two women became greatly increased. They shoved and threw earth into the grave as rapidly as possible, a veritable cascade which fell on Temarau's head and face, covering nose, ears, eyes. There was a movement then from Temarau — a jerking of the head as to throw the dirt off, but they redoubled their efforts and he could not.

It was more than Sarah could stand and, the rock hammer still in her hand, she fled back toward Kaumo, whipped by branches of slender saplings and slapped by leaves, hardly feeling them. She burst into the clearing and startled the four women by the fire. They leaped to their feet crying out fearfully and one snatched up the baby lying on the ground beside her. Another gripped the wrist of the little girl Cacaih, and yet another, the arm of the boy Kaiwa. They ran from the apparition that Sarah seemed to be as she charged toward them with a strange weapon in her hand.

Sarah jolted to a stop not believing what she saw here. The blood pounded in her head and for an instant she thought she might faint. The fire had been built up larger and chunks of red meat were impaled on sharpened sticks which themselves were stuck into the ground and leaned inward over the fire so that the meat would cook. On *pacova* leaves spread over the ground was other meat, a great deal of it, and to one side a pile of entrails. They were the gruesome remains of the Nhambiquara warrior. She saw legs and arms that were severed at each joint, some with large chunks missing from them. She saw the separated hands and feet and the large bloody lump that was the heart. And she saw the head, lying on its left side, eyes half open. All this she saw in a mere instant. In that same instant a horrifying knowledge struck her with such force, she actually staggered a few steps, nearly falling.

"Oh, my God," she whispered aloud, "they're *cannibals!*"

She reeled and dropped the rock hammer, buried her face in her hands and screamed – a long piercing cry that stilled the chittering of small birds in the underbrush. The women who had fled were making loud urgent cries from the forest behind, in the direction from which Sarah had entered the clearing. She heard answering cries and knew they were coming.

Sarah ran as she had never run before, her pumping legs thrusting her in headlong panicky flight along the path leading to the river. Before she could reach it she heard someone coming behind, leaves swishing with the passage, feet thudding on the earth.

"Sa-rah! SA-RAH!"

It was Juma's voice. She ran even harder. The river loomed ahead and she raced to the landing beneath the suspension bridge and threw her weight against the prow of the canoe with a great shove. It slid more easily than expected and she fell. The current tugged at the stern of the *montaria*, pulling it outward and she nearly lost it. She grabbed at the prow and caught it with one hand.

Juma burst into sight, running hard, his blowgun in one hand. He saw her and called again, telling her to stop, but she ignored the command. She literally sprawled into the *montaria* full length, rocking the little craft violently, nearly turning it over. It shot out from shore with the momentum of her plunge.

Breathing heavily, Juma lurched to a stop at the shore, his face contorted. "Come back, Sa-rah. No one will hurt you. Come back!"

She did not reply, did not even raise her head. She just lay there gasping, feeling the boat turn as the current of the Ituí caught it and spun it downstream. Behind, Juma was still calling urgently.

"Sa-rah. The Nhambiquara will kill you if you go down that way. Come back. SA-RAH . . . !"

The voice became muted and then lost with distance and still Sarah lay outstretched in the bottom of the *montaria*. Her back was heaving with violent sobs and the bile rose in her throat, threatening to strangle her. A vision of that ghastly scene in the clearing came to her and she raised herself, clung to the low gunwale and vomited into the river.

She was weak, gasping again, when she finished and sat in the bottom of the boat, slowly regaining control of herself. Far behind she could still see a portion of the suspension bridge over the river, but then another bend in the river obliterated that view. The walls of foliage rising on either shore towered silently over her but they no longer frightened her. Others things had been much more frightening. There was a sense of stolid peace to the majestic trees and she was relieved at being back among them, alone.

She looked back upriver and was sure she would never again see Juma. She thought of their times together, how he had helped her and, despite what had occurred back at Kaumo, she was saddened.

"Good-bye, Juma, and thank you," she murmured. "*Eheh ahoh putareheretamo koteh*" — I am going away to my own country.

Chapter Ten

SARAH FRANCIS WAS BOTH RELIEVED and frightened at being on her own again. During the first hour of floating in the *montaria*, her mind drifted as aimlessly as the canoe. The horror of discovering that the young man with whom she had been staying, and upon whom she had been depending for over a month, was a cannibal rose up time and again to haunt her. The image of his burying Temarau alive was hardly less disturbing. The fact that it had been at Temarau's own request made little difference. The barbarism of it revolted her.

Underlying everything was the terrifying knowledge that she was evidently floating into the territory of the Nhambiquara. The perils in the surrounding jungle paled compared to peril by humans and she gazed with only mild curiosity at the numerous caimans floating in midstream or along the edges of the river as the current carried her ever farther downstream. Far behind her she could hear the throbbing of a *manguare* and she wondered if it were Juma sending a message to another village about her escape, wondered if she would be waylaid by Indians ahead. After a while the sounds ceased and she found herself drifting mentally as well as physically.

It was hunger more than anything else that brought her back to the reality of her situation. That, and the fact of the rapidly waning afternoon. She had to think about where she was going to spend the night, and this jolted her into the strong awareness of here and now. Fully aware of her predicament, she began watching the river ahead more closely, alert for a sandabar where she might stay during the dark hours, as she and Juma had done before.

Although there was still a good bit of daylight remaining, the sun had long since gone out of sight behind the screen of trees along the west bank and she was traveling in shade. Infrequently, as the *montaria* drifted close to one shore or the other, or headed for one of those swirls indicating a hidden underwater snag or boulder, Sarah dipped the paddle and changed her course enough to avoid the potential danger.

Another half hour passed before she came in sight of a sandbar, but her initial elation at the sight became disappointment as she came closer and discovered it was alive with resting caimans. They were so abundant that at times smaller ones lay across the bodies of the larger animals and they regarded her with cold crocodilian eyes. Most often they remained where they were as she passed but every so often they stood high on squat legs and lumbered into the water, swimming toward the little canoe with calculated interest, only to stop and watch her with baleful stares from a dozen feet away before submerging. Sarah was thankful when at last she left the extensive sandbar behind.

The problem was still with her, however: Where

could she spend the night? The thought of continuing to drift along like this was totally unappealing. Juma had told her that no one traveled on the river at night because of the increased dangers — striking an unseen obstacle could easily turn the boat over with deadly results; there were occasional rapids to contend with where clear vision far ahead was an imperative.

At last, with the first trace of twilight beginning to dim the sky, she pointed the *montaria* into one of the little *igaripe* indentations along the west shoreline, similar to the one she and Juma had entered where they had subsequently found mushrooms and the large black bird he had called *piuri*. This little creek, however, was somewhat narrower, and it was only with difficulty that she forced the boat through the initial dense growth cloaking the river's edge. Time and again she had to pause and lop away intervening vines or branches with her machete. At one point, just where the heavier cover gave way to the more open gloom of the rain forest interior, a large log lay across the waterway. The stream had cut a little ravine here with low, steep banks and the water surface was a couple of feet below the log. In order to pass it she had to lie on her back in the bottom of the *montaria* and pull herself under the log to the upstream side.

The *igaripe* was so narrow that at times the sides of the *montaria* brushed along the banks and she knew there would be no way to turn it around, but was confident that, when the time came, she could merely float the craft backward until she reached the Ituí again. A hundred yards or more past the log spanning the stream she came to a place where the bank had caved in, forming a natural place to pull up the canoe and wedge it.

With the dusk rapidly deepening, Sarah stood on the ground and looked about, searching for anything that might be food. A small grove of *pacova* trees was close by and she walked to it at once, but it was bare of bananas. Far in the distance a troop of *guaribas* was howling in noisy chorus making her wish fervently she had some monkey meat. The longing brought to mind her father and his comment about the futility of wishing, and a small smile touched her lips.

After a moment Sarah clenched her teeth and moved on, making sure she would be able to find her way back to the canoe. As the gloom increased, however, she realized she was going to find no fruit here and turned back toward the *montaria*. A spongy, fern-bedecked log caught her attention and she walked to it, immediately chopping into it with her machete as Juma had done, being watchful for snakes. The grubs were there, many of them, along with a few of the enormous adult beetles with five-inch horns. With a faint sense of revulsion she put a dozen of the grubs into her pouch.

Returning to the canoe, she picked up branches as she walked, watching for one of the anthills to find some tinder, but it was getting too dark and she could not see any. Nor were there any *bacaba* palms from which she could get kindling material from the midrib of the broad leaf. She dumped the armload of wood in a pile on an open spot of ground close to the canoe and squatted, breaking the smaller branches, positioning them in a little cone-shape for lighting.

There were eight matches left in the metal container and she scratched one aflame on the side of the machete and touched it to the base of the wood. It didn't take fire well at all. The area where she held the lighted match blackened and smoked; one of the twigs burned briefly, then went out, along with the match. She tried again, and then a third time with the same results.

It was getting too dark to see well but she took one of the larger, dryer branches and used her pocketknife to cut thin shavings from it until she had a hand-sized pile. To these she touched another lighted match and they burst into flame. Quickly she placed small twigs on top and larger pieces atop those, but the shavings burned themselves out without doing more than scorching the twigs and she had to begin again. This time she was more careful and cut a much larger pile of shavings before carefully placing twigs upon it. The fifth match flared but went out at once and, disgusted, Sarah tossed the matchstick onto the pile and tried another. This time she was successful and in a short while had a cheery blaze going. Carefully recapping the last two matches, she replaced them in the pouch. She sharpened a branch and impaled four grubs on the end of it.

They swelled and split, sizzled and crisped very quickly in the living fire but she held them over the flames too long and the thin dry branch burned through and dropped into the middle of the fire. She remembered then that Juma, as well as the women at Kaumo, had cut green saplings for spitting food. It was too dark now to try to find anything so she sighed and cut another spit from the greenest branch she had and tried again. This time she kept them higher above the flames and though the branch blackened and smoked, it did not burn through and she was able to cook the grubs without losing them.

Sarah cooked and ate them all without pause, at one stage giggling abruptly as she considered the picture she made: a young city girl clad only in crude garments of barkcloth, barefoot, sitting cross-legged before a tiny fire in the vastness of a trackless wilderness, roasting and eating fat beetle grubs and liking them. She wondered what Vicki Francis would think if she could see her daughter at this moment, and she giggled again, knowing her mother would be appalled. She finished her meal but was still hungry and toyed with the idea of going back to the log for more grubs but was afraid to move about in the darkness. The fear increased when, very faintly, she heard the throb of a log drum. Her uneasiness grew when she could not tell from which direction the sound was originating.

She drank from her canteen and then reentered the canoe. Stretching out in the bottom of the *montaria* she tried to settle herself for sleep, but it was so hard she could not get comfortable, so she returned to the fire and lay on the ground. That was when she first noticed the mosquitos. Until now there had been few of the pests about and wherever she and Juma had encountered them — he called them *carapanas* — they simply moved away from them to another area. This time there was no moving away and they descended upon her in swarms. She rubbed herself liberally with her diminishing supply of cream repellent. It helped for a while, but then they were back again and she repeated the process, feeling the numerous welts already springing up on her flesh.

This time, after applying the repellent, Sarah donned her poncho and lay back down, tucking it snugly around her. For a short while it worked but then she was attacked again on face and neck. Once more she applied repellent using the last of it and this time pulled her head inside the poncho, leaving her feet and ankles uncovered which were soon bitten savagely. It was a night of pure torment and she wound up moving away from the dying embers, sitting with her back against a medium-sized tree, feet tucked under, and the poncho tentlike over her. There was little rest for her this night. Even after the *carapanas* gave up in the small hours of the morning, she was still miserable with the itching left in their wake.

Sarah slept only fitfully at best and was weary and depressed when the distant howling *guaribas* heralded the dawn light seeping weakly through the overhead labyrinth of leaves and branches. The fire was dead and when full awareness returned to her she looked around fearfully, half expecting to see Juma and his people or the Nhambiquara creeping up on her. No one was there. She relieved herself, discarded the clump of *kahpahk* from her panties, and noted it was not stained. Her first menstrual period was apparently over and Sarah was glad she didn't have to concern herself about that, at least.

Marking trees with her machete as she walked, Sarah moved deeper into the forest looking for something to eat. Some squabbling scarlet macaws on the ground led her to a scattering of Brazil nuts and she put a couple of dozen in her pouch. A few minutes later some parrots, rustling about in the foliage of a palm which Juma had called *assai*, attracted her attention and she found the ground beneath the tree strewn with a greenish-yellow cherry-sized fruit. The parrots were eating them and knocking down a good many undamaged. Sarah picked them up eagerly, feeling they would be safe to eat. She bit into one and found it had only a thin coating of pulp over a hard kernel, but the pulp was tasty and she ate a large number of them. They stained her fingers, lips and mouth with a violet color similar to the stain from black-berries, but she didn't care about that.

She had hoped to find a *massaranduba* tree to drink some of its milk but was unsuccessful. The only other thing she found edible was a young palm of the kind Juma had opened for the heart, which had tasted like a combination of celery and cabbage. It took her a while but she chopped the tree down and, after a lot of hard work, got the heart out of it — a cylindrical chunk of vegetation the color of ivory and weighing over a pound. She placed it in her pouch and, perspiring from her efforts, followed her blazes back to the *montaria* and started downstream.

As she approached the large log stretched over the stream she gave an involuntary cry and quickly stopped the boat by thrusting a paddle against the water-cut bank. Lying atop the log not over twenty feet from her was a mottled yellow and black shape thicker than her own body. It stretched back out of sight, well up on shore behind the bulk of the log. It was the largest snake Sarah had ever seen and she knew it was an anaconda — the snake called *sucuruju* — not only from the small one seen on the boat trip from Cruzeiro do Sul down the Juruá River, but also from the huge one she had seen many times in the reptile house at Chicago's Lincoln Park Zoo. That one was purported to be twenty-four feet long, but it was small compared to the one she was seeing now.

A thick coil of the body hung low over the water near one shore and the head of the reptile, almost a yard in length and very broad, rested on the surface of the log above midstream. The head was turned away from her and the snake appeared to be staring at something she could not see. What the snake was intently watching then came into view — a caiman of considerable size, swimming up the little *igaripe*. At first she could not tell just how big it was, since most of its body was underwater, but a momentary glimpse of the end of the tail showed it to be about eight feet long. The head was very wide. She caught a look at the broadest part of its back as it crawled over a submerged log or some other obstruction, and it appeared to be about three feet across. The gaze of the caiman was locked on Sarah and, from its determined actions, she knew it was coming at her to attack. In this narrow, shallow *igaripe* there was no way to maneuver away from it, so she scrambled to her feet, intending to get up on shore and move away.

The *montaria* tipped and she lost her balance, then half leaped, half fell toward the shore. The lower part of her body fell into the water and she hugged the shore with her arms, pressing her chest against the bank, attempting to scramble up. Immediately the caiman put on a burst of speed, throwing up a small wake, and its jaws opened several inches exposing a ferocious array of large cone-shaped teeth.

Sarah screamed and struggled harder to climb up onto

the shore but her movements splashed water all over the bank and it became slick mud, thwarting her efforts. The caiman surged under the creek-spanning log. That was when the anaconda struck. The snake's head flashed down and the gaping jaws gripped the big animal just behind the eyes. Instantly the caiman hissed piercingly, its mouth open to full measure as it spun its body furiously. The caiman's turning wrapped the coils of the anaconda around the scaly body in three powerful loops, but still the serpent's tail remained out of sight. A tall thin tree, growing from behind the log where Sarah could not see, began shaking vigorously and it was evident the snake had wrapped its tail around it and was holding on. Another loop of the anaconda's great muscular body fell from the log and pinned the frantically flailing tail of the crocodilian against the other coils.

The adversaries held this way with little movement for a long time as the jaws of the caiman, the only thing it could move, opened and slammed shut with heavy thuds time and again. The incredibly muscular coils of the *sucuruju* bunched and compressed as they tightened around the caiman until the jaw movements ceased. The bone-crushing strength of the coils forced the caiman's air from its lungs in great wheezing sounds and, unable to inflate them to breathe again, the large animal quickly suffocated.

Long after the caiman's movement ceased, the anaconda maintained its unbelievable pressure and then the muscles tightened in the snake's lower body and gradually pulled the coiled upper body and its heavy load back to the shore. They were on the opposite side from where Sarah had finally managed to reach dry ground. She was standing there, stupefied by the unfolding tableau. Even after getting well upon shore, the anaconda maintained its incredible grip on the caiman for a long while. Then the tail portion of the snake relaxed its hold on the tree which had given it leverage, and slid over the top of the log to where the main part of the body was located.

Slowly, ever so slowly, the coils relaxed. Not until they were free of the caiman's body and there was still no movement did the jaws of the anaconda release their hold on the caiman's head. For the first time since the battle had begun, Sarah was able to see the full length of the snake, and a thrill of awe went through her. Even though it lay on the ground in loose folds, the great length of it was apparent. Stretched out straight it would have to be upwards of forty feet long. There was no way for her to estimate its weight except to think again of the twenty-four-foot specimen seen in the zoo. That particular anaconda had weighed close to three hundred pounds. But this one was so much thicker and longer it had to weigh three or four times that much.

Sarah no longer felt any sense of danger for herself, only a strong curiosity to observe what would happen next. She remained standing motionless on the bank, forgetting her own wetness and muddiness, giving no thought to moving away or to the problems still facing her. She was being privileged to watch a drama of nature few people had ever witnessed and there was no way she could tear herself away from it.

For several minutes the snake lay motionless beside

the upside-down carcass of the caiman. Then its head moved closer to it. The tongue flicked out and touched the caiman's side and gradually moved toward the head. Upon reaching the snout the anaconda's mouth opened again and began engulfing it. Large as the snake's head was, it seemed impossible to Sarah that it could open wide enough to swallow the caiman whole.

Where the head of the caiman grew broader at the great jowls, the jaws of the snake disconnected and spread to meet the need. First the right side of the snake's head would advance several inches, grip and hold; then the left side would move up, pass the hold on the right jaw and continue a few inches farther. In this way the gigantic reptile was, in essence, walking its body over its prey to swallow it. There was a little difficulty and maneuvering when it came to the caiman's forelegs, but they were only a temporary hurdle. Slowly they were thrust backward until they lay flat against the caiman's sides and then the jaws walked over them as well. By the time the anaconda reached the broadest middle portion of the caiman, half an hour had passed and the snake's head was improbably distended. Without pause it continued to swallow and now there was a huge lump behind its head, extending into its body. The serpent paused once for five minutes to rest, then began swallowing again and, just slightly over an hour from the time it began swallowing, only three feet of tail still extended from the snake's mouth. A convulsive series of muscle ripplings moved down the snake, shoving the engulfed body of the caiman toward the stomach. With that, the last vestiges of the tail slid out of sight into the anaconda's mouth in one steady movement. The snake gaped its jaws wide several times, reconnecting the separated jawbones, and its head resumed its normal appearance.

The great lump in its body was now over a third of the way down the snake's length and the anaconda's head swung back and forth several times, its tongue testing air and ground. It began moving forward slowly and in less than fifty feet pulled itself into a loose coil in a sheltered area between two high flanged roots belonging to one of the larger trees. Its head settled into the midst of the coilings and the tongue stopped flicking out and in.

Slowly and carefully, Sarah reentered the *montaria,* which was wedged against both shores, and straightened it so it was floating free once again. She stood carefully in the boat and looked a final time at the anaconda. A peculiar exaltation filled her at having been a part of the stark drama and she knew she would never forget one instant of it. In a way, the *sucuruju* had saved her life, yet she knew as well that had the caiman not appeared, had she not seen the great snake and instead glided under that overhanging log, it could well have been she rather than the caiman in the anaconda's stomach at this moment. It was just one more of the hazards she had learned about and luckily avoided.

The light *montaria* poked backward out of the brush at the mouth of the *igaripe* and into the open water of the Ituí. As soon as the entire craft was clear, Sarah carefully turned herself around inside the boat and took a seat closer to the stern. She picked up the paddle and began to use it with slow, measured dips, letting the current do most of the work, avoiding snags as she had seen Juma avoid them, staying in midriver most of the time.

There were more caimans than ever in the river,

chunks of barely animated logs clustered near the over-hanging forest screen near shore and less abundantly in the open water. They watched as she passed, occasionally one or another moving a few feet toward her before stopping. Some appeared about as large as the one eaten by the anaconda, but mostly they were smaller.

The day became one of paradox: an unending mo-notony of dipping and thrusting the paddle, while at the same time an excursion punctuated by stirring, unex-pected and often very beautiful glimpses of wildlife. The paddling did not bother her and she preferred it to merely sitting still and drifting. It was something to do and it was hastening the time when she would get *some-where*. The knowledge lay heavy in her mind that ahead was Nhambiquara territory and there was nothing she could do but what she was doing now — heading directly into it. She tried to envision what she would do if she encountered them. Would they chase her in their own dugout canoes? Would she not even know they were aware of her presence until one of those deadly darts suddenly pierced her skin?

"Take it as it comes," she told herself. "That's what Dad would have said."

The beauty of what she was seeing was counterpoint to the apprehensions she was experiencing. The sandbars were now more frequent, but not all of them were rest-ing places for the caimans. On some, the level white sand had no marks at all except for the tracks of wading birds or turtles. Often, veritable clouds of butterflies fluttered in dizzying patterns over one particular area of such bars for no apparent reason and the glitter of the iridescent colors under the midday sun became a kaleidoscopic fantasy. On one of the bars a brilliant orange and black ocelot stood and calmly watched her pass only thirty feet away without taking alarm. It cocked its head and looked at her. Sarah wanted to take the beautiful cat up in her arms and stroke it.

Turtles were everywhere, sunning themselves, not only on the sandbars but also on any purchase sturdy enough to hold them. They were large, smooth-shelled turtles with shells as much as three feet long and two feet wide. Many times a half dozen or more had crowded up onto a log sloping into the water from shore, but in all cases they were extremely wary and as soon as the canoe came within fifty feet, even if Sarah sat unmoving, they tumbled into the water with loud plops.

Once, in midafternoon, a little company of squirrel monkeys was playing in a treetop high over the river when a harpy eagle unexpectedly shot out of the foliage beneath and snatched one in its powerful talons, disappearing again almost immediately in other foliage. The other monkeys screeched in terror and fled, but a young one lost its footing and plummeted. It hit the river with a splash and hardly began to thrash wildly on the surface before a caiman grabbed it and submerged, leaving only a faint string of bubbles. There was no mercy in the Amazon balance of nature but neither was there cruelty. Death was a part of life here; no animal wanted to be killed, but when that occurred, others continued their lives as before, taking only brief note of the incident, perhaps even learning something from it. When man was not involved, nothing died without reason, and nothing that died was wasted.

With a strange detachment she had not experienced

before, Sarah wondered if she would die here, if the Nhambiquara would kill her or some other tragedy befall which she could not survive. She knew it was very possible, even likely, yet the thought did not at this moment engender a great fear; only a sadness, should it occur, that she would not have had enough time in this life.

It would have helped had Sarah known how far downstream it was to the Nhambiquara territory. In not knowing, it was a constant drain upon her; an anticipation that around every bend of the river she would encounter savage Indians intent upon her destruction in some grisly manner. To compensate, her mind attempted to nullify the possibility. Since she had no real choice about the manner of her travel at this point, to be wracked by fear over what lay ahead was debilitating. She drifted.

Every so often Sarah tried to backtrack in her thoughts over all that had transpired, but everything was melding into one great unending dream — at times lovely, at times nightmarish. She tried to calculate how long it had been since she left the Emerald City ruins, but could come up with only an approximation; somewhere in the vicinity of six or seven weeks, she guessed. How, then, could she still be alive? This was the jungle where lost travelers of much greater strength and experience than she were killed or died of exposure within days of becoming lost; a jungle where even the Indians did not normally travel beyond specified boundaries because those who did had a way of not ever being seen again. It was even more difficult trying to estimate how far she had traveled. She felt as if she had walked scores of miles. Whatever the distance was, it was hardly in a straight line. Even the river travel, faster and certainly easier, was difficult to estimate from a standpoint of distance. The Ituí often looped back and forth in serpentine convolutions; at times she could drift for an hour or more and yet, in direct-line travel, be only a few hundred yards from where the measurement began. At other times the channel narrowed and became faster, more direct, and then an hour would find her five or six miles farther than she had been. There was just no way of telling with any accuracy.

Sarah was not in terribly good condition. Sometimes she went a little hungry, but usually she found food enough to keep her going. Sometimes she avoided jeopardy through good luck, but more often through depending upon the forest lore learned from Juma. Her left big toe had become swollen and painful, though she could not remember having hurt it. Her arms and legs were peppered with scratches and welts. Fierce thorns which Juma called *jacitara*, meaning "the terrible," did the most damage and, early on, had been responsible for the rapid destruction of her clothing. They were also the reason she often had to replace the barkcloth garments she now wore. The *jacitara* was a palm, though it looked more like a vine as it extended itself in a writhing manner through undergrowth sometimes for seventy feet or more. Dreadful thorns grew along its entire length, the worst being at the tips of its numerous long switches, each of which hardened into a needle-sharp curved hook. The sand flies called *piums* continued to be a nuisance, sometimes of monumental proportions, along with mosquitoes. Fortunately, both pests were localized in specific areas and one had to learn to endure them until the area was passed. It was bad for her when she ran out of the cream repellent at last, but she had learned to gather mud from the banks of the *igaripes* and carry it with her on a *pacova* leaf in the bottom of the canoe, smearing it thickly on face and arms and legs whenever she encountered the pests.

On the third day after beginning her solitary downstream journey, she pulled into an *iragipe* to gather fruit and mud and was in the process of moving back toward the Ituí when an unusual sound she could not identify caused her to stop. She held the *montaria* utterly still behind some dense brush and, camouflaged by the mud she had already applied to herself, watched, deeply afraid, as four large *inyahns*, each having three Indians, paddled upstream, unaware they were passing within fifty feet of her. She was sure they were Nhambiquara.

Late in the afternoon of the fourth day, certain that by now she had somehow managed to pass the Nhambiquara stronghold unnoticed, she was looking for an *igaripe* to head into for the night. As she began rounding a bend in the river she saw, a quarter mile ahead, a suspension bridge much like the one at Kaumo, but in better condition. Instantly she reversed direction and, when the bridge was out of sight, moved in toward shore and stopped, clinging to the vegetation along the left bank to keep from drifting. Her heart was hammering wildly and for the moment she was verging on panic. If the bridge was there, then almost certainly a village was nearby as well.

"Think, Sarah, *think!*" The words were in her mind, but they were in the voice of her father and she calmed herself with an effort, taking deep gulping breaths as her pulse gradually slowed. She thought.

Turning the *montaria* around and paddling upstream was no answer. Where would she go? It had been about an hour since she passed the last *igaripe*. It would be dark before she could get there. Even if she could find it in the darkness, the problem would still exist. Sooner or later she would have to pass the village. Besides, she had seen the four *inyahns* moving upstream. Suppose they came back? She shivered at the thought. There seemed to be only one answer: attempt to float past the bridge — and the village, if there were one — unnoticed.

Sarah considered holding on here, waiting until after dark, but then where would she be? There would be no way of finding safe shelter after dark and Juma's warning of the dangers of nighttime travel on the river haunted her. No, she had to pass now. If she could do that without being seen, she could then find a safe place for the night somewhere below before darkness set in in earnest.

A sick dread filling her, Sarah relinquished her hold on the vines and paddled to midstream. There she put all her strength into the strokes and the light boat surged forward, once bumping slightly as it touched an underwater obstruction. Less than three minutes from that time she was approaching the bridge. Where it attached to a great tree on the west bank there was an insignificant clearing and no one in sight there. On the east, however, the clearing was expansive and ten or twelve canoes, both *montarias* and *inyahns*, were drawn up on shore. A large palm-thatched shelter was there as well, a simple affair of four posts with a framework at the top over which palm fronds had been overlapped. A broad path led eastward into the forest.

Two Nhambiquara Indians were by the canoes — a man and a woman — engaged in unloading some fish and two large clumps of bright yellow *pacovas* from one of the *inyahns*. Their backs were turned toward the river and, for a moment, Sarah thought she might be able to slip past them. In the next second, her worst fears were realized — not only did the two on shore turn and see her, but from around a bend a thousand yards downstream, three *inyahns* hove into view, four men in each.

In that fractional space of time Sarah's mind raced, but she became outwardly calm. A bit of dialog from some nearly forgotten conversation with her father came to her. "People tend to be afraid of people who are afraid of them," Ian Francis had said. "Even if you're scared silly, don't let it show. Meet them head-on with a friendly attitude and they're likely to respond in kind."

On the heels of that thought her paddle strokes changed and the *montaria* angled directly toward the landing. As the two Nhambiquara stood watching, stunned, she ran the canoe ashore beside their *inyahn* and stepped out, smiling. She spoke in Juma's tongue, hoping they would understand her.

"Hello," she said boldly. "My name is Sa-rah."

Chapter Eleven

THE NHAMBIQUARA MAN was well built and middle aged, with small yellow straws protruding from holes in his nasal septum and upper lip. He wore a necklace and bracelets of human teeth, but his face and body were neither stained nor tattooed. The expression of complete surprise remained on his face.

"It is just a *kunyimuku*," he said wonderingly.

The woman with him did not reply and Sarah saw she was quite young, no more than three or four years older than Sarah herself. In front of her, the woman held a stick upon which were three fair-sized fish, impaled through the gills, one of them still flopping weakly. She dropped them and Sarah saw she was in an advanced state of pregnancy. She wore no ornamentation of any kind and both she and the man were nude except that, in addition to his necklace and bracelets, he wore a waist-band of thin knotted vine to which a knife was attached. His hand was hovering close to the weapon. When he spoke again it was softly, the incredulity still strong in his voice.

"*Tameh ekyheyeh hychuy*" — You are not afraid of us. It was a statement, not a question.

Still with what she hoped was a pleasant expression, Sarah shook her head. "No, I am not."

His hand fell away from near the knife and a faint smile moved his mouthcorners. "I am Epini," he told her, "and this is my daughter, Garca."

The young woman also smiled faintly and cocked her head to one side. "I do not know such a name as Sa-rah," she said, "but I like it."

"*Apotare haho heiruchuy?*" — Do you want to go with us? Epini put it as a question, but Sarah had the feeling that at this point she really did not have much choice in the matter. Though she was uncertain about what lay ahead, at least they had not killed her immediately and in that there might be hope. Ridiculously, the thought sprang into her mind, *Yes, take me to your leader*, and her smile became more genuine. She merely nodded.

Epini took his blowgun out of the *inyahn* and handed it to Garca, who had picked up the fish dropped a moment ago, so that she could carry it as well. He then gripped the two heavy clusters of *pacovas*, placing one under each arm. He tilted his head toward the broad path.

"Marec, our village, is this way."

He strode off. Garca indicated that Sarah should follow and she fell in behind. The three *inyahns* from downstream were just putting in to shore as Sarah and the others lost sight of the river. Within a minute they came to an expansive clearing dominated by such an imposing structure that Sarah sucked in her breath. It was a rectangular building about one hundred feet long and sixty wide. The top of its peaked roof was very nearly a hundred feet high. Thatched with palm fronds dried to a light tan, the roof sloped very steeply and its lower edges were no more than three feet above the ground. A peculiar latticework of neat design covered the entire front of the structure except for the spacious, open doorway.

"This is our *maloka*, where all our people live," Epini explained.

A number of children were crawling or playing on the bare earth before the *maloka*, and as soon as they saw the trio approaching they let out a cry that brought a large crowd of people streaming out of the doorway. Like Epini and Garca, they were naked except for waistbands on the men. They were all talking at once and one of their number, a heavily muscled man of about fifty, stepped forward. His cheekbones were not prominent, nor were his black eyes in the least oblique. His features were strong and his expression, at the moment, was stern.

"Who is the one with white skin?" he demanded of Epini.

"A *kunyimuku* named Sa-rah, Chamakani. She was in an Aramoki *montaria*, going downstream. She understands our words."

"You have white skin," Chamakani said severely, "but you are Aramoki."

"No," Sarah spoke up, "I am not Aramoki. I come from far away. A different country. I became lost in the forest and Juma found me above the great *pancanda*. He is Aramoki. He took me to his village, Kaumo, but I became afraid there and took his *montaria* and came downriver."

"You did this by yourself?"

"Yes."

Chamakani was impressed and there was a murmuring from the crowd which silenced as the headman continued. "Why did you flee from them?"

Sarah hesitated. "It is as I have said — I was afraid."

"What made you afraid?"

This time her hesitation became a long pause. Beside her, Epini placed the bananas he was carrying on the ground. Garca put the fish down beside them and Epini's blowgun across the two clumps of fruit. Sarah felt the fear rising in her again. She put it down with great effort. Suppose these Indians were also cannibals? She steeled herself to reply honestly but before she could speak, Chamakani prompted her.

"*Tameh ekyheyeh hymbireta,*" he told her gently: Do not be afraid of my people. "We will not harm you. Why were you afraid with the Aramoki?"

"They buried a man alive!" Sarah blurted. "And they killed another one. They cut that one into pieces and were starting to cook him. They were going to *eat* him."

"What was his name?" The question came sharply from Epini.

"I don't know. They didn't say. He never spoke."

"How did they kill him?" It was Chamakani speaking again.

"A . . . a dart, tipped with *wourali.*"

"What did the man look like?" Epini asked, his manner tense.

Behind them, from the trail leading to the river, emerged the dozen men whom Sarah had seen coming from downstream. They stood silently, listening to the exchange.

"He wasn't very old," Sarah said. "Just a young man and he had a big crooked scar. Here." She indicated her abdomen and side with a diagonal movement of her hand. Instantly there was a gasp from Garca and her father placed a hand on her upper arm. The crowd rumbled, and Chamakani's features tightened.

"That was Iwuateh. He was Garca's *berekauh*."

Sarah was shocked and she turned and took Garca's hand. "I'm so sorry," she said softly. "I didn't know he was your husband."

"Bring the white girl inside," Chamakani said. He turned and moved through the crowd into the *maloka* with most of the gathering following him. Several of the women came to help carry the bananas and fish. One of them led Garca into the dwelling.

"Come with me," Epini directed Sarah, now carrying his own blowgun. He walked toward the *maloka*, Sarah after him. It was very dim inside and a bit smoky. The interior was one huge room and the high roof was held up by a series of smooth straight tree trunks, each about a foot in diameter and without bark. Crossbars from these, of smaller timbers, helped support the roof sides. Numerous small fires burned at intervals along each side and Sarah saw that each, apparently, was the fire of one family and that all the Nhambiquara lived inside this same building. Each family had as its quarters a compartment of the same size and shape. A larger compartment at the rear belonged to Chamakani and his family.

The two hours that followed were a period of penetrating questions put to Sarah as she sat on the dry, hard-packed earth in the center beside Epini, with most of the men and some of the women seated in an expanding rectangle around them. They wanted to know everything about her: where she had come from, how she came to be in the rain forest, how she had managed to survive her long stay with Juma at the falls and, especially, her brief time with Juma at Kaumo. Chamakani reiterated that they would not hurt her, although he pointed out that had she attempted to flee from them at first encounter she would probably have been killed.

Long before the questioning was over it had become dark and, while some light came from the many flickering family fires, the middle portion, where Sarah was being questioned, was illuminated by the burning of a succession of cherry-sized fruits from the *ucu-uba* tree. That fruit had a paper-thin brown shell. When fire was touched to it, it burst into a bright flame which sizzled and popped giving off a sooty smoke and a material which often dropped in small burning globules to the ground. Each of the fruits would burn for about five minutes. A dozen of them, impaled on the long spine of a *javary* palm, having one end lighted, produced a fine torch that burned for an hour without attention. Eight of these torches were lighted, illuminating the big room rather nicely.

Sarah was fed well — fruit, meat and fish, along with a strange mealy sort of bread. She was not sure what she was eating but didn't really care. It was filling and tasted good and that was all that mattered for the time being. The questioning continued as she ate but, upon finishing, an encompassing drowsiness came over her. The full stomach was gratifying, making her cozy and comfortable. The experiences she had endured left her emotionally drained and her head kept nodding. At last Epini led her to his compartment along one wall and she stretched out there beside Garca. She was asleep by the time she had drawn her second breath.

In the days and weeks that followed, Sarah learned a great deal about the Nhambiquara. She learned that the eating of human flesh was by no means unknown here among her new friends, but it was far more a ritual process than among the Aramoki, who ate it whenever possible — not only ritually, but as a food source. Among the Nhambiquara, three different parts of an enemy were eaten if that enemy were a famous leader or an especially brave fighter. The men would eat the enemy's heart to give them the enemy's strength and the brain to give them his wisdom, while the women would eat the genitals to acquire greater fertility. Nor was the process of burial alive unknown to the Nhambiquara.

Such burial was reserved for those who requested it because they could no longer take care of themselves, usually as the result of incurable illness or injury, or because of advanced age. It was considered an honorable and even desirable form of death, but was never forced upon anyone. When it was explained fully to Sarah it seemed to make more sense than her own civilized people's manner of keeping the very ill and hopelessly incapacitated alive through technology long after they should have died normally or long after they wanted to die.

During these weeks Sarah and Garca became very close. As much as she had previously learned from Juma, she learned far more from Garca and her parents, Epini and Kolliri. Garca often took the time to explain things to her in great detail and, once again, Sarah was like a sponge, absorbing the information and retaining it with a facility that surprised the Nhambiquara. She had become something of a celebrity and was always treated respectfully by everyone. About a hundred persons lived in the huge *maloka* and it was difficult, at first, for her to get over the discomfiture produced by being among so many people who did not wear clothing, but before long she hardly noticed.

On the second day her swollen big toe had become worse and was very painful. She limped badly and Garca shook her head after examining the toe closely.

"*Chigoe*," she said. "It will get worse unless we take it out."

"But what is it?" Sarah asked. "I don't remember sticking a thorn in my foot or anything like that. What's a *chigoe*?"

"It is a tiny creature, Sa-rah. So small you can hardly see it. It lives in dirty places and waits for people to pass. Then it climbs up on their feet and burrows in under a toenail. That is why we keep our ground clean. We do not often get them here, but our warriors who attack the Aramoki sometimes come back with them. That is probably where you got this one. In Kaumo. They are very bad. Once under your toenail it lays eggs. That is what is causing the pain. The eggs swell up like a little bean and they must be taken out quickly. If they hatch, the little *chigoes* eat the flesh and spread farther and deeper and become very bad. Some people who did not take them out right away have died."

"Can you take them out of my toe?" Sarah was very concerned.

"No, I cannot, but our *paje* can." The *paje*, Sarah knew from Juma, was a sort of medicine man.

"It is very painful," Garca continued, "but we have something that will ease that pain for you. It is called *parica*."

She gave Sarah a small cup of the pasty material, greenish-yellow in color, which she instructed her to eat. Sarah scooped it out on the blade of her pocketknife and tried it. The taste was bitter and rather nauseating. Only with difficulty was she able to down it. In ten minutes or less she was enveloped in a strange sense of euphoria, aware of what was going on around her but largely numbed to outside physical sensation. When Sarah had finished, Garca summoned the *paje*, who came with a small reed basket. As if in a dream, Sarah watched him spread a foot-square mat of woven grasses and place his instruments on it — a sharp, thin-bladed knife, a clump of *kahpahk*, a rattle made from a gourd, a vessel of watery brown liquid and a long, thin black thorn.

The *paje* was a wizened old man with deeply wrinkled skin and bright black eyes. Sarah expected he would be toothless but when he smiled she saw that his teeth, though stained purple, were in very good shape. He shook the rattle over her foot several times, muttering strange incantations Sarah could not follow. He picked up the knife — a hammered piece of metal affixed in a handle — expertly sliced the tip of her toe, penetrating a half-inch into the flesh. Blood spurted and Sarah jerked at the sight of it, though she felt no more than a slight stinging sensation. The *paje* chanted in a singsong manner as he dipped a clump of the *kahpahk* into the brown liquid and applied it to her toe. Very quickly the bleeding and stinging stopped. He continued the sound as he peered into the wound and nodded in a satisfied way. He then dipped the black thorn into the liquid and thrust it up in the wound toward the toenail, probing carefully. Very skillfully he worked out a white pea-sized nodule.

"That is the *chigoe* and her egg-bag," Garca whispered. "The *paje* must be very careful not to break it and set the eggs loose. If that happens, then each will hatch and cause even more trouble."

Sarah breathed a sigh of relief as the egg sac was removed unbroken and tossed into the fire. The *paje* daubed the whole wound again with the brown liquid, pushed the edges of the incision together and wrapped *kahpahk* around the whole toe, tying it snugly with supple palm fiber.

"For two days," he instructed Sarah, "you will have pain, so you must eat a little more of the *parica* each time it hurts. Do not walk for five days after that and then you will be well."

It happened as he said. It was almost more than she could bear for Sarah to eat the pasty *parica* and each time she put it off until the pain became all but unbearable, then ate a small portion. It always made her feel sick, but after a while the nausea would pass and the pain was gone. By the end of the week the wound was fairly well healed and she could walk again.

During the time Sarah was off her feet, Garca cared for her in a very competent manner and was insatiably curious about Sarah's past life and the wonderful and strange civilization she had come from. Others of the Nhambiquara, men as well as women and children, were always hovering close to hear her talk and answer their questions. They were a simple, basically happy people with a great deal of affection for one another and with strong family ties.

One of the peculiarities of these people was that whenever the men had to make long trips, which they seemed to do frequently, this was indicated by a swelling of one cheek. To Sarah, it looked as if an epidemic of abscessed teeth had settled in. She soon discovered the swellings were caused from a strange concoction prepared from certain leaves; a concoction held in one cheek.

"It is called *coca*," Epini explained to her one day, when she asked about the lump in his cheek. "I am going away to hunt in the forest for a few days. The *coca* keeps me from becoming tired and does not let me become hungry. Therefore I can hunt more and go farther and not have to stop so often. And if my hunting is successful, it lets me carry loads of meat home which I could not carry except with the help of *coca*."

Together, Epini and Garca showed her how it was made. The main ingredients were the leaves of the *coca* bush and the *setico* tree. First the fresh *coca* and *setico* leaves were hung near the fire until dry and brittle and then pounded into a rough powder in a bowl. To this were added the ashes of burnt begonia leaves and the whole mass was then placed in a sack of finely woven, very tough grasses. The sack was tied to the end of a stick and thrust deep inside a smooth wooden cylinder. It was banged back and forth against the walls of the cylinder and a refined powder seeped out through the sack fibers, falling to the bottom. This powder, scooped up on a bone carved into a spoon, was put into one side of the mouth where it became an oblong, rather nauseating looking lump. It gradually dissolved and was swallowed with the saliva.

"We always use it on our way to fight our enemies, too," Epini told Sarah, "for in using it we not only do not suffer hunger or fatigue, but it also takes away the pain of any injuries we receive in the fighting."

The *coca* did not seem to diminish any awareness on the part of the user, nor in any other way have possibly harmful side effects. The same was not true of the beverage they drank called *kaapi*. This was evidently some sort of hallucinatory drug, for when the men drank it they became not only mildly intoxicated, but also went into a sort of ecstatic delirium.

"Have you ever tasted it, Garca?" Sarah inquired. "What's it like?"

Garca rolled her eyes and shook her head. "Do not even think it, Sa-rah," she replied. "It is not allowed that women ever drink *kaapi*. We are not even allowed to touch with our fingers the vessels and implements used to prepare it. It is said we would die if we did so."

"But how is it made, Garca? What does it come from?"

"It is first a root, but we are not told of what tree or plant. That is forbidden, too. The roots are pounded by the men until they are shredded and they are thrown into the *kaapi* bowls — very special bowls with red and white designs of great mystery. Such bowls must never be washed. They must not even be emptied all the way. Not ever. I do not know all that is done to the crushed roots, but water is added to them and something else and they are allowed to stand for a long time, until the liquid smells very strong. Then it is dipped out in small portions and drunk by the men. My father says it is the most bitter thing he has ever tasted, but it also makes him feel as he has never felt before and see things he has never seen before."

"It also," said Epini, who had just come up to them from somewhere in the dim interior of the *maloka*, "allows us to see into places far away and know what is happening there." He had returned from his hunt in five days, he and his companion having almost filled their *inyahn* with the meat of tapir and monkey from far downstream. "When Chamakani last drank some," he continued, "he spoke of the dreams it gave him and he told of being in the land far toward where the sun rises where a tribe called Pira Parana lives. He said that even while he watched, their headman, Choluyac, had suddenly fallen over and died. Only a few days ago we learned from a messenger from that tribe that this was what happened, on the very day that Chamakani drank the *kaapi*. We do not drink it often. Too much can kill the drinker. But we drink it on special occasions. Soon we will be having such an occasion and you will see."

"What is happening then?" Sarah asked.

"Many of our men are preparing to go to war and it is important to hold the dance first."

"Why do you war with the Aramoki or other tribes, Epini?" Sarah questioned, "Isn't there any way you can make peace?"

"They make war on us and so we make war on them,

Sa-rah," he said. "It has always been so. When they were stronger they killed and ate many of our people. Now we are the stronger. After our last attack on them we left them very weak and we were content to make war on them no more. Garca's husband, Iwuateh, was sent to them to make offering of peace, but they killed and ate him. This calls upon us to avenge his death."

"But you prefer peace and harmony, don't you?"

"Of course, but sometimes our enemies do not allow us peace and harmony. Sometimes even our own people break our rules by which we live and must be punished."

"Do you have many rules, Epini?"

"No, not many, and they are simple and obeyed." He paused a moment, thoughtfully, then continued. "I will tell you our rules as they are learned by all our children and obeyed by everyone. When everyone pleasantly obeys Chamakani — or whomever else might be leader — everyone enjoys perfect peace and quiet. Envy is a worm that gnaws and consumes the insides of him who is envious; therefore, he who envies another injures himself. He who kills another without authority or just cause condemns himself to death. It is very just that he who steals from his neighbor should be put to death. Thieves can demand no mercy nor is there any to be given. The man who is patient in adversity and kind at all times is noble and to be honored. Bravery is admirable, but foolhardiness inspires only contempt. The *paje* who is ignorant of the medicine and the virtue of herbs necessary for him to use must learn all, until he knows well the plants which are useful as well as those which are harmful. If he does not, he may no longer retain the honor of being *paje.* Drunkenness, anger and madness go together; the first two are self-inspired and to be stopped, but the last is perpetual and to be pitied. Those are the rules we live by and they are good. Now I must see to the meat we have brought back."

Throughout the remainder of that day and on the several days which followed elaborate preparations were made. Meat and fowl and a meal called *mandioca* were cooked together in great clay pots and set aside for later use. Large numbers of fish were smoked and hung on vines inside the *maloka* — children were kept busy swishing flies and other insects away with feathery palm fronds. Great quantities of *kaapi* were made, along with vessel after vessel of a sort of beer called *kashiri*. It was the *kashiri* which the women made. They also made large numbers of thin round cakes of mashed-together *mandioca, kara* — a white tuberous root — and *makashera*, a sort of sweet potato. These were baked on flat clay pans to the point where they were almost burned. Then, after they cooled, the women chewed them up but instead of swallowing, spit them out into the large vessels, to which a small amount of *pupunha* palm fruit, mixed with larger amounts of water, was added. With two days of fermentation, the brew was ready to be drunk. It was the most popular drink among the Nhambiquara.

When the festival preparations were almost completed Garca went into labor. That had been anticipated and a matting of palm screening was set up to enclose the compartment where Garca lived with her father and mother. No one was allowed to enter except members of the immediate family but, since Sarah had been more or less adopted into that particular family, she was allowed to stay. Epini at once set about digging a hole two feet deep near the outside wall. Garca's mother, Kolliri, tended to her daughter and Sarah helped wherever possible. Garca remained very calm, obviously suffering with the spasms, but rarely making any sound other than sucking in her breath.

Kolliri, a very heavy woman with round, genial face and pendulous breasts, would not allow Garca either to lie down or stop moving, nor would she allow her daughter anything further to eat or drink until after the birth. Kolliri walked her around the compartment until she was weary and then Sarah took over and walked with Garca, her arm around the pregnant woman's back to help support her. For hours they did this and, to help her through the time, Sarah kept her talking, asking her questions about childbirth and the raising of children.

"Why must we keep you moving, Garca?" Sarah queried at one point.

"It would be very bad to lie still, Sa-rah. The baby would be born lame or blind or otherwise not perfect." Garca shook her head and smiled. "Do not be concerned. It is tiring now, yes, but I will have much time later to rest. For eight days after the baby is born I must lie still and not be left alone. I hope it is a boy who will grow up to become like Iwuateh. He was a good man."

Tears began filling her eyes at thought of him and Sarah steered the conversation to another subject. "How long is it before anyone else here will be allowed to see the baby, Garca?"

"There is no time to wait. They can come and see the

baby as soon as it is born, and when they come they will bring little gifts which I am to keep for him." She paused briefly, gasping, then moved on and continued. "But all who come will enter the doorway quickly and not stand in front of it. If someone stands in the doorway, the child will get a cloud in his eye."

"Will you feed him your own milk?"

"Yes — for two rainy seasons and two dry seasons. After a while, even though he is still feeding from my breast, once each day I will give him a mixture of honey and *ukubu*, which is the urine of a small boy. That is very important for him to become strong and clever."

"Well, at least during those eight days you will be able to get a lot of sleep."

"No! I am not allowed to sleep in the daytime. If you sit by me and talk, which I hope you will do, it will help to keep me awake. For those eight days I am allowed to sleep only at night. After that I may sleep anytime. That is when my feet will be tied up in palm leaves so that when I walk I will not get sickness through my feet and pass it on to the child through my milk."

"Have you picked out a name for the baby?"

Garca was shocked. "Oh, no. The baby will be named by my mother. If it is born at night, Kolliri will go outside to look at the stars. If it is not born at night, she will wait until darkness comes and then she will go outside and look at them. It is from how the night sky looks that the future of the baby is known, whether good or bad. A bright red star overhead is a very good sign and the baby will live long and become much loved and respected by all."

"Well, what kind of name will your mother give him?"

"If it is a boy, she will name him after someone very important, like Chamakani or the *paje* or after a great warrior. If it is a girl, she will name her after someone from our history who was very wise or someone who is famous or who is good and can heal and help people."

By the time Garca had been kept walking for five hours and the contractions were close together but still the baby had not been born, both Kolliri and Epini were becoming concerned. Epini went out and came back with a log which he placed on the floor. They directed Garca to climb upon it and jump off, time and again, not cushioning the impact with bent knees, but striking the ground stiffly, jarringly. Sarah held Garca's hand as she did this to help prevent her falling and Garca spoke through clenched teeth.

"I hope the little one comes soon. If it does not, they will have to do more to make it come out."

Sarah didn't think she really wanted to know what these measures would be, but still heard herself asking how.

"They will take my shoulders and shake me very hard. Sometimes this causes the nose to bleed very much and hurts the head. If still it does not come, I will have to drink *kuhehku*, which is made of chopped up pieces of bird feathers mixed with sweet oil from the *ruhtuk* tree and wax from honeycombs which has been broken into little bits."

Fortunately, the treatments Garca mentioned were not necessary. Just short of six hours from the onset of labor, delivery began. Kolliri put Garca into a sitting position on the log and instructed Sarah to get behind and help hold her up. She rocked the lower part of Garca's body on the log until the baby's head appeared, held it gently until the shoulders were free and then supported shoulders and head simultaneously while the rest of the baby slipped out easily.

At once the baby — a girl — began crying. Kolliri and Epini smiled and she handed the infant to him carefully, making certain no part of the child or her umbilical cord touched the ground.

"If the little one should touch the ground at all at this time," Kolliri told Sarah, "she would forever be unhappy." She cut the cord so that it was very long and this portion too Epini took carefully in hand to prevent its brushing the earth. He set the infant in a large bowl having an inch or so of tepid water and held her firmly as Kolliri bathed her, both of them being very careful that not a single drop of water touched her head. This accomplished, they wrapped the baby in a soft covering of barkcloth. Kolliri handed the bundle to Garca who eagerly held her new daughter to her left breast and guided the nipple into her mouth. The crying ceased as the baby suckled, comforted not so much by the colostrum seeping into her mouth as by the very act of sucking.

Garca made no effort to rise from the log but remained sitting, legs spread wide. The babe's sucking caused the uterus to contract and the spasm delivered the placenta. This too, Kolliri took into her hands and handed to Epini, who washed it thoroughly in several changes of water, beginning with the water in which the infant had been bathed. While he was doing this, Kolliri hovered near her daughter and granddaughter, making elaborate artificial motions of sewing the infant's mouthcorners closed, telling Sarah this was so the mouth would remain permanently small. In order to accomplish this, the baby was forced to stop nursing for a few minutes, giving vent to her displeasure in resounding squawks.

As soon as Epini completed washing the placenta, it was sewn shut by Kolliri, placed into the hole Epini had dug at the onset of Garca's labor and the successive bowls of water used to wash it were poured over the top. Into the same hole a small amount of *coca* powder was sprinkled. Then special leaves, twigs and small nuts were dropped in and the whole collection was buried.

Sarah had assisted, after the expulsion of the placenta, by washing Garca thoroughly and now the new mother and daughter lay together where Garca normally slept. She was making a crooning sound and the baby was still suckling happily.

"She needs to suck," Garca told Sarah who had come to sit beside her. "It does not matter that no milk is there yet. When the time is right, the milk will come."

Sarah nodded and watched as Kolliri went out the palm-matting doorway, announcing she was going to consult the clear, star-studded sky for auguries.

"Will she be gone very long?" Sarah asked Garca.

"No. She will know quickly. Then she will return and announce what this little one will be called."

"What about the cord? I noticed it was very long. Doesn't it have to be tied off or something?"

"In three days, when it has dried, it will be cut off close to her. A small piece of it will be given to me and I will keep it for a year. The rest will be burned." Garca looked at Sarah and smiled. "It is night and I am very tired. I think I will sleep now."

Sarah was both shocked and pleased when Kolliri returned and declared with evident pride that Garca's daughter was born under an auspicious sky, that she would always be very happy and have a tiny mouth — and that her name was Sa-rah.

It was, Sarah thought, unfortunate that Garca, because of her confinement, had to miss the festival. Held two nights later, it was an unusual and exciting event. By late afternoon a wide variety of foodstuffs had been placed in baskets of different shapes made from flattened *maranta* stalks, and on *pacova* leaves and plaited rush mats called *tupe*, at the end of the room toward Chamakani's compartment. There were *abacates*, oranges, pineapples, papayas, melons, squash, breadfruit, beans, mangoes, bananas and *ignames* — a sort of yam. In addition there were scores of calabashes, specially blackened and polished on the inside, to be used as drinking cups. They would be dipped by the participants into the dozen large vessels called *tucanas*, each containing about twenty gallons of *kashiri* — there were also vessels containing *kaapi*, but fewer in number since only the men would be drinking that. There were great varieties of fish, smoked and baked; dozens of large turtles called *pitiu*, which had been roasted in their own shells, the shells then split; a multitude of meat chunks from tapir and armadillo, agouti and sloth, peccary and paca and capybara; a half hundred or more roasted birds, blackened on the outside, juicy and sweet within.

A whole series of musical instruments had been placed at intervals and the afternoon was broken by a weird and raucous series of trillings and tootings, rattlings and thumps as each was tested for the night's performance. There were two types of drums, both made with stretched animal skins; one of these tautly covered the open end of a hollow log upon which a drummer would sit and tap it with his fingertips and knuckles; the other was hide stretched tightly over a wooden hoop. This latter instrument, when slapped with the hand or thumped on the knee, had a peculiar high taborlike tone. Large calabashes, each with dried ivory nuts inside, produced rattling sounds, high pitched or low, depending upon the size of the calabash and its contents. Numerous bamboo panpipes were there, some with as few as three tubes, others with as many as eleven, each tube producing a single note and, when played in succession, producing a haunting, eerie sound. Another pipe, a single piece of reed with one end plugged, sounded much like the piccolo. The *turé* was a single large horn constructed of a long, thick section of bamboo tapering down to a small mouthpiece in which there was a split reed, and the notes it gave off were deep and mournful. Finally, there were some very unusual trumpets, each having a hollowed *pashiuba* palm mouthpiece lengthened by rolls of thin bark. These instruments came in pairs with each pair different in size and the notes of each instrument mellow and true and individual in its tone. When played in concert, they seemed to trigger a vestigial, primitive emotion in Sarah.

An hour before sunset everything was in readiness and the Nhambiquara emerged from their separate compartments. The men still wore nothing except a string around the waist, but now it was a gaily beaded one of tiny fruits and nuts in bright reds, greens, yellows and browns. Some of the men had their entire faces and bodies coated with bright red *carajuru* powder spread on them by the women. Atop the red color they had been painted with blue dye from *senipapo*, applied by twig brushes marking three parallel lines at each stroke. Those men not colored this way had daubs and streaks of deeper red *ucuru* dye on their bodies and wore necklaces of teeth from caimans, jaguars, peccaries and humans. Each wore, on one leg only, a circlet of rattles around the ankle, and a good many had red, green, yellow or blue macaw feathers in their hair. A few thrust such feathers into the permanent holes in their nostrils and lips. Some of the women were clad in loose skirts of colorful feathers and a few wore the dried horns of huge *asserador* beetles around their necks, but the majority wore nothing except anklets and bracelets of shiny berries, small black nuts, and teeth. None of them were painted. Those with infants carried them in basket-weave containers called *aturas* slung on their backs and secured over the mother's forehead with a broad, tightly tied ribbon made from the soft inner bark of the *monguba* tree. The children sat grouped to one side, some of them painted and ornamented like their parents and almost all of them wearing necklaces and bracelets of the polished wood of the *tucum* palm and the strung molars of small mammals.

The women sat in an elongated oval in the center of the *maloka* while the men formed a line around them, twelve feet away. A drum began to throb and pipes tweedled sweet clear notes. A dozen torches of *ucu-uba* fruits were lighted and began to sizzle and drip flaming stearine drops to the floor where they continued to burn until they were ash. The air became hazy with smoke.

The lights attracted mosquitoes. They were bothering Sarah badly until Epini called to his wife, whereupon she brought him a dark, green-skinned fruit the size of a plum. Sarah had seen many of them on the forest floor and had, before meeting Juma, cut one open to see if it were edible. It had smelled slightly repulsive and the white pulp did not look appetizing, so she had thrown it away untasted. Now Epini showed her the fruit, calling it *genipapo*. He cut it in half and instructed her to rub the juicy pulp on her skin wherever she was being bitten. She did so and not only experienced relief from the bites already suffered, but the mosquitoes no longer landed upon her at all. It was a better repellent than the commercial cream she had been using — its only drawback was that it turned her skin a faint blue.

"That is no problem," Epini told her. "As long as the skin is blue, no insects will trouble you. They do not like it. In five days the blue will peel away, leaving your skin as before, taking away even the black spots left by *pium* bites. Then you can put it on again as you need it. Always keep one or two *genipapo* in your pouch."

It was good to know and Sarah resolved to get some of the fruit the next day. She returned her attention to what was going on inside the *maloka*.

Seated on the floor between Chamakani and Epini,

Sarah had already been given a large quantity of *kashiri* to drink from a calabash and her ears were buzzing, her face flushed with excitement. Both men were sharing a gourd-shaped pipe with a long slender mouthpiece into which they first blew with a great puff of the cheeks before sucking in smoke.

Chamakani gave a signal with one hand and a slender young man of about twenty-five strutted forward importantly into the space between the men and women. On his left arm was a shield woven of thin bamboo strips on a framework and interlaced with long colorful plumes. In his right hand he held a long, beautifully polished war lance, the tip sharply pointed and barbed, hung with other feathers and the opposite end bell shaped, containing seeds which rattled as he struck the shaft of the lance against his shoulder with every fourth step.

This dance master began a lilting sort of chant that silenced the instruments, the chant then picked up by the men, who repeated it with intermittent stampings of their rattled left legs. In perfect cadence they raised bamboo staffs with large thick ends and thumped them to the floor with heavy thuds. One by one as he passed them, the men began falling in behind him, imitating his movements and cries, striking the ground harshly with each step of the right foot. A strong beat established itself and stirred the listeners, many of whom swayed to it.

Sarah herself experienced a strong atavism and felt her own body swing to the primitive throbbing rhythms. At first the chanting sounds had been unintelligible to her but soon she began to understand the words and strained to hear them better. In perfect accord the chant was made, enlarged by the voice of each man who newly stepped into the line.

> *Come, little sisters, come.*
>
> *Our faces and bodies are painted with beautiful colors and designs.*
>
> *Come little sisters, come.*
>
> *We have donned the plumage of all the wondrous birds of the forest.*
>
> *Our shoulders are covered with the teeth of the jaguar, who prowls through the forest at night, and with teeth of Huitoto, whose bite is even worse.*
>
> *Come, little sisters, come.*
>
> *The birds and beasts of the jungle could not escape us; they flew or ran but our darts and arrows were quicker.*
>
> *We are the Nhambiquara. We are the men.*
>
> *Come, little sisters, come.*

When the chant ended, all the men were in the moving line and, at a given signal, the women raised their voices in a high trilling sound which continued until their breath was gone. The women then came to their feet and each selected a man with whom to dance, though by tradition the man could not be the woman's husband. Standing behind the man, the woman placed her right hand on his right shoulder and once again the line, now double, moved forward, swaying, stamping, shuffling, rattling, thumping until a full circle had been completed.

The sounds of the instruments rose as accompaniment and where before they had been cacophonic, they now merged in a wild primeval harmony and the dance pattern changed. A few men remained standing inside the circle, their voices raised in long quavering wails attuned to the pitch of the instruments, while the couples in line took three short sideways steps to the left, two steps marking time, three more steps backward and two to the right, repeating the whole movement over and again, the circle gradually enlarging until they were nearly to the compartments area. Finally, with a heavy thumping of the drum five times, the dance ended.

Bodies were streaming with perspiration from the efforts and all were talking at once. They crowded up to the food and drink, gulping down great draughts of *kashiri*. The food disappeared as if by magic — the men finishing their eating before the women began — and when all were filled, the dancing began once again, though not so extensively as before. When it was finished, copious amounts of *kashiri* were quaffed, with some of the men now beginning to imbibe *kaapi*.

Individual men moved in turn to the center of the room and regaled their audience with tales of their great prowess during hunts for peccary and jaguar and tapir, their fierceness in warfare, the number of heads taken as trophies. While this was going on, incredibly large cigars, two inches thick and up to three feet in length, were lighted and puffed upon, handed from man to man down the line.

By this time the *ucu-uba* fruits were burning out and new spikes of them were lighted. Heavy poles were driven into the ground in four places and coated thickly at the top with a viscous pitch which was set afire. The flames from these lighted the whole interior very brightly, causing great flickering shadows to dance macabre waltzes on the interior of the roof.

As consistently more of the *kashiri* was drunk, it became frequently necessary for the imbibers to go outside and urinate. The women moved out and in silently, but the men always announced their intentions loudly. A man would rise and give a semblance of a bow to his neighbors left and right.

"I will now," he would say in a formalized pattern, "leave your company and go forth into the night and pour out my stream of *ukubu* in the forest."

Invariably, the reply would be the same, given with inebriated gravity: "May you do so mightily."

Upon his return he would announce to each of his neighbors individually that he had, indeed, relieved himself mightily, whereupon the reply was always, "It is good that you have done so."

Late in the night Sarah sagged with weariness and, unknowingly, leaned against Epini and fell asleep. He placed an arm around her, sat quietly that way, taking *kashiri* when it was handed to him, but otherwise not moving.

Sarah awoke as dawn was breaking and still the festivities were continuing. Some of the assemblage had drunk themselves into a stupor, though not many, but among the men the *kaapi* had taken effect and they were speaking in elevated terms of wondrous things they were seeing and of the successes ahead. Talk of the continuing war with the Huitoto broke out and soon the younger men were leaving and walking into the darker portions of the great room, only to return moments later armed with javelins and shields, bows and blowguns. They gathered together under three or four separate leaders and enacted a mock attack upon the enemy, crouching, stalking, looking, creeping, finally rushing with maniacal cries to thrust and jab, aim and fire. It was all very confusing and terribly realistic; what had, at first, been exciting for Sarah, became terrifying and she cowered from the spectacle until once again Epini placed his arm about her shoulders and told her not to fear, that the frenzy of real attack was reserved for their enemies.

"Very soon," he told her, "nearly all of the young men you see here, as well as some of the old, will move again against Kaumo. The Aramoki are weak now and we would not have attacked them again, for they are no longer a threat to us, except that they killed and ate Iwuateh, husband of my daughter, and this calls upon us for revenge."

"Will you be going with them, Epini?" Sarah asked, her voice still frightened.

He threw back his head and laughed. "You did not understand from the dance? Not only will I go, I will be leading them!"

Chapter Twelve

It was the third day after the great festival held in the *maloka* that about half of the Nhambiquara men set off upstream on the Ituí to avenge the death of Garca's husband, Iwuateh. Where previously broad straws had been worn by each warrior in the holes of his lips and nasal septum, now these had been replaced by peccary tusks — a symbol of the march into battle. The whole population turned out to see the warriors go. Sarah was with them as they stood on shore and watched the five boats paddle off with strong coordinated strokes that sent their *inyahns* slicing neatly upstream through the strong current of the river. Each boat contained four or five warriors, all under command of Epini, who was in the lead boat. They expected to be gone for seven or eight days.

In the six weeks since she had been with them, Sarah had come to know practically everyone in the village, from the youngest to the oldest. She had also learned to appreciate their customs and culture. They were sensitive people, caring deeply for one another, imbued with intelligence and humor as well as courage. The many hours she had spent with Garca before and after the birth of little Sa-rah had been filled with talk and it came with something of a shock when Sarah realized that she could not only speak their language fluently, but could understand nuances that had heretofore passed unnoticed. She even found herself thinking in their language, since there were many concepts not literally translatable into English.

Much as she had learned from Garca and Epini, it was from Kolliri that she was gaining the deepest insights into the tribe and its customs. Sometimes Kolliri sat beside Sarah and Garca and talked for hours, holding the two enthralled with her stories of the past and her knowledge of this rain forest world. The customs and folklore of the Nhambiquara were her special interests and she loved to speak of them and answer questions about them. Sarah was especially interested in how the children were raised from infancy to puberty. Kolliri always had the answers. The customs were sometimes charming and sometimes deeply rooted in superstition and tradition. Yet, little by little, Sarah came to realize that even those that at first seemed the most outlandish often were based on very sensible foundations.

The fact, for example, that a baby must never be allowed to touch the ground or it would forever be unhappy was reasonable when its basis was understood. A wide variety of parasitic creatures, some relatively large and some all but microscopic, lived on and in the soil and babies were particularly vulnerable to them. *Chigoes*, such as the one dug out of Sarah's toe, were only one such creature, but there were many others of which to be cautious. Just as the earth was filled with potentially deadly or at least debilitating organisms, so too was water, and water was not allowed to touch a child's head before the age of three. Nevertheless, many of the beliefs were so alien to Sarah that it was difficult for her to grasp the basis for their having become custom.

That was brought home in force as Sarah and Kolliri walked slowly back to the *maloka* together after seeing the warriors off. While the boats had still been in sight, a peculiar bird, long-legged and essentially black, with a sharply curved beak, had alighted on a dead branch at the top of a tree across the river and issued a peculiar whining cry. Kolliri had looked stricken at the sight of it and Sarah asked why.

"That is the *caracara*," Kolliri told her. "Seeing one at any time is an omen of bad fortune. Seeing one at a time like this, especially when it gives that cry, is a warning that death will soon come to someone close."

There was nothing to say to that and they walked in silence, among the others, the remainder of the way back to the *maloka*, Kolliri steeped in thoughts about her husband, and Sarah filing away in her mind the belief about the *caracara*, to take its place with the other beliefs she had learned here. At the moment it seemed to make no sense to her but she was not prepared to scoff. Were she inclined to do so, all she had to remember was how at first she had thought the belief was ridiculous that a baby would be unhappy all its life if it touched the ground, until she correlated that belief with the fact of parasitic creatures on and in the earth. Nevertheless, this *caracara* belief just learned was no less mysterious to her than were many of the others.

If a pregnant woman lifted up a small child, for example, it was believed the child's nose would stop up. To circumvent such a possibility, the woman must lie on her back and put the child on her legs and then, holding its wrists, draw the little one up across her body to her face and then blow in its nostrils. During its first year, no child could be taken out into the field or forest, for then it would become ill, shrivel up and ultimately die. No child, until age three, could be allowed to look at anything dead, human or animal; but if it occurred, then the child, to preserve it from bad luck, had to be wrapped for two days in the twice sun-dried leaves of the *munu-maya* shrub. If a baby somehow came into contact with the ground, to forestall the unhappiness such an event augured, he or she was required to eat a mouthful of that soil; the earth itself was appeased by burying, on the very spot of ground the infant touched, such things as *coca*, *kashiri* and *kaapi*. Until the age of three, no child must be left alone at night, and until that age it must carry on its back a little bundle containing a small knife and various herbs to protect against ill winds. A child could not be permitted to cry overnight, for if it did so, *Lari-lari*, an impish spirit would come.

Not all of the beliefs involved children. Everyone in the village was firmly convinced of the actuality of the forest spirit *Cucupira*, the wild man who was said to be responsible for all unaccountable noises. This being was described in many ways, but most often as being essentially man-shaped, covered with reddish-orange shaggy hair and living in trees. Sometimes he was said to have a scarlet face and feet like a peccary. Often the Nhambiquara would tremble with fear at unknown sounds in the forest attributed to *Cucupira*, and to ward off danger from him they would plait young palm leaves into a circle and hang this ring from a branch in the path they had to walk.

When Sarah asked Kolliri where the tribe came from, she responded that long ago all the Indians of the forest had been of the same tribe. "But then there was strife and the people separated and went their own ways and learned to dislike one another and make war among themselves." She wagged her head sadly. "That is not a good thing, but that is the way it is and we must live with it. Before that split, when we were all one people, we came to this forest from a great water far toward the morning sun. To get there, one would have to travel many days down our river to where it joins a larger river, then down that one to where it joins the largest river anywhere. That river flows into the sunrise and finally pours itself into the great water which has no far shore. Once, long ago, a powerful monster from that water lived at the place where the largest river empties into the great water. He built a vessel and came up the river, bringing with him birds of many different kinds. After several weeks of travel he became stranded on an island and was surrounded by *jacares*, who lay in the water and showed him their big teeth and prevented him from leaving. He became hungry and knew he would soon die, so he breathed into the nostrils of each bird with him and set them free. They flew into the forest and while they stayed in the trees they remained birds, but when they touched the ground they became people, and that is how we began."

The caiman — *jacare* — was a crocodilian involved
as a major character in much of the Nhambiquara folklore. It was Chamakani who told Sarah the legend of
how the *jacare* almost succeeded in preventing man
from having fire.

"Long ago," he said, as he sat with Kolliri and Sarah,
while Garca nursed her infant, "the tribes in the forest
did not know about fire. But a great god sent fire down
to the earth for their use, giving it first to the Tarianos
who lived then on the Ariari River far to the north. All
the other tribes sent representatives to see this great
wonder. Then the *jacare* offered to take the fire and dis-
tribute it among the tribes so that all mankind could
have the benefit of it. The Tariano were foolish enough
to give it to him and when the *jacare* swam to the middle
of the river with it, he sank. All mankind grieved over
this loss and they asked the animals to help them get it
back. The frogs gave a banquet to which they invited
the *jacare,* but he was sly and came only to the door,
and when the frogs croaked too soon over their success
at luring him, he went away swiftly. Then mankind
asked the old lizard, who was the *jacare's paje,* to help,
and the lizard went to him. In the way medicine men do,
he blew and sucked all over the *jacare's* body, pretend-
ing to treat him for illness, but actually trying to discover where the *jacare* hid the fire. He found smoke,
but not the fire. Then the white *japo* bird, who is very
wise, offered to help, but even he could not find it.
Finally, mankind went to the black *japo* bird, who has
a curved beak, and by using this beak, the bird located
the fire in the very tip of the *jacare's* nose and the black

japo snatched it and returned to man. Since then we have been very careful with it and that is why we never allow the principal fire inside the *maloka* to go out."

The day after Garca's confinement ended, Sarah joined the majority of women and a number of men, including Chamakani, as they paddled downstream on the Ituí toward an extensive sandbar — called a *praia* — about a mile below the village landing. Garca and Sa-rah stayed behind at the *maloka* with some others. The group traveled in the remaining *inyahns* and *montarias*, leaving behind on the shore a post decorated with leaves and feathers tied to the top. This, Chamakani explained to Sarah, would tell the absent warriors where they had gone, if those men returned before the business on the sandbar was completed. That business was *pitiu eh kua praia*, a term Juma had once used and had not explained beyond the fact that it meant "turtle time on the sandbars." Now she would learn what it was.

On the way to the sandbar, Sarah rode in an *inyahn* with Kolliri and Chamakani and the leader's wife, Joli, along with a pleasant-looking, temporarily lame young man of about twenty named Puapeh. He was chatty and friendly and Sarah liked him very much. Several times already, Sarah had brought up with Kolliri and Epini the subject of getting back to her own people. Was she a prisoner here, or would the Nhambiquara help her get home? They were sorrowful that Sarah wanted to leave them. She had become well liked by them and the other Nhambiquara in Marec. They did not want to see her go but, no, she was not a prisoner here. She had come to them of her own will, a guest, and if it were her desire to leave, they would speak with Chamakani about it.

Now, Sarah having put the question to the headman, Chamakani's brow furrowed and he was not pleased. "Why," he asked, "would you want to leave us? Do you not like us?"

"I do like you, Chamakani, and I like Garca and Kolliri and Epini and the others, but I am lonely for my own people, just as you would be lonely for yours if you were to find yourself away from everything and everyone you knew."

Chamakani nodded slowly. "I can see that. Yes, any of us would be lonely without his family and his way of life. But we cannot take you back to your people. We do not travel above the *pancanda* upstream, which you saw, or below the dangerous *pedral pancanda* downstream." He referred to an area a week's journey down the Ituí, where the river squeezed between mountains and became a roaring rapids. "It is said that no *inyahn* or *montaria* which enters that water can ever return. Where the water goes after that, we do not know, but our legends say that again, in time, it becomes a river like this but larger. It is filled with many dangers. We know that far down that river there are other tribes and people whose skins are not white like yours, but with lighter skins than ours; they are people who cover their bodies. Sometimes these people have tried to come into our country and hurt us, but we have not allowed them to do this. They are dangerous. By throwing thunder they have killed a few of us, but we and our brother Nhambiquara from other villages like Marec have killed many of them and so they do not come anymore." His voice became sad and very serious. "They might hurt or kill you if they saw you."

The fact that the people Chamakani spoke of wore clothing and could "throw thunder" stirred an excitement in Sarah which she endeavored to hide, since those people were obviously enemies of the Nhambiquara. But clothing and guns meant a higher degree of civilization and Sarah was sure if she could get to them, then somehow she would get home. She kept her voice calm as she responded.

"I am glad you have warned me, Chamakani, but even if they are a danger, I will have to face it, if that is the only way to get back to my own people. Perhaps they fear you and would kill you if they could, just as the Aramoki do, but the Aramoki did not hurt me and you did not hurt me, so maybe the people below would not hurt me either."

"That is possible," Chamakani admitted, nodding at her logic, "but they are more powerful than the Aramoki and more dangerous and it would be a great risk for you. If you stayed among us you would be safe. Eventually one of our young men would take you as his wife — perhaps Puapeh —" the young man grinned at his chief — "and you would have a family here and forget your other life."

Sarah was touched by his earnestness. She noticed that both Kolliri and Joli had tears in their eyes and was taken by surprise at the emotion that rose in her own breast. They were good people, kind and simple and warm. The prospect of remaining with them was by no means abhorrent. Kolliri and Epini had become almost like parents to her and Garca like an older sister. She was sure she could be happy with them. After all, her father was dead and she certainly did not want to go live with her mother. Where, then, could she go if she did get back? The sort of life Chamakani and his people offered here could be very pleasant and she was sure she could adapt to it even better than she already had, but even as she thought of these things, Sarah knew she could not remain.

"It would be nice to stay here, Chamakani. Kolliri and Epini and Garca have become like my own family, but my heart tells me I have to leave. Will you help me?"

Chamakani nodded sorrowfully. "Yes. As much as we can. We can give you food and you can take the *montaria* you brought here, which we will mark. That way, other Nhambiquara you may meet will know you are not Aramoki and that you are under our protection and they will not harm you."

"When would you go away from us, Sa-rah?" It was Kolliri who spoke up now.

"Soon as possible, Kolliri, but not until after the warriors return. I would not go without first saying goodbye to Epini."

They were quiet for the remainder of the boat ride. The sandbar to which they paddled was the largest Sarah had yet seen, almost a mile long and sixty feet wide. A smaller one was located on the opposite bank, half the length and less than half the width. There were few *jacares* in this portion of the river, their lack due to little cover in which the caimans could hide to unexpectedly snatch prey. The sand was so white that at first it hurt Sarah's eyes from reflected sunlight.

The boats all put to shore and immediately men, women and children leaped out carrying baskets of various sizes. Sarah was strongly curious about what they were going to do. Right away they found several little excavations which looked to Sarah like rat holes. The men and women plunged their arms into the holes and in a couple of instances pulled out huge iguanas which were each, including the tail, close to five feet long. Others managed to escape, bursting up from the sand and running with great speed to the water where they plunged in and swam away quickly, followed by the laughter of those who had failed to catch them. Usually they swam on the surface, but two or three went beneath the surface. Their hind legs were long and powerful and often as they ran they leaped like frogs. The two captured iguanas were each tied by a hind leg in one of the boats.

"*Tyu-assu*," Chamakani told Sarah. "Very good to eat. We will keep them alive until we wish to eat them."

Very timid, they were nevertheless fearsome-looking creatures like miniature dragons, with an array of fleshy protuberances beginning at the back of the head and running all the way to the tail. Their green bodies were peculiarly flattened side to side, in a leaflike configuration. Diagonal dark stripes ran down the sides, giving the illusion of the ribs of a leaf and Sarah nodded when Kolliri told her that they spent most of their time in the trees and could hide among the leaves so well that it was very difficult to see them.

"Sometimes the *tyu-assu* sit on high branches over the river," Kolliri went on. "When they see a boat, they jump and hit the water with a big splash. It will frighten you much if you are in the boat and do not expect it."

"What kind of meat do they have?"

"You said you had eaten the large black bird called *piuri*, Sa-rah. It is like that in color and tastes almost that good. Its bones are like the bones of a bird."

"The *tyu-assu* are what we came here to get, then?"

"No. A few weeks ago this sand was underwater because the river was much higher. Then the dry season came and the river began to drop. This will last for four moons. Then the little rains we have now will become more and in six moons they will become every day and very heavy and the river will grow big again. But here, because the sand has come out of the water and it is now the time of *jahy uruahnhu*" — full moon — "it is time for the *pitiu*. They have come by many hundreds in the night and under the light of the *jahy* they have laid their eggs here."

Sarah looked around but could see no indication of turtle eggs. "Where are they, Kolliri, buried?"

"Yes, buried very well. We must look for them."

"How?"

"Come. I will show you."

As the others were already doing, she and Sarah walked through the sand. It was reasonably firm under their feet, but at one point Sarah's bare foot sunk nearly to the ankle and she gave an exclamation and jerked away.

"Ah, good!" Kolliri said. She called loudly, alerting

the others, then continued. "You have been first to discover where a *pitiu* has laid her eggs. That is a very good omen for you. It means you will have good luck for a long time to come. Since you are now determined to go away from us, I am happy it is you who found the first."

The others crowded around and Kolliri told Sarah that, having found the first turtle nest, it was her place to dig into it and find the eggs. "The sand will be soft and the eggs will be buried as deep as your elbow."

Sarah dropped to her knees and dug in the softer sand while those around her murmured happily and offered words of encouragement. The hole she made was not quite elbow deep when she encountered the eggs and drew out two of them. They were gray-white, perfectly round and about the size of golf balls. The shells were not brittle like that of a bird's egg but firm and elastic in character. Loud enthusiastic cries erupted from the crowd and Kolliri took one of the eggs from her, tore it open and poured off the albumen into the sand. The yolk, remaining in shell, she handed back to Sarah and told her to eat it. Sarah did so and found the taste not unlike the yolk of a hen's egg, but a bit oilier. She didn't think she would care much to subsist on them.

As Sarah ate the egg, Kolliri began digging in the same hole, bringing up three or four eggs with each handful. Others in the party were stepping about carefully, seeking the soft sand spots indicating more of the nests. They found one, then another, then a multitude. Soon nearly everyone was digging in his own nest hole. At the nest Sarah had discovered, Kolliri withdrew a total of one hundred thirty-one eggs and approximately as many were in each of the other nests.

The eggs were carried to the water in baskets and washed, then replaced in the baskets and taken to a special small *montaria* that had been towed along. There they were dumped into the bottom of the boat and two children, a boy and a girl about ten, rinsed their feet free of sand and stepped in among the eggs. Chanting in harmony they stamped on the eggs, crushing them and squirting their contents into the boat's bottom, then picking out the empty shells and throwing them away. As more eggs were collected they were washed and dumped into the boat, there to be crushed like the others. Hundreds were saved in baskets to be taken back whole, but thousands were put into the *montaria* for mashing. When they were finished, the yellowish mess in the canoe bottom was ankle deep and two inches of water was poured over them. It was then left to season in the direct rays of the sun.

They rested for several hours, eating and drinking, conversing and sleeping. In late afternoon they began stirring. A layer of oil, lighter than the water, had risen to the surface and was skimmed off with mussel shells and poured into clay vessels. This, Kolliri told Sarah, would be used for many purposes, among them lighting the interior of the *maloka*, rubbing down the skin of arms, legs, feet and hands to sooth cracks and insect bites, and soaking animal hides to soften them for tanning and for later use as pouches. In just such pouches brought along, the watery residue of yolk material was ladled carefully, and the pouches were tied shut with palm-frond fibers. This would be used later in cooking. When empty, the small boat was tipped on its side and thoroughly scrubbed out with sand and water.

When they returned to the village dusk was settling. Excitement had risen among the party when they discovered, at the landing, that the canoes of the warriors had returned. Everyone, including Sarah, was loaded with their day's efforts and moved quickly with their burdens to the broad clearing dominated by the *maloka*. A large fire had been built outside next to a pile of sand and some large flat stones. Warriors and a few women were clustered about it and one of the men, a squat, extremely broad-chested man stood and approached them. Chamakani stopped, Kolliri, Joli and Sarah behind him and the others clustered close behind them. Kolliri set down her load and put an arm around Sarah's shoulders, holding her close. The warrior had by this time stopped a few feet in front of the headman.

"Welcome home, Behtyuc," Chamakani said. "You brought war to our enemies?"

Behtyuc bobbed his head once. "We brought war to them."

"Do we rejoice or do we sorrow?"

"We have strong measures of each." The brawny warrior lowered his eyes a moment, then looked up again, his gaze steady on Chamakani's. "They were many more than we expected. The Aramoki were few, but their boy-man, Juma, had gone to the Huitoto village of Sehlok and more of them than there were of us had come back with him to fight us. Because of precautions taken by Epini, we surprised them and killed more than half. Those who were left then fled and we did not chase them. We brought back thirteen of their heads, including the old one, Jarana, of the Aramoki. The rest were mainly Sehlok."

"That is the news for rejoicing," Chamakani said, but his expression was grim. "Now tell me that which inspires sorrow."

"One of their warriors killed Epini."

Sarah sucked in her breath and the blood pounded in her temples. The grip of Kolliri's arm over her shoulder had tightened with pressure nearly painful to her and she looked up at the woman. The round face was expressionless but Sarah could feel the trembling that had struck her. The lips barely moved as she spoke.

"The black *caracara* cried as they left but I did not know he cried for my husband. Stay with Chamakani, Sa-rah. I must go to Garca."

She dropped her arm and moved with steady pace past the headman and warrior, looking neither left nor right. In a moment she had vanished into the dim interior of the *maloka*. Chamakani had heard what she said and stepped backward a pace, placing a hand gently on Sarah's shoulder. He responded to Behtyuc's remark with a single word.

"How?"

"As we were landing a lookout in a tree shot an arrow through his chest. Epini made no sound. He fell from the boat and did not come up. Though we later looked for his body, we could not find it. There are many *jacares* in the water. We think they found him."

Chamakani's eyes glinted overbright and when he spoke his voice was bleak. "The warrior who killed him?"

"I killed him with my javelin. He thought he was well hidden, but there was a small space between branches where the spear in my hand, tipped with *wourali*, could go and I sent it there. His life had gone away before his body fell."

"You brought his head?"

"I brought it."

"You will prepare it."

"The fire is ready, and the vessel. We waited only for you."

"Then begin. There will be no eating or sleeping until it is finished." Chamakani stepped closer to him and gripped his shoulders. "I commend your arm and your eye, Behtyuc. You have gained much honor for this and you now take Epini's place."

He leaned forward and placed his mouth to Behtyuc's nostrils and blew very hard. It was the greatest recognition that could be paid him, the headman having blown into the warrior all his strength and sagacity. There was a deep, approving murmur from the crowd and all knew what it meant. Though Kolliri was now without husband, Garca without father and Sa-rah without grandfather, all three women would hereafter be his responsibility and he would move with his wife and small son to Epini's quarters and care for them as Epini would have done. He would also assume Epini's role as the village's chief warrior. These were responsibilities he accepted with humility and gratitude.

"Assemble everyone," Chamakani said as he stepped back. "Form the ring. Let those with burdens," he continued, turning to face the party behind him, "place them where they belong and then join the ring. Then the preparation may begin."

There was a flurry of activity as the vessels and

pouches and baskets filled with oil and egg yolk and whole eggs were stowed away inside the *maloka*. At Chamakani's gesture, Joli and Sarah followed him into the structure and directly to Epini's compartment. Kolliri sat on the floor, one arm around Garca, whose head was against the large breasts and at whose own breast the infant Sa-rah was suckling. Both women's cheeks were streaked with tears, but they made no sound. Chamakani squatted before them and touched their heads in turn, including the baby's, then told them what Behtyuc had told him.

"I have blown into his nose, Kolliri," he concluded, "and Behtyuc will move into Epini's space with his family. Your families will merge and become one. He will hereafter provide for you."

Kollini nodded. "I and my family are honored. Our family strength will be increased and we are thankful."

"Come, then, to the ring where they are waiting. They have made ready the fire and the *hankeyaahn*."

They were the only ones left in the *maloka*. With gravity they walked outside, Chamakani and Joli leading, Kolliri and Garca, with the infant, next, then Sarah. It was getting dark but the fire shed considerable light. All the people of Marec had seated themselves in a ring around the fire, leaving room at one side for these six. Behtyuc was squatting beside the fire, which had been built upon white sand. He rose as they sat down, touching each of his new family in turn on the head, including Sarah.

Beside the fire were two *pacova* leaves with the head of the slain warrior who had killed Epini sandwiched between them, facing the fire. The fire itself had been built around an odd conical pot of red baked clay — the *hankeyaahn* — eighteen inches in diameter at the widest and eighteen inches high. It rested on its apex and had been propped upright with stones, allowing the flames access to the greatest possible surface. To Sarah it looked like a strange flowerpot of some kind. The pot had been a quarter filled with cold water straight from the river.

Facing the fire, Behtyuc took the covering *pacova* leaf off of the severed head. He set the head upright, propping it between his knees. Sarah, seated between Joli and Kolliri, was a dozen feet from where Behtyuc was kneeling and she was repulsed and thankful she could not see the head too well. Whatever gruesome thing they planned to do, she did not want to see it; yet, at the same time, she watched with morbid curiosity.

Behtyuc and the head were garishly illuminated in the flickering firelight and no one moved or spoke as he took the sharp-bladed *parati* from his waistband. He carefully parted the hair straight down from the crown to the base of the skull, then slit it to the bone all the way down the line of the part. Quickly and deftly he pulled the skin back on both sides and, using the knife sparingly, peeled it off the skull much as if he were pulling a stocking off his foot. He had to use the knife more frequently to cut tissues at the ears, eyes, nose and mouth. Flesh and muscles all came off with the skin, leaving the skull naked, with the eyeballs and teeth still attached to it.

From a basket beside him, Behtyuc took out a bamboo

needle and fine strong palm fibers and swiftly sewed up the incision he had made, leaving the neck opening untouched. Digging into the basket again he withdrew three thin two-inch bamboo splinters with which he impaled both lips to hold them together, tying the top portion of each sliver to the bottom with a strand of palm-leaf fiber. He then concentrated on the other openings, beginning with the eyeholes. The upper eyelids were pulled down. Tiny bamboo pegs, sharpened at both ends, had their lower ends stuck at the eyecorners and upper points used to prop up the eyebrows to keep them from falling into the eye cavities. The nostrils and ears were plugged with tightly rolled wads of *kahpahk*. The purpose of all this, Joli whispered to Sarah, was to hold the features in place during the succeeding operations.

"*Paranah!*" Behtyuc ordered, without looking up from his work. Immediately two men brought pots of water and filled the conical *hankeyaahn* to the brim. While they did so, Behtyuc filled the boneless head with dry sand from the pile beside him, stuffing the neck opening with great wads of *kahpahk* to keep the sand in and, in turn, holding the *kahpahk* from coming out by skewering the neck opening with a half-dozen intersecting bamboo splinters. He then dropped the prepared head into the water, eliciting a general satisfied sighing from the onlookers.

Within half an hour the water in the *hankeyaahn* had been brought to within a fraction of the boiling point. That was the critical moment. The head had to be removed before the water actually boiled or the flesh would soften and the scalp become scalded and cause all the hair to fall out, neither of which was desired. Forked out with a two-pronged stick, the object was exhibited by Behtyuc and there were loud cries of approbation. The head had shrunk to about one-third its original size.

Four men helped Behtyuc move the hot *hankeyaahn* onto a broad piece of bark and while one balanced it, the other three pulled on the bark, dragging it away toward the edge of the clearing.

"What are they going to do with it?" Sarah asked Joli, fascinated with all that was occurring. The initial revulsion she had felt was gone and she had become interested in this bizarre ritual.

"They are taking the *hankeyaahn* to the river and will throw it in when they get there." Joli's eyes were wide and bright with excitement. "It is too sacred an object to be used for anything else."

As soon as the pot was out of the ring of people, several other men helped toss new wood on the fire to heat the sand upon which the fire had been built. When extremely hot, the sand was scooped up by Behtyuc on the base end of a palm frond that had been beaten flat when green and forced to dry that way. It took six scoopings of the hot sand poured into the neck opening to fill the head. Then, using doubled *pacova* leaves to protect his hands, Behtyuc used a heated flat stone from the fire to press along the flesh of the head, almost as if he were ironing it.

Time and again the sand inside the head, cooled and greasy, was poured out and fresh hot sand poured in and the process repeated. Each time the head was smaller than before. A dozen or more of the flat stones were always in the fire being heated and as soon as the head had been filled again, Behtyuc resumed the ironing. Because of natural oils exuding from the contracting pores, the hot smooth stones slid over the skin of the face as smoothly as does an iron over linen damask.

Throughout the night and into the early dawn light, the process continued. The last filling of the head was done with hot coarse pebbles instead of sand, Behtyuc constantly rotating and tilting the head from side to side to prevent the stones from burning the curing tissues. As he did so, he used *kahpahk* to wipe away the minute amount of oil still exuding from the face, daubing it up as soon as it appeared until it was no longer evident. All the grease and oil had been cooked out and the head was now somewhat smaller than a croquet ball. The skin was only a little darker than it had been during life and as hard and tough as tanned leather. The hair, though it had not changed at all, seemed unusually long for the size of the head.

It was at this point that Chamakani rose and went to Behtyuc. He took the small object from him and inspected it carefully, murmured his approval and patted the back of the warrior's neck. Once again he blew into the man's nose and the villagers hooted and cried and smacked their hands against their knees. Chamakani handed it to the man in line nearest to him and that man looked it over closely, nodding at the excellent job of headshrinking Behtyuc had done. He then passed it to the man to his right.

As the head was being passed around, Chamakani came back and squatted before Kolliri and Garca. He smiled broadly. "It is finished," he said. "None I have seen has looked better, Kolliri. Every feature is there, every hair, every scar. Even the expression may be the one he wore. When it comes into your hands, it is then yours to keep and Epini's death will, at that moment, have been fully avenged."

The shrunken head continued to pass from hand to hand, but each to receive it was anxious to study it well, so it was a long while before it fully circled the ring. The morning air was bright and cool by the time the head reached Garca, to Kolliri's left, and the young mother turned it over and over, peering closely at the features of the man who had slain her father. At last she nodded and handed it to Kolliri.

"Behtyuc could not have done better, Mother."

Sitting to Kolliri's right, Sarah craned to look at the head, marveling at how small it was. As Chamakani had said, every line, every scar, every feature was as intact as it had been when the warrior was alive. The eyes were closed, as if in sleep, and, as Epini's widow turned it in her hands, Sarah saw it generally but not specifically; not until Kolliri turned it in such a manner that Sarah saw the left ear was in two sections. Only then did she look at it very closely. Only then did she unmistakably recognize it as Juma's head.

Chapter Thirteen

ALTHOUGH SHE TRIED to control herself, Sarah Francis was not successful. Her recognition of the shrunken head as belonging to Juma was too much. Waves of nausea rose, threatening to strangle her, and she was blinded by the tears that filled her eyes. She lurched to her feet, one hand clenched to her mouth and staggered out of the ring of people, only managing to take a dozen steps before she stumbled and fell. She tried to crawl but even that became too much and she held herself on hands and knees, retching violently. Having had nothing to eat since late the previous afternoon, there was little to regurgitate but the vomitive spasms continued and she became dizzy, almost faint, with the effort.

Vaguely she was aware that Kolliri and Garca had come to her and that Chamakani had lifted her in his arms and carried her inside the *maloka*. She was trembling uncontrollably when he placed her on the mat where she had been sleeping since coming here. Tears, without accompanying sobbing, flooded from her eyes in great quantities. She didn't remember much of what happened after that.

The Nhambiquara did not associate her sudden sickness with the sight of Juma's head. Their only interpretation was that some illness inspired by evil spirits had manifested itself, attacking her with such devastating force, the *paje* was summoned at once. He came with his pouch and basket, first giving her a small quantity of bitter green juice to drink, a concoction made from the roots of *marupá-mira* and *quassia*, sprinkled lightly with a powder derived from pulverized seeds of *pajurá* and *puchury* beans. He crawled all around, placing his hands on her here and there to exorcise evil spirits. He lighted a large cigar made by rolling tobacco in folds of *tauari* leaves, blowing the smoke upon her stomach, which seemed to be the origin of her discomfort. At last, using his final magic which always had such impact on those who were watching, he fumbled in his pouch and, unseen by anyone, slipped a long, slender white root from a bromeliad into his mouth. He mumbled strange incantations and then leaned over the recumbent girl and pressed his lips to her abdomen, lifting the skin with the suctions of his mouth. When he finished, the *paje* straightened and, in view of all, drew the root from his mouth as if it were some bad worm he had sucked from Sarah's stomach, exhibiting it for all to see, then casting it into the fire where it shriveled and blackened.

Sarah fell asleep and dreamed a series of disconnected vignettes involving her father and Juma, giant stinging ants and gaping-jawed caimans, her mother and Epini. When she awoke in late afternoon, Garca and Kolliri were there close beside her, as were Behtyuc and Chamakani and Joli. All were concerned about her but Sarah, weak and a bit disoriented, assured them she was all right now. The villagers praised the great skill of their *paje*, who strutted about with self-satisfied importance.

A meal had been prepared by Kolliri, and Sarah ate with them. During the course of it she announced to all, directing her remarks to Chamakani, that she wished to leave first thing in the morning. They were sorrowful but resigned, promising they would prepare things for her. After a good night's rest of dreamless sleep, Sarah arrived at the landing in the early morning light to find her *montaria* well loaded with supplies — numerous fruits and nuts, *mandioca* cakes, smoked fish and meat. Even a large clay jug containing about a gallon of *kashiri*.

The entire population of Marec had turned out to see her off and the parting was far more wrenching than Sarah had anticipated. She had come to have a profound affection for these people and once again, as in turn she embraced Garca and Kolliri and Chamakani, she wondered why she was leaving, why she just didn't stay with them and become a part of their lives and make them a part of hers. She promised that one day she would return and they urged her to do so, saying she would always be welcome.

With their final farewells and warnings of the dangers facing her still hanging in the air, Sarah climbed into the *montaria* and sat down. Chamakani himself thrust the boat far out into the current. Sarah's cheeks were wet as she dipped the paddle and straightened the canoe. Each time she swiveled around to glance back, they were still standing there, continuing to wave until finally the current of the Ituí swept her around the first downstream bend and they were gone from sight.

A great loneliness touched Sarah as the green walls of the jungle closed in to create a world of her own. Yet, at the same time, she felt a strong exhilaration. She was on her way at last, enveloped in a world of nature. She viewed with interest and appreciation the things which earlier had terrified her because she didn't understand them. Her senses were keenly alert to everything around her and few things passed unnoticed. By scent alone she could tell when she was close to a *pacova* or *paunapa* grove. Her ears collected and identified the sounds of various birds and mammals calling or moving in the treetops or through the underbrush. Her eyes cataloged the variety of life every foot of the way traveled, recognizing the plants and trees and knowing whether they were good or bad or of no importance, seeing and recognizing the macaws and toucans, parrots and curassows and hoatzins as they flew across the river ahead or perched in the riverine growth, watching curiously as she passed.

Sarah was not foolish enough to believe she now knew all about the rain forest and would have no trouble surviving. What she had learned was only a small fraction of this world, yet she was filled with great self-assurance, convinced that by continuing to utilize the advice of her father to think and remain calm, by continuing to rely on the forest lore she had gleaned from Juma, by continuing to bear in mind the warnings of the Nhambiquara, by continuing to have the courage to do what needed to be done, to think and to have confidence in herself, she would survive.

The days on the Ituí passed pleasantly enough, always with much of interest occurring, but without great peril. Rains continued to come nearly every day, but they were relatively gentle compared to what she had experienced earlier, and were shorter in duration, usually coming during midday. Sarah did not mind paddling along in the rain, dry enough beneath the shelter of her poncho. It was very ragged and no longer the protection it had been earlier, but it still served her well.

Late each day she sought out the faint indentation in the jungle cover which indicated the mouth of an *igaripe* and pulled into it carefully, conscious of the fact that such creek mouths were favorite places of anacondas and larger caimans. She encountered these animals often enough but always kept her head, backing away carefully, finding another place to pull into. She had learned to spread *pacova* leaves to sleep upon or to make impromptu shelters over leaning trees or buttressed roots, and she rubbed *genipapo* juice on herself to ward off *piums* and mosquitoes.

An unending drama of life and death sustaining the balance of nature in this most wild of worlds continued around her day and night. She watched, absorbing and learning, ever less frequently making mistakes or errors in judgment. Every leaf and branch and twig carried a message for her and every sound had its meaning. Afloat or afoot, she had become skilled in the art of survival in a terrain where survival was a monumental undertaking. She was always alert, always ready to react swiftly to whatever happened, often intuitively avoiding situations that ranged from merely uncomfortable to downright deadly.

The Nhambiquara had warned most emphatically of the extensive rapids ahead which marked the northernmost limits of their territory. The *pedral pancanda*, they had said, was seven or eight days downstream by boat and, while not a lofty, powerful waterfall such as the *pancanda* marking their southern limits where she and Juma had stayed, it was, in many ways, just as dangerous.

"As soon as the waters swiften," Chamakani had told her soberly, "you must pull ashore, leave your *montaria* and continue your journey through the forest. No *montaria* ever returns which enters the *pedral pancanda;* no person who enters it is ever seen again."

Much as she was conscious of the danger, watching for it, she came upon it with devastating speed. The Ituí was still broad and its surface unbroken for as far ahead as she could see — about a mile. At that point it curved out of sight beyond the screen of vegetation. Far beyond that she could barely make out the tops of tree-cloaked slopes and she was sure it was in that hilly area where she would encounter the rapids. She decided to go as far as the bend and study the river from there, perhaps going a little farther if it were still safe to do so. Halfway there the current speeded up appreciably and a niggling concern touched her. Still, she was sure she could reach shore any time she chose. Three-fourths of the way to the bend the current had become very swift and she began to question the wisdom of continuing, but hesitated about thrusting the *montaria* to shore.

When she at last reached the bend in the river it was too late. The light *montaria* shot along with ever quickening pace and when she tried to move in toward shore, she succeeded only in turning the craft athwart the current where it bobbed along in midcurrent unresponsive to her frenzied paddling. With a real fear blooming in her, Sarah realized she had waited too long and was now committed to the increasing power of the current. Only with phenomenal effort was she able to straighten the boat so that it was pointing downstream.

White water was ahead as she rounded the bend, not much at first, but a scattering of jagged rocks rearing their slick black masses from the surface with the river frothing at their sides. The shores passed by on either side in a blur but she had no time to even glance at them. Her eyes were glued on what was ahead and she was using every measure of concentration to avoid the worst areas. With the white water came the sound, growing ever louder: the splashing, dashing, swelling thunder of a great river confined in too small a channel and struggling to burst its bounds. It was overwhelming and Sarah's whole world became no more than roaring water and incredibly powerful current.

She entered the rapids in midmorning after floating for about three hours, but during the first ten minutes in the rapids she traveled much farther than she had all morning. The shorelines were becoming very craggy, with little vegetation clinging to the iron-colored rocks. The channel continually narrowed as the Ituí was enclosed between steepening hills.

There was no exhilaration to the ride, no excitement, no thrill of trying to best a force of nature. For Sarah, there was only a grim determination to somehow remain upright, to somehow avoid colliding with crushing force against boulders. Time no longer had meaning and nothing existed except water and rocks and the will to survive. At one point the *montaria* shot over a drop of four or five feet and smashed into the water below with jarring force that all but stunned Sarah. The boat somehow managed to stay afloat. Time after time the hardy little dugout struck glancingly against rock edges or bumped and rolled over tar-black boulders swelling the surface. A lighter canoe of fiber or metal could not have withstood the pounding taken by the *montaria* and a larger *inyahn* could not have negotiated the quick turns combined with narrow passages between rocks. Over and again the canoe spun around in a circle. Sometimes it traveled backwards, sometimes sideways, as Sarah strove with all her strength to straighten it. Her efforts with the paddle helped only slightly, but that was important enough.

A dozen times or more the craft should have turned over or been smashed apart or Sarah thrown from the boat, but somehow it didn't happen. There were a few less turbulent areas during which she only held the paddle as a rudder and rode with great speed. At other times, the powerful Ituí became compressed from a normal width of about two hundred yards to a gushing torrent passing between sheer cliff walls less than thirty feet apart and the boat shot along with the current at a blinding pace. Once she passed three naked Indians standing on a flat-topped boulder against the shore and they stared with slack-jawed wonder at this apparition that had appeared where no boat had any right to be. One man's mouth opened and closed as he shouted something, but whatever he said was lost in the continuing thunder of the water.

It was not through any skill on her part that Sarah survived the incredible passage, only a matter of pure chance and fantastically good fortune. Close to two hours had passed from the time she entered the rapids until she left them behind and the rocks diminished and disappeared from the shorelines and then from the water itself. Gradually the current slowed and the Ituí relaxed and stretched, spreading itself to comfortable width once more. The forest crowded to the river's edge and birds sang. The nightmare had ended. How many miles she had traveled, Sarah had no idea. Certainly, it had to be what normally would have taken two or three long days of floating, maybe more.

Sarah slumped in the bottom of the boat, wholly exhausted, thinking she ought to eat something but too weary to bestir herself. She slept. Not until late in the evening did she awaken, frightened at the encroaching darkness. Black skimmers with long narrow wings flew a fraction of an inch from the water, their lower beaks slicing through the surface with razor neatness. She looked about anxiously but there were no sandbars here, nor were there any signs of *igaripes*. The river was alive with caimans, their average size considerably larger than that of those in the Nhambiquara territory. Though their baleful stares fixed on her as she passed, they only watched without moving to attack. Darkness fell rapidly and there was no choice but to float through the night and hope for the best.

She was hungry and ate a good portion of smoked fish and thin pieces of smoked and dried meat hardly less tough or more tasty than shoeleather. She also ate some fruit and drank enough *kashiri* to become a bit giddy. The night was moonless and though the stars shone brightly, the darkness on the river was impenetrable to her eye. Large fireflies with dull, glowing red center light framed between two green lights on their sides blinked in the shore growth. Myriad luminous insects dotted the foliage with quick spots of brilliance or lingering glows. She had the sensation of a multitude of eyes tracking her passage. Many of the sounds were familiar, but as many more were unknown to her and terrifying in their mystery. Once in a while, the *montaria* was bumped from below and, though she was sure it was probably caused by underwater snags, she envisioned huge caimans passing underneath the light craft. She passed the hours in mortal dread of one of the crocodilians' bursting up from beneath, overturning her and snapping those great jaws closed around her body.

Off and on during the night she was awakened by loud splashes, sometimes very close to her. In one instance, a large caiman erupted from beneath the surface gripping a huge thrashing fish in its jaws, and the brief struggle before they sank from sight sent droplets spraying over her. An hour or so before dawn she caught the smell of smoke and a few minutes later saw the glow of a fire on the left shore. She remained perfectly still, watching. The fire was in the midst of a small clearing. In a circle around the fire were the recumbent forms of a dozen people whom she took to be Indians, although at least three of them were wearing trousers. The others were bare except for cloth bands encircling their waists, running snugly between their legs. As nearly as she could tell, they were all men. If any were awake, there was no sign and she drifted past without one of them so much as stirring. Nevertheless, her heart was beating very rapidly and the fright remained with her for a long time.

At dawn the forest came alive with the fearsome howls of *guaribas* and several times she spied them through the branches. Herons and egrets and roseate spoonbills perched in sullen solitude on low branches overhanging the water. Iridescent birds and butterflies flitted about in the growth fronting on the river, and lumbering caimans came ponderously out of the water onto bars that were now mixtures of mud and sand. A few times caimans surfaced in front and watched the boat approach, sinking from sight as it neared. The river here, she noticed, was no longer the clear brown it had been for so long, but had taken on a dingy hue. Gulls and terns flew low over the surface, occasionally crying out.

She ate more of the fruit for her breakfast but the remaining small amount of smoked fish and meat did not smell right and she decided it had finally gone bad, so she pitched it overboard. Instantly the water erupted with a frenzy of activity as a substantial number of foot-long oval-shaped fish attacked the debris with a startling voraciousness. When she dipped her paddle to pull away from them, they attacked *it*. Two were lifted out of the water with the implement, gripping the wood with powerful heavy jaws filled with a horrendous mouthful of triangular teeth. They had beautiful silvery-white scales peppered with small black spots. The tail and belly were bright red, as was an area around the gills. She shook them off but not before she recognized them as the scourge of the Amazon Valley, the piranha. They were always the peril depicted in grade-B movies as attacking explorers in the Amazon, and she had seen several of them in a large aquarium at Bill Ware's pet store — which he mischievously advertised as . . .

B. WARE — PETS

After that she was very careful not to get her hands near the water. She remembered hearing or reading somewhere that the piranhas were not beyond leaping out of the water and attacking a hand held near the surface. Rinsing hands off in the water or trailing them as the boat moved along was practically an invitation to lose a finger or thumb.

Shortly after noon she found a fair-sized *igaripe* opening, slightly muddy in color. Pulling in, she paddled for thirty or forty yards before the dense growth on both sides diminished and the forest became more open. The creek split around a large rock with a flat surface fully covered by a thick matting of bright green moss. Sarah wedged the boat so that it would not pull free, climbed atop the rock and stretched out. In moments she was asleep and did not awaken until early evening. Until nightfall she just sat there watching and listening, drinking in the always-same yet ever-changing aspects of the forest. There was a warm appreciation in her for the beauty to be found here, an understanding of the complex and delicate interlocking of life, both plant and animal, a love for all it was and all that it harbored. She hoped it would never change, that its pristine loveliness would never be destroyed. Later, with the strident sounds of crickets and tree frogs swelling around her and the booming wail of an Amazonian owl filling the air nearby, she fell asleep again and slept through the night undisturbed.

During the next nine days she continued her drifting, only once passing through rapids — a very mild and short trip negotiated without any great problem. She stopped when necessary to find food in the forest, once digging up a couple dozen turtle eggs which she ate sporadically as she drifted. The *igaripes* emptying into the Ituí were consistently larger and muddier, and on the morning she left the moss-covered rock, in the first hour of traveling, she passed a huge river entering the Ituí from the west. Yesterday, just after dawn, it was the Ituí itself which merged into a much larger stream coming from the southeast.

She tended to stay close to the overhang of brush along one shore until she saw, just as she rounded a bend, a squirrel monkey leaning down to pick a leaf out of the water. It saw her and froze. In that instant a gigantic catfish with a mouth as large as a bushel basket burst from the water and engulfed the hapless monkey. The swiftness and unexpectedness of it unnerved Sarah and she paddled the *montaria* closer to the middle of the river.

The Ituí was now enormous, fully four hundred feet wide, very fast and considerably more muddy. It was still not finished growing. In midafternoon today yet another river entered from the left. Only a few hours after that, while Sarah was looking for a place to put up for the night, she spied ahead a man-made construction leading out into the water. As she approached, wary of what she might find, she saw that it was a rude pier of sorts. Her eyes widened and her heart accelerated when it dawned on her that it was constructed of sawed planks.

She pulled up to it and found its level was well over her head and that a wooden ladder would give her access to the top. She tied the canoe firmly to the pilings and climbed the ladder. The bank was high here, solid mud and nearly perpendicular, leveling off to flat ground ten feet above the water. It was to the flat ground that the pier was attached and she moved across it cautiously. There was a clearing here and she stepped into it. Behind a dense screen of *pacovas* heavy with fruit, she saw a house; not a grass hut or a *maloka*, but a small house, its weather-grayed clapboards badly warped, its window frames askew, its door missing. But a house!

"Hello?" She said the word tentatively, rather softly. There was no response. She said it again, louder this time, but still no one replied. Hesitantly she climbed the four steps to a small veranda and knocked on the doorframe. Nothing. She stepped inside and a rat scurried across the floor to disappear into a crack in the back wall. The house was empty.

There were only two rooms, one evidently a tiny bedroom in which a mildewed hammock made of manufactured cord was hanging, strung from wall to wall. The rest of the interior was one sizeable room, a combination kitchen and living room. Two battered chairs at a well-scarred table were the only furnishings other than the hammock. In one corner were several large black balls of material and she looked at them closely. They were soot-stained rolls of crude rubber. This was evidently an abandoned rubber camp.

Deciding to sleep in the house tonight, Sarah went to the *montaria*, returning with an armload of fruit, which she put on the table. Going back outside, she plucked a half-dozen bananas. Her mind was in a turmoil. A house! A table and chairs! Civilization! Without warning she was crying and then she was laughing at the same time. Civilization! She had made it. She was going to be safe.

After eating she climbed into the hammock with some difficulty and settled herself for sleep, but was too excited, and her eyes kept popping open. She watched curiously in the waning light as a tarantula as large as her hand crawled across the floor beneath her and around the doorframe into the other room. The rat returned, or another just like it, and was joined by four others. She heard them climbing up onto the chairs and table to get at the remains of her fruit. Their shrill squeakings and pattering of feet were unnerving. The jungle's night sounds were less audible inside the house, but there were other sounds here, coming from the rafters, from under the floor and from the other room — sounds which she could not identify — and she found herself attributing them to *Cucupira*, the Wild Man Spirit. She grew increasingly bothered by the close and heavy air. The hammock was not so comfortable as she had anticipated, and no matter what position she got into — and there were few from which to choose — the discomfort increased. At last she sighed and stepped down in the darkness, her foot touching a furry body. Her sharp exclamation merged with the squeal of the rat as it scampered across the floor and into the other room.

Sarah couldn't take any more. She stamped her feet

and cried out to frighten away anything else that was here and felt her way along the walls to the door. The freshness of the air outside was a relief and the familiar sounds of the night now came to her more clearly and were reassuring. She lay down on the planking at the foot of the dock and slept the night there, but her sleep was fitful at best and she awoke many times.

In the first light of dawn she was back in the *montaria*, moving downstream. Here and there during the day she passed other dilapidated piers and isolated huts or houses, but all were empty. She spent the night as she had the last, on one of the piers. It was not until late in the afternoon of the next day that she glided around a bend in the river and saw a huge river, somewhat larger than the one on which she was floating now, joining this one from the west. What she saw next, on the right bank, was immeasurably more important — a town.

It was a fairly large place with over a hundred houses on high stilts, and three large, well-made docks. At the smallest of the docks was a dirty white steamboat of considerable size. Two very big buildings which looked like warehouses dominated the waterfront and, beyond them, she could see the spire of a small church. Quite a few stores were visible along with a variety of signs. And there were people, many people, moving about. They wore shirts and trousers, blouses and skirts and many even wore shoes. Numerous vultures, like black stringless kites, spattered the sky high above, soaring elegantly on motionless wings.

She was seen within seconds and she heard shouting in the same language that the men of Cruzeiro do Sul had spoken — Portuguese. A crowd was collecting at the largest pier and she headed the *montaria* that way. By the time she was nearing it, at least forty or fifty people had gathered.

Sarah was abruptly aware of her appearance. Her barkcloth blouse, the fourth she had made, was so tattered it was hardly any covering at all, and the skirt of the same material was little better. She was embarrassed and for a moment stopped paddling, took the crumpled poncho out of her pouch and shrugged into it.

A young man had climbed down the ladder at the end of the pier and was perched there waiting for her. As the canoe touched the pilings he gripped the bow and tied it firmly with a length of cord hanging down from above. He said something to her but she shook her head, unable to understand him.

"Do you speak English?" she asked.

He merely shrugged and held out his hand to her. She put down the paddle, moved to the bow and placed her hand in his, letting him help her to the ladder and then up. When she reached the top the crowd had grown to about a hundred and everyone was talking at once, shouting questions and comments at her, none of which she understood. She shook her head again and held up a hand.

"Wait," she said, "I don't understand you. Please, is there anyone here who speaks English?" It had been so long since she had spoken English herself that the words seemed strange in her mouth.

A pleasant-appearing bearded man in an open-fronted white shirt and slightly stained, unpressed pants stepped forward. Middle-aged, he was of medium height and rather slight in build. In a genteel manner he removed a thin black cigar from his mouth and bowed slightly to her.

"I speak English," he said, with only a very slight accent. "I am Roberto Elvas da Barca. How may I assist you?"

"I've been lost. I need help."

"What is your name and where have you come from?"

"My name is Sarah Francis. I came from up the river. I've floated down a long way."

"Down the Javari?" He pointed to the larger river that entered from the west. "Do you mean to say you have floated all the way down from Repouso by yourself? How did you get around the waterfall?"

Sarah looked where he pointed and shook her head. "No, not that river, this one." She pointed up the river she had just descended.

Roberto da Barca was even more amazed. "The Itacuaí! But there are no towns up the Itacuaí."

"I was not on that river all the way. I was on another. It joined this river from the west. That was four . . . no, five days ago."

His jaw dropped and his eyes opened wide. "The Ituí? You have floated down the Ituí? But how? From where? Where do you live? Where did you begin?"

"I live in the United States," she told him, "but the last town I was in before coming downstream to here was Cruzeiro do Sul."

It was too much for him to contain and in rapid-fire dissertation he explained to the crowd what she had told

him. When he concluded by naming the town of Cruzeiro do Sul, his audience was flabbergasted and again
everyone began talking at once.

"Please," Sarah shouted over the din, "Mr. da Barca,
can you or someone help me? I don't even know where
I am. What town is this?"

Roberto da Barca raised his hands to hush the crowd
and when they quieted he smiled at her and nodded.
"Of course we will help you. This town is called Remate
de Males. In English, that is The End of All Ills."

Sarah smiled. "It's a good name."

Roberto Elvas da Barca nodded. "It has probably," he
said softly, "never been a more fitting name for anyone
than it is for you. Come along, Sarah Francis. We shall
see what can be done about getting you home."

Epilogue

ABOARD THE VARIG BRAZILIAN Airlines jet, Sarah Francis watched the last of Brasília's modern buildings pass from sight. To the west were cultured fields of large farms and ranches. In only a short while these gave way to the unending jungle, scarred in various locations by new construction and road cuts as civilization nibbled its inexorable way into the vastness of the greatest forest on earth.

She leaned back in her seat, wriggling to get adjusted more comfortably, unaccustomed to the sensation of the new clothing she was wearing. The airliner was taking her to Miami and from there another would carry her directly to O'Hare International Airport in Chicago. The events of the past two weeks had exhausted her and she thought back over what had occurred since her return to civilization at Remate de Males.

Her survival in the jungle and her long savage journey had become a major news item not only in Remate de Males but, rather quickly, in Manaus, Brasília, Rio de Janeiro and then throughout the world. Much as she had been relieved to reach Remate de Males, she found the town unpleasant. With few exceptions, her feeling for the people there was the same. It was a bustling community of not quite a thousand inhabitants with the rubber industry ostensibly its principal business. In a way it was, but only as an adjunct to the more lucrative business of smuggling contraband.

The Javari River was the border of Brazil and Peru and, far from official centers of constraint, Remate de Males was a brawling outpost where drunkenness and murder were all too common. The majority of the people were ugly-tempered opportunists, suspicious of everyone. The nearest fiscal post was the town of Santo Antonio over three hundred miles downstream on the Amazon. A fantastic amount of contraband crossed the border between Brazil and Peru at Remate de Males, as great quantities of fine Peruvian rubber were exchanged for Brazilian rum, tobacco, farina, dried meats, beans, coffee, sugar and other items — all without the required duties being paid. Customs officers on hand were aware of the abuses but too afraid for their own lives to more than voice token objections. The worst was the trafficking in human lives. Regularly, forays of men, tough and brutish, penetrated the jungle and attacked Indian villages, bringing back so-called "volunteers" to work for the rubber barons, called *caucheros*. They were paid a pittance for difficult and dangerous work, suffering the exploitation in mute misery.

Two days after her arrival at Remate de Males, Sarah had been placed aboard the dirty white steamship *Pyrineus* by Roberto Elvas da Barca, bound for the large city of Manaus almost a thousand miles downstream. It had been a singularly unpleasant ride. The filthy little ship was terribly overcrowded — a few owners and *cauchero* overseers of rubber plantations, but mostly a surly, unwashed collection of Brazilian and Indian rubber workers in ragged clothing; drunken and diseased men who had spent months in the jungle seeking out and tapping the *caucho* trees for the valuable sap which ultimately became crude rubber. Among the latter were a large number of the more or less enslaved Indians coerced or kidnapped from their isolated forest villages in both Brazil and Peru. Accustomed to being lashed, beaten, kicked and otherwise cruelly treated, the Indians were a frightened, cowering lot with no vestige of pride or dignity remaining, bound to the work they did through a company-store policy which quickly put them into debt from which they could never emerge. They had no real liberty and no respected rights. Sarah had watched, appalled, as the overseers came past and harshly mistreated them for no apparent reason. When, three days into the downstream cruise, one of the Indians died, the overseers were summoned. Despite the pleas of another Indian who was the dead man's friend or brother, they unceremoniously picked up the body and tossed it overboard into the Amazon.

Because of having to move slowly through numerous exposed snags in the ship channel, the *Pyrineus* took over twelve hours to move the forty miles down the Javari to where it emptied into the ochre-colored Amazon, carefully negotiating the outer fringe of a great whirlpool at that point that had sucked down many boats in the past. Sarah was astounded at the incredible size of this mightiest river on earth. It was miles across where they entered; so wide it was not possible to tell whether the far shore were mainland or an island. This was the great muddy river that carried one tenth of all the running water in the world and its immensity and power boggled the imagination.

It took nine days and nights to reach Manaus, a modern city of one-third of a million inhabitants, three degrees south of the equator, at the point where the second largest Brazilian river, the Negro, added its great volume to the Amazon. The mouth of the Amazon was still a thousand miles downstream from Manaus.

The regional governor, Antonio Rochedo, took Sarah into official protection, heard out her story with unabashed astonishment and spread the word not only in Manaus but by radio messages to Brasília and Rio de Janeiro. From the capital city came directions: Sarah Francis was to be flown there at once. It had been done.

In Brasília, an incredibly modern city carved out of the wilderness, Sarah was interviewed for three days by government officials and the press. She even dined with President Humberto da Silva and his minister of state for external relations, José Peregrino. Official contact was made with the United States government to arrange for her return home and, overnight, as the international wire services spread the story, Sarah Francis became a celebrity. Many articles about her appeared in newspapers and magazines — a human interest story that also enlivened radio and television news broadcasts everywhere.

At last she had been given complimentary first class boarding on the Varig airliner for the flight to Miami, where she would be met by her mother in what the press was speculating would be a joyful reunion. Sarah was not particularly pleased at the prospect. Now, sitting in the plush comfort of the airplane, she looked through the pages of yesterday's *New York Times* and *Washington Post* containing stories about what they were calling her "escape from the savages" and her "amazing odyssey." She was surprised to see pictures of herself — one a Maine West High School yearbook photo, another taken only two days ago in Brasília. There was a picture of her mother being interviewed at O'Hare prior to her departure for Miami, with the caption:

Sarah's Mother Prepares for Reunion with Her "Little Lost Darling"

Sarah shook her head and her lips curved in a slight smile. She would, of course, be returning to Chicago to live with her mother — a thought which would have caused her great distress not many months ago. Now it did not. The experiences she had undergone had tempered her, made her far more capable of accepting what had to be, imbued her with a sense of tolerance and understanding far beyond her years. Now, she knew, she could cope with anything, endure and adapt to whatever might be required — not just as a role being played, but with patience and quiet strength. Without realizing quite how it had happened, Sarah Francis had, in a few short months, crossed the threshold into womanhood, both mentally and physically. She was still only thirteen, yet she possessed now a maturity that few of her age had acquired; a maturity and strength of character that many in their lives never acquired.

She raised her eyes a moment, briefly returning the smile of the stewardess, who was just then passing down the aisle. This actuality of returning home excited her in some respects. It was, after all, the culmination of what she had striven for with single-minded determination ever since leaving the Emerald City ruins. Yet, it was tempered now with a pervading sadness and unease.

Sarah returned her attention to the newspaper and a bleakness grew in her as she turned the pages, noting that the newspaper was filled with the usual fare: a new war was feared in the Middle East; terrorists had bombed the Rome airport; a French airliner with two hundred passengers aboard had been hijacked and was presently en route to an unknown destination, suspected to be Algeria; a famine was sweeping India and thousands were dying; a new border incident had occurred between Russia and China and a hot war appeared imminent between the two giant nations; an assassin had narrowly missed in his attempt to murder the new president of Kenya; rapes and muggings had reached an all-time high in the United States; the drug problem was reaching crisis proportions in the ten largest cities of the United States; the city of Chicago had just had its two hundred seventeenth murder for the current year, fewer than half of which had been solved; child-molesting and wife-beating were increasing sharply; air pollution; water pollution . . .

"Savages," the newspapers had called the Indians Sarah had encountered. She threw the paper down disgustedly and stared out the window at the clean, unbroken jungle sliding past far below. She thought of the loveliness of the rain forest's dim interior, the beauty of its unspoiled rivers and magnificent thundering cataracts, the simplicity of life among its inhabitants, the generosity of nature.

"Ladies and gentlemen," the voice of the pilot on the intercom filled the compartment, "if you care to look below you'll see that we are just now passing the Amazon River, largest and most powerful river in the world."

He began to repeat the announcement in Portuguese, but Sarah was no longer listening. Her forehead was pressed against the window and no one heard the words she murmured.

"Roberto da Barca told me the town was called Remate de Males — The End of All Ills. He forgot to say it depended on whether you were going upstream or down."

Printed in the United States
65392LVS00003B/168

9 780595 181711